MW00635101

Retsbol Rises

An Abenaki Lobster Tale

JAYNE ROWE JONES

illustrations by THOMAS BLOCK

Retsbol Rises
An Abenaki Lobster Tale

ISBN 13: 978-1-938883-65-1

Illustrations by Thomas Block

designed and produced by
Maine Authors Publishing
558 Main Street, Rockland, Maine 04841
www.maineauthorspublishing.com

Manufactured in the United States of America

To Joey Larracey, JL 73,
whose smile might have faded
but whose memory
will remain in our minds
and our hearts forever.

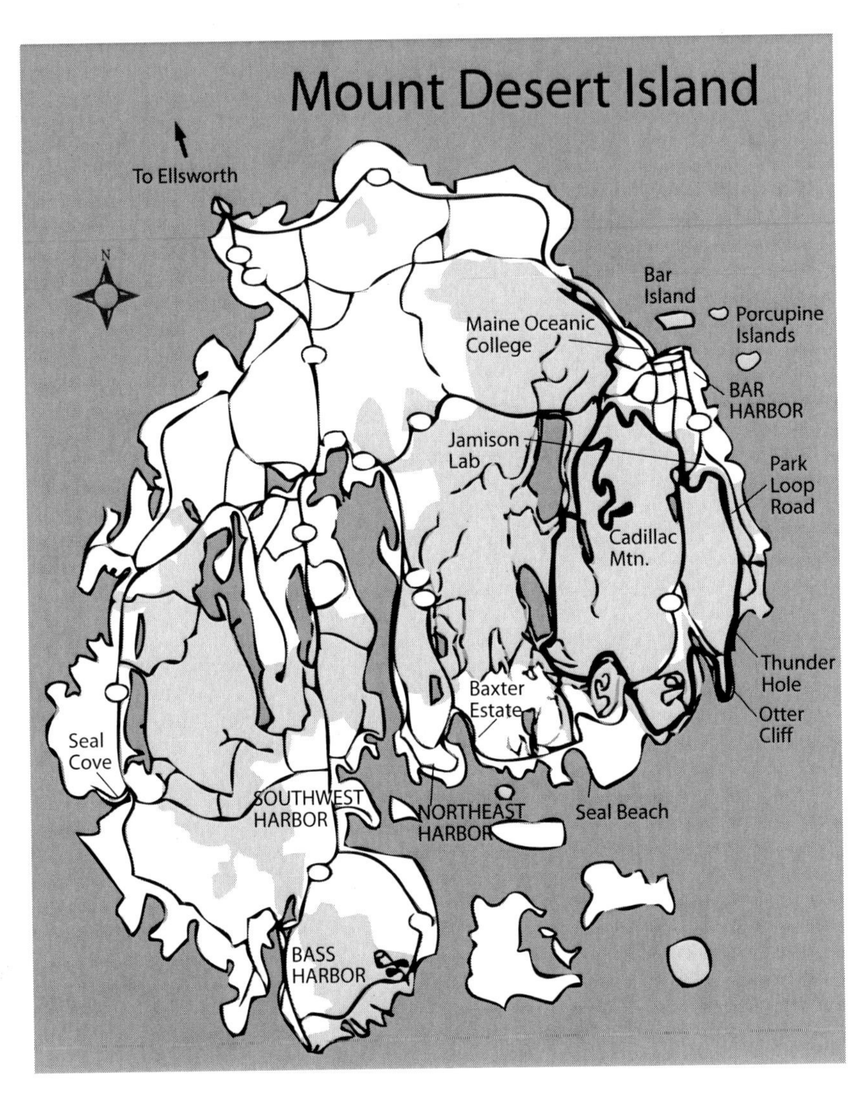

Lightly shaded area indicates Acadia National Park Land

CONTENTS

"Will you walk a little faster?" said a whiting to a snail,
"There's a porpoise close behind us, and he's treading on my tail.
See how eagerly the lobsters and the turtles all advance!
They are waiting on the shingle—will you come and join the dance?
Will you, won't you, will you, won't you,
will you join the dance?
Will you, won't you, will you, won't you,
won't you join the dance?"

"You can really have no notion how delightful it would be
When they take us up and throw us, with the lobsters out to sea!"

—LEWIS CARROLL, "The Lobster Quadrille"

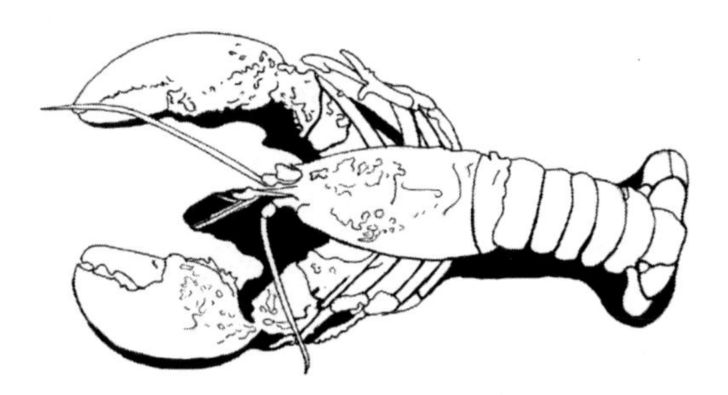

Prologue

Clawman heard the familiar squawk of seagulls flying overhead as they finished their daily task of searching for food. He gazed up toward the sky, and in the distance he caught the majestic bald eagle as it retired to its nest perched high above on the cliff at Porcupine Island. A good sign, he thought. The gods must be happy now.

A low mist rolled up on the beach with the waves as if to escort him to his destination. Soft chanting and the rattling of many seashells could be heard coming from the people, his people, praying that all would go as planned, as he carried his canoe toward the sea. The birch bark canoe had been crafted by his own father as a gift when Clawman was made chief of the Abenaki tribe. His father would be very proud of him tonight, and Clawman felt his presence in spirit as he descended to the water's edge. Members of the tribe patted him on his back, head, and arms when he passed by. His ceremonial clothing, so carefully stitched by his wife and daughters with thousands of shells, made him appear larger than life for this momentous occasion. The noise from the shells hitting one another as he walked seemed to be saying, "Clawman, Clawman, Clawman."

His uncle, Bluesky, the eldest member of the tribe, was waiting for him to present the final adornment, a headdress made of deerskin from the last big hunt. It was covered completely in lobster claws offered to the Abenaki from the Retsbol tribe. Bluesky held the headdress to the sky and shouted an Abenaki blessing: "Nakaki nee, Nakaki nee."

Bluesky's eyes filled with tears as he placed the sacred headdress upon Clawman's head. Clawman kissed his uncle's hands and then felt for the amulet pouch he always wore around his neck for protection and guidance. He would need both of these tonight because soon the covenant ceremony was to take place and the agreement between the tribes made official. He gave the canoe a quick shove and swiftly stepped into it and began to paddle to Seal Cove, the meeting place agreed upon by both tribes, Abenaki and Retsbol.

The canoe glided across the choppy water of the ocean. Clawman had paddled this same journey too many times to count, but on none of the prior trips was he filled with both excitement and sorrow. The last bit of pink could be seen as the sun was setting, signaling the end of another day. Wistfully, Clawman thought about tomorrow, when the sun would rise again, and Acadia Island would be a changed place, a place without the company of the Abenakis' dear friends.

Clawman's canoe slid across the sand as he leapt onto the beach at Seal Cove. His heart was pumping from the paddling and his own nerves, but his amulets comforted him. They were presented to him as a young boy by his grandfather: a gray wolf paw for strength, an owl talon for wisdom, a deer tail for grace, a puffin feather for devotion, and a moonstone for hope. Clawman could sense the power from these five talismans and felt stronger and more confident as he bent down to retrieve the granite wheel wrapped in deerskin in the bottom of the canoe. He hugged this beautiful offering, hand carved over weeks out of the pink feldspar granite found throughout the island. He traced the five chosen shapes painstakingly etched out of the hard stone. Yes, he thought, as he reached into his deep pocket, he had personally collected all the ceremonial amulets that soon would fit perfectly into the wheel.

Suddenly the wind blew and the mist parted to reveal a lone teepee on the rocks to the left of the beach. Smoke swirled out of its top, and Clawman identified several shapes taking form as the fog lifted even more.

Long shadows projected outward on the walls of the animal-hide teepee. Clawman knew that one of those shadows belonged to the great Retsbol leader, BigClaw. BigClaw was true to his name and stood almost seven feet, a full foot taller than Clawman. As the flap of the teepee opened, Clawman glimpsed a small table made of driftwood in the center of the teepee and, on top, the most beautiful rose quartz orb he had ever seen. As he entered, he bowed to BigClaw and the orb. The ceremony had begun.

Lobster fact: *The State of Maine has special laws to protect the lobster fishery. There are both minimum and maximum size measurements for harvesting lobsters. The minimum size is designed to make sure that all lobsters are mature enough to breed at least once before they are harvested. The maximum size limit is set to protect the breeding stock. A minimum size lobster will weigh around 1 pound, while a maximum size lobster will weigh between 3 and 4 pounds.*

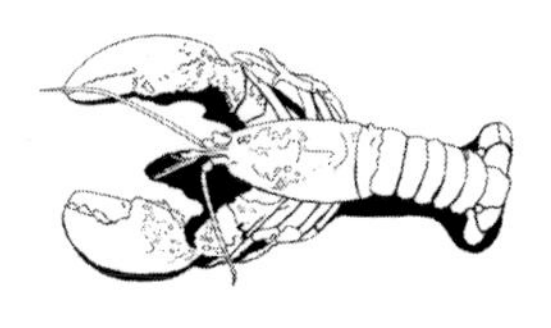

Chapter 1

The Birthday Party 1957

Barton Thuya Baxter III was thirteen years old today. His father, Barton Thuya Baxter II, had promised Barton a special surprise on this day and he couldn't wait. Maybe it was his own car or perhaps his own plane, he thought as he stuck his finger in the coconut icing that Cook was mixing for his cake.

"Now, none of that Master Barton," Cook said as she slapped Barton's hand away. "Your friends will be here soon, so why don't you go outside in the garden and wait for them to arrive."

Barton took one more lick while fiddling with his blond hair, a nervous habit, smiled naughtily, and left through the back door of the kitchen, slamming it as he went.

"He hasn't got any friends," muttered the cook's assistant, Millie.

"Now, Millie, be kind," Cook said as she frosted the enormous cake with her equally enormous hands that had frosted many a cake over the fifty years she had served the Baxter family. "He may be trouble, but his father—and there never was a kinder boss from here to Boston—tries hard to keep the young lad in line, especially since the Missus died so many years ago." She plopped a large dollop of fluffy icing on top of the cake.

"He's trouble all right, that one. Trouble with a capital *T*," said Millie as she tidied up her traditional black-and-white maid's uniform.

Cook's head turned at the loud ring of the front doorbell. "That will be the gardener bringing the children up for the party. Butler Harrison will answer the door. Run along quick now and make sure the garden is all set for the party."

Millie made a face and reluctantly left with a quick curtsy. "Yes, Cook."

The gardener, Mike O'Leary, dressed in overalls and a straw hat, had rung the bell of the stately Baxter mansion, or "cottage" as the wealthy liked to refer to their summer homes along the rocky coast of Mount Desert Island in Maine. Normally Mike would have come around back to the kitchen and had a hot cup of tea with a biscuit graciously presented by Cook. But it was not to be today, since today was the young boy's birthday. Next Mike unlatched the back of the wagon, and straw and children tumbled onto the cobbled stone walkway. Some of the children had never been to the house before, which sat up high from the center of town, Northeast Harbor, and could not be seen from below. Several mouths dropped open as the children turned to see the beauty of the Baxter estate, an estate so grand that it almost commanded quiet. Today was no exception: a hush fell over the children, and, as if on cue, from around the corner came a splendid white horse carrying Master Barton himself.

"Welcome to my home for this grand celebration of my thirteenth birthday," Barton said as he twirled his hair. Barton was a pale, thin boy whose blond hair seemed to constantly fall into his light blue eyes. No matter how much cream he applied to hold his hair down, it always ended up spilling over the side of his face. Besides being a rather undisciplined and mean-spirited child, Barton had the annoying habit of wrapping the back of his hair around his right index finger whenever he was nervous or excited. Cook called this "twiddling." She always knew when he was lying or being particularly ill-behaved because his twiddling seemed to intensify. The last few days Barton had twiddled so much that Cook thought he might develop a bald spot. She knew that he was eager for his special gift and was hoping that he was more excited than mischievous.

Regardless, she was keeping a watchful eye on him and wasn't afraid to inform Mr. Baxter if she felt he was up to no good.

"Follow me," Barton commanded, and the twenty or so guests moved behind him and his horse as they rounded the house to the back and the impressive garden, well-tended by the gardener. The Baxter Thuya garden had the reputation of being the most beautiful garden on the island, and Mike O'Leary took a great deal of pride in this fact. The weeding, the mulching, the pruning, the replanting, and the watering were all done lovingly by Mr. Mike O'Leary and someday would be done by Mike O'Leary and Son. Gardener Mike knew Patrick, his son, also had the love of the land in his heart and believed that he would make a fine gardener and partner someday. It was good for the spirit to work the soil, really feel it in your bones, he thought. Nothing grounded you more to Mother Earth than the simple acts of digging, planting, watering, and watching things grow.

While Mike was enjoying the fruits of his labor, Barton was thinking he would like to make his horse trample all over the prize lupines that encircled the property. He felt the garden was stupid and silly. Other employees of his father might be afraid of him, but Barton knew that Gardener Mike most certainly was not and would most definitely tell his father about the lupines if he crushed them. Barton didn't want to risk not getting his special birthday surprise that his father had spoken so much about. Today was finally the day that Barton would get exactly what he deserved, and he wasn't about to do anything that would spoil this day.

As one can imagine, Barton was not a well-liked child. The children who attended his party did so because their parents, most of whom worked directly for Barton's father, coaxed them. His father owned most of the town of Northeast Harbor along with properties and businesses in Boston and New York. Barton's father was a generous and kind man. Unfortunately, his wife had died from influenza when Barton Thuya Baxter III was just a few days shy of his seventh birthday. Some might say that Barton's bad behavior was a result of losing a mother when he was just a lad, but others would argue that he was just born mean. Plain and simple, they would say, Barton was bad to the core.

The children promptly engaged in the festivities that were arranged for the celebration. There were pony rides, sack races, and bowling on the green at one end of the garden. In the center of the yard, the guests could bob for apples, play croquet, or be entertained by the several hired clowns and acrobatic performers. The outside tables were laden with all sorts of delicious foods that Cook and Millie had prepared. Potato salad, fresh fruit, locally grown corn, hot dogs, and hamburgers were piled high on banquet tables placed in the shade. But what impressed the partygoers the most that sunny afternoon in 1957 was what was cooking underneath the steaming seaweed situated at the edge of the garden. Barton's favorite meal was steamed lobsters with lots and lots of butter. And since Barton normally got what he wanted, Gardener Mike and a few helpers from the Northeast Harbor Lobster Pound were steaming lobsters along with clams for all the children.

It was a spectacular birthday celebration that any child would have loved. Any child, that is, except for Barton. He had a melancholy look as he searched the crowd of guests. Why wasn't she here, he wondered? While the children were participating fully in the merriment, Barton sat quietly under the shade of an old oak tree. Finally, his face lit up as he spied Amelia Legere standing in front of an enormous wooden door adorned with carvings of creatures indigenous to the island. The garden was surrounded by a tall cedar fence, which had several doors similar to that which Amelia now admired. Each door had unique carvings etched by local artisans, many of them Native Americans from the famous Abenaki tribe. Amelia herself was a member of this tribe known for its love of the land. Her grandmother, Little Gull, had created quite a stir by marrying a French lobsterman from Machias. But that is for another story.

Amelia, who tended to be serious about everything, was seriously studying the door as she reverently touched some of the carvings. Next Barton watched her walk toward a clump of lupines and allow her fingers to gently caress the stalks of the colorful plants, her favorite. For her sake and her sake only, he was glad that he hadn't destroyed the flowers. Barton also knew that Amelia preferred lemonade over root beer, hot dogs over hamburgers, and sunrise over sunset. Barton was mean through and through, but his heart, small that it was, did have a soft spot for Amelia "Little Bird" Legere. He cared for Amelia immensely. Her beautiful smile, her dark brown eyes, her genuine goodness along with her bravery besotted Barton. He didn't know why, but he felt better when Amelia was around, and now that she had arrived, he felt that the party could finally start.

Barton smiled, something he rarely did unless it was a roguish smile, and walked over to the thirteen-year-old girl with the two long, dark braids with soft blue ribbons that hung down the length of her back. As he approached her, his smile turned back to a frown as Patrick O'Leary, the gardener's son, dressed in dusty overalls, appeared in the doorway. Amelia's face broke into a grin as Patrick presented her with a lupine of her own that she graciously stuck into the pocket of her pinafore. Patrick was also thirteen, and just as Barton was chided for his bad behavior, Patrick was praised for his excellent behavior. This, coupled with the fact that Amelia seemed to enjoy Patrick's company more than Barton's, resulted in Barton's deep dislike of Patrick.

"I didn't think you were able to come to my party since you still had to help your father with the pruning of the perennials, Patrick," teased Barton.

"Your father specifically asked that I be allowed to come today. It has something to do with a surprise," Patrick replied.

"Well, don't get too excited, Patrick. The SURPRISE is for me, the birthday boy, not you," Barton retorted with glee.

"Barton, you don't have to always be so rude," said an exasperated Amelia.

Then, without any warning, the skies darkened and the wind howled. A quick storm, which is so common to this coastal

Maine town, poured down on the party. Children and servants ran about gathering presents, food, and other treats while Barton looked on from the back terrace, nice and dry, not moving to help Cook or Gardener Mike or Millie or anyone, for that matter. Why should he help, he thought. This was his party, and besides, he didn't want to get his new shoes wet.

The celebration continued in the main house, which certainly was large enough to accommodate the visitors. The cake that Cook had so meticulously decorated did survive the rain, and it was brought to the ballroom to be served. The children sang "Happy Birthday" to Barton after he blew out all fourteen candles, one for each year plus the traditional one to grow on. Millie and Cook handed out the rich chocolate cake with the coconut cream frosting to the eager children, who politely thanked them both and sat on the floor of the marble-tiled ballroom. Soon thereafter the Blue Hills Fair Players, consisting of several clowns and acrobats, performed a magical show, and the children shrieked with laughter and cried out in amazement. Cook and Millie stood in the back of the room, satisfied that the party was going well. Mr. Baxter would be happy, thought Cook, and that pleased her tremendously.

Patrick and Amelia had been friends since they were born. They lived near each other in the only modest section of Northeast Harbor. Amelia's father, Lucien Legere, was a close friend of Mike O'Leary. Lucien was an excellent lobsterman who loved the sea as much as Mike loved the land. The children had grown up together, and now, with both at the beginning of their teenage years, their friendship had deepened into something more. They sat side by side in the main house while Patrick finished eating an extra plate of cake given to him by Millie. Amelia pulled the lupine from her pocket.

"You said you were going to show it to me at the party," Patrick said with a mouth full of cake garbling his words.

Amelia giggled and then got serious. "You're right, I did promise, but only because I want to show it to you and not because you want me to. You do recognize the difference, don't you?"

Patrick swallowed the last bite of cake. "Yes, of course, I understand."

Amelia tucked the lupine behind her ear and reached around her neck with both hands. She lifted the rawhide string over her head, raising the leather pouch attached to it from beneath the front of her dress. "This is my amulet pouch, given to me by grandmother. I don't remember when exactly, but I think I have always had it. In my clan we use these to hold our chosen amulets and wear it around our necks to protect us from harmful spirits and to give off positive energy to those who are close."

Patrick then reached behind his head and removed his own necklace, handing it to Amelia. "This is for luck and protection," he said. "It's a St. Christopher medallion. We Catholics believe St. Christopher guides and protects us, too."

Amelia flipped it over and gingerly traced the raised image of St. Christopher. She carefully handed it back to Patrick. "Thank you for showing it to me. It is very beautiful." Next, Amelia slowly opened her leather pouch and poured the items out into her own hand. She held each one as she explained what they were and the power they held. She reminded Patrick that he could view them—not touch, mind you—but view: a silver sand dollar for peace, blue sapphire for clarity, green tourmaline for healing, and an eagle feather for knowledge.

"See how tranquil you feel when you look at them?" she asked Patrick, who nodded in agreement. "This last one," Amelia continued as she held up a single bear tooth, "is for bravery."

"Wow!" exclaimed Patrick.

"My grandmother, Little Gull, always says that you don't choose the amulets, they choose you," she said. "I know she's right because I always feel better and more connected to my people when I have them."

Patrick gazed at Amelia's amulets and smiled. "I only have the one," he said, examining his own medallion. "Do you always have five?"

"Yes," said Amelia. "Five is significant to the Abenakis because most important rituals take place at five-year intervals.

At five we officially enter the young child stage, at ten we learn hunting and other essential skills, at fifteen we cross over into young adulthood, and so on throughout our lifetime."

"Neat," said Patrick.

Both kids were so engrossed in what they were doing, they didn't notice that Barton had entered the room. When he saw them with their heads close together, anger filled his young body. Silently, he approached them and stretched his right hand out and slapped Amelia's palm filled with her precious things from underneath. Her amulets sprang high into the air, then hit the floor and scattered across the room.

Patrick jumped up as Amelia yelled, "Barton! How could you?" Barton laughed and ran off. "Oh, he is so mean," cried Amelia with tears prickling her eyes.

"I'll help you find them, Amelia," Patrick said. Both children began crawling on the floor to retrieve Amelia's treasures.

Just then, Millie appeared in the doorway. "There you two are," she said. "I have been looking all over for you." Patrick and Amelia stopped what they were doing and stood up.

"Mr. Baxter is waiting for you in the garden cottage. Hurry," she urged. "You know how he doesn't like to wait, and Cook will have my head if I don't get you there lickety-split."

"We better go now, Amelia," Patrick said. "Mr. Baxter wants us."

"But my amulets," she protested.

"I'll help you look for them as soon as we're finished."

Amelia was reluctant. "I don't like to be without them," she said and crouched back down to the floor to look.

Patrick, who was visibly uncomfortable as he had been raised to respect his father's employer, said, "We don't want to keep Mr. Baxter waiting. He's a busy man. He has something important to share with us. Remember? He told us the other day." Patrick bent and took Amelia's hands. "I promise we will come back here and find them all, as soon as we're finished with Mr. Baxter."

"Come on you two, shake a leg. You've got to go, now. Move it!" an impatient Millie demanded. All three left the room, Millie, nervous that she didn't find the children soon enough, Patrick, excited to hear what Mr. Baxter wanted to tell them, and last, Amelia, anxious that she was leaving her amulets.

Choices made can't be undone later even if one wishes with all his might. Each action leads to a reaction, which leads to another consequence and so on and so forth. Amelia and Patrick and even silly Millie had no inkling of what was to come as a result of the incident in the ballroom—an incident that will be forever remembered and forever desired to be forgotten.

Lobster fact: *Lobster is a very healthy food that can be cooked a variety of ways. Perhaps the easiest way is to boil it in a big pot of water.*

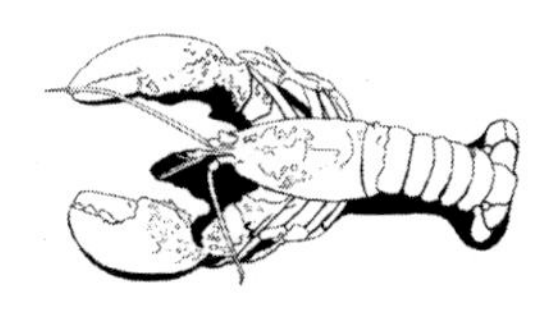

Chapter 2

The Present: Something Given, Something Taken

Amelia and Patrick entered the cottage, breathless and excited. This guesthouse was located on the edge of the Baxter property. Most everyone associated with Mr. Baxter knew that he preferred the simplicity of this cottage to the grandeur of the Baxter mansion. The cottage, although small, had warmth and spectacular views of the garden and ocean harbor. It was furnished in rustic décor, with dark Oriental carpeting, walnut wood paneling, and floors of wide pine planks. An impressive grandfather clock was located in the corner of the foyer, and above the doorframe were two large rowing oars inscribed with Bowdoin College Class of 1936. The door to Mr. Baxter's study was closed.

Amelia and Patrick sat together on a bench while staring at the door to Mr. Baxter's office. As was her habit, Amelia absently reached for her pouch and then remembered it was no longer there. "Patrick, I don't like being without my amulets. Promise you'll help me look for them when we finish with Mr. Baxter."

"Promise," he said and crossed his right index finger over his heart. Amelia smiled. The two children remained silent for a few minutes until Patrick spoke. "What do you suppose he wants to show us? I've been thinking about this all morning."

"Perhaps it has something to do with Barton," Amelia suggested.

Barton, who came bounding around the corner, twirling

his hair, disrupted them. "Of course it has something to do with me. It's my birthday! I told you not to get too excited," he said.

At this moment the door to the study opened, and Mr. Baxter appeared with his arms opened wide. Mr. Baxter was a tall man with a head of thick, light-gray hair. He had a very pronounced moustache, which he groomed impeccably each day before his morning stroll in the garden. But what was most memorable and always present was his warm smile, which he generously gave to any passerby. Amelia always felt that if Santa Claus had a younger brother, Mr. Baxter would be him.

"Welcome! Welcome! Come in and sit. So good of you to join me," he said. His greeting was so enthusiastic that his visitors appeared to melt from his kindness. Even Master Barton's surly disposition softened around his father. Mr. Baxter instructed the children to come into the study and motioned to them to sit in the three chairs placed in front of his mahogany desk. This was Mr. Baxter's favorite room. He often spent long hours here conducting his business, answering correspondence, or just reading from his vast library as he watched the harbor below. In addition to his desk, the room held two deep leather sofas and several comfortable overstuffed chairs. Prints and maps embellished the walls, and there was a large schooner in a bottle resting on the mantel over the stone fireplace. Several pairs of binoculars along with a spectacular telescope were at the ready for whenever Mr. Baxter wanted to view the comings and goings of harbor life. A massive painting of an aerial view of Cadillac Mountain and the Porcupine Islands was hung directly behind Mr. Baxter's desk. The three children did as they were asked and sat down, waiting patiently for the great man to begin.

Mr. Baxter lowered his large frame into the chair behind his desk. His grin was replaced by a more serious face, which instantly changed the tone of the room. Patrick was so excited that he could barely sit in his chair, choosing instead to place most of his weight on the front part of his seat. Amelia trembled slightly in anticipation. Barton opened his mouth to say something, but his father silenced him with a wave of his hand.

For once Barton obeyed and closed his mouth. Next, Mr. Baxter opened the top drawer of his desk and pulled out a tarnished jangle of keys, playing with them for a bit before clasping one with his left hand. He placed his closed fist in front of the children, palm down, and beamed, looking like a child who had just broken into the cookie jar. He slowly turned his hand over and opened his fingers to reveal a small brass object shaped like a lobster tail. Amelia let out a little "ah" sound.

Mr. Baxter said, "It's nice to see you, Amelia and Patrick, today on this very special day, a very special day indeed. I hope you have been enjoying yourself despite the rain. It wouldn't be Maine in July without a storm blowing through now and again to keep everyone on their toes." Patrick and Amelia nodded in agreement, almost too anxious to move.

Barton couldn't help himself and blurted out, "What is it, Father? What is my special surprise?"

Mr. Baxter pursed his lips together and raised his right eyebrow at his son, which quieted Barton immediately. His father continued, "On my thirteenth birthday, my father called me into this very study, much like I have done here today. Unfortunately, I did not have any brothers or sisters or even close friends to share in what I was about to discover, but you three are a different story. Since Mrs. Baxter, God rest her soul, and I were blessed with only one son, Barton, I have been observing you, Amelia, and you too, Patrick. And I have been impressed with what I have seen."

"Thank you," said Patrick.

"Yes, thank you," echoed Amelia.

"Amelia, your love of this island and the traditions of your people, both the French and the native Abenaki Indians, is commendable." At the mention of the word *Abenaki*, Amelia frowned with the memory that her amulets were still scattered on the floor of the main house.

"And Patrick, much like your father, who has served this family as head gardener for many years, you have his magic touch and truly, as they say, a green thumb. You take great pride and care in all living plants, both nurtured and wild. I am equally impressed with your integrity and honesty, which should serve you well as you continue on your journey throughout this world."

Barton's face turned sour while listening to the praise given so generously to his young friends. "Barton, I have not forgotten you, son, especially on this momentous occasion of your thirteenth birthday." Barton sat taller in his chair. "Your mother would be delighted to see the fine young man you have become. You have a natural business sense and a keen understanding of the workings of many of the Baxter industries. Just be mindful to keep your overconfidence in check, and I guarantee you much success."

"I'm not too confident, it's just that..."

"Barton, enough, please, let me continue."

"Yes, Father."

"What I am about to tell you in this room today must be something that you and you three alone keep to yourselves. It will be your responsibility to understand and believe this sacred story and protect"—the children each gave Mr. Baxter a puzzled look—"yes, protect it from others who might want to use it for their own advantage. I was trusted with this care and this history on my thirteenth birthday, and how I wished that I had someone to share it with. You children, well really, young adults, are the perfect threesome to be the keepers of the tale. So, without further ado," Mr. Barton stood and faced the picture of Cadillac Mountain. He tugged at the right side of the picture frame causing it to swing open. Behind the picture was a safe. While pressing his ear against it, Mr. Baxter turned the tumbler left, then right, and then left again. He opened a door, which revealed a smaller door with a tiny handle. The door had a shape cut out of it in the center. He held up the brass lobster tail, displaying it proudly to the children. He then placed it in the center of the door, where it fit perfectly into the space. He turned the tail to the left and the door clicked open.

Amelia and Barton had joined Patrick on the edges of their chairs to see what was behind the door. What magnificent thing was waiting for them to find out about, to keep secret, and to keep protected? The anticipation was so great in that room back in 1957 that one could almost touch it in the air. Mr. Baxter slowly reached into the safe and pulled out three books, which were actually parchments bound together by leather straps on either end. Each parchment was approximately eleven by fourteen inches, the size of a legal pad, and about two inches thick. The parchments looked old, like they were made of animal skin.

Amelia recognized it right away and blurted out, "It's deerskin, isn't it?" Then she quickly covered her mouth, feeling that maybe she had broken the mood by speaking.

Mr. Baxter said, "Yes, that is correct, Amelia. They have a deerskin covering with paper primarily made from birch trees, which is what they used back then."

"Back when?" asked Patrick. He too couldn't contain his enthusiasm, and even Barton added, "Yes, back when, Father, back when?"

Mr. Baxter held his other hand up to hush the children. "Let me tell you the story, and then you can ask me all the questions that you want. I can't guarantee that I will be able to answer them all; in fact, I can guarantee you that I won't. I also want to say that what I am about to tell you may seem improbable. You may choose to believe or not believe. I want you all to know that I believe unequivocally what I am about to tell you, and I hope that when I am finished you too will be believers. Now, a long time ago—when, actually, it is hard to say—just know that it was a very, very long time ago, the Abenaki Indians inhabited this island. They lived in harmony with the plants, the animals, the moon and the stars, the ocean and lakes, and even the lobsters."

"Lobsters!" Barton burst out.

"Yes, even the lobsters," Mr. Baxter said. "Old Indian lore would tell us that the lobsters, like their Indian brothers and sisters, walked on land, upright, side by side. They each took care of their territory and lived in complete accord without conflicts or strife. As each tribe began to grow, the demands for the land increased. Disagreements began to happen, and clashes developed where they never existed before. Something needed to be done before these minor problems escalated into major problems. The two great leaders of the Abenaki and Lobster tribes met and formed an agreement, or covenant, if you will. The covenant stated that the lobsters, since they could live on both land and water, would return to the sea and let the Indians take over the island. The lobsters would retreat to the water only if the Indians agreed to follow the creed and care for the land, taking only what they needed for their own survival and working to make sure that all plants and animals would have their rightful place to grow and flourish.

"Great rejoicing and great sadness ensued for several months after the decision had been made. Man and lobster had existed together for centuries, and both would be sad to have to separate, yet they all knew it was the only smart solution.

"Supposedly on the final day the lobsters were to spend on land, the two leaders held a sacred ceremony and presented a beautiful orb along with other special gifts as offerings to the gods of Cadillac Mountain. The orb was then buried deep within the heart of the mountain, where it currently resides. As long as the orb remains undisturbed and intact, the lobsters know that man is taking care of the land and they will remain in the ocean. If, however, something were to happen to the orb, the covenant would be broken, and the lobsters would come back to take over the land."

"Wow!" Amelia said.

"Jiminy," croaked Patrick.

"Incredible!" Barton said.

"I would agree with all of you," Mr. Baxter said. He then focused his attention on Amelia. "Amelia."

"Yes, sir?" Amelia replied earnestly.

Mr. Baxter lifted the top parchment off of the pile. "This parchment includes information about how the gods were appeased along with the offerings and sacrifices that both tribes made in order to solidify their pact. It also includes many drawings and Abenaki writings that you might find interesting. I am giving this to you because I recognize that you are a deeply spiritual person connected to her ancestry with pride and bravery. I trust that you are the right keeper of this sacred information." He handed the book to her and she took it reverently.

"Oh, yes, Mr. Baxter. Thank you, sir, thank you so very much." Amelia stared at her book in amazement.

"Patrick," Mr. Baxter began, "I have watched you grow into a fine young lad. You have great respect for the land and the plants that make this area beautiful. This book that I am about to give you includes information about the steps the Indians were to follow to take care of the land and the certain plants they would choose to grow that would be beneficial to both man and animal. I can't think of another person so deserving of receiving this parchment today." He handed the second parchment to Patrick, who accepted it with gratitude and sincerity.

"I don't know what to say. I am honored, thank you."

Mr. Baxter finally spoke to his beloved son, Barton. His face lit up as he looked lovingly at his only child. "My dear Barton. I am so proud of you today on your thirteenth birthday. It seems like only yesterday that I held you in my arms when you were born. Your mother would also be proud to be here today," he said as his eyes became misty. Barton twiddled his hair intently.

"This last and final book is for you. This parchment contains specifics about where the orb is hidden in the base of Cadillac Mountain as well as several maps showing the pathways that exist under the entire mountain range on the island. This is the most important book of the three. If this ever gets into the wrong hands, the outcome could be catastrophic."

Barton's father lifted the third and final parchment up and tenderly handed it over to his son. Barton reached his hands out to receive his gift, the most important of all three. With his fingertips inches away from touching the book, Barton asked, "How much do you think I could get for the orb on the open market, Father?"

When these words popped out of Barton's mouth, everything that followed happened in a flash. Amelia and Patrick turned to face Barton, each holding their own treasured parchments in their laps, their mouths opened wide in shock at what Barton had just said. Mr. Baxter's own stunned face showed both disgust and shame. Within seconds, he grabbed the book from Barton, turned around, placed the revered document in the safe, banged the safe doors shut, spun the lock, and returned the beautiful painting of Cadillac Mountain to its previous position on the wall. Barton protested, but his father interrupted him.

"I'm sorry. I obviously misjudged you. You are definitely not ready to receive this special present today, not at all. I don't know if you will ever be ready!" And with those last words, he strode out of his office and slammed the door behind him.

Lobster fact: *Centuries ago, lobsters were so plentiful in North America that Native Americans used them to fertilize their fields and to bait their hooks for fishing. In the colonial period, lobsters were considered "food for the poor" and were served to children, prisoners, and indentured servants.*

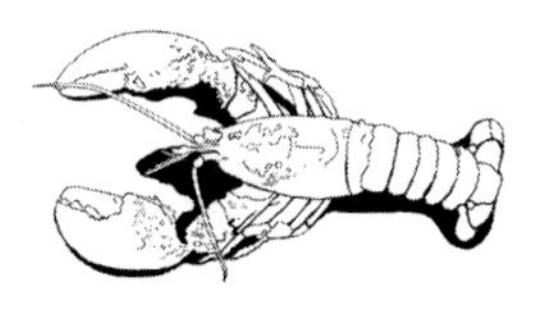

Chapter 3

The Door Opens

Amelia and Patrick were outside in the garden, looking at their books. The rainstorm had passed over and blue sky and sunshine had returned. "This has to be written in the ancient Abenaki language," Amelia said. "I will have to ask my grandmother; she might be able to tell me what it all means."

"My book is full of pictures of plants and flowers. This must be a blueberry bush, and this is definitely a lupine," Patrick said while running his fingers over an open page. "Do you believe it?" Patrick asked Amelia.

"I'm not sure what I believe, but I believe the ancient people believed in it or they wouldn't have created these books. This is their history, and it is very important to them."

"I can't imagine a walking, upright lobster. My mother could make a whole lot of lobster pie from a six-foot lobster," Patrick said. Amelia giggled.

"Look at this drawing," she said as she pointed to the picture in her book. "This is obviously a lobster claw and this one must be ..." Her voice trailed off as she rotated the book to look at the image from a different angle. Patrick bent his head lower and said, "A bear tooth."

Amelia felt for the pouch around her neck.

"Oh, my gosh! I forgot to get my amulets," she cried as she jumped up from the rock wall they were sitting on. Patrick stood to go with her, but as they walked down the stone path, Barton leapt out from behind the fountain.

"Ah ha!" he yelled.

"Barton, don't do that!" shouted Amelia.

"Yeah, Barton," Patrick said.

"Yeah, Barton," mimicked Barton. "What were you two doing? Looking at your stupid books?"

"They are not stupid; you're just jealous because you didn't get to have yours now," Amelia said.

"My father will give it to me whenever I want it. He always gives me what I want when I want it."

"He didn't seem like he was going to give it to you any time soon," said Patrick. "He seemed pretty upset with you."

"That's just an act. He'll come around. You'll see. I always get my way sooner or later." With one hand Barton twiddled and with the other he slyly reached around Amelia. "In the meantime, I will just have to take this," he said and he snatched one of the ribbons from Amelia's braids.

"Hey, give that back!" Amelia said.

"You'll have to make me," Barton cried with glee, and he ran down the garden path. Amelia sped after Barton with Patrick right behind. Barton was swift, but Amelia was faster, and she reached him and grasped the ribbon with her right hand, holding her book tightly with her other hand. Patrick arrived quite winded with his cheeks flushed from running.

"Barton, cut it out, just give it back to Amelia."

Barton yanked hard on the hair ribbon and ripped it out of Amelia's hand. He was taller than both Patrick and Amelia and waved the ribbon in the air as they both unsuccessfully reached for it. As they pushed him back, they all found themselves at the end of the path, where the brush was much thicker and the light was greatly diminished.

"Give me back my ribbon NOW!" yelled Amelia and shoved Barton.

Barton bumped up against a thick wooden door over which vines had grown. When he hit the door some of the vines were pushed aside, revealing words etched in the door that read:

Rain, sleet, snow, or hail
Let no man pass this trail
—ABENAKI

They all paused to read the words as they had done countless other times while playing in this wonderful garden. Barton moved toward the other two, visibly shaken by the realization of where he had ended up during the chase. Patrick also backed up as if in awe of the door. "We better turn back," said Patrick. "My father made me promise that I wouldn't go near that door. Come on, Amelia."

Barton, relieved that Patrick seemed to be more scared than he was, regained some of his cockiness and nonchalantly passed the ribbon to Amelia. "Here's your silly ribbon, Amelia." He pointed to the door. "That is just a dumb Indian legend. You can't be scared of that, scaredy pants Patrick."

"It is not a dumb legend!" Amelia said. "This door is closed to protect sacred ground, sacred Abenaki ground of my ancestors!"

Patrick was now more nervous than before and his voice quaked. "We need to get back to the party, Amelia. Come away from the door."

Barton, with an evil smirk, said, "Yeah, Amelia, listen to what Patrick says. You always do anyways. No one cares about the stupid old Indians and their stupid sacred ground anymore either."

This was the straw that broke the camel's back as far as Amelia was concerned. She thrust Barton out of the way and stood firmly in front of the door. "This is not stupid; you're stupid. The Abenaki tribe was here on Mount Desert Island long before you and your family and will be here long after you're gone!"

Barton stepped closer to Amelia, his fear now gone and replaced by arrogance. "If you are so proud of your ancestors, then why don't you just go through this stupid door and visit them!"

"Don't listen to him, Amelia. Let's just go," implored Patrick.

"Are you afraid, Amelia?" taunted Barton.

"I am most certainly not afraid," Amelia said as she reached toward her neck to feel for the familiar pouch that was not there. Her face flashed concern, but only for a second before she added, "I just don't like to break the rules of the ancestors."

"Besides, the door is locked anyways," Patrick said confidently, and they all looked toward the door and the oversized padlock secured to the handle. What followed next was unbelievable. In what seemed like slow motion, the padlock began to swing, screeching as it rubbed against the door, scraping the weathered wood. The lock gave a final shudder and fell to the ground with a thud. All three stopped in their tracks.

"Let's get out of here, fast!" Patrick cried and turned to head in the opposite direction.

"I guess you're right, Patrick. Let's go," Amelia said and backed away from the door.

"Oh, right, good-bye, you chickens. Buck, buck, buck," clucked Barton. "Chickens, big chickens."

Amelia, enraged, shouted, "I'm not chicken!" And she pushed hard on the massive wooden barricade. It breathed a loud creak and opened slowly. The children waited in anticipation, holding their breath, yet nothing happened. Nothing happened at first, that is. But after a few moments, an eerie white light appeared through the crack, followed by a dense, yellowish mist.

"Amelia, don't!" shouted Patrick.

"Go on, I dare ya," said Barton.

The door sighed open wider, and the mist thickened and darkened with each passing second. Cries along with streaks of white light came streaming out of the opening and encompassed the children. Barton and Patrick flailed their arms wildly at the mist, but Amelia remained motionless. The ominous fog soon left the boys, seeming to reject them, but it wrapped and twisted itself completely around Amelia's small frame, lifted her off her feet, and moved her closer to the open doorway. Amelia finally snapped out of her trance, but it was too late.

Her cries could not be heard, drowned out by the shrieks and screams coming from the invading vapor. Patrick tried desperately to seize her arms, clothing, anything he could get his hands on, but could not break the shield the mist surrounded her with. Barton stood as if frozen to the ground, shocked by what he was witnessing.

"Amelia!" Patrick shouted, as tears streamed down his face. With both his fists he beat at the mist, but he was unable to break through. Amelia struggled in vain to move, but all she could do was mouth the words, "Patrick, help me." With that final plea, her book dropped to the ground. The mist changed to black, sucking her behind the door, which closed with a slam. The padlock jumped back up from the ground and locked. Amelia was gone.

Lobster fact: *Until the early 1800s, lobsters were caught by gathering them by hand along the shoreline. Lobstering as a trap fishery started in Maine around 1850. Today Maine is the country's largest lobster-producing state.*

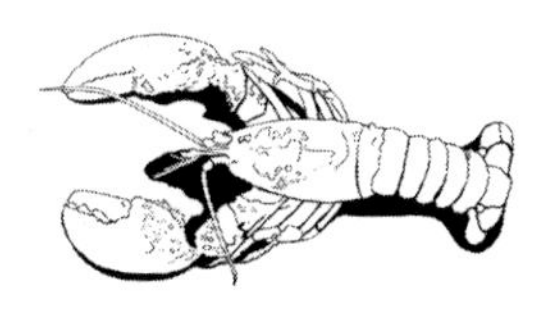

Chapter 4

Small Friends Work Together

One can only imagine the commotion that occurred after the mystical Abenaki door slammed shut and Amelia vanished from sight. Two thirteen-year-old boys running and screaming was not that uncommon a sight; however, Cook, Millie, Mr. O'Leary, Mr. Baxter, and even some of the birthday guests knew immediately that the cries coming from Barton and Patrick were anything but common. Everyone stopped what they were doing and dashed outside. Patrick's father thought the boys had uncovered a beehive and smiled to himself thinking Master Barton much deserved some bee stings. Mr. Baxter grabbed a rifle from the den wall in case the boys were being chased by a black bear. Cook grabbed the only weapon available to her, her broom, to beat off whomever or whatever was causing the boys so much distress, while the party guests huddled together in fear. No one could have imagined what was behind the boys' screams. Amelia was gone, disappeared, vanished, and as Patrick explained, "sucked up through the mist of the door never to be seen again!"

The boys' implausible story prompted Mr. Baxter and Mr. O'Leary to investigate the padlocked door. In a flash, Mr. O'Leary sprinted back to retrieve the small Snow and Nealley axe he kept hanging on the shed wall and used mostly for banging in garden stakes. He gave Cook a look, and she blessed herself and went into the house to call the sheriff. The authorities arrived, and the party guests departed. The other gifts were never opened. Cook, who had taken great pride in making the triple-layer chocolate cake with the coconut cream frosting, decided no one much felt like celebrating anymore, and tossed the rest of it in the garbage. Thus Barton's thirteenth birthday ended, ended with the gift that never was and the party that never finished and the girl who never returned.

With all the commotion right after the boys fled screaming toward the main house, no one noticed a squirrel and two particularly strong and determined chipmunks silently scurrying to the now padlocked door. Amelia's precious book, the book that described the amulets offered to the gods to seal the covenant, lay on the grass, on the exact spot where she dropped it right before the unthinkable, the unimaginable, and soon to be unspeakable thing happened to her. This small trio crept noiselessly from their wooded domain and looked cautiously around. With a nod from the squirrel, all three pushed Amelia's parchment behind the juniper bush that flanked the door.

Lobster fact: *During World War II lobster was considered a delicacy, and thus was not rationed. Lobster meat filled the increasing demand for protein-rich food, and because of the boom of the wartime economy, people could afford to buy it. There was a decline in lobster purchases immediately after the war, but lobster consumption quickly rebounded, almost doubling between 1950 and 1969.*

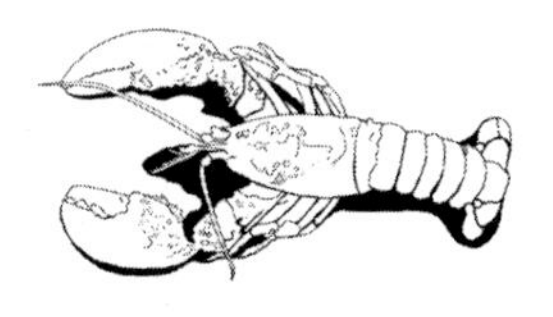

Chapter 5

Return to the Scene of the Crime

While the full July Blood Moon rose over Northeast Harbor, Moon Violet, just fifteen, Violet's mother, Little Bird, and Violet's uncle, Raven's Wing, crept soundlessly along the path to the sacred door. At the door all three began to dance and chant softly. Dancing and chanting, chanting and dancing into the wee hours of the morning. The intended outcome was twofold: to ward off the evil spirits and to ask for Amelia's return. Just as the first blush of pink appeared in the sky, Raven's Wing beat his small drum three times. Moon Violet and her mother stopped their dancing. Moon Violet got down on her hands and knees to push back the branches of the juniper bush and retrieve the book that had briefly belonged to her cousin Amelia. Moon Violet raised it high over her head, while her uncle sprinkled it with a fine powder made of ground seashells, moose antlers, and dried berries, which he took from a small vial he carried around his neck. Little Bird lovingly dusted the book with a pine branch. The ceremony ended just as it had begun, quietly, respectfully, and solemnly, and then the three participants retired as the morning light brightened. The book had been appropriately cleansed and purified and would be preserved until the next owner was revealed.

Lobster fact: *Maine lobstermen have traditionally managed their share of the resource through unofficial lobstering ter-*

ritories. In any port, the lobstermen have an informal, often unspoken agreement about where each member of the community may lay traps. All the members of one community lay their strings of traps in one direction, such as north to south, so they don't tangle their lines in someone else's.

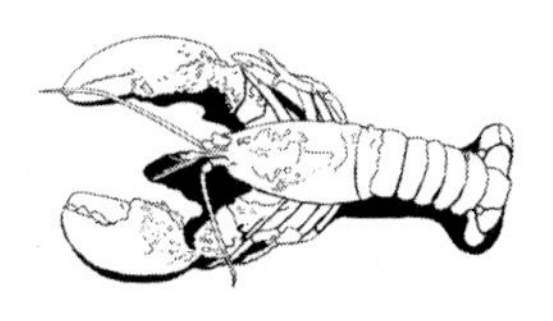

Chapter 6

Boston Aquarium, Penguin Feeding 2012

Twelve-year-old Ani Banke climbed down the ladder leading into the penguin infirmary tank at the Boston Aquarium. Ani's father, Dr. George Banke, was the visiting marine biologist at the aquarium, and Ani hoped to follow in her father's footsteps someday. Penguin feeding was Ani's favorite time. Today was an especially exciting day for Ani because she had been given special privileges to work with the critical care rescue penguins. These are penguins flown in from all over the world to receive treatment at Boston Aquarium's hospital under the direct supervision of Dr. Banke. Ani, in a wet suit, stopped halfway down the ladder to adjust her navy Boston Red Sox hat on top of her wavy, light blonde hair. Then she sprang off the ladder, splashing when she landed in the water. She greeted her father with a big grin. She had been waiting for this moment all week. Her father, a tall man with dark, curly hair, followed behind his younger daughter with a full bucket of fish. Dr. Banke was a true scientist. He knew he wanted to pursue marine biology when he was a child growing up on Cape Cod, and first learned about the creatures living under the sea from clamming with his grandfather in Harwich, Massachusetts. He studied at Harvard University for his undergraduate and graduate degrees in organismic and evolutionary biology. He used to tell Ani that salt water, not blood, pumped through his veins. It was his attempt at humor, which Ani thought was more corny than funny, but regardless she idolized her father.

As they waded to the fake rock in the middle of the tank, Ani was oblivious to the penguin stench and penguin waste covering the rock. She was on a mission, a mission to help the penguins. Ani's father unzipped the front of his wet suit and pulled out a flip chart. He read the names and numbers of the penguins listed across the top. Each penguin had been tagged with a specific number that corresponded with Dr. Banke's chart. All of the staff took turns naming the penguins based upon their individual personalities. And, yes, even penguins had their own style. The greedier penguins, upon seeing the bucket, had already swum over to Ani and her father. They knew the drill, and the drill meant food. Bossy was the first to arrive, number T-60.

"Ah, Miss Bossy, always the first to eat," said Dr. Banke, chuckling as he reached in the bucket and retrieved a few smelts. Bossy approached Dr. Banke with her mouth wide open. One, two, three, she swallowed the fish as fast as he could hold them up to her. Ani recorded the feeding on the chart. Next up was Kitty, so named because she looked like she had whiskers. She was one of Ani's favorites because she normally wanted to swim around Ani and play. Due to her illness, a virus that affects only penguins, she was not too interested in her food. Skillfully Dr. Banke picked her up and held the fish in front of her face. She wiggled her head as Dr. Banke dangled the fish back and forth. Eventually Kitty stopped moving and like a dutiful school child, she opened her mouth wide to eat her allotted fish. This process continued for some time with father and daughter utterly engrossed in their task of checking the tags, counting the smelts, and feeding the penguins.

Finally, only one penguin remained to be fed, Cottontail. He looked like a mix between a penguin and a strange bunny with feathers on his backside. Cottontail was not thriving, which concerned Dr. Banke. He gently scooped up Cottontail and said, "Come on, little fellow. We really want to see you eating some fish today." He held the smelt in front of Cottontail, but the penguin twisted his head away. "Ani, check his data again for me, please."

Ani reviewed the chart. "It looks like he hasn't eaten in the last week, Dad."

Her father frowned. "I don't have to tell you that this is not good, not good at all," he said as he unsuccessfully tried to feed Cottontail again.

"Dr. Banke," an announcement came loudly over the intercom system. "You're needed in the sea turtle tank."

"Ani, I have to go. The sea turtle is ready for his procedure. See if you can have any luck with our friend here. I'll be right back." Dr. Banke positioned Cottontail tenderly on the rock. He handed the bucket of fish to Ani and climbed out of the tank.

Ani cautiously approached Cottontail and took a fish in her right hand from the bucket. Slowly she raised her left hand and placed it on Cottontail's back. Cottontail didn't move, but instead appeared to be staring directly into Ani's deep blue eyes. Ani kept her eyes locked on Cottontail's as well. She spoke softly to him, so softly that it was almost a whisper.

"Come on, little buddy. You heard my father. You really need to eat something today. Not a lot, just a little something." Cottontail curled his head tightly into his chest. "I know you might be feeling lonely and maybe missing your family and your friends, too. I promise you if you eat something today, you will start to feel better, and then you can get out of this small tank and join the rest of the penguins."

It was as if Ani was able to read Cottontail's mind, for as she spoke, he inched closer to her, as if he really was listening to what she was saying. Ani resumed her quiet cajoling. "So, Mr. Cottontail, what's going to happen is that I'm going to take this delicious looking fish." She raised the fish to her nose and sniffed. "Smells great, too." She wrinkled her nose in disgust. "And you're going to open your cute little penguin mouth and eat him. Any questions?" she asked, not waiting for a reply. "Ready, set," she held the fish directly in front of Cottontail's mouth, "go!"

Cottontail straightened his head, blinked his eyes twice,

and opened his mouth wide. Ani dropped the fish in, and it slid smoothly down Cottontail's throat. Mission accomplished.

Lobster fact: *Lobster shell disease, caused by a bacterial infection in the carapace, has become considerably more common in recent years. A new type of shell disease was observed in New England in the late 1990s, when temperatures were higher than in previous years, and it has been steadily moving north toward Maine and Canada.*

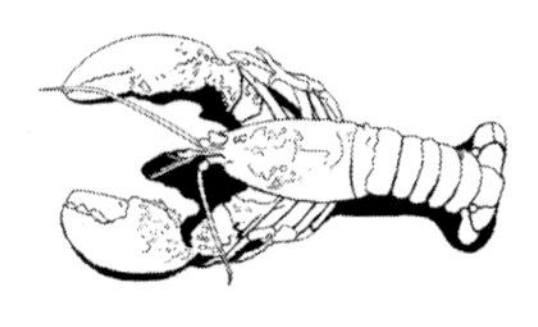

Chapter 7

Mount Desert Island, a Death

The grandfather clock in the hallway struck twelve midnight, "Bong, bong, bong." The noise could be heard up the staircase. "Bong, bong, bong," the clock continued, measured as always and precise. As the twelfth bong rang, the nurse checked the pulse on her patient, a very, very old man lying in a narrow bed with the covers tucked neatly around his chest.

Dr. Maynes checked her watch and wrote on his medical chart: Twelve midnight, June 2, 2012. "Better let his son know," she said with a frown.

The nurse assisting Dr. Maynes agreed and left the bedroom. Moments later Barton Thuya Baxter III dashed into the room. He looked from the old man in the bed to the doctor and then back to the old man.

"I'm sorry for your loss," said Dr. Maynes.

Barton had a sorrowful look on his face as he approached the bed. He reached up and twirled his now gray but still full hair. Time had been kind to Barton. He was tall and thin, but still quite healthy and still quite terrible. He paused and looked at his father. "Well, you certainly took your time, Father," he said with a sneer.

His unkind comment shocked the doctor and nurse. Next, Barton reached around his father's neck and pulled out the chain that lay underneath his pajama top. Barton's sneer now resembled a grin. There were several keys at the end of the chain. "Ah, ha!" he said. "Now, Father, you have no choice but to give me what is rightfully mine. I have waited for fifty-five years to get my special birthday surprise, and you can't do anything about it, anything at all." He feverishly flipped through the keys, his tugging and pulling causing old Mr. Baxter's head to wobble side to side as he searched for what he wanted. Finally, Dr. Maynes stepped in,

"Here," she said, "let me help you with this," and she gingerly removed the chain from around his father's neck and handed it to Barton. Barton seized it without as much as a thank you. Swiftly his hands moved over the keys.

"It's not here," he cried. He said it again, much louder this time. "It's not here! What have you done with the key? Where is it?" he shouted at his father. "Where is it?" Barton shook his dead father's shoulders roughly. "It's mine, I tell you, mine!"

"Now, sir, I know you must be in shock at the death of your beloved parent," said Dr. Maynes, "but he was ninety-eight years old. You need to get a grip."

Barton's hair twiddling increased, and he glowered as he shouted, "You must have it! I know he gave it to you."

"I don't know what you're talking about, Mr. Baxter," the nurse said.

"Perhaps you would like something to calm you down," the doctor offered.

Barton became even more frantic and moved back toward his father and shouted, "You can't keep it from me! You just can't. I win, I always do. You just wait and see what I do now!" And with that, he stormed out of the bedroom and slammed the door shut, rattling the pictures on the bedroom wall. Soon, the thump, thump, thump of his feet going down the stairs faded out.

The doctor and nurse exchanged glances. The nurse hurried to the small window overlooking the road below. "He's gone," she informed the doctor. Dr. Maynes cautiously removed a brass chain from around her own neck and held it up to her recently deceased patient. The light from the bedside table shone on it, casting shadows on the bedroom walls.

"I kept your promise, Mr. Baxter. It's safe with me. Now,

rest in peace, my kind man, rest in peace," said the doctor, raising the chain up toward heaven.

On the end of the chain, dangling in the light was the key that Barton was looking for, screaming for, pleading for. The key that eluded him all these many years. This was no ordinary key, however. This key was made of brass, centuries earlier, forged into the shape of a lobster tail.

Lobster fact: *Based on the descriptions of lobsters seen by fishermen in colonial times, lobsters sometimes lived to be about 150 years old. Not surprisingly, when the lobster industry began in the 1800s, the life expectancy of lobsters decreased. The oldest lobster officially recorded lived to the age of 100 years.*

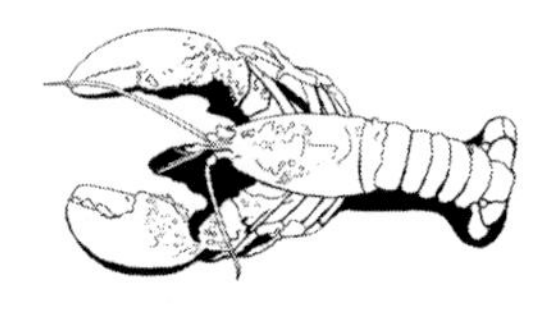

Chapter 8

The Will

"We are just waiting for one more person before I begin to read the Will and Testament of Barton Thuya Baxter the second, who died yesterday after a long, drawn-out illness," said the mayor of Bar Harbor, Mayor Peterson, while finishing up his favorite lunch, a lobster roll. As he spoke, a bit of lobster fell from the end of the toasted bun onto his lobster tie. "Nuts," he sputtered while picking up the lobster meat with his chubby fingers and placing the bite back into his mouth.

Mayor Peterson was a large man, a very large man who enjoyed eating and lobsters and lobsters and eating. His office was cluttered with everything lobster. He had a lobster clock with a lobster claw that moved back and forth with every second that it ticked, a nautical chart with the details of all the traps lying underneath the sea waiting to catch their prey, and a lobster ceiling fan that circled overhead while his guests drank their coffee from red lobster mugs. His desk featured every lobster gadget imaginable: lobster-themed pens, pencils, snow globes, and note paper shared space with plastic, glass, stuffed, plush, and blowup lobsters. Even his drapes were made from fabric covered with lobsters, which matched his tie. Behind his desk loomed a seven-foot cardboard cutout lobster wearing a sash that read *Bar Harbor Annual Lobster Festival, July 14–July 21*.

The mayor impatiently looked at his watch, lobster of course, and frowned. "Nancy," he said to his assistant, "we're going to have to get started here because I am sure our fine guest has other important business to attend to." The mayor looked at the older man sitting opposite his desk, taking a sip from a very large mug with a lobster claw handle.

"No. No, sir. I have all the time in the world. My curiosity hasn't been this alive since, well, I can't remember when is all," said Patrick O'Leary as he took another sip. "I am in no hurry at all."

Patrick O'Leary, now reaching sixty-eight, had aged quite well. Garden work with plenty of manual labor and fresh air had been good for his body and his soul, for that matter. He still had the same ruddy complexion with brown hair, a little thinner and a little grayer but hair nonetheless. He wore a clean but broken-in pair of work boots, rumpled khaki pants, and a blue button-down shirt with his trademark lupine flower in the lapel.

"Yes, yes, I am curious, very, very curious," he repeated to no one in particular. He smiled a private smile that might have indicated he knew more about this meeting than he was willing to let on.

The mayor, in his usual rushed manner, gobbled down his lobster roll, handed the empty red-checked basket to his assistant, and started rustling through the papers. He cleared his throat and loudly read, "I, Barton Thuya Baxter the second, being of sound mind and body ... "

A loud bang outside the office followed by rapid footsteps interrupted him. Nancy jumped up to open the office door, but the visitor was quicker and practically knocked her down as he pushed his way into the room. Barton Thuya Baxter III had arrived!

"Hello there, mayor. Sorry for the delay. Pressing business. Couldn't be helped. Let's just cut all the small talk. I am fully aware that as the only surviving heir of my beloved father, I am to inherit it all: the business, the investments, the property, and, most important, the garden cottage. So let's not waste my time any further, and let me sign on the dotted line." Barton grabbed at the papers on the mayor's desk. He had yet to recognize the gentleman sitting quietly in the room, still smiling the knowing smile. Unlike Patrick's good health gained by working the land, Barton's health had been maintained by money, power, and influence over others. Jetting off to exotic vacations, having servants always at his beck and call, and simply bossing everyone around had instilled vitality, vigor, and vanity tenfold. His piercing blue eyes seemed to have lost whatever warmth they had in his youth, only to be replaced by steeliness.

"Now wait just a snail's tail's minute, Barton," protested the mayor. Barton glowered at him. "I mean, Mr. Baxter. Your father specifically requested that you be present at the will reading along with my fine guest here, Mr. Patrick O'Leary," the mayor said as he swept his doughy hand toward Patrick. Barton's head snapped up quickly at the mention of Patrick O'Leary's name, and he pivoted toward him in amazement. A look of panic passed over Barton's face so quickly that only the sharp eye of the mayor's assistant, Nancy, noticed the flinch. The panic immediately switched to a look of surliness. Barton's skinny lips curled into a snarl.

Patrick greeted Barton calmly and coolly with an air of indifference: "Hello, Barton."

Just the mere sound of Patrick's voice seemed to enrage Barton. "What is the meaning of all this, mayor? It is ridiculous to have him here," Barton cried as he pointed a long, slender finger at Patrick. "Why would we need to have the gardener here, unless of course, my father wanted something mowed, but seeing as he's dead, I don't think Patrick is necessary. Never fear, I will continue to make sure to maintain the gardens as we Baxters have done for generations. Consider yourself fired, Patrick. Don't let the door hit you on your way out." Barton cheerfully dismissed Patrick with a wave of his hand as if shooing an annoying fly off a bowl of fruit.

"Now, let's all just stay calm and rational here, Mr. Baxter. Sit, sit, please sit down and let me read the will as dictated to my father, who was, of course, your family attorney, by your father on July 25, 1957." The mayor shuffled the papers on his desk. Barton winced at the mention of July 25, 1957. Patrick also reacted to hearing the date of the will.

A subdued Barton softly said, "July 25 is my birthday; 1957 would have been my thirteenth birthday. My father threw me a big birthday party. There were balloons, ice cream, and even a pretty white pony. I liked the pony." His voice became almost childlike, and Barton sat down. "My father took back the present he gave me."

Patrick sat up straighter in his chair and nervously touched the lupine in his lapel. In his eyes the smallest hint of tears began to form.

"Yes, yes, Barton, that was a long time ago, and I'm sure you had a lovely birthday party, but now let's get back to the will," the mayor said.

As the mayor read the will, Barton vacantly stared out the lobster-curtained window. He raised his right fingers to the nape of his neck and twiddled his hair for only a second, then slowly lowered his hand and placed his fingers in the right front pocket of his jacket to feel the familiar softness of a hair ribbon. Once the fingers made contact with the object, Barton let out a long, near silent sigh.

"As predicted, Barton, your father has left you, as the only surviving heir, the following: stocks, bonds, canning factory, Baxter properties including the apartment in the Back Bay in Boston, Massachusetts, the house in the Caribbean, and the estate in Northeast Harbor at 13 Baxter Lane," the mayor read.

"Great," Barton said. "Finally it's all mine, and my father's library, too." By now he had let go of the ribbon, and with his mind back onto his inheritance, his arrogance returned.

"Let me clarify that the estate includes the main house, the pool, the tennis courts, the stables, and the property surrounding all of the above mentioned," the mayor said. "The cottage and the cottage garden are bequeathed to Patrick O'Leary to care for on behalf of the Friends of Acadia National Park. The contents of the cottage are Patrick's alone to do with as he sees fit."

Barton leapt to his feet and shouted, "What? This is absurd! Let me see those papers. The garden cottage is supposed to be mine." He grabbed the papers out of the mayor's hands.

"I've been waiting fifty-five years to get my hands on my birthday, er, the cottage." Barton scanned the will. "This is not to be borne. Giving the cottage to Patrick, unbelievable! My father was an old coot. He was ninety-eight years old when he died. He didn't know what he was doing." Barton tore up the will. "My lawyer will be in touch with you!"

"Now, Barton, you know I've already filed a copy of this with the state, so ripping it up won't make a difference," the mayor said calmly.

"I can't believe this! It's your fault," Barton yelled while glaring at Patrick. "This must have been your plan all along. Convince my doddering old father to bequeath the cottage to you. And I know why. You always blamed me for what happened on that day." He stuck out a finger at Patrick, but Patrick remained silent and just stared at Barton.

The mayor pulled out a small security box from his desk and took a key from his breast pocket. He unlocked the box and lifted out a brass lobster tail, which he handed over to Patrick. Patrick took the key from the mayor and put it in his shirt pocket.

Seeing this, Barton raged at a fever pitch. "That key was supposed to be mine!" he screamed shrilly. "You will be hearing from my lawyer!" he threatened again as he swept out of the office. The mayor, Patrick, and Nancy were left speechless by the spectacle, a silence only to be broken by the lobster clock striking noon and the lobster claw swinging back and forth twelve times.

Lobster fact: *Lobsters have been around for approximately 500 million years. They are depicted in the art or folklore of many cultures. The Romans featured lobsters battling octopuses on mosaic floors. Turkish warriors wore helmets with a design based on the lobster's armor plating.*

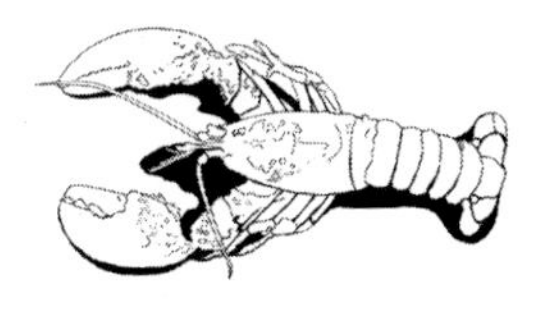

Chapter 9

Theft in the Garden

A tall, thin man carrying a satchel and dressed in black approached the back door of the small garden cottage on the estate of Barton Thuya Baxter III. He reached into the satchel and pulled out a pair of needle-nose pliers. He opened the utility box door on the side of the house and clipped the exposed green wires, extinguishing a small red light in the box.

"Ah, good," whispered the man. From under his black cap, he turned on his headlamp. Again he reached into his bag and this time retrieved a small hammer. Two quick blows on the corner windowpane shattered the silence of the evening. The man punched his gloved hand through the broken opening and turned the latch of the door from the inside. He pressed his head against the door and listened for the click, click as the lock released from the latch. He removed his hand, shook off the remaining glass, and opened the door. Once inside he used the light from his headlamp to scan the room. As he rotated his head, the light lingered on a picture of Barton Thuya Baxter II holding a big fish, and then on a picture of a young bride and her groom getting into a carriage. "Mother," muttered the man as he placed the picture face down.

The light stopped on the last picture in the row. It featured three children: Patrick, Barton, and Amelia in the middle. A pony and balloons were in the background, indicating that it was taken on Barton's thirteenth birthday. The birthday when the gift was given and then taken, when Amelia was there and then not.

The gloved hands smashed the frame and pulled out the photo, ripped it in half, and crumpled the portion with Patrick, throwing it on the ground. Carefully the man traced Amelia's outline before placing the picture inside his breast pocket. He approached the door of the study of Mr. Barton Thuya Baxter II. He tried the handle, but the door was locked. The man slammed his body against the door, but it didn't budge. "Ouch" he cried, rubbing his right hip with his gloved hand. Next he tried kicking in the door. One, two, three times he tried, but to no avail. Finally, one last kick and the door gave way. He was in. Once again, the light scanned the room, but this time more quickly, stopping at the painting behind the desk. He swiftly moved there and tugged at the painting. It swung away from the wall, exposing the safe. A third trip to the satchel produced a bomb. Smiling, he attached the two ends of the small device to the outer safe door. The bomb was designed to detonate ten seconds after he activated a button on his watch. He knelt behind the leather sofa across the room and pushed the button. A deafening boom reverberated across the study. The room filled with smoke, but the man had already opened the side window. The bomb was just strong enough to rip through both safe doors, and as he approached what remained, the man fanned the smoke away and plunged his hand inside the hole.

"Finally, finally, I have waited and waited, and finally I get my birthday present," he cried childishly. Triumphantly he held the deerskin parchment over his head while dancing around the smoky study of his recently deceased father.

"Ow!" he winced as pain surged through his hip. "Owie," he said again. Yet the pain did not stop his jubilation. He continued his dance, but this time he swung only his hands and stood still and rejoiced. "Mine, mine, mine, all mine!"

Lobster fact: *While lobsters do not possess any kind of receptor akin to human pain receptors, they do have stress receptors. Most scientists believe that lobsters have a sophisticated nervous system and that they can feel pain.*

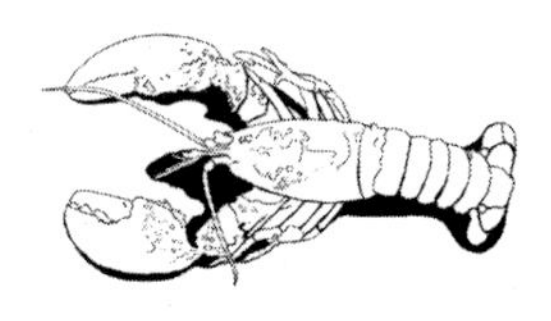

Chapter 10

Academia and Arrogance Assemble

"Bert, as a college trustee and personal friend of the president of Maine Oceanic College, I am sure that you will be willing to help me with my request," Barton said as he sat down without waiting to be asked in the Bar Harbor office of Professor Sol, chairman of the Department of Native American Studies.

Sol's office walls were adorned with Native American artifacts ranging from tribal masks and spears to ancient drawings and tapestries. Several shelves around the room buckled with books, books, and more books. Additional stacks lined the floor space in front of the shelves. In fact, the only space available to put anything anywhere was Professor Sol's neat as a pin desk, where he sat. Behind him hung his college diplomas: the University of Maine bachelor's degree in American Studies shone brightly next to his Princeton doctorate in Native American Studies.

"I was informed that you are the expert on the Abenaki Indians," Barton said without giving the professor a chance to respond. "I want you to look at this and tell me what it means," he demanded as he shoved several papers toward Sol.

Professor Sol reached for the copies with his left hand as his small dark eyes widened. Bert Sol was a tall, bony man with flaming red wiry hair that he kept cropped short close to his small ears. Closer inspection of those ears revealed a small earring on the lower left lobe that resembled a tiny white barnacle. But Sol's barnacle could be viewed only by those who got close, really, really close. Professor Sol, a man with a prickly disposition, didn't allow anyone to get close, no one, not ever.

Barton observed that Sol's right sleeve was pinned up and tucked into the folds of his shirt. "What happened to your arm?" he asked.

Nervously, Professor Sol said in a tinny voice, "Boating accident, when I was younger."

Barton rudely didn't respond, as he asked only out of a momentary curiosity, but since the reply was uninteresting to him, he promptly returned to the point at hand. "Well, can you tell me what it says?"

Professor Sol carefully examined the papers Barton had given him. He flipped them over and over, looked at them sideways, upside down, and right side up again. "Oh my, my, my, this is most unusual, most unusual for sure," he squeaked while turning the pages again with his only working hand. "Where did you say you got this?"

"I didn't," replied Barton coolly. "It came from a present." He paused. "A birthday present from my father."

"Right," Professor Sol said, seeming to understand that the where and how was not meant for him to know. He changed his tactic. "I was just asking because it might give me more information about the writings if I could see the source. I also would like to say that if the source was original, meaning the authentic writings from this tribe, then it would be an invaluable ancient artifact..."

"I don't care about ancient artifacts. I just want to know what it all means!"

Professor Sol timidly replied, "Oh, yes, well then, let's see here." Sol pulled out a magnifying glass and looked more closely at the words on the paper. "You might want to get comfortable. This may take a while," he said. "I might have to copy some of these papers, if that is all right with you." Barton nodded, rose from his chair, and moved behind the professor's desk as Sol scrutinized the documents.

"These writings indicate that this is from the Abenaki tribe a very long time ago."

"I could have told you that, Sol. I want to know WHAT

DOES IT SAY?" Barton shouted.

"This drawing here," the professor said, pointing to what looked like a mountain with a wave across it and weird squiggles and dots below, "represents Cadillac Mountain, or as the Abenaki once called it, 'Eagle's Nest or Eagle's Perch.'"

As the professor continued deciphering and explaining, Barton only half listened. For Barton was devising a plan. A big plan. A plan he had been planning for nearly fifty-five years, ever since his father had given him the parchment and then ripped it out of his hands so forcefully. Barton was going to find the orb, the sacred covenant, and then he was going to sell it, sell it to the highest bidder. The more he thought about his plan, the greater his smile grew. Grinning, he reached up and twiddled his hair and leaned in closer to Sol to find out where his fortune lay.

While Barton was planning, Sol was also planning, interpreting and planning, but planning nonetheless. Professor Sol knew that the pages Barton had given him were copies of a rare Abenaki artifact. So rare, in fact, that no one was even sure of its existence. Rumors, speculations, and conjectures were all that most of his colleagues were able to boast. Sol always knew the truth, however, and today he held in his one hand the proof he needed. This discovery was just short of a miracle, and Sol was at the center of it all. Like Barton's, his lips, too, formed a tight, little smile.

Lobster fact: *Like people, lobsters exhibit "handedness." Some lobsters have the crusher claw on the right side, while others have it on the left.*

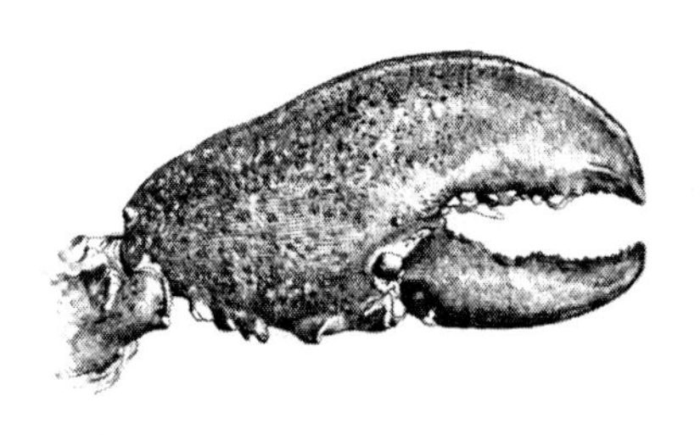

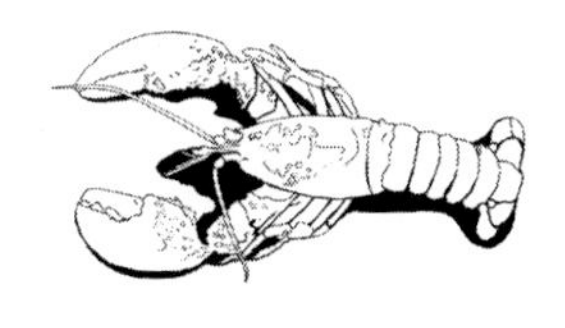

Chapter 11

Another Theft

Barton finished his breakfast in the formal dining room while the clock over the mantel chimed six in the morning. An awkward, timid servant, fully clad in butler's attire, waited patiently behind Barton's chair. Sorenson had worked for Mr. Baxter for only a few months. The last butler had lasted just a day. Sorenson had thought it would be adventurous to move from the West Coast to the East Coast. He never imagined that his adventure would come from trying to avoid being yelled at by his boss instead of exploring the beauty of the Maine coast. Sorenson had an itch on the side of his face, a face that was thinner than when he first arrived since his nerves made it impossible for him to eat, but he knew better than to scratch for fear he would disrupt his boss's newspaper reading. Sorenson had learned this lesson yesterday and had spent the better half of his morning being reprimanded by Mr. Baxter. Sorenson clenched his angular jar tight and prayed the itch would go away soon.

Barton took a last sip of orange juice from a crystal goblet and patted the corners of his mouth dry. An older, plump woman with a kind face entered from a side door and removed Barton's plate while the butler helped him pull out his chair.

"Mrs. Pollinger, Sorenson and I will be going to the basement to work on something that doesn't concern you or anyone else in the household for that matter. I don't want anyone bothering us, or they will be asking for immediate dismissal. Do you understand?"

"Yes, sir, perfectly," replied Mrs. Pollinger, and she exited the same door she entered while giving a sympathetic eye to Sorenson, as if to say, "good luck." Sorenson acknowledged her concern ever so subtly.

"Sorenson, follow me at once!" Barton barked, and he briskly walked out of the dining room and made his way through the house. Barton's legs were so long and limber that his gait was unusually fast and even more so today as he appeared to be on a very important mission. Sorenson had to hop, skip, and run to keep up with him. Barton passed through several rooms, each beautifully decorated and filled with antiques. Finally, he reached the library, where shelves filled with books from floor to ceiling lined the room. A large portrait of Barton's father hung over the stone fireplace.

"Close the door," he ordered. "Lock it, too, and come over here." Barton pulled down the left sconce of the pair that bordered the fireplace. The fireplace rolled to the side to reveal narrow, granite stairs leading downward. Barton took hold of a lantern that hung from the top of the stairs.

"Step lively. I have a busy day today as always ..." Barton's voice trailed off as his head disappeared around a curve. Sorenson scurried after Barton and cautiously began his descent. Barton walked down, down, down the gray stairs, stopping occasionally to check the papers he had pulled out of his breast pocket.

Sorenson was confused and started to protest. "Sir, do you think you could tell me where we are going? I don't seem to recognize this way to the cellar. I am wondering if you wouldn't want to use the other staircase, the one from the kitchen."

"Save your breath, Sorenson. The air quality gets poorer the lower we go, and yes, we are going lower, much lower according to this map," he said as he held up one of the papers that he had carelessly torn out of the precious Abenaki parchment.

"Now, here we are. It's behind the furnace over there. I remember my grandfather telling me something about hiding the moonshine behind this during the time of Prohibition," Barton said as he felt behind the bulky black furnace. "Where is it, where is it? Ah, here it is. I knew it had to be here. All roads lead to Baxter eventually, isn't that right, Sorenson?" Barton extracted a small handle buried within the cement wall. "Now, pull on this, Sorenson," Barton commanded. "I believe a door should be attached to this handle."

Sorenson did as he was told and after several attempts, accompanied by huffing and puffing, the outline of a door emerged. Barton became impatient with Sorenson and practically knocked him out of the way. "Let me do it. You are too weak!" Barton pulled on the handle, straining with all his might, and practically willed the door open with his determination and spite.

With a loud creak and groan, the door emerged from the confines of the wall and opened. As it did so, the temperature dropped, and Sorenson buttoned up his jacket. A fine mist appeared, caressing both of them. Sorenson licked his lips. "Salty," he whispered to himself.

Barton said, "I heard you, Sorenson, and I don't remember asking you any questions. However, you are correct; it is salty. We are getting closer to sea level, and the salt from the ocean permeates the air." Barton inhaled deeply. "It is elixir to the Baxter family. I can feel my blood pumping. Nothing like it!" Barton twiddled his hair and moved down the passageway, a narrow tunnel with water-soaked walls that echoed with his rapid footsteps.

Sorenson was skeptical and frightened, but he could do nothing but follow his employer. The air smelled damp and moldy and tickled Sorenson's nose. He was allergic to mildew. Moments later, with Sorenson getting more and more anxious with each slippery step, he blurted out, "Is that the ocean that I am hearing?"

Barton mimicked him with a singsong voice, a habit he developed when he was younger. "'Is that the ocean that I am hearing?' You can relax, Sorenson, we are perfectly safe and you will remain so if you obey my orders and do what you are told."

"As always, sir, I always do what you ask of me," Sorenson said.

"I know this of you, Sorenson, and that is why you were chosen to assist me on this very exciting and interesting adventure. An adventure so secretive that if you ever tell anyone of the existence of the door, these caverns, and what we are about to do, you can rest assured that I will have you eliminated for good. Comprehendo?"

"Per, per, perfectly."

"I thought so, Sorenson. Now, we are wasting time. Let's get on with it. I've already told you, I have a lot to do today."

Thirty minutes later, Barton found himself at a junction. Standing in the center, he turned toward three tunnels, each leading in a different direction. He consulted the map. "There, this is the one," he said looking at the center tunnel, "or maybe it's this one," he exclaimed, examining the tunnel on the right. This passageway emitted a low mist, yellow in color. "Mist, yes, mist, yellow mist, this must be the one," he cheered as he disappeared into the fog.

"Wait, wait for me," cried Sorenson.

The two men were swiftly surrounded by the vapor. The roar of the ocean increased and soon the sound became deafening. Barton had to crouch, as the ceiling had dropped a few feet. Sorenson's only advantage here was that he stood four inches shorter than his boss.

"It has to be here," Barton said as he referred to the map. "Turn around, Sorenson, and let me have your back." Sorenson dutifully obliged. Barton talked low to himself. "Sol said this meant near Thunder Hole, around this bend here." His fingers traced the map and pushed into Sorenson's back. "Which leads us to here, the crossroads, and now this is mist and this is yellow, and this looks like..." Barton picked up the map and rotated it counterclockwise, counting each of his steps out loud as he walked. "One, two, three, four, and five!" he finished, quite pleased with himself. "It should be right here," he cried and flapped his arms in the air. The mist parted to reveal a raised circular slab with several designs etched around the perimeter.

"What have we here?" Barton giddily asked, not expecting an answer. He approached the tablet, which was about the diameter of a bicycle tire, and waved his hands again at the invading mist. This time, when the mist parted, it revealed a singular, egg-shaped orb carved from rose quartz.

"Ah, ha! It's true! My father was telling the truth all along. Oh, how I would love to show this to him," he exulted as he grasped the orb that he had coveted for most of his lifetime. "At last!" he shouted loudly in order to be heard over the ocean waves beating on the cavern walls. He raised the orb straight out in front of him in elation. Victory was sweet, but only for a few seconds as the yellow mist swirled around them and then turned as black as charcoal. The smell changed from mold to decay as a loud creaking emanated from below, and both men watched the granite tablet sink down, level with the cavern floor. Barton's face registered slight concern while Sorenson looked absolutely terrified.

"Time to leave, Sorenson, let's go," Barton said, and he brought the orb closer to his chest and while doing so, twisted it ever so slightly. What he saw within the orb almost caused him to lose his balance and drop it to the ground. A girl with two long braids and brown eyes blinked back at him.

"Amelia!"

Lobster fact: *Lobsters come in several colors besides the usual blue green (their shells don't turn red until they are boiled), including blue, yellow, red, and white. Some even come in two colors, with half the shell one color and the other half a totally different color.*

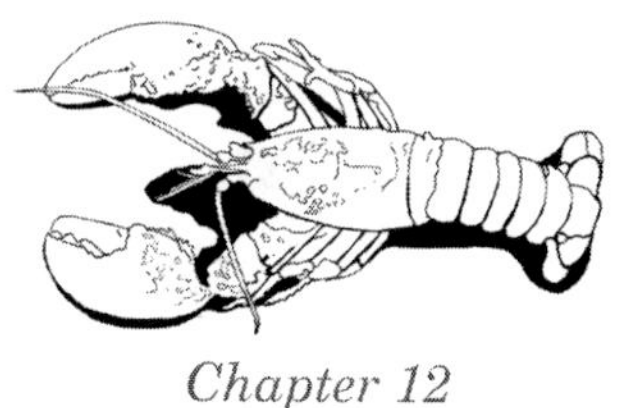

Chapter 12

Something Odd Is Happening

"Do you have that chart, Ani?" Dr. Banke yelled as he pulled on a green rope at the end of the dock on the grounds of the Woods Hole Oceanographic Institution in Massachusetts where the family lived.

"Yes, I do, Dad. It's right here," Ani shouted back as she held up the chart. Ani was dressed in a sweatshirt and jeans with tall, red rubber boots. Her hair was tied up in a high ponytail that swished back and forth each time she responded to her father. She perched on the rocks at the edge of the dock. "We haven't seen any since last Tuesday, remember, Dad?"

"Are you sure about that, Ani?" her father asked, tilting his head sideways.

"Positive, Dad," she said as she tapped the chart with the marker attached by a string to the clipboard. "See?" She waved the clipboard that held the chart.

"Well, there's bound to be something in Number five. I loaded it with extra fish heads," he said as he finally yanked the lobster trap from the ocean floor. The trap landed with a crash on the long dock. Dr. Banke unfastened the trap door and peered into the main holding area, the parlor. Nothing was in the trap. No lobster and no fish heads. "This is most unusual," Dr. Banke said as he closed the trap door. "Hand me that chart, Ani. I need to check it myself." He reviewed the pages for several minutes, flipping to past records clipped underneath the top sheet.

"It's been over two weeks since we have seen any lobsters.

This just doesn't make any sense," Dr. Banke mumbled to himself as he walked back to the end of the dock and stared out over the vast ocean.

Ani peered below the surface. The water was calm, and she could almost catch her own reflection while the tide gently lapped back and forth. She noticed a starfish clinging to the side of a rock. She called to the starfish, "Hello, little fellow. How ya doing?" Ani was unaware of the two seals floating patiently under the dock, their large black eyes following her every move. Soon, they silently submerged, not wanting to be seen. Ani watched as the starfish detached one tentacle from the rock and shook it back and forth. She spoke out loud to the starfish since her father was absorbed in his research. "It looks like you're waving to me."

Ani lay down on her stomach on the dock and hung her head over the side to look at the ocean floor, a favorite pastime of hers. At the exact moment Ani swung her head down, the seals reappeared. Both parties were shocked to be staring at each other.

"Ahhh," Ani cried and jumped up. The seals barked and hastily dove and disappeared.

"Ani, stop screaming. You're going to scare off the lobsters and all the fish for that matter," Dr. Banke said. He rushed from the end of the dock to her side.

"Dad, it's just that, well, there was this starfish and then the seals, and they scared me and … " She didn't finish her sentence as her father's annoyed look told her to stop talking.

Thankfully, just then Eliza called from the house. "Hey, you guys, dinner is ready. Come and get it while it's hot!"

"Right, let's eat. I'm starving, Ani. This lobster problem is serious, honey, and well, I just can't have you goofing around while I am trying to figure out what is happening, okay?" He put his arm around her back.

"Okay, sorry, Dad." Ani smiled apologetically. They looked to the sky as they both heard the distant sound of a helicopter.

"Must be a Coast Guard rescue. Let's go and see what concoction Eliza has cooked up for us tonight," said Dr. Banke.

“I wouldn’t be too excited, Dad. You know Eliza can only make macaroni and cheese from the box or spaghetti.”

“Two of my favorite meals,” a bemused Dr. Banke said.

Lobster fact: *In one study, researchers put a camera in a baited lobster trap and monitored it for twenty-four hours. Many lobsters entered the trap, and more than half nibbled at the bait, but surprisingly, 94 percent of them walked right out. In one twelve-hour period, lobsters made over 3,000 approaches to the trap, but only 45 entered, and only 5 were trapped, 3 of which were under size. So out of more than 3,000 approaches, there were only 2 salable lobsters!*

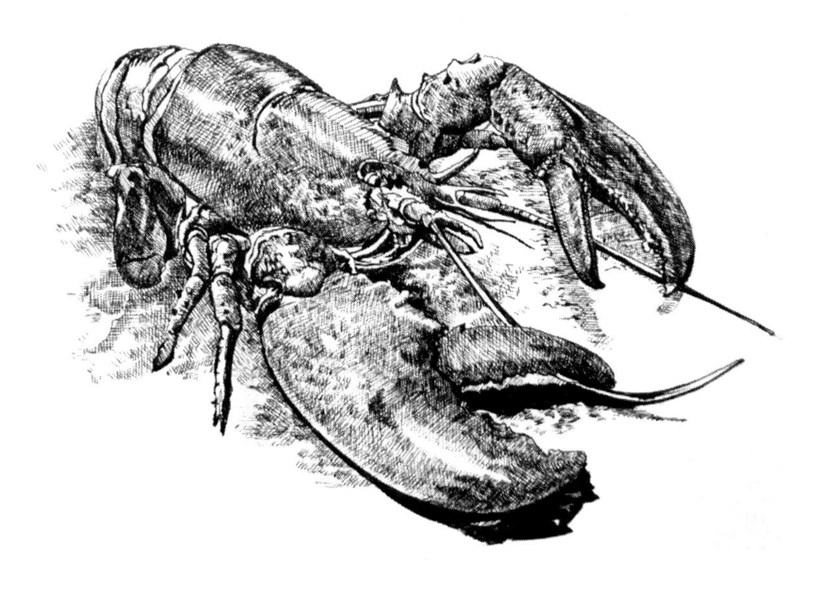

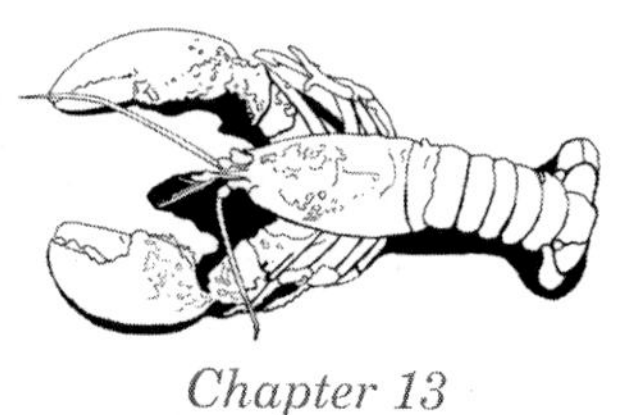

Chapter 13

Thirteen, Take Two

The Banke family sat around a large rectangular table littered with half-eaten dishes of very orange looking macaroni and cheese. Windows on all sides of the simple but elegant two-story house afforded amazing views of the ocean. Ani's paper napkin was crumpled on top of her plate to hide a large helping of the congealed orange pasta. "This is a great birthday dinner, Eliza, but I'm stuffed," Ani said to her fifteen-year-old sister. Where Ani was fair skinned and blue eyed, much like her mother, Eliza had dark hair and green eyes, more like her dad. Eliza and Ani were close sisters even though they had completely different tastes. Eliza tended to have a more dramatic personality and added this drama to her style of dress. Ani, on the other hand, was more levelheaded and relaxed. Regardless, the sisters enjoyed each other's company most of the time.

Dr. Banke reached for the large bowl in the center of the table. "This is a particularly superior batch of macaroni tonight, Liza. I must have some more," he cheerfully said as he scooped up the orange glop. The macaroni had now hardened and stuck to the bottom of the bowl, so when he tried to pull the serving spoon out, the entire bowl lifted off the table.

"What have we here? I guess I will just have to eat the entire bowl. That is, if I can get the spoon out of it." He laughed.

"Dad, it's not funny," cried Eliza, but she couldn't help laughing along with her father.

"Really, Eliza, Mom would be extremely proud to see what

you have done with her recipe," Ani said and giggled.

"Oh, come on, guys, it isn't that bad!" Eliza argued half-heartedly."Well, the cake won't have you laughing; it is going to be perfect," she said as she cleared the table. "Help me with the dishes even if it is your thirteenth birthday today, Ani."

"I don't know if I will have room for cake since I'm so full from my dinner," Ani choked out while laughing even harder. Eliza stuck her tongue out at her younger sister.

"All right, that's enough. Let's all clean up together." Dr. Banke pushed his chair back and headed to the sink with the macaroni and cheese still stuck to the spoon and bowl.

The Banke family finished the cleanup together, except for the pasta pot, which definitely needed to soak overnight. Family tradition dictated that the birthday person gets blindfolded and led to the sofa to await the cake and presents. Tonight Ani was escorted to her seat by her father, who gently pushed her onto the couch while Eliza put a ridiculous birthday hat on her head, which was actually a large birthday cake complete with fake, glowing candles with little jingle bells for flames. Each time Ani moved, the bells jingled and Ani giggled. Then her father turned off the lights.

"We are ready, Eliza," called Dr. Banke.

Eliza entered the living room with an enormous white cake, which looked quite solid despite the earlier pasta fiasco. The cake was lit up brightly with fourteen candles, which illuminated Eliza's face, making her look ghostly.

"I am the birthday ghoul," Eliza said in a ghoulish voice.

"Eliza! Cut it out," cried Ani, whose movement and speaking caused the candles on her head to jingle loudly.

"Let's sing, Eliza," said Dr. Banke. What followed was a loud and off-key rendition of "Happy Birthday." Ani blew out all the candles in one breath. "Make a wish, sweetie," Dr. Banke reminded Ani.

"I bet it is to not have to go rock climbing in New Mexico," Eliza said.

Ani giggled again and shook her jingling head in agreement. "I will never tell," she said.

"Let's do gifts now," cried Eliza as she switched the lights back on.

Dr. Banke selected a large box from the coffee table and handed it to Ani. "Now this might not be your first choice gift, but I know it is something that you can use."

Ani smiled sweetly. "Thanks, Dad." She tore off the brightly colored wrapping paper. "It is kind of heavy, Dad."

"Yes, it should be, it should be."

Ani lifted the box lid off with great anticipation. She loved presents, and her parents made a point of always giving unique and special gifts to her and her sister. Her face was flushed with excitement only to change to disappointment when she viewed the contents of the box: a pair of climbing boots, clamps, ropes, and gloves, all to be used for a rock-climbing trip that the family would be taking next month. Ani's mother was an archaeologist and was leading a dig in New Mexico for the entire summer. Ani, Eliza, and Dr. Banke would be joining the other Dr. Banke to help the team with the dig site, something that Ani was looking forward to much more than the family climbing trip.

"This equipment will be perfect for you and will help you feel more secure and give you a chance to overcome your fear of heights," Dr. Banke said.

"If you say so, Dad," said an unconvinced Ani.

"Open my present now, Ani! I just know you're going to love it!" Eliza said as she handed her a newspaper-wrapped box. Ani ripped through the paper to find a large flat box with a clear plastic covering. Ani's brow began to frown only slightly so as not to hurt her sister's feelings.

"Makeup," she said flatly. "I don't really use makeup, Eliza, but I guess, I mean, I guess, I could start ... " Her voice trailed off unconvincingly.

Eliza grabbed the box from her sister's hands and read, "For the fashionista! Complete with directions that anyone can use! See, that's you, Ani, anyone!" Eliza continued with great enthusiasm, "Kit includes five blushes, twelve eye shadows, four eye pencils, four mascaras, two lip pencils, and look, Ani, they even have a small mirror for application. This kit is even better than the one I have," she said while looking longingly at the jeweled colors of the makeup.

"Why don't you keep it for me, Eliza? Study up on the directions and later you can teach me the techniques." Ani rolled the ripped wrapping paper up into a ball and threw it at her father, who deftly caught the wad and winked at her.

"Well, if you insist." Eliza grinned.

Ani rose from her seat trying to mask her disappointment in her birthday gifts. She was a sweet girl who, unlike her older sister, preferred giving gifts and wasn't the type to get too caught up with what she received as a present. At this particular moment, however, she was feeling sorry for herself that her mother was not there, especially because she always knew the perfect gift for Ani. Perhaps Mom had been too busy with the demands of the dig to remember her today, her thirteenth birthday of all days.

"Not so fast, Ani Dani," cooed her father, using his nickname for her. "I seem to remember one more gift. Now, let's see, where did I put that?" Dr. Banke searched the room before he reached under the sofa that Ani was sitting on and extracted a large box decorated in bright turquoise paper. "Here it is," he said as he placed the box in Ani's hands.

"Oh, it must be from Mom! Is there a card? Read the card, Ani. She always writes the best cards!" squealed Eliza. Sure enough, taped to the top of the box was a cream-colored envelope with Ani's name written in her mother's familiar handwriting. Ani happily tore the envelope off and opened the card. "Read it out loud, Ani," Eliza demanded.

Ani read, "*Dearest Ani, Happy 13th birthday, a magical birthday for my magical daughter. You are a delightful daughter, dear one, and I am so proud of you and who you have become. Your father and I want to wish you much joy, happiness, and adventure now that you have become a real teenager. We know that you will succeed in whatever you try but please remember the journey is more often the memorable learning experience, so focus on that instead of the desired outcome. I am* *sorry that I am unable to share this monumental birthday with you, and I can't wait to see you next month.*

Much Love, Mom

P.S. I came upon this book while rummaging around an old store in Montezuma. I found the drawings and etchings quite interesting, and I hope that you do too. We can try and decipher the meanings when you get here.

Love ya Anipoo! xo xo."

Ani opened the lid and pulled out a large package wrapped in brown paper held together by a thick rubber band. She slowly slipped the band off, and the paper unraveled to reveal a rectangular book tied closed by a rawhide string. Puzzled, Ani untied the string and opened the first page. "Wow," she exclaimed in barely a whisper. "What do you think this is?"

"It looks dirty," Eliza said while crinkling up her nose.

Dr. Banke slid closer to examine the book with Ani. "Whatever it is, this looks very old. It might even be Native writings."

"Wow" was all Ani could say. Slowly and reverently she opened the pages of her present. Ani could make out some of the drawings. "This looks like a lobster claw," she noted while pointing to a picture that did in fact look like a lobster claw. "This one over here looks like a wing of a bird, perhaps a hawk or falcon," Ani exclaimed, not able to hide her excitement.

Dr. Banke touched the outer cover. "This feels like some kind of an animal skin, and the paper is more like a parchment, paper used by ancient people."

Ani sprung up from her seat with her strange present. "I need to do some research right away! Dad, Eliza, this has been the best birthday ever!"

As Ani scurried to her room, in Maine a woman lit a tapered candle. As the smoke billowed greater than usual, the woman encircled the flame with both hands, and the smoke blew up and around her torso and head. She chanted softly, knowing that Amelia's book had been delivered to its new owner. Relishing the knowledge, now, she could only pray, and pray she did into the night, keeping vigil by the candle, chanting and praying until the sun rose over Cadillac Mountain.

Lobster fact: *Before Europeans settled in America, Maine Indians preserved lobster meat by sun-drying or smoking it, a practice that wasn't common among Europeans.*

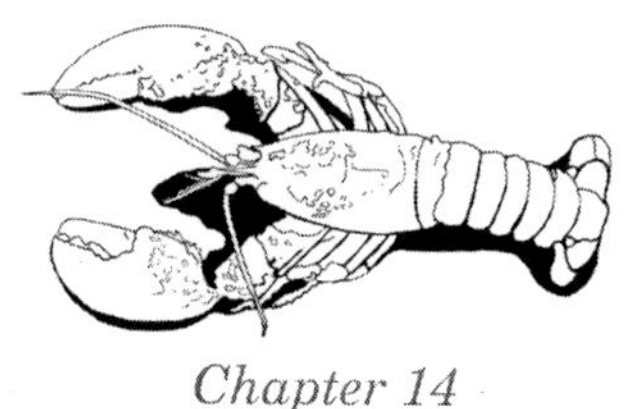

Chapter 14

A Surprise Request

Ani had just settled into her favorite spot in her room, a hammock suspended between her two closet doors allowing her a view of the ocean while holding a new mystery novel. Ani loved to read, especially mysteries, and she couldn't wait to tackle this latest installment about a secret society and the problems surrounding the secrecy. Ani had barely turned to the second page when she heard a loud noise that she couldn't immediately place. As she climbed out of her hammock and ran to the hallway, she practically slammed into Eliza, who also had left her bedroom to find out about the noise. Ani could see that her sister had wasted no time opening up her present, as her face was almost unrecognizable under a slab of makeup.

Eliza immediately said, "I know, I know, a little too heavy on the mascara."

"A little? I think you used the wrong adjective here, Liza." Ani chuckled.

The girls were interrupted by Dr. Banke, who yelled up at them from the bottom of the stairs. "Hurry, girls. I have never seen this before!"

"What is it, Dad?" both girls cried simultaneously.

"A helicopter and it is landing in the side yard!" Dr. Banke was correct. A helicopter was landing not more than thirty yards from their home, one of several on the Woods Hole property. A security car drove up the shell-covered driveway with blue lights flashing. Two security guards well known to the

Bankes exited the white jeep. They hurried over to Dr. Banke and the girls.

The younger of the two guards, Kenneth, spoke first. "The director called us a few minutes ago and informed us that a helicopter would be arriving."

"What's this all about, Kenneth?" the doctor asked.

"We don't know, sir," replied the second security guard. More rotund and slightly balding, Dwayne seemed out of breath with the excitement and the rush that orders from the director caused. "We only know that the folks coming need to speak with you immediately, and Kenneth and I are to offer our assistance if necessary."

The helicopter made its way to a landing, creating a storm of wind, sand, and small rocks. Once the blades stopped whirring, Ani could make out the name inscribed on the helicopter door: Jamison Laboratory, Bar Harbor, Maine. Two people got out of the backseat and were waved over by Kenneth and Dwayne.

As they got closer, Dwayne spoke first, shouting to be heard. "Hello, I am Officer Chisholm and this is Officer Billings," he said in his most formal voice as he pointed to Kenneth. Kenneth nodded, also looking more official than Ani had ever remembered. Dwayne continued, pointing to Dr. Banke, "This is Dr. Banke and his two daughters, Ani and Eliza." The girls smiled and Dr. Banke reached out his hand to the two visitors.

"I am Dr. Emily Clemens and this is Dr. Simon Belanger," said a middle-aged woman with a pleasing face and welcome smile. She had light brown, shoulder-length hair that she wore pulled back into a ponytail. She was raised in Tulsa, Oklahoma, but came east to study psychology at Hobart and William Smith College. That plan changed after her freshman seminar class, entitled "Biology, Ecology, and Your Food," when she caught her first fish from Lake Seneca and instead of eating the smallmouth bass, dissected it. From then on she was hooked and moved from fresh water to salt water while pursuing her doctorate at Maine Oceanic College. She hadn't left the area since. Dr. Clemens extended her hand to Dr. Banke. "Hello, nice to meet you."

Dr. Belanger, tall and angular with a ruddy complexion and deep voice, spoke next while offering his hand, too. "Sorry for the intrusion, old chap, but this visit is of the utmost importance, I dare say." His phrasing and his accent gave away his British origins. He had studied at the University of St. Andrews in Scotland, majoring in classics. Upon completing his undergraduate degree, he traveled the globe until his money ran out. He ended up in Boston and eventually received his graduate degree in marine biology from Boston University. He connected with Dr. Clemens at a marine biology conference in New Zealand, where she convinced him to come to Maine and study the *best the sea has to offer*. He did and hadn't regretted his decision for one minute. "I am not a fan of heights nor helicopter rides for that matter. I believe it would be best if I could sit myself down at the present or I fear I am soon likely to keel over," he said with a grin. Ani immediately liked him.

After Dr. Banke, Dr. Belanger, Dr. Clemens, and the girls, who had helped with refreshments, were seated comfortably in the living room, Dr. Banke said, "So what brings you both here to see me?"

Dr. Clemens opened up her briefcase and pulled out a folder. "We were informed by the director that you are the leading authority on crustaceans and their migratory patterns. I also know that you are familiar with the research that we conduct at Jamison Laboratory in Bar Harbor, Maine. Primarily we are focused on medical research. However, our oceanographic division also conducts regular research known as RECI, Research, Experiment, Confirm, and Inform, which is all part of the town/gown relations. We monitor the sea and wildlife for the National Park Foundation and the local fishermen in order to assist in the enjoyment of the park for our visitors and the sustainability of the fishing industry for the many registered fishermen."

Dr. Belanger piped up, "Last week I received an interesting report from RECI lobster team. Hand him the first report,

Emily," he said. She passed Dr. Banke the report and pointed to a specific section of the document.

"Now, you can clearly see a change from June 2," she said, "to the present report, which I received this very morning, June 18. Same location, Bar Harbor, and same traps scattered randomly up and down the coast from RECI."

With a puzzled face, Dr. Banke said, "Odd," while flipping through the RECI report. "Why, just this afternoon, my daughter Ani and I made a similar discovery with our few traps off our own dock."

"It's true," cried Ani.

"You did?" said Eliza.

"Odd?" said Dr. Belanger.

"Only our catch appears to be decreasing, not increasing," Dr. Banke said. "I plan on conducting additional tests tomorrow. I want to get to the bottom of this myself."

"Which is exactly why we are here, Dr. Banke. Jamison Lab, with permission from the Woods Hole director, wants you to find out what is going on," said Dr. Clemens.

"And we need you to do it quickly before, before, well, before it just gets bloody out of control," chimed in Dr. Belanger.

Lobster fact: *Scientists say that ocean circulation may explain why populations of lobsters and clams are sparse in some rocky coastal areas that would seem ideal for these crustaceans.*

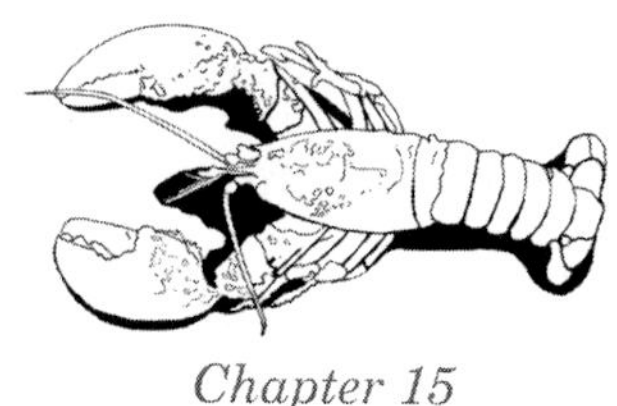

Chapter 15

Summer Plan B

"100 bottles of beer on the wall, 100 bottles of beer," sang Dr. Banke in a brassy voice.

"No, Dad, please, I am begging you, not that one again," moaned Eliza while gazing out the car window en route to Mount Desert Island, Maine. Their minivan was jam packed with Dr. Banke's research gear, boating supplies, clothes, food, and also Eliza's numerous bags. Eliza was not a light packer. Two bright orange kayaks were tied to the roof, and their bikes were attached to the back of the vehicle.

"You take one down, pass it around, 99 bottles of beer on the wall," sang Ani.

"No more!" cried Eliza.

"Come on, Eliza, it won't be that bad. You'll have fun, meet some new friends, perhaps have an island adventure," said Dr. Banke.

"Yeah, Eliza. Listen to this," Ani said and read from an Acadia National Park brochure, "*The park encompasses 35,000 acres of beautiful seacoast, rocks, islands, forest, lakes, and mountains for all to enjoy. Acadia is among the top 20 most visited National Parks.*"

"Ugh," groaned Eliza.

Ani ignored her sister and continued, "*In 1913, President Woodrow Wilson set aside 6,000 acres (within what is now Acadia National Park) as Sieur de Monts National Monument. With the acquisition of more land and private support and funding, in 1919 President Wilson signed an act establishing*

Lafayette National Park. In 1929 the park's name was changed to Acadia."

"Dad, please, make her stop."

"Eliza, relax. Go on, Ani," urged Dr. Banke.

"Here is something interesting that even you might like, Eliza. *There are over 120 miles of trails for hikers to enjoy in Acadia National Park. Trails vary from short, level surf walks, to the steep Precipice Trail.* Maybe you and Dad could climb that one together while I stay below and take pictures."

"How high is the Precipice Trail?" asked Eliza as she grabbed the brochure out of Ani's hands.

"Eliza! I am not finished with that."

"Girls, come on. Eliza, give that back to your sister." Eliza pouted in the front seat. She was extremely disappointed she was not going to New Mexico and had been adamant about not wanting to go to Maine. Eliza, despite being a glamour cat, loved rock climbing, the higher the better, and she was really looking forward to the trip out west. After the visit from the Jamison Laboratory scientists, it was decided that Dr. Banke would take the girls to Acadia since the other Dr. Banke was too busy at the moment with her own project to supervise her daughters. The parents agreed that spending time on Mount Desert Island would be more enjoyable and more practical for all involved.

Ani, on the other hand, was ecstatic about these new plans. Not only was she relieved that she didn't have to go rock climbing in New Mexico, at least not for a while anyway, she was thrilled with the idea of spending her summer in a national park where the sea meets the mountains. Ani loved all living things, especially sea life. Like her father, Ani couldn't wait to begin exploring the park. She also knew that her father would become completely engrossed in his own research, allowing the sisters to investigate their new surroundings alone.

"Ani." Her father's voice brought her back to the moment. "What else does the brochure say?"

"Let me see now… Hey, this is interesting. It's about Native Americans on the island: '*The Abenaki tribe inhabited the*

Island of Mount Desert and survived by farming, fishing, and fur trading with the French settlers. The arrival of the French in the early 1600s brought increased fur-trading opportunities but also devastating illness. The Maine Abenaki tribe was hit very hard during the year of 1617, with a fatality rate of 75%, and the population of the Eastern Abenaki fell to about 5,000.' That is horrible, Dad."

"You might be able to conduct some research on your birthday present while we are on the island, Ani. Maine Oceanic College, which is located in Bar Harbor, has an extensive Native American collection and library."

"With all this excitement, I forgot about the book Mom gave me," Ani said as she reached into her backpack and gingerly pulled out her gift. "Can I go there today, Dad, first thing?"

"We'll see," said Dr. Banke. "Let's just get there and then we'll see."

"Hey, I just saw a store, and they say they have lobster ice cream. Gross!" shouted Eliza.

Dr. Banke pulled into the next parking lot and turned the car around. "We definitely have to try some of this!" he said.

Lobster fact: *Ben & Bill's of Bar Harbor invented Lobster Ice Cream in the 1990s to demonstrate to shop patrons that they do, without a doubt, make their own ice cream. Since its debut, the ice cream has been featured in numerous newspaper and magazine articles and on several television shows. Lobster Ice Cream is butter-flavored ice cream. Ben & Bill's buys cooked lobster meat from a local lobster pound, chops it up, butters it, and folds it into ice cream. During the summer, hundreds of people daily sample this unique treat.*

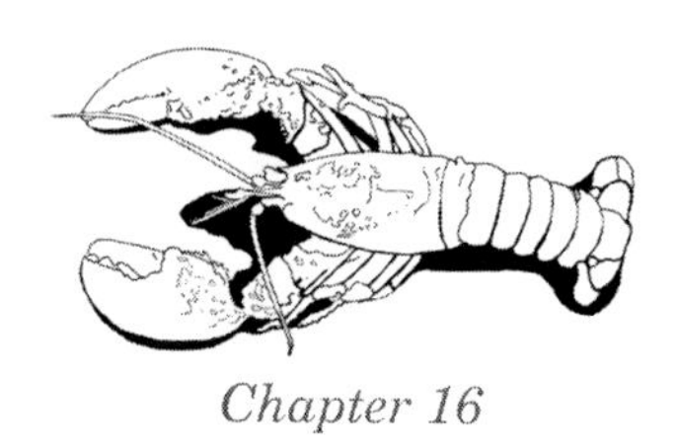

Chapter 16

Northeast Harbor and Spidey Boy

Dr. Banke stopped the car in front of the road named Baxter Lane—PVT.

"What does *PVT* mean, Dad?" Ani asked.

"*PVT* means private, stay out. That means riff raff go home and all others," Dr. Banke said while consulting his map and turning down the road.

"Uh, Dad," Ani asked nervously. "Why are we going down here if it is so private?"

"Because, surprisingly, this is where we are staying," replied Dr. Banke while once again consulting directions on a piece of paper from Emily Clemens. "Wow, look at this," he said quietly as all three, even Eliza, noticed the splendor of the long and winding driveway flanked by stone walls and large, sculpted trees. The well-manicured lawn behind the walls was a rich, forest green color that resembled a luxurious carpet more than a field of grass.

"Who else lives up here, Dad?" asked a now interested Eliza. "Anybody famous?"

"Yeah, Dad, who does live up here and why are we staying here?"

"Some guy by the name of Baxter or Barton, something like that. Somebody rich enough to have an entire road named after him, but not so famous that you know who he is."

The car slowly approached the main house on the property. The Baxter homestead was a grand estate built in the late 1800s. The house was a cedar shingled mansion with several porches, porticos, and balconies designed to enable the inhabitants to relax, get out of the rain, or simply enjoy the view of the harbor down below. The circular driveway boasted a view of impressive gardens with a mixture of perennials and annuals in a remarkable array of colors. To the left of the house, Ani could see a tennis court and behind that a beautiful pool surrounded by a flagstone patio and a wrought iron fence with an ornate letter "B" positioned in the center of the gate.

"Will we get to use the pool, Dad?"

"I don't think so, Eliza."

"Bummer," she said.

Ani agreed. "Yeah, bummer, how come?"

"Well, first of all, we are not staying at this Baxter person's mansion, but rather at another guest cottage that just happens to be on the estate. Our cottage is managed by The Friends of Acadia National Park and we're to meet the caretaker, who will show us around and such. And also, from what I have heard about this rich fellow, I don't think we will be getting any invitations to join him for tea."

"Great, that sounds just great," said Eliza. "We get to stay on the grounds of this beautiful house and not use the pool and not use the tennis courts. Yeah, I would much prefer to be here than with Mom in New Mexico."

"Enough, Eliza. Ani and I already know how you feel." Dr. Banke sighed as he pulled the car to a stop in front of a large wooden door some distance from the mansion. All three exited the vehicle and retrieved their own duffel bags and a few of Eliza's, and headed for the door. Ani reached it first and noticed the intricate designs that lined it.

"Hey, Dad, look at the carvings on this door. They kind of look like some of the drawings in my book from Mom."

Dr. Banke put his bags down to get a closer look. "Why, I think you're right, Ani. We might want to ask the caretaker about the history behind this door and whether there is a tie to some Indian craftsmanship. It certainly is impressive."

"It just looks heavy to me," said Eliza. "Could someone open this thing up? My arms are killing me here." Dr. Banke lifted the latch and pushed. What was behind the door amazed the Bankes and left them temporarily speechless: the most beautiful garden imaginable. As they approached the charming cottage about fifty yards away, their feet crunched down on rose-colored stones that covered the raked pathways throughout the garden. Each path was lined with flowers of varying heights, sizes, and colors. Small markers stood in front of the plants, informing the lucky viewer of the Latin name of the plant after the common name.

Ani's gaze traveled eagerly down the row. "Bluebell Blueflower – *Campanula rotundifolia*," she read. Some she recognized, but many she had not seen before. Dr. Banke too was walking from plant to plant, crossing from one side of the garden to the other, admiring the beauty and abundance of plants. Even Eliza was secretly enjoying the splendor of the garden.

Their senses of smell and sight were so overloaded they failed to notice the commotion occurring behind the plants, low to the ground and high up in the trees. A number of woodland creatures, primarily chipmunks, woodchucks, and squirrels, were also experiencing heightened awareness of sights, smells, and sounds. Their excitement was electric, and soon others who were called to the garden to verify the arrival of the *special one* joined this small group. After much animal chatter, which consisted of squeaks for those who cared to listen, it was decided that the smallest squirrel would follow the party to verify that the *one* had in fact arrived. Unbeknownst to most humans, squirrels run subterfuge on a regular basis in order to distract *Homo sapiens* from seeing what really happens in the animal kingdom. This particular squirrel started his task immediately and ran close behind Dr. Banke, Ani, and Eliza. Eliza spotted him first, but his appearance barely registered on her personal radar screen, as she was more concerned with the weight of her bags. The squirrel needed to get close enough to make eye contact, but not so close as to disrupt the natural flow. The trio continued toward the cottage while the squirrel ran back and forth, up and down, behind and in front.

Soon, the heaviness of Eliza's luggage could be borne no

more. Her bags slid off her shoulders and landed with a loud thump on the path. She slumped her body onto one of the suitcases and called after her sister and father, "You all go ahead. Don't worry about me. I'm just fine."

Ani and Dr. Banke did not even hear her. Eliza rested her back against one of the stone bird feeders scattered about the garden. She closed her eyes for only a second and then a barely detectable noise caused her to open them suddenly. She was surprised to find two small eyes staring right back at her. A gray squirrel was peering down from the feeder and looking right at her.

"Get away!" yelled Eliza. "Scat, shoo, go!" she said even louder as she bolted upright. The squirrel scurried away down the path and then disappeared, ducking under a rhododendron bush. "That was weird," Eliza said. She heard a low chuckle coming from a stand of oak trees about five yards to her right. Her curiosity piqued, she left the trail and walked toward the trees, prompting a great rustling of leaves and branches.

"Is someone up there?" Eliza asked timidly from the base of the largest tree. This place was starting to give her the creeps, and she wasn't sure if she really wanted a reply. She waited for a few beats before looking up, trying to spot where the laugh had come from. She heard and saw nothing and decided to go back to her luggage, which had toppled over when the business with the squirrel happened. Not two steps away from the tree, Eliza heard that annoying chuckle again. She lunged back to the tree and called up, "I hear you laughing so get down here and show yourself or I'm, I'm coming up." Eliza slipped off her flip-flops and started up the tree. Her pronouncement caused an even greater movement of leaves and branches than before. "Show yourself!" she demanded, while inching herself up to the lowest branch of the tree. About fifteen feet higher, the weight of who or what was above her caused one of the branches to dip low enough for Eliza to see, only for a flash, what was at the root of all the commotion. She was so startled by what she thought she saw—Spider-Man—that she lost her grip and landed squarely on her backside. She stood up hurriedly, ignoring her pain, and dusted off her seat. She sprang around to the other side of the tree, but knew she was too late. All movement and noise had stopped from directly above, yet she thought she detected activity in the birch trees that lined the garden and the start of the encircling woods. She was interrupted by her sister's exasperated voice.

"Eliza, what are you doing? We can't climb trees now. The caretaker is waiting to show us around." Ani picked up a few of Eliza's bags. "Here, let me help you."

"You won't believe me if I tell you what happened, but I'm going to do it anyway. I think I just chased Spider-Man away from the garden."

Ani giggled. "You're right, I don't believe you. I'm sure it was just a large bird or a squirrel."

"That reminds me. I think a squirrel was following me, too. This place is bizarre. I'm calling Mom and begging her to let me fly out to New Mexico."

"A squirrel, seriously, Eliza?" Eliza grabbed the remainder of her bags, and both girls trudged down the walkway. They were met by their father and an older man wearing a denim shirt, khaki pants, and a green Acadia National Park hat. He stared stoically at Ani and Eliza.

"Girls, this is Patrick O'Leary. He is the caretaker of the cottage, the one I was telling you about. He also is the man responsible for this profusion of color as he is the head gardener," an impressed Dr. Banke said.

"Afternoon," said Patrick in a thick Maine accent with a tip of his hat to Ani and Eliza. This was not a friendly tip but more a tip of obligation.

Dr. Banke continued the introductions. "The taller of the two is Eliza, while this here is Ani, my younger daughter."

"Hello," the girls said.

An awkward silence followed until Dr. Banke said, "Why don't you show us inside, Mr. O'Leary, and then we would all love a tour of the garden."

Patrick did not reply. Instead he unceremoniously opened the front door and held it for the group to enter; he, however, remained outside. The cottage was truly a cottage in every sense of the word. The walls were lined with light wood paneling, and the rooms were decorated comfortably and tastefully with a rustic yet coastal theme. Ani detected a scent of pine and old books mixed with a pleasant fragrance that must be coming from the bouquet of wildflowers placed in a vase on top of a low bookcase to the right of where they stood.

The first floor consisted of a small entryway, a kitchen, a living room, and a beautiful library. Ani planned on spending time in that room. Eliza was dismayed to learn that there was no TV. There were three rooms upstairs, two bedrooms and one small office. The girls' room had two twin beds with white eyelet bedspreads. A small vase of flowers adorned the bedside table along with a white lamp. The ceiling was slanted on one side, which gave the room an even cozier feel. Ani thought the room probably hadn't changed since the cottage was built. She already knew where her favorite spot would be, the reading bench underneath the solitary window that overlooked the harbor. She couldn't wait to get to her mystery. Eliza made a face once her father had proceeded to his bedroom down the hall.

"It smells musty in here, and the gardener guy is creepy."

"I think this place is perfect!" Ani said. Dr. Banke popped his head in and announced that Mr. O'Leary was going to give them all a garden tour soon and they were to finish bringing up the rest of their things. The girls sprinted down the twisted staircase to retrieve their luggage. Mr. O'Leary was still outside, but he had picked up Ani's backpack from the stoop and was staring at the parchment that was slightly sticking out of the corner. Ani noticed his interest and reached up to take it from him just as he was about to touch the book.

"Thank you, Mr. O'Leary, but Eliza and I can get the rest of our bags," Ani said as she retrieved her backpack from him. Mr. O'Leary remained silent and unmoving. As the girls ascended the stairs, Eliza muttered under her breath to Ani. "My creepdar is ringing loud and clear."

"Creepdar?" whispered Ani.

"It's short for creep radar, creepdar." Ani nodded in agreement. The garden tour began behind the cottage house. Mr. O'Leary spoke with the quiet authority of someone who clearly was master of all that the eye could see. His pride and love for the garden was evident once he started explaining the number of employees who worked the garden, twelve in total, along with the number of plants, flowering bushes and trees, bird feeders, wishing wells, and gazebos. Dr. Banke and Mr. O'Leary soon were involved in a lively conversation about the methods both organic and chemical that eradicated the red lily leaf beetle, and the girls naturally lost interest and lagged behind the adults. Eliza was on the hunt for the possible reappearance of her Spider-Man buddy while Ani took out a notebook in order to write down the names of plants that she was interested in learning about.

"Eliza, tell Dad that I will be right along. I want to sketch the bergamot, better known as bee balm."

"Okay, but hurry up. Dad said he was going to take us to dinner after the tour, and I'm starving," Eliza declared before following the pathway to their father.

Ani sat down in front of the plant and began drawing. She was a curious observer of all living things, and as a result, she turned out to be quite an artist. She took her time as she carefully outlined and shaded the shape of the petals and then the leaves and long stem of her subject. She enjoyed the feel of the sunshine on her face and the smell of the flowers mixed with the pine and sea air. She took a deep breath and let out a slow sigh, relishing the moment. A twitch at the base of the plant broke the spell. A squirrel sat behind a cluster of multicolored snapdragons.

Ani smiled warmly at the creature. "Sorry to be intruding on your space. I promise to leave just as soon as I'm finished here." The squirrel cocked his head and stared at Ani from behind a large leaf. She mimicked his movements and stared back at him with a widening grin. A few seconds turned into a solid minute. The squirrel blinked once and then twice before turning and running farther behind the snapdragons. Mission accomplished, the squirrel thought, verification complete.

Ani rejoined her family and the gardener. They had come to what appeared to be the end of the property, and Ani noticed that the trees were thicker, blocking out the sunshine almost completely. The walkway ended at a thicket of overgrown shrubs and brambles that seemed out of place with the rest of the well-groomed garden.

"Oh, good, Ani, you're here. Mr. O'Leary was just reviewing a few safety rules for all of us to follow."

"Rules?" Ani asked.

"Yes, rules," declared Mr. O'Leary in an exasperated tone. "Stay on the paths, do not pick the flowers, do not throw stones into the wishing wells or fountains because it clogs up the filters, no pets allowed at all times, and, most important, stay away from this part of the garden." He pointed at the overgrown area in order to emphasize this. "It's not safe and no place for kids!"

Eliza was right, Ani thought, he is a creepy and also kind of an angry man.

Lobster fact: *The Heliconia rostrata is known as the lobster claw plant because of the shape of its bracts. It has red and yellow flowers and is considered a tropical plant, so it must be grown in pots in colder climates (such as Maine) and protected during the winter.*

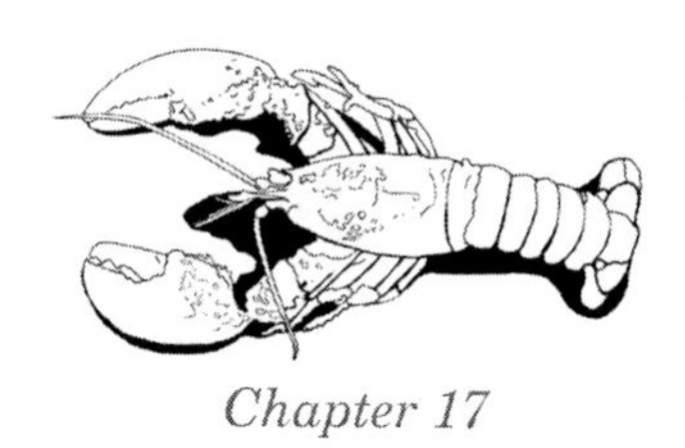

Chapter 17

JL 73

Eliza and Ani strolled casually behind their father and Dr. Belanger along the pier in Bar Harbor. They passed a forty-three-foot sailboat with the inscription The Jackson Five. "Jackson Five," laughed Dr. Banke. "I haven't thought of them in years."

"What is Jackson Five?" asked Ani as she climbed on board the RECI vessel *JL 73* carrying her backpack, which she hadn't let out of her sight since arriving in Maine, and a Jamison Lab cooler. One of the team members, TJ, a summer intern, helped Ani with her supplies. "You've never heard of Michael Jackson and the Jackson Five band? You know, 'A.B.C., It's easy as one, two, three.'"

Ani and Eliza couldn't help but notice that TJ was cute. He had light curly hair with aquamarine eyes, a muscular build, and a mischievous grin. Ani gave him a smile and blushed a bit, too. She was grateful for the Red Sox hat she selected to wear today and bent her head down so TJ wouldn't notice her pink face.

"Ouch, you're hurting my ears," said another young man, Ben. Also quite good looking, he was tall with short dark hair and a great smile. Eliza looked up when she heard his voice, playful and commanding. She was in a snit because her father had informed her that this boat trip was not a chance for her to work on her tan in her bikini and made her leave the lounge chair she found in the shed back at the cottage. After seeing TJ and now Ben, Eliza's mood changed. This trip might actually be fun, she thought.

"Your voice is even worse," said TJ as he took the cooler from Ani's grip.

"Important research materials?" Ani asked casually.

TJ pushed the button on the side of the cooler that released the lid, which slid open to reveal several bottles of Old Soaker Wild Blueberry soda. "No, not really, just Ben and I are addicted." He winked at her.

"You both are tone deaf. Do you have to compete on everything?" asked Dr. Clemens as she climbed down the ladder from the top deck. She was dressed in sandals, cargo shorts, and a Jamison Lab T-shirt.

"Where did you come from?" asked TJ.

"She's always doing that," said Ben. "She just shows up everywhere."

"Eyes in the back of my head, Benjamin," she said.

"Just like my Moth ..."

"Don't say 'mother,' Ben, don't say 'mother,'" scolded Dr. Clemens.

"Sorry," Ben said.

"I see you've already met Ben and TJ," she said. "These two Blueberry soda–obsessed young men are part of our college summer intern program. TJ is studying at Dickinson, and Ben, here, is from my alma mater, Hobart and William Smith."

"Lucky for us we were assigned to work with RECI," TJ said.

"And now, we get to help figure out why the lobsters are coming, the lobsters are coming," Ben joked.

Eliza giggled a bit too loudly. "Like Paul Revere, 'the British are coming, the British are coming.' You're like so funny." Ani rolled her eyes at her father. Eliza was about to enter full-blown flirt stage and it was not going to be pretty.

"You boys game for another go round?" Dr. Clemens asked. She looked at Ani and Eliza. "These smart college boys have been trying to figure out what *JL 73* stands for since coming aboard in May. The first one to guess correctly owes the other one a full shore dinner at Stewman's Lobster Pound."

TJ said, "I figured out the whole story." He pulled a piece of crumpled lined paper from his shorts pocket and read, "'Josette Lawrence, famed opera singer in the early 1900s who summered in Bar Harbor and performed to a sold-out crowd songs from *The Marriage of Figaro* in the Bar Harbor Opera House on June 21, 1914.' It was reported that wealthy patron of the New York art scene Harrison S. Simpson was so besotted with Ms. Lawrence's talents that he donated an undisclosed but substantial amount of money to the founding of Jamison Laboratory in her name with the stipulation that a research vessel be named after her in the future. And 73 represents the number of times he proposed marriage to her before she finally agreed. Take that, Ben. I'm picking out the largest lobster in the pound," TJ proclaimed, licking his lips.

Ben immediately jumped in with "Nice try, TJ, but you are wrong! Stand back and listen to the master unveil the true meaning behind the name of the ship. *JL* stands for Joshua Littlefield, wealthy shipbuilding tycoon, born in 1873, yes, that's right, *tycoon*, from Belfast, Maine, whose ancestors, the Littlefields, and I emphasize the word *field* here not *little*, were early landowners of several places across Maine. Including, now pay attention, TJ, including, a large parcel on MDI that was generously donated to C. C. Little, no relation here, in 1929, founder of Jamison Labs, originally known as Roscoe B. Jamison Memorial Laboratory. Looks like someone owes me a lobster dinner, and that someone is you," he finished and pointed at TJ. The two argued while Eliza and Ani stood by, obviously amused by the boys' demonstrations.

"Looks like peanut butter and jelly for both of you," said Dr. Clemens. "Good effort, though, boys. Your college professors would be impressed, but not me because you both are incorrect. We can try again next time we launch. Now, get to work."

After the boys returned to preparing the research supplies, Ani approached Dr. Clemens. "Can you tell me what it stands for? I promise I won't tell Ben or TJ."

Emily Clemens smiled and leaned in conspiratorially. "*JL* simply stands for Jamison Laboratory and *73* stands for the year the ship was commissioned. Nothing more." She glanced up at TJ and Ben. "It has been driving those two fellows crazy."

Ani giggled and said, "Are you ever going to tell them the truth?"

"I'll tell them, all right, but not until the end of the summer. I'm having far too much fun hearing their answers."

The *JL 73* was a seventy-five-foot marine research vessel equipped with air time access routes via nautical programs, onboard digitalized charts that automatically figure charts, tides, and currents, and sophisticated sonar and GPS receivers, which helped the ship to navigate and detect sea life. Also, the vessel included a two-man, completely independent submersible view craft, a micro marine hospital, and a fully equipped galley kitchen.

The RECI team, Dr. Clemens and Dr. Belanger, the six crewmembers, consisting of the captain, the first mate, the engineer, a communication specialist, an apprentice shipmate, and a cook, along with the three Bankes departed Bar Harbor at approximately nine in the morning. The purpose of the mission was twofold: to give Dr. Banke a firsthand account of the RECI team's findings, and to conduct additional experiments requested by Dr. Banke, for example water depth samples, temperature, randomized tests of additional sea life such as cod, flounder, bluefish, and stripers, and retrieval of RECI lobster traps.

The view of the harbor was spectacular. As the boat passed the breakwater, Ani could see the town of Bar Harbor and the famous cliff walk starting at the Bar Harbor Inn, several other "cottages" dotting the landscape, and magnificent Cadillac Mountain, over 1,500 feet above sea level. Ani couldn't wait to visit the summit. Dad had promised they could do that later that day. Even though Ani was afraid of heights, she didn't mind driving up to the top. Now, looking at the precipice jutting out toward the water's edge, she could make out a couple of lone rock climbers. Her body involuntarily shuddered thinking about that climbing experience. She knew she would not be joining Eliza and her father when they attempted that trail.

Ani turned back toward her father and the rest of the crew busy at work. TJ and Ben were donning lobster fishing attire, long rain boots and slickers, as they were the lucky ones to pull up the traps. Dr. Banke, clipboard in hand, was getting a briefing from Dr. Clemens.

"That is one of our buoys there," she said, pointing to a buoy with a hot pink and black stripe. "We didn't have much choice on color."

"It certainly is easy to spot in the water," Dr. Banke said.

"Get ready to grab this, TJ," commanded Dr. Belanger. TJ moved into action with a lobster trap hook.

"Stop now, John," Dr. Clemens called to the captain. "You see, what we have been finding is an abundance of lobsters. Normally, we might find five or six per trap, but lately, we have been finding twenty to twenty-five. This phenomenon has been reported all over the island."

"As I mentioned to you during your visit to Woods Hole, I have discovered the exact opposite, as my catch has dwindled down to nothing," said Dr. Banke.

The boat slowed and TJ easily reached the buoy. He grabbed it and flipped it over. "RECI-25B," he called loudly to Ben, who checked off the RECI number on his clipboard.

"RECI-25B, got it!" replied Ben.

"Very efficient," said Dr. Banke.

"They've watched too many crime shows and have turned this lobster situation into some kind of FBI incident," Dr. Clemens said.

The remaining crewmembers, except for Eliza, who was trying to catch some sun on the starboard side of the boat, gathered around TJ and Ben. Ani tried to get closer, too, but was blocked by her father. She tugged on his jacket and he turned around and kindly scooted her in front of him. TJ was helped by Ben and the two pulled up the rope attached to the buoy. Ben, who obviously was quite the joker, hummed the theme song from *Jaws*.

"This feels kind of light, Dr. Clemens," declared TJ.

"What do you mean, light?"

"As in," TJ made a final pull only to reveal nothing but the frayed rope. No trap was attached to the bottom. TJ continued, "As in so light there is nothing at the end."

"Odd," said Dr. Clemens.

"Let me see that, please," Dr. Banke asked. He brought the rope close to examine it. "Hard to tell what could have caused this, knife or animal? We should get this back to the lab to run some tests. Can I cut this off?"

"Why, of course," she replied. "Ben, cut the rope to the buoy." Ben did as he was asked and placed the rope into a plastic bag, which he sealed with tape and tossed into one of the Jamison Lab waterproof storage containers.

"Why don't we pull another trap and see what we find," suggested Dr. Banke. As the vessel headed due east, Eliza reclined on top of a large cooler using her backpack as a headrest and read her new fashion magazine. "Hey," Eliza exclaimed as a large swell crested over her, dousing both her and her glossy pages. As she reached for her towel, her eye caught something bobbing in the waves, but in a flash, it was gone. She dried her lap off and cast another furtive glance out at the sea, and this time she did notice something, something like a… "Wow," she called. "It's a seal, I see a seal!" She pivoted to share the news with Ani and her father, but could see they were engrossed in something at the other end of the boat. Eliza searched for the seal again, and sure enough, she spotted him. She watched for a minute or two knowing that soon the boat's speed would be too fast for the little guy and he would fall out of sight.

Why is he not getting any smaller? she thought. I shouldn't be able to see him at all. Eliza now noticed a second seal. "I think they're following us," she said out loud, but again, no one was near to hear her. When she looked back, the two seals were joined by two, no, three more seals. "One, two, three, four, five, six, six seals!" she said louder this time. She was about to get her dad when to her surprise something jumped up behind the seals and, just as quickly as it appeared, went back under.

"What was that?" Eliza squinted and concentrated on the water behind her. There, there, and there, one, two, three, four porpoises positioned behind the seals and all following the *JL 73*. Eliza couldn't believe her eyes. She counted the seals again and discovered that now there were ten of them, while the porpoises had also increased in number. Soon birds appeared, circling and diving close to the swimming mammals. Eliza picked out seagulls, cormorants, and even two bald eagles. She grabbed her camera and took pictures as fast as she could click and shoot. Behind the boat, and now on the side, were birds, seals, porpoises, and maybe even a mako shark or two. It was wild, amazing, and strange. After Eliza felt she had taken enough pictures, she ran to Ani and yanked on her sister's wrist, pulling her away from the RECI team.

"Eliza, what are you doing?" an annoyed Ani asked.

"Come see. I can't explain it to you. You just need to see it. That weird animal thing is happening again."

"What weird animal thing?" Ani said as Eliza dragged her to the back of the boat.

"This weird animal thing," replied Eliza, pointing to the growing sea-life menagerie.

Ani's mouth dropped open in amazement. "Oh, my, wow!" was all she could manage. The *JL 73* came to an abrupt halt to retrieve another trap, and the seals also stopped and just floated and bobbed in the waves. The porpoises continued their dance behind the seals. In and out, in and out of the water they leapt. Ani was jostled out of her incredulity by the cries of the birds flying overhead. She waved at them and the squawking increased dramatically. Meanwhile, TJ and Ben pulled up the second lobster trap.

"How does it feel this time?" Dr. Clemens asked.

"Heavy, very heavy," grunted TJ. With a final forceful tug, the boys hoisted the trap up and heaved it onto the deck. Salt water flowed out of the trap as the scientists peered in.

"Unbelievable," declared Dr. Banke.

"More than a few days ago," said Dr. Belanger.

"Lobster roll here I come," joked Ben while he stared at the lobster trap overflowing with lobsters. Legs, claws, tails, and antennae were poking out of every opening imaginable.

Dr. Clemens put on her thick protective gloves and cautiously opened the trap door. At least three times the average number of lobsters, weighing perhaps four or even five pounds each, tumbled and rolled out onto the deck, their orange-green color contrasting sharply with the whiteness of the ship's surface. But the clacking noise of claws pinching open and shut and spindly legs moving wildly to right their bodies was barely audible above the cacophony coming from up above.

"Dad, you've got to see this. Come quickly!" Eliza shouted. The urgency in her tone caused everyone to stop what they were doing and follow.

"Ani," called Dr. Banke when he saw his younger daughter standing among the swirling sea birds with the whirling ocean behind her littered with sea mammals.

Ani twirled around at the sound of her father's voice. "Dad, look!" Ani swept her hand out, and as if on cue, a large minke whale sprung out of the water and splashed down hard, soaking the crew and the deck of the *JL 73* with its spray.

Lobster fact: *Losing a string of lobster traps to a storm or having a line accidentally cut by a propeller can be costly. There is no such thing as insurance for lobster traps, which cost about fifty dollars a trap, so losing an entire string is not cheap. Lobstermen may average a thirty percent loss of pots per season.*

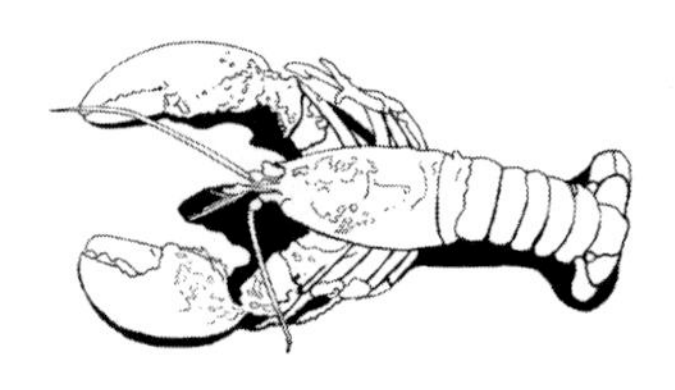

Chapter 18

Lobster Roll, Lobsters Stroll!

The *JL 73* docked at the pier. Ani, Eliza, and the rest of the crew unloaded the supplies from the boat. "Eliza," Ani said softly while carrying a plastic bin to the Jamison Lab minivan, "What did you mean when you said, 'weird animal thing is happening again'?"

Eliza dropped the bin she was toting and sat down on it with a sigh. "You know what I'm talking about, Ani. The weird animal thing that always happens when you are around, and well, lately, it just seems to have gotten weirder. Or have you forgotten the animal fracas that we all just witnessed?"

Ani sat down next to her sister. "No, I haven't forgotten," she said. "It was pretty strange."

"Remember when we went camping in the White Mountains and the same chipmunk with the torn ear was following us for three days? Or the time when we were in Yellowstone and that falcon kept circling us like forever? Or just this spring, when we were kayaking on Lake Winnipesaukee and the loon with the really ginormous neck swam next to us for most of the trip?"

Ani smiled. "So?"

"So, that's not normal. Other families don't get pursued by wildlife. I used to think it was because Dad is so calm and well, earthy like. But now I'm not so sure."

"Not so sure about what?"

"I don't think it's because of Dad anymore. I think it has

something to do with you."

"Me?" Ani said, incredulous.

"Come on, girls, stop lazing around. We could use your help here," said Dr. Banke, arms laden en route to the van. The girls groaned but listened to their father and hoisted their bins.

TJ and Ben were also helping to load the van. Eliza pulled out her mirror and checked her appearance.

"Look at my hair. I'm a mess! Quick, Ani, give me an elastic." Ani pulled an elastic off her arm and handed it to her sister. Eliza flipped her head upside down, causing her brown, curly, and now frizzy hair to swing violently. She efficiently swept her hair up in a high ponytail and then stood abruptly. She consulted her mirror once again and made a face.

"This will have to do. I hate all this humidity. It just makes my hair look like a frizz ball. Why am I not in New Mexico? Who cares about lobsters anyway?" Eliza applied a new coat of lip gloss.

Ben and TJ came around the corner of the van. "It was nice meeting you both," said Ben. "We're going to head back to the lab now. An intern's job is never done."

"Yeah, we have a lot of lobsters to eat," said TJ.

Dr. Clemens heard him from the front of the van. "TJ!" she cried.

"Just kidding," he yelled back to her.

"Have fun. Maybe we'll see you around sometime," TJ said. Eliza giggled.

"That'd be great," said Ani.

"Bye," said Ben. The boys got into an open-air jeep along with Dr. Belanger and headed back to the lab.

"They were so cute," lamented Eliza as she watched them drive away. Once everything was stored in the van, the girls asked their father if they could walk to the harbor beach next to the pier. They had both noticed a lot of people on the shore, and they wanted to get closer to see what was going on. Dr. Banke agreed since he was occupied with arranging the bins and the other collected data before the van departed.

"All right, girls, but don't stray too far. I want to get back to the lab soon to run some tests."

"Run some tests on what? Find anything interesting?" A tall thin man asked, appearing out of nowhere. He flashed a smile producing a slice of lemon covering his teeth, presumably from the frozen lemonade drink he held.

"Excuse me?" asked a puzzled Dr. Banke. "Do I know you?"

"I don't think so, not yet anyway," replied the man. "I'm Barton Thuya Baxter, the third, at your service."

"Oh, hello," said Dr. Banke and extended his hand. "Girls, this is Mr. Baxter. He owns the estate that we're staying on."

"Charming, charming," said Barton.

The girls smiled halfheartedly and then stared at their father. "Oh, right, girls. You may go now, but remember, not too far."

"Bye," Eliza called as she backed away from the group.

"Yes, bye," said Ani. "Nice meeting you, Mr. Baxter." Barton and Dr. Banke watched the girls skip down the pier to the granite stairs that led to the beach.

"Delightful girls," said Barton.

"Thank you."

"I must correct you on your information, Dr. Banke. I am the owner of Baxter property, which includes the roadway, the main house, the tennis court, and pool along with the immediate surrounding land. However, unfortunately, my poor senile father left the cottage and the garden to the care of the gardener and Acadia National Park," Barton said as he twiddled his hair. "No worries, though. I plan on getting it all back very soon."

"I, I didn't know. Nevertheless, the girls and I appreciate the opportunity to stay on your property. It is beautiful, so thank you."

Barton waved his hand dismissively. "As I was saying, did you and the RECI crew find anything interesting?"

Cautiously, Dr. Banke said, "I'm not sure what you are talking about, Mr. Baxter. We were just touring the harbor."

"No need to be coy with me, Dr. Banke. I know all about

why you are here. As a long serving member on the board at Jamison Lab and owner of Baxter Industries, which includes several lobster and fishing enterprises, I am fully aware of what brings you to the island."

"Baxter," said Dr. Clemens while carrying a cooler to the back of the van. She set it down and opened the lid to show Barton the lobsters retrieved from the traps. "This was just from one trap."

"Impressive," Barton said. "What do you think, Dr. Banke?"

"Well, it certainly is too early to say," he said.

"Yes, of course. I understand that these things take time. In the meanwhile, the lobstering business seems to be a boon for those of us here."

"I guess it all depends upon how you look at it," said Dr. Clemens. "Regardless of who does and who doesn't profit from this migration, something isn't right here, and with the help of Dr. Banke, I am sure we will figure it out soon enough."

Ani came running down the pier, her arms swinging wildly and her pigtails bouncing up and down with each step.

"Dad! Dad! Hurry, you need to see this," she cried and tugged on her father's arm.

"What is it, Ani?"

"All of you, you have to see what is happening on shore! It's the lobsters. They are at the edge of the water line and some are even on the beach."

"I'll get my camera," said Dr. Clemens.

She opened the front door of the van and Ani, Dr. Banke, and Barton headed for the beach. Word seemed to have gotten out as a number of other spectators were already gathered there.

Eliza greeted the party at the bottom of the stairs. "Dad, you have to see this. It's, it's amazing!"

"Dr. Clemens, Dr. Clemens," Mayor Peterson called from the sidewalk above the stairs. "What are you doing about this? This has gotten out of hand." They looked up to see the mayor's assistant, Nancy, two male police officers, and the mayor huffing and puffing his way to the stairs. "I just got a call from my nephew who said lobsters were congregating on the beach. On the beach! What are we to do? Tourists are not going to want to come here and go to the beach with lobsters crawling all around them. Kids can't swim in the water and build sand castles, and oh, this is bad for business, bad, bad, bad." He wiped the sweat from his forehead with a handkerchief. "Not to mention the lobster festival event happening next month. Dr. Clemens, you assured me you would get to the bottom of this. ... " His voice trailed off once he noticed Barton. "Barton," he nodded.

"Mayor," Barton acknowledged coldly. The mayor marched down the stairs.

"Mayor, this is Dr. Banke, the scientist who has come to lead the investigation," Dr. Clemens said. The two men shook hands.

"Officers Kiley and Perry." The mayor nodded his head toward the two men standing behind him. "And my assistant, Nancy Murphy."

"You will have to move back now," one of the officers said to the onlookers.

"Thank goodness you are here, Dr. Banke," the mayor said. "Nancy," he commanded, "call Joe at Public Works to get down here with the truck, the coolers, and the large snow shovels and brooms."

The group pushed their way through the growing crowd. Several other police officers and town officials arrived. Soon orange cones were arranged on the sand and yellow police tape was stretched between the cones to keep the observers at bay. Dr. Banke motioned to the girls and pointed for them to stay back behind the tape. Ani took a few pictures with her camera.

"Mom is not going to believe this," Ani said.

"Why won't Dad let us get closer?" complained Eliza. "I mean we are the ones who told him to come, and it's just lobsters. They can't eat us."

"You know Dad. Safety first," Ani said.

Dr. Banke was the first to reach the water. He couldn't believe what his eyes were seeing. Lobsters were everywhere along the beach, which stretched the length of a football field. As the tide rolled in, more lobsters washed up on shore, only to be dragged back by the tide. Back and forth, back and forth, tide and lobsters, in a constant struggle to dominate each other. The town workers had now reached the beach and shoveled up the lobsters and put them in holding tanks other workers carried down the granite stairs. Some men had brought industrial-sized brooms and swept the lobsters back into the water. Several lobster boats hovered in the harbor, dropping and hauling traps up as fast as they could. More and more people arrived, their curiosity piqued by the commotion and police cars. A few brave souls slipped under the yellow tape and scooped up lobsters with their bare hands. Once this happened, others followed suit, and before long more than twenty people had joined in the lobster picking. A few "ouches" and "it pinched me" were heard.

"This is getting out of hand," declared the mayor. "Officer Kiley."

"Sir?"

"Call in the auxiliary. We need to evacuate the beach immediately before the press arrives. This is not good for business."

"What?"

"I mean before someone gets hurt, of course. Now get going!"

Kiley shouted, "All right, folks, put down the lobsters and move away from the shore!"

Sirens blared as a few more police cars, two fire and rescue vehicles, and an ambulance arrived on the scene. Mr. Baxter, not surprisingly, had pushed his way through the people and to the front with Dr. Banke and Dr. Clemens. Ani was unable to hear what was being said because of the click-clacking of the claws, the roar of the surf, and the noise from the crowd. Dr. Banke, his back to the ocean, consulted with Dr. Clemens. Ani could see only Mr. Baxter's profile, but he looked as if he was grinning. Puzzled why he might be amused by this unimaginable scene, she noticed a good-sized lobster with a large claw reach out of the water and attach itself to the bottom of her father's pants.

"Dad!" yelled Ani. "Dad!" But Dr. Banke didn't hear her. "Dad!" Ani yelled louder this time but to no avail. By now, the lobster had pulled its entire body out of the water and was about to clamp onto Dr. Banke's calf. Without thinking, Ani burst under the yellow tape and ran to her father, kicking up sand as she sprinted. "Watch out! There's a lobster on your leg!"

Dr. Banke saw the orange crustacean, *Homarus americanus*, clinging to his pants. He shook his leg. "Off, get off," he demanded. But the lobster wouldn't let go.

"Dad," said Ani. "What's going on?"

Only one man with a big secret truly understood why the lobsters were coming to shore. He alone observed that the sound of Ani's voice put in motion all that happened next: the lobster stubbornly attached to Dr. Banke's cuff simply let go and dropped to the water. Moreover, the lobsters on shore, which had managed to get past the throng of workers desperately trying to corral and push them back from whence they came, also receded into the rolling surf.

Coincidence? thought Barton. Perhaps, yet perhaps not. After witnessing the lobsters' hasty retreat, he knew he would need to devise a special plan, a plan to get to know the family who was staying on his estate, especially the young girl with the curious name.

Lobster fact: *To protect themselves from predators, lobsters "march," just as fish swim in schools and birds fly in flocks. In a lobster march, dozens of the crustaceans walk close together in long rows.*

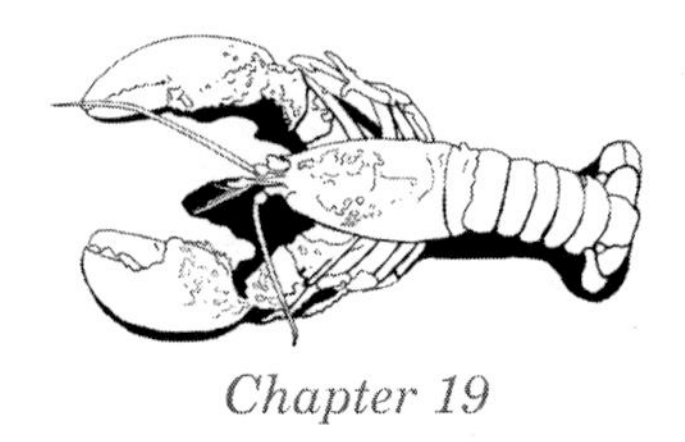

Chapter 19

Kanake-kee

Dr. Banke rang the doorbell at the Baxter estate. Beethoven's "Ode to Joy" chimed lively.

"Funny," he said to his daughters, "Mr. Baxter doesn't strike me as a Beethoven fan. I see him more as a lover of Gustav Mahler."

"More like *Phantom of the Opera*," said Eliza. The door opened and Sorenson greeted the Bankes.

"G-G-Good evening," he stammered. "Welcome to the Baxter estate. I am Mr. Baxter's butler, Sorenson. Let me show you to the sitting room."

The main entryway was richly decorated. Silk wallpaper featured a repeating peacock pattern in a pale mauve color. The black marble floor was polished so brightly that Ani could see her reflection. Fittingly, an enormous crystal chandelier was suspended grandly in the middle of the double buttress staircase. Ani noticed several antique vases filled with beautiful flowers that could only be from Mr. O'Leary's gardens. The smell from these flowers was wonderful—a combination of lavender, rose, and even vanilla. There was also a solitary silver vase, holding a single lupine. Odd, she thought, but odd seemed to go hand in hand with Mr. Baxter.

"Mr. Baxter," spoke Sorenson hesitantly. "Sorry to interrupt you, sir, but Dr. Banke and his daughters are here."

"That will be all, Sorenson. Tell the cook we will be sitting down for dinner soon. We wouldn't want the kids to be up past their bedtime now would we?"

"Very good, sir," replied Sorenson.

The sitting room had a coastal theme. Blue and white plates rested on the white, carved mantle, and comfortable chairs upholstered in blue and white toile surrounded a round coffee table. As Ani inspected the table more closely, she saw that it was not an ordinary coffee table. It was about four feet in diameter with the base a solid knotty pine, painted white. The top of the table was covered by thick, clear glass with a raised wooden border. Several interesting items lay underneath the glass: a couple of gems, a shell, a feather, and what looked to be an animal tooth. These were surrounded by pieces of sea glass. Different hues of blue, green, and white glass encircled the center, creating a mosaic pattern that resembled a pinwheel.

"I see you like my table," said Barton.

"Yes, sir," said Ani. "It is unusual."

"Something my father helped me build." He paused. "To remind me of my fri … ah, never mind," said a wistful Barton. "Cocktail, Dr. Banke?"

"That would be nice," said Dr. Banke. "I'll have what you're having."

While Barton mixed the drinks, the girls took a seat on the sofa across from the fireplace.

"Ginger ale, girls?"

"Yes, please," said Eliza.

"Yes, thank you," said Ani.

"That was strange business with the lobsters yesterday afternoon," Barton said. "Any further ideas, Dr. Banke?"

"No, nothing yet. We have some theories, but really, it's too early to say for sure. At the moment, the lobsters seem to have backed off a bit. Perhaps this was just a fluke and all will go back to normal soon."

"Yes, well, perhaps," said Barton. "However, it did make for an interesting story in the Maine papers, the *Bangor Gazette* and the *Portland Post* or I could say my papers, since Baxter Industries owns both of them. It was also covered in the *Boston Globe*, and the *New York Times*," he gloated.

"Well, it was a rather unusual occurrence, and one could see why it would make the papers," Dr. Banke said.

"I particularly enjoyed this picture on the front page of the *Globe*, Dr. Banke. Where is that? Ah, here it is," Barton said, enthusiastically retrieving the paper from a magazine rack next to his chair. He read, "'Dr. George Banke, world's foremost crustacean scientist from Woods Hole and the Boston Aquarium, confers with Jamison Lab scientist unaware that a lobster is ready to pounce.' This is a very good shot of you, wouldn't you agree, Dr. Banke?" Barton handed the newspaper with the picture to Dr. Banke.

"I was, well, I get very engrossed in my work, and I …" an embarrassed Dr. Banke said. "Don't I get engrossed in my work, girls?"

"All the time," agreed Eliza. Ani nodded.

Sorenson entered the room and announced, "Dinner is served."

Then a sizeable Rottweiler barked and nudged his way around the butler and bared his teeth in front of Dr. Banke, growling menacingly.

"I told you to keep him in the kitchen," Barton said. "Now get him out of here this instant, Sorenson!"

"Come along, Beauregard, come here, boy," Sorenson timidly said.

"He won't listen to you if you speak to him like you're frightened. How many times do I need to tell you this, Sorenson?"

"I'm sorry, sir," replied Sorenson, now more meek than before.

"Beauregard, no growl! No bark! Heel!" commanded Barton. Beauregard ceased and sat at once. Barton parted the pocket doors, which folded neatly into the wall. A formal dining room was revealed, set with china, crystal, and newly polished silver.

"Shall we?" asked Barton. "I hope you like lobsters. The cook has prepared her famous lobster casserole."

Dr. Banke inched little by little away from Beauregard.

"Nice doggy," he cooed. Beauregard snarled. Dr. Banke was not generally afraid of animals, but this dog was particularly intimidating, and he wasn't going to take any chances. "Eliza, Ani, just walk slowly and I'm sure we will be fine."

Eliza strode completely around the coffee table and behind Barton's chair to avoid being close to the beast. Beauregard's eyes monitored her every move. Ani copied Eliza's footsteps and was relieved the dog did not move. Once seated in the dining room, Ani realized that she had left her ginger ale on the coffee table.

"Excuse me. I left my drink in the other room. I'll be right back." I hope, she thought. Ani walked carefully into the sitting room. She swiftly perused the area, but Beauregard was not to be found. Feeling relaxed, she reached for her glass and then heard a low growl coming from behind. Enough, she thought, and boldly turned to face Beauregard.

"Now cut that out, Beauregard. You know that you're scaring everybody, and well, it just isn't nice. As my mother always says, no one likes a bully." Beauregard stopped growling and hung his head as if in shame. Softly now, with more kindness in her voice, Ani praised the dog. "Now that's more like it." She patted him on the top of his head. With this tenderness, Beauregard became putty to Ani's touch and collapsed to the floor, resting his large head on her flip-flops. Ani had made a friend.

The lobster casserole was delicious. The combination of asparagus, lobsters, leeks, and corn bread was absolutely amazing. Barton was of the generation in which children were seen but not heard, so he spoke directly to Dr. Banke and ignored the girls. That was fine with Ani and Eliza, as they simply enjoyed the meal. As Barton rambled on about lobsters and fishing and more boring topics, Ani's new friend wouldn't leave her side, or rather her legs, since they bonded in the sitting room. Throughout the meal, Beauregard had gently and sometimes not so gently tugged at her pant legs, flip-flops, and now even her toes. She eased his head away.

"Shoo, get away, no," she whispered.

"Pardon me?" asked Barton.

"I'm sorry," she said once she realized that he was addressing her. "It's just that …" She giggled as Beauregard removed her flip-flop with his mouth.

"Ani," her father said, giving her a look to indicate that he didn't find her behavior appropriate.

"Sorry, I, um." She giggled again, this time because the dog was licking her toes. "I or we or may Eliza and I be excused? We need to use the ladies room."

Eliza said, "No, I don't." Ani gave her sister a kick in her shin. "I mean, yes," Eliza said. "May we please be excused?" Dr. Banke frowned.

Barton coolly replied, "Yes, of course. It's around the corner and down the hall, fourth door on the left."

"Thank you," said Ani and she got up from her seat. Eliza reluctantly trailed her younger sister.

"Why do I suddenly need to go to the bathroom?" she asked once they were out of earshot of the dining room. Eliza spied Beauregard halfway up the grand staircase. Ani nodded toward the dog.

"It's Beauregard. He, um, wants to show us something," she said.

"Oh, right, here we go with the W-A-T," Eliza said.

"W-A-T?" asked Ani.

"Weird Animal Thing," Eliza said, shaking her head in disbelief.

"We're coming, boy," Ani said to Beauregard.

The dog, now aware that both girls were behind him, playfully bounded up the massive staircase covered with plush royal blue carpeting. Lining the walls were many oversized portraits whose eyes appeared to be following the girls. Eliza looked at the pictures and grimaced. Ani could tell she was getting creeped out again. "Come on, Eliza. I'm sure he just wants to show us his dog bed."

"I hope that's all he wants to show us. These portraits and their eyes."

"I know," agreed Ani.

The landing at the top of the stairs was impressive. A large mirror framed in gold leaf hung in the center of the hallway with two uncomfortable but expensive-looking gold chairs on either side.

"I don't see Beau anymore," said Ani.

"Good, now can we go?"

The dog appeared from around the corner and barked.

"We're here," Ani said.

After passing a few doors farther down the hallway, Beauregard planted himself in front of a dark paneled one and whined.

Ani cautiously opened the door and entered what looked to be a library, much like the one in the guest cottage. This library, however, was huge and overflowing with books, multiple clocks ticking loudly, hourglasses, three telescopes angled at the harbor, glass vases, antique toys, ornamental trays, and framed coins, along with two large sailboats in glass bottles placed side by side on the marble mantel. Piles of newspapers and magazines littered the enormous mahogany desk centered in the room. The walls were covered with paintings, mostly portraits but also several sea scenes of lighthouses, ships, and ocean storms. Ani recognized one painting of the Baxter Thuya garden cottage dwarfed by the Baxter estate. Several black and white mounted photos adorned the side table to the left of the door. Ani walked over and picked up one of them—a picture of three children, about her age, she guessed, from a long time ago. The girl had braids and a very friendly smile. Beauregard yanked on Ani's pant leg again.

"Okay, Beau, what is it? What is it, buddy?"

"Now you're talking to the animals. Great, just great. I promise you this, Ani, if he talks back to you, I am leaving pronto."

"Eliza, everyone knows that dogs can't talk. Seriously now. Stand by the door in case Mr. Baxter or that nervous nellie Sorenson shows up."

"The dog might want to show us a bone or something that he's buried in here or perhaps he just wants us to find his missing tennis ball," Eliza said to calm her nerves. "I don't think Mr. Baxter would like us to be in here, Ani. I think we should go back now, and I, I really, really don't want to miss dessert."

"Must you always think about food? Now get to the door, please," Ani said.

Grudgingly, Eliza obeyed. She made up a little song while inspecting the hallway for any activity. "Here we are, in this creepy man's house, hoping the scary dog will show us something, but we don't know what, and I am being bossed around by my very bossy younger sister."

"Eliza, I can't concentrate!" Ani said.

"You know I need to sing. It helps me relax."

"Oh, all right, sing, but not so loud."

Eliza started up her song again, this time softer. "Now here I still am, still in the creepy man's house." Eliza switched to low humming. Ani focused her attention on Beauregard.

"Show me what you want to show me, Beau. Come on, buddy, what is it?"

The dog cocked his head to one side, licked Ani's hand, and pranced regally over to the built-in cabinet behind the desk. Ani followed him while Eliza hummed. Beauregard jumped up on his hind legs, stretching his body a full five feet high, and placed his two front paws on the top cabinet door. He looked at Ani and whined.

"Hurry up, Ani! Open it and let's get out of here."

"Do you hear something, Eliza?"

"Just my own heart pumping, but now I feel like I need to pee."

"Eliza, knock it off. Keep looking."

Beauregard now clawed at the door, his nails scratching the dark paneling. His whining intensified. Ani pushed him down gently. "I'm here. It's okay," she said soothingly. She pulled the brass doorknob, but it wouldn't budge. "It's locked."

"Of course it would be locked. I could have told you that. Rich people always have everything locked, especially this guy," hissed Eliza. Ani slid her fingers along the side and bottom of the door. "What are you doing now? The door is locked.

Let's just go," begged Eliza.

"I read something about this in one of my mystery stories. A panel had a secret latch that opened the cupboard if you pushed on it just right."

"Hello, that was a story, not like now, where we have been led by a killer dog upstairs to break into a locked cabinet. What am I saying?" Eliza said. "This sounds like an old Nancy Drew story. Next you're going to start calling me Bess and ask for a bobby pin."

"There, I feel something, this hinge here," Ani said. "It's loose. Now, I think if I just push here like this." A click came from the hinge, and the locked cabinet door popped open, only an inch, but open nonetheless. Ani smirked at Eliza. "Told ya."

"Whatever," Eliza said. Beauregard jumped up on Ani, shoving her against the cabinet.

"Easy, boy, down," Ani commanded, and the dog dropped to the floor. Ani opened the cabinet and it was completely bare, which surprised her since the room was so cluttered.

"What's in there, Ani?"

"Nothing, nothing that I can see." Beauregard rose up again and pushed his head into the back of Ani's thighs, letting out a louder whine. "I can't see the top shelf completely," she said to both Eliza and the dog. Ani rolled the desk chair over and climbed on it to get a better look.

"I don't see anything," she said, sweeping her hand along the shelf. "Wait a minute. I feel something. I just need to move it a bit. It's heavy, whatever it is." With both hands and on tiptoes, she grabbed it. Slowly, she lowered her arms, swiveling in the chair, and faced Eliza. "Come help me, Eliza. I can't get down. The chair is too wobbly."

Eliza hurried to her sister. "What is that?"

"I don't know, but it must be something sort of valuable, I imagine, since it's covered with this velvet cloth," Ani said. Beauregard yipped and bumped into the chair, moving it and causing Ani to shake the object. "Quick, Eliza," Ani said. "Take it from me before I fall."

Eliza placed the object on top of the desk. Ani jumped

down off the chair, and both girls stared at the black velvet covering. Ani slid the drapery off. What occurred next happened so fast and was so strange that even later that night in their beds the girls still weren't sure what they saw and what they heard. However, Eliza was right, something weird *was* happening and not just with the animals, and somehow, some way Ani was a part of it, whether she wanted to be or not.

Underneath the covering was a pink egg-shaped object about ten inches tall and eight inches around, resting in a silver trophy or loving cup proclaiming "1st Place Northeast Harbor Regatta, 1964."

Eliza pulled it out of the cup and shook it really hard. "I know what this is. It's a snow globe like the one Dad brought back from the Seattle Aquarium. You know, the one with the Space Needle inside and the floating sea turtle." She stopped shaking it and placed it back in the cup.

"Eliza, be careful. I don't think this is a snow globe," said Ani.

"Then what is it?"

"I don't know, but now we need to wait for the liquid to stop moving."

When the swirling subsided, the girls were not prepared to see what they saw. Trapped inside was a small person, more like a Barbie-sized person, with brown hair tied back in two braids, and wearing a blue dress covered with a white pinafore.

"Oh my goodness," Ani said.

"This must be some sort of trick," Eliza said. The girl blinked, and both girls reeled backward. Eliza shrieked.

"Don't be afraid," the girl said. Ani and Eliza stared back, wide-eyed and motionless. "I don't have much time. They're coming soon."

"Who's coming?" asked Ani as she found her voice.

"Lobsters are on the move, Kanake-kee, Kanake-kee!"

"Kanake what?" Ani asked.

"Kanake-kee, use the present, my present, the present!" the doll girl pleaded. "Lobsters ... beware of Retsbol. Help is near, Kanake-kee!" Beauregard barked and ran to the door. Using his large head, he shoved it closed. The girls looked up in alarm. They knew what was happening: Mr. Baxter was coming. "Help me, help us all," the voice trailed off. Ani threw the cover back over the object. She jumped up on the desk chair, and Eliza carefully handed the orb to her sister. Ani rose up on her toes again and swiftly returned it to its previous position.

"Girls, where are you?" their father's voice called out coming down the hall.

"Beauregard?" Barton called sternly.

"Hurry, Ani, hurry!" cried Eliza. Ani leaped down from the chair, closed the cabinet door, and tucked the chair back behind the desk.

"What can we say? Why are we here?" Ani said. Eliza shook her head. She had no answer. Beauregard barked and growled as the door handle turned.

"Ani, Eliza, this is no time for games," demanded Dr. Banke, sounding stern.

The dog barked louder and growled even more menacingly than before. Ani got it! She ran next to her sister and pulled her back against the fireplace mantle.

"Act scared," she whispered.

"Act? I'm already terrified by what we just saw," Eliza whispered back.

Mr. Baxter, Dr. Banke, and Sorenson sprang into the room. Beauregard barked, growled, and bared his teeth at the girls, saliva dripping from his mouth.

"Dad," cried Eliza.

"The dog, he chased us up here and wouldn't let us move," Ani said, running to her father's arms.

"Beauregard, heel!" yelled Barton.

Eliza also ran to her father.

"Sorenson, take the dog downstairs at once."

"Certainly, Mr. Baxter," Sorenson answered feebly. "Beauregard, come here!"

The dog growled one more time at the girls and stared at Ani. She nodded ever so slightly to him, and he backed down and trotted after the butler.

"My apologies for the beast," Barton offered while fingering his hair. "I don't know what has gotten into that dog. He has been all out of sorts since, well …" Barton stopped speaking as his eyes narrowed and focused on the cabinet door. The girls followed his gaze and to their alarm saw that the cabinet door was ajar. Shoot, thought Ani, I didn't close it tightly enough. Barton strode toward the cabinet. "Well, since my father passed away several weeks ago." Barton reached the cabinet and quietly closed the door. Click-click sounded the latch. He glared at Ani who, as tempted as she was to turn away, met his stare head on. He might suspect them of finding his secret orb and the imprisoned tiny girl, she thought, but he didn't know it definitively. Beauregard made sure of that with his growling and barking.

* * * *

Kanake-kee, Kanake-kee, what does it all mean, Ani wondered as she lay in bed later that night. Eliza was right. Dad wouldn't believe us if we told him. Really no one would. Who is the girl and how did she get in the orb? Why would Mr. Baxter have her? What was she talking about? What was Retsbol? What present? None of this made any sense. Finally her eyes closed and she drifted off with the sound of the ocean in her head and dreamed of snow globes, strange places, and presents.

Somewhere, locked in a cabinet, covered with a dark cloth, another girl was awake, awake and praying. Kanake-kee, Kanake-kee, she thought as she too eventually succumbed to sleep.

Lobster fact: *Lobster Casserole*

Melt 1 stick of butter in an 8 ½ x 11-inch nonstick pan

Layer: 2 cups of cooked lobster meat
1 lb. blanched, diced asparagus
½ cup sautéed leeks
Sprinkle 2 cups crumbled cornbread on top

Bake covered at 350° for 20 minutes (cornbread should be lightly toasted)

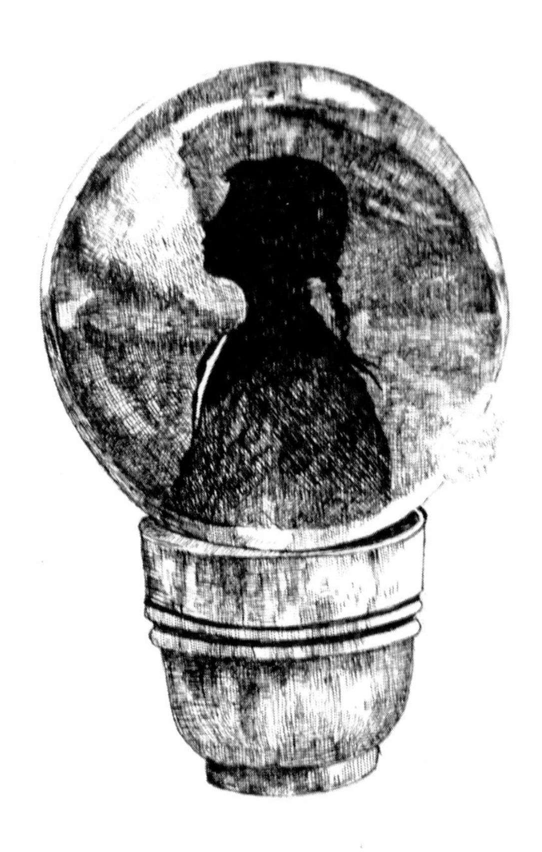

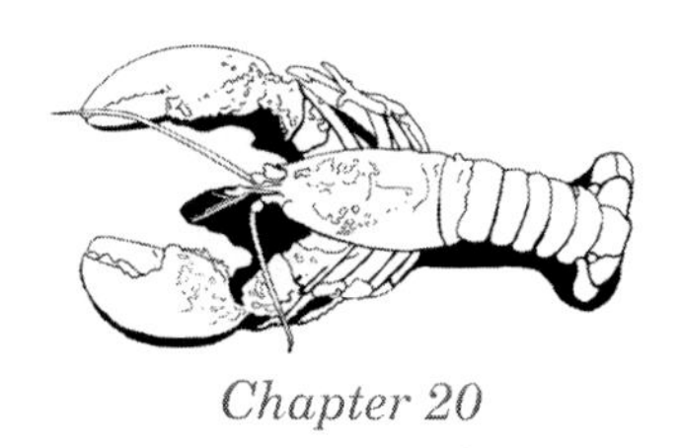

Chapter 20

Professor Bert Sol, Take Two

"Ani, please pass the milk," Dr. Banke said. Ani's head rested wearily on her placemat. She didn't move. "Ani, milk, please," he asked again a little louder.

"Oh, what, milk?" Ani said groggily. "Here you go, Dad." She passed the pitcher to her father.

"You need to get some more sleep tonight and stop reading your mysteries so late. I saw your light on at midnight when I came up to bed."

"Yes, I guess you're right." Ani yawned.

Eliza entered the kitchen, dressed and ready for the day. She gave her father a kiss. "Good morning Dad, Ani," she chirped.

"Well, someone certainly got up on the right side of the bed this morning."

"You always say that, Dad. Mom too. My bed is against the wall. I can only get out on one side," said Eliza.

"I just meant that you were happy, that's all."

"I am happy because I finally woke up. I had the weirdest dream about being chased by the scary dog and finding a snow globe with a talking gir … "

Ani snapped her head up and squeezed Eliza's wrist tightly.

"Hey, Ani? Ouch, I was just telling Dad about my dream and ouch," Eliza said again as Ani's grip intensified.

Ani glowered at her sister.

"That's funny, Eliza," Ani said. "I also had weird dreams

last night."

Dr. Banke ignored the exchange between his daughters and stopped eating his breakfast cereal. "Did you find something peculiar in Mr. Baxter's library last night? I thought you said Beauregard kept you pinned to the fireplace."

"He did, Dad, he did. It was terrible, all those gnashing teeth and drooling balls of spit. Scary and disgusting," said Ani.

"Well, girls, I have a lot to do at the lab today, so I think I will be gone most of the day. I spoke with Patrick the gardener, and he will be around the cottage garden today if you need anything. You are free to go and explore, but please be careful. Stay out of trouble. Especially stay away from that dog Beauregard."

"No problem," said Ani. "We will be sure to stay far away from him."

"Do you have any idea what you are planning on doing today?" Dr. Banke asked.

"We are thinking about biking over to the library. Eliza needs a book for school, and I was going to see if I could do some research on the present that Mom gave me."

"That sounds like a good idea," said Dr. Banke, resuming his breakfast.

"That's it, the present, my PRESENT," blurted out Ani. The tiny girl mentioned the present. She must be talking about my present from Mom, Ani thought.

"Yes, Ani," a confused Dr. Banke said. "Yes, it is your present. I think that was quite clear when Mom gave it to you, so you really don't have to yell at us about it."

"Sorry, Dad, it's just that, well, I love it so much and I got carried away," Ani said. Kanake-kee does sound Indian, she mused, and Dad thought that some of the pictures could have been drawings from Native Americans.

"Hey, girls, why don't we put your bikes on the rack, and I can drop you off at the library on the way to the lab. Then you can get something to eat in town, do some exploring and bike home or wait for me to finish at the end of the day"

After they finished eating their breakfast, the girls agreed to clean up. Ani made sure to grab her backpack, which contained a notebook, index cards, pens and pencils, and, most important, the birthday present. The three got into the car and headed for the town of Bar Harbor on the opposite side of the island.

Bar Harbor, incorporated in 1774, was the most touristy town on the island. Great hotels, fantastic restaurants, ice cream shops, and several souvenir businesses lined the streets. As was the norm for this time of year, the harbor was filled with visitors who were enjoying their summer vacation with trips to Cadillac Mountain and Sand Beach, biking on the carriage paths, and munching on lobster rolls. Eliza spied a shop that she just had to check out, so Ani visited the library by herself.

Ani loved libraries, and the library in Bar Harbor was spectacular. The main room was huge with high vaulted ceilings. To the right were granite stairs that led up to research periodicals and special collections, according to the sign. The center circulation desk was also made from stone and curved in a large semicircle, accommodating several librarians to help check out books to patrons, answer questions and phone calls, and welcome visitors. Ani approached the desk with great enthusiasm.

"Hello, dear, may I help you?" asked an elderly woman dressed in a sensible navy blue skirt with a matching cotton cardigan. Her nametag said "Judith Starke, Head Librarian." Ani couldn't have been more pleased.

"Yes, thank you, ma'am," Ani said. "I am interested in researching Native Americans, especially specific tribes that might have been from this area."

"Well, you have come to the right place. That would be the Abenaki people, so let's go upstairs to Special Collections. We have an entire section dedicated to Wabenaki and Abenaki Indians," the kindly librarian said.

After an hour of Mrs. Starke's time, Ani sat at a large table surrounded by piles of books about Native Americans. She had hand-copied a few of the drawings from her book at home, which she had cautiously shared with the librarian. Ani wasn't sure why, but she felt the need to be protective of her manuscript. Mrs. Starke barely flinched when looking at Ani's pages. She had a mission to do and research was its name.

Ani learned that Mrs. Starke had been a librarian at the Bar Harbor Library since 1968, the year she graduated from the University of Rhode Island with a degree in Library Sciences. She had welcomed technology at every step of the way. However, true research with actual books, and not something found electronically, was the only research that she could respect. Ani was grateful for her knowledge. With a burning intensity, Ani pored over the books. She had to find out what her present meant so she could help the tiny girl in the orb and understand the connection with the lobsters.

"Where is Eliza?" she sighed. She had promised Ani she would assist with the research. Most likely she was trying on a dress she just had to have. She did love to shop.

A few more hours passed and Ani rubbed her face and stood up to stretch her legs. Unfortunately, her research had been only somewhat useful. She was fairly sure that the writings in her book were linked to Maine Indians. The book entitled *Maine Native Americans, Then and Now*, by Dr. Bert Sol, had proved to be the most informative. His book had etchings from the Wabenaki and Abenaki tribes indigenous to Downeast Maine and parts of eastern Canada. The drawings were from early cave paintings found primarily at the base of Cadillac Mountain, the tallest peak on the eastern seaboard and just a few miles away in Acadia National Park. Ani hoped that she would be able to see those drawings firsthand. The author also said that translation of the Abenaki language was incredibly difficult. He compared the Abenaki alphabet to that of the Chinese. Great, thought Ani. However am I going to figure out what the book, my present, says if I can't figure out the language? Ani kept hearing the tiny girl's voice: "Help, help me, Kanake-kee." None of the books that Mrs. Starke had found for Ani included any information about the spoken and written language. As far as Ani could tell, her book contained only drawings. Ani was tired, frustrated, and hungry. Just then Mrs. Starke tapped her gently on the shoulder.

"Finding everything you need?" she asked.

"Sort of. I did find this one book," Ani said and picked up

Dr. Sol's volume. "This had the most helpful information."

"Yes, I am not surprised. He is a leading authority on the Abenaki Indians. A great lecturer, too. You should try to hear him while you're on the island."

"Does he live here?" Ani asked.

"Why, yes, dear. He's a professor at Maine Oceanic College about a mile from here on Eden Street. I imagine that he would enjoy pontificating ... I mean sharing his knowledge with you."

"Thank you, Mrs. Starke, thank you very much." Dr. Sol right here in Bar Harbor, how wonderful, Ani thought.

"You know, you could take this book out if you established a temporary guest library card. Why don't you follow me downstairs and I can take care of that for you?" A few minutes later, an efficient Mrs. Starke had indeed issued Ani her temporary library card, checked out her book, and given her the phone number and address of the professor. Ani left the library with a lilt in her step. Now to find Eliza, she thought. Soon the girls reconnected and talked about their morning over pizza. Eliza had purchased some bargains that she just had to show her sister.

"This one I bought for you, Ani," she said proudly while reaching into one of her many bags. "Ta da, isn't this hysterical?" She shook out a red cotton T-shirt that depicted a sunbather on the beach about to be pinched by an enormous walking lobster. The words "Welcome to Bar Harbor" with the "Bar" crossed out and "Lobster" written instead topped the T-shirt. "Funny, huh?" Eliza laughed.

"Eliza, this is horrible." Ani smiled. She had to admit it was pretty funny.

"Did you find anything out?' her sister asked, biting into a hot slice of pepperoni pizza.

"Yes, yes I did," Ani said and then launched into what she discovered at the library. Eliza grabbed the book from Ani's hand and flipped through the pages.

"This guy certainly is wordy," she said. "Check this out," she added, holding up his picture on the back of the book. "He's got the nerd thing going on nicely here. Groovy argyle vest."

"Soon you can meet Mr. sweater-vest man in person," Ani said. "I made an appointment with him when you went to the bathroom. Finish up because we need to be there in twenty minutes." Eliza wrinkled her nose at her sister.

"You promised you would help me and besides, Dad wouldn't want me to go alone."

"Oh, all right, but you have to admit I'm right about the nerd thing."

The two girls got on their bikes and headed west out of town to Maine Oceanic College. Mrs. Starke was right: the school was only a mile away. The property had been the estate of a Mrs. Attebury, who donated the buildings and the grounds upon her death in 1970. Since then, the college had grown in size, acquiring land and buildings along the way. The campus was a wonderful mix of old and new nestled along the rocky coast. The girls biked through the main gate and followed the signs to the Rowe Building, home of the Department of Native American Studies and Professor Sol's office.

A bored student intern who barely looked up from the book she was reading greeted them. She buzzed Professor Sol. "Yeah, it's Sophie. The caller is here. Yeah, okay." To Ani and Eliza she said in a flat voice, "You can sit if you want. He'll be out soon."

"Thanks," said Ani and both girls sat down on the wooden bench across from the intern's desk. After only a few moments, the door to Professor Sol's office opened and out came the man himself. Eliza made an audible gasp. He was wearing the same argyle sweater-vest from his book cover photo. Ani worried that Eliza would start to lose it and end up laughing throughout the entire meeting. She gave her a stern look as if to say, *Get it together*. She held out her right hand to shake and said, "Hello, I'm Ani Banke. This is my sister, Eliza. Thank you for meeting with us."

Ani was not prepared for what happened next. Professor Sol shifted his body slightly left revealing that his right white cotton sleeve was pinned up at the elbow. His right arm was missing! He awkwardly stretched out his left hand. Ani shook it with her right as did Eliza, who was visibly uncomfortable. His missing arm squelched her amusement over what he was wearing.

"Sorry. Boating accident as a child," he said, shrugging. "Nice to meet you both. Let's go into my office and see if I can help answer your questions. Sophie, please hold all my calls," he said to the lifeless girl behind the desk.

"Yah" was all the girl could get out before going back to her book.

Ani and Eliza sat in the two collegiate black chairs in front of Professor Sol's desk. The office was completely cluttered. This was not what Ani had expected, but nothing had been what she expected since coming to the island. "Now, girls, tell me how I might be able to help you," he said while easing himself into his desk chair.

"As I mentioned on the phone, I am working on a project for school, and I figured since I was going to be on Mount Desert Island for most of the summer, I might as well get a jump on it and do some research while I'm here," Ani said as she had rehearsed to herself earlier. Eliza put her hands in front of her mouth so Professor Sol wouldn't see her smile. "I'm particularly interested in how the Abenaki communicated both with drawings and words. I found your book in the library." She pulled the book out of her backpack, causing the parchment to shift and one corner to peek out.

"I see," Professor Sol said, sitting a little straighter in his chair and obviously flattered by the mention of his book.

"I was hoping you might recommend another book that might help explain the language. You know, things like the Abenaki signals, sayings, and any other communication methods," Ani continued.

The professor leaned back in his chair for a few seconds and then swiftly got up and moved toward one of several overflowing bookcases. Again, using his left hand, he passed over several books. "No, no, not that, no," he said to himself. "Ah, here it is." His hand rested on a particular volume. He tilted his head to the left to better read the spine: "*New England Native Americans: Their Origins and Language Development*, Dr. William F. Merriam, God rest his soul." He straightened up, retrieved the book, and returned to his seat. "Here, this might help you. You are welcome to borrow it while you're here on MDI." He handed the book to Ani.

"Thank you," she said while thumbing through it. "This looks great."

"Speaking of which, what brings you here?"

Eliza piped up, "Our father is doing research for Jamison Lab. He is studying why … "

"Why mice are drawn more to the taste of honey than to real sugar cane," Ani said. "He's a scientist." Eliza looked confused and Ani shook her head at her and pleaded with her eyes for her to go along with the lie she just told. Earlier at the library, Ani had overheard several townspeople talking about the incident with the lobsters. People seemed anxious and uncomfortable about outsiders in particular coming to investigate the goings on in their town. She just didn't want to share any more information than she had to about what she was doing, even to this kind professor.

"Do you speak Abenaki?" asked Eliza.

"Eliza? We really should be going," Ani said nervously while rising from her chair.

"Somewhat. The language is not really used anymore. As they say in Latin, *Sola lingua bona est lingua mortua.* The only good language is a dead language." He smiled at his own joke. "I am the leading expert on all things Abenaki. Why do you ask?"

"Just curious. I heard a phrase from the gardener at the place we are staying and

it sounded Indian or maybe even French, 'Kanake-kee'?"

"Eliza, that's enough. We have to be getting back now," Ani said.

"What did you say?" asked a more curious Professor Sol.

Ani stomped on Eliza's foot.

"Ani!" Eliza cried and rose out of her chair.

"Sorry, I'm sorry," Ani said unconvincingly.

"I'm not familiar with that expression. Are you sure you heard it right? Who said this again?"

Ani laughed. "Eliza, you're so silly. I heard him, too. He

said 'kayak key.' He was looking for the key to the bunkhouse in order to get the kayaks out for Dad. Thank you for your time and for your book. I'll just put it in my backpack along with your book that I borrowed from the library, and we will get out of your way." As she was about to grab the book, Sol's left hand shot out and his thumb and index finger pinched the volume before Ani knew what happened.

"Here you go," he said and handed it to her.

"Thank you," she said, startled by the speed and dexterity of his fingers.

Professor Sol walked around his desk and stood next to the girls. Ani had her back turned toward him as she struggled to close her very full backpack. Without thinking, she took all the books out of her bag and piled them on the chair.

"I can't close it," she said. "I need to organize it better." She replaced her notebook and index cards first, then her day planner, Professor Sol's book, and the book by Sol's mentor. The remaining item left on the chair was the present from her mother. Sol stared at it.

"What's this?" he asked, reaching around Ani to pick up the parchment.

But Ani's hand was quicker this time. She snatched the present from her mother and shoved it into her bag, zipping the backpack shut in seconds.

"Something my mother found for me in New Mexico. Old wagon trail recipes for things like flapjacks and well, things like old wagon trail food." Ani wasn't sure why she didn't want to share the book with Dr. Sol. He was an expert on all things Abenaki, after all, but for some reason, she was leery. Maybe later she would be willing to, but not now. She wanted to do her own research, and if she got stuck, she would ask to visit with Professor Sol again. She wondered how much he saw of her book.

"Sounds interesting," said Professor Sol.

"Yes, it is," said Ani.

"Extremely," said Eliza, who had no idea what her sister was talking about. After the girls had thanked Dr. Sol, said their good-byes, and were back on their bikes, Eliza asked Ani, "What was up with the old wagon flapjack talk?"

"I just didn't want him to see the book. I mean, he seems perfectly fine and very helpful. It's just that, well, I don't know."

"Sounds like a good plan to me because you know my rule."

"What rule?" asked Ani.

"Never trust a man who wears a sweater-vest!" And Eliza laughed.

Lobster fact: *Many kinds of lobsters possess the ability to voluntarily lose a limb. Like many other crustaceans, lobsters can detach a limb that has been grabbed by a predator. Sometimes they are able to grow a replacement limb; this process is known as regeneration.*

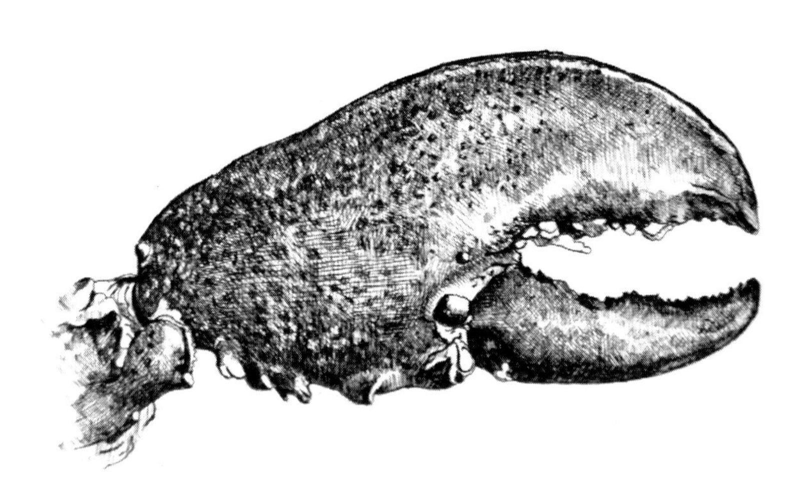

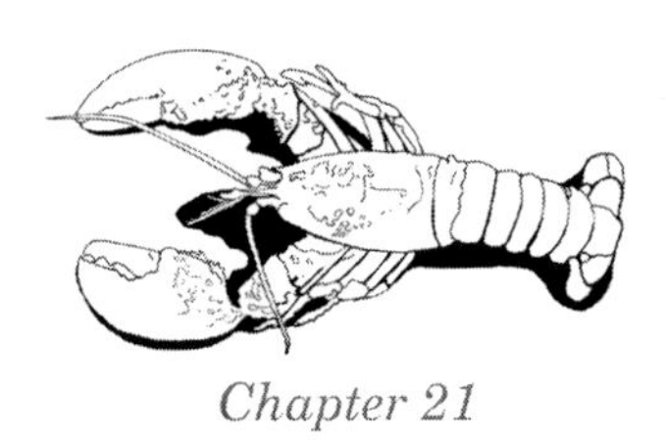

Chapter 21

Spidey Rides Again

The girls returned to downtown Bar Harbor to hang out in the park where they planned to meet their father. Eliza declared that she was hungry again.

"Ani, I'm going to get an ice cream," she said after noticing the Mount Desert Island Ice Cream Shop on the other side of the park. "Do you want to come with me?" she asked.

"No, you go though. I want to look at this book that Dr. Sol gave me." She plopped down on the inviting grass.

"You've got all afternoon," Eliza said. "You know how Dad gets when he's doing his research thing. It will be amazing if he picks us up at the end of the summer." She laughed and left to get her ice cream cone.

Ani was glad to have a few moments alone. She couldn't wait to dig into the book from Dr. Sol. She pulled it out of her backpack along with the parchment. Like her father, Ani also got engrossed when doing research. So much so that she didn't notice that Eliza had returned with a large, sea salt caramel ice cream cone, melting all over her arm. Eliza sat down next to her sister licking the dripping ice cream. Out of the corner of her eye, Eliza spied a ginger-haired boy riding a red bike, pedaling around the park square. Eliza looked back at her sister, who had not even acknowledged her. Nor had Ani's head moved as she bent over her books, flipping between the two sources. Eliza resumed eating. She glanced up to enjoy the view of the busy harbor and recognized the tall ship the *Martha Thomas* from one of the boring brochures that Ani had read to her and her father when they were traveling to Maine. The ship was sailing into the harbor from a sightseeing cruise, and Eliza was struck by the beauty of the sails blowing in the wind. She moved her eyes back toward her cone, only to see the boy go whizzing by on his red bike again. Eliza didn't think much about it. However, by the third time she noticed him, her curiosity, which wasn't normally too great, had been piqued.

"Check out this boy," she said, tapping Ani on the shoulder. "Watch how he keeps going around the park."

"Huh? Oh, you're back," Ani said and returned to Dr. Sol's book.

"Here he comes again. Strange. Do you see him?"

"What? Who?" Ani popped up from her research.

"That boy there, with the ginger hair and the red bike and the ... " Eliza didn't finish her statement. She jumped up and dropped her cone to the ground. The boy in question turned his head at the exact moment she walked determinedly toward him.

"You there, boy!" yelled Eliza, pointing a finger at him. "Hey, can you stop please?"

Upon seeing Eliza, the boy abruptly faced the front of his bike and pedaled as fast as his legs could manage. Ani now was close behind her sister, trying to figure out why Eliza was so interested in this boy on the bike.

"Stop. I said, STOP!" Eliza demanded louder this time, but by now the boy had increased the distance between them.

"What's going on?" asked Ani.

"I just had a hunch," Eliza said. Both girls watched as the small boy pedaled around the corner away from the harbor and the park. Just then, the wind from the shore blew particularly strong, causing the zip-up sweatshirt the boy was wearing to lift up from the back, revealing a red shirt underneath with black lines. Spider-Man had been found.

"Come on!" cried Eliza and ran after the boy. Ani followed her older sister and soon passed her. The boy was pedaling up the hill now and slowing down while Ani, a running enthusiast, gained on him.

"Stop, Spidey boy, stop!" Ani cried breathlessly at him. But hearing her words so close behind him only increased his speed. Ani was within reach as they both came to the top of the hill. She knew she had to make her move now for once he reached the top of the hill and began his descent on the other side, she would never catch him. She pushed herself and willed her legs to move faster and reached out to grab at whatever was in range. Her fingertips grazed the back of his Spidey shirt, but she wasn't close enough to get a good hold on the material. Her hand slipped down and landed on the back of his seat, which was empty since now the boy was standing up while pedaling with all his might to move him and his bike up the hill and away from the girls. Within a few feet of the top, Ani lunged at her target again, desperately trying to clamp down on something. To her surprise she was able to get part of the boy's bike license plate, which was already dangling by one side. Ani pulled hard, but had to run even faster as the boy now dragged her along behind him. His bike wobbled to the right and then the left before straightening.

"Gotcha," Ani cried, but the remaining twine from the license plate broke free and she fell backward and landed on the pavement with the plate in her hand. Eliza almost tripped over her, and, looking very red in the face and very much out of breath, bent over with her hands on her knees and rested. Both girls looked up as the boy and the bike crested the hill and disappeared behind the library. Ani stayed on the ground and viewed the name on the plate. "Roonie?"

It took Eliza a few moments before she could speak. "I knew it was him. Spidey boy is alive!"

"Well, this proves one thing," said Ani.

"What's that?"

"I definitely run faster than you."

Lobster fact: *Lobsters have five pairs of legs, the front pair of which end in claws. They also have delicate leg-like limbs on their abdomen called swimmerets, which, not surprisingly, are used for swimming.*

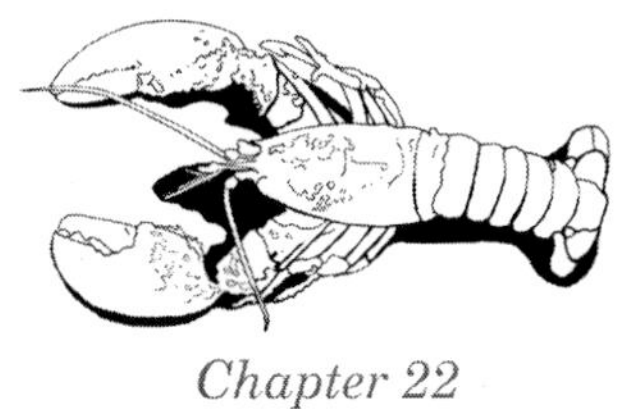

Chapter 22

Research Intensifies

Ani couldn't stop thinking about her present, the visit with Professor Sol, and the girl in the orb. The girls had returned home on their bikes, as their father had indeed become so involved in his work that they tired of waiting and went home without him. While Eliza napped in their bedroom, Ani tiptoed down the stairs and quietly exited out the kitchen door. She headed for the circle of Adirondack chairs in the corner, placed strategically by a large, shady elm tree. She retrieved the book from Professor Sol and the mysterious present from her mother and soon was lost in her own inquiry. The professor's book by his mentor included an Abenaki alphabet, and Ani kept that page open with a rock.

"This is fantastic," Ani said. She flipped to the middle of the parchment and found the drawing she was looking for, a sun with five rays above what appeared to be a mountaintop. Ani pulled out a stack of note cards, a method of note keeping that her mother had taught her. *Sometimes, Ani,* she could hear her mother's voice in her own head, *you need to feel the research in your hands in order to figure out what you are looking for*. She wrote on her first card the words *Cadillac Mountain* and then copied the drawing from the parchment with the triangle with the rays slanting down from the sun.

Ani continued in this manner for the remainder of the late afternoon, decoding the ancient drawings and creating note cards. Eventually the combination of waking up extremely early and the warming sun proved too much, and she close her eyes and fell comfortably asleep surrounded by note cards and books. A steady breeze washed over Ani, further guaranteeing a sound afternoon nap. A few yellow note cards escaped from the top of her stack, which by this time was quite high, and lifted up by the wind, danced away from their owner, landing elsewhere on the Baxter property.

Unbeknownst to Ani, Spidey boy, aka Roonie, had come back to the Baxter estate and climbed silently and efficiently up the old elm tree, which was providing a protective covering for him to do what he liked best: spy!

While Patrick was bent over an unfortunate mildewing black-eyed Susan, one of Ani's note cards attached itself to the purple balloon flowers in front of him. Patrick picked up the card and read Ani's handwriting: *Three Islands now known as Porcupine Islands,* followed by her rudimentary copying of the parchment drawing of three oblong shapes placed side by side. Patrick stood up and saw another note card, this time attached to a row of cosmos. He took the card, which read *Sand Dollar* with a drawing of a circle with an open star in the center. The wind blew stronger, and Patrick caught another card in midair. This one read *Bald Eagle*, followed by a half circle with a wide *V* underneath.

"What the blazes?" Patrick mumbled as he followed the path of yellow cards, reading and walking at the same time. He couldn't quite figure out what these all meant, but something in the back of his old mind was giving him an odd feeling, and he wanted to get to the bottom of what or who was behind them. Soon he came upon the Adirondack chairs beneath the black elm tree, planted by his own father when he was just a lad. My, wouldn't Father be pleased to see how lovely the elm has grown, he thought. Patrick scooped up another card, this time resting peacefully on the carpet of green fine fescues and read the word *Thunder Hole* with a drawing of an upside down *V* surrounding a solitary circle. By this time Patrick was about fifteen feet from Ani, who was still sleeping soundly. It took him a moment to recognize the daughter of the scientist, and he cautiously approached the circle of chairs. After three long strides Patrick nabbed another card, just a few feet from Ani's bare toes. The words were hidden and Patrick turned the card over to reveal what he now surmised was the girl's writing: *Lobster Claw* with a drawing of a single right facing claw. Patrick looked closer at the sleeping girl and noticed the books resting on her lap. A tingling started at the base of his neck and moved swiftly down his forearms and legs. He felt the hairs on his skin rise up and dizziness washed over him. This can't be, he thought to himself, or can it? He rested his hand on the chair to Ani's left and waited for the dizziness to subside.

Meanwhile, Roonie, from his perch in the elm tree, was planning to climb down and search the girl's backpack to see if he could recover his bike plate. But Patrick, and yes, he knew who Patrick was since his Aunt Kate worked for Mr. Baxter at the main house, was going to ruin his plans, he thought disappointedly. Roonie did not care too much for the old gardener. He didn't want Roonie climbing any of the trees on the property, even though they were the best trees to climb in all of Northeast Harbor, and they had the best branches and the best views of the harbor. Feeling suddenly protective of the girl he had spent the last few days spying on and angry with Patrick for showing up and messing up his plot to get his nameplate, Roonie pulled a rock from his pocket. Fortunately, he collected unusual things, mainly sea glass, shells, and rocks, and usually had several on him. Roonie squinted, closing his right eye to get a better aim, and threw the rock square at Patrick's back. "Bingo," he whispered.

In his surprise at being hit from above, Patrick thrust his body forward and he bumped into Ani's leg. "Ouch," Patrick blurted and looked up. The outburst from the gardener and the bump to her leg woke Ani and her eyes flew open. She was startled to see the "creepy gardener," as Eliza called him, standing so close. She quickly closed her precious book and leapt to her feet.

Patrick had a good idea where the small rock had come from and yelled, "Roonie, I know this is your doing. Come down here this instant!" But by this time, Roonie had already swung to the next tree, and within moments he would be onto the next and then the next, easily working his way to the edge of the tree line. And then he would do what he did best, disappear.

"Roonie?" Ani said. "What's going on? Can I help you with something, and who is Roonie?"

Patrick was ashamed of himself for letting some silly girl with her silly drawings upset him so. Still holding the collected note cards, he said, "Roonie is an annoying boy from town whose aunt is employed by Mr. Baxter and who apparently does not understand the words *No Trespassing*, and these cards were littering my garden." He handed them to her. "See that this doesn't happen again." He stormed off.

Ani took the cards in confusion. She opened her notebook to a clean page and wrote Roonie's name followed by *annoying boy according to gardener* in her neat handwriting.

Patrick also was confused. Confused about why the girl would be writing those cards, and what those cards and drawings meant. He had seen those drawings before, a long, long time ago. A time he must not and would not think about. He had to be mistaken, he just had to be. His eyes were getting worse, and he was an old, old foolish man, he thought. Surely she could not be in possession of the book, Amelia's book. Or could she?

Patrick opened the door of the garden shed behind the cottage house and pulled the string that dangled in front of him, illuminating the tidy room. He lifted a dirt-covered tarp off the potting bench to reveal a small old-fashioned trunk. He then took a key from his breast pocket and opened the lock. Patrick raised the lid, which revealed a green plastic trash bag with a thick rubber band holding it secure. Barton would never think to look in here for his book, which is exactly why Patrick had placed it here, covered with gardening tools these many years. He smiled, feeling proud of his ability to trick Barton. He gingerly removed the rubber band, unwrapped the trash bag, and exposed his own deerskin parchment given to him on that day that held so much promise and hope for Patrick, but ended with so much horror and sorrow. Lovingly he opened the front cover and found a pressed lupine flower. He picked this up and brought it to his nose. The smell was gone, but not the memory. He remembered it all as if it were yesterday. He opened the pages searching for something, what he wasn't sure, but he continued to the back of his book and stared down at the two pages before him.

"It can't be," he said out loud. Patrick's own book contained several of the same drawings that he found scattered throughout his garden on little yellow note cards copied down by a young girl, who for some unknown reason had the book. Amelia's book? And now it was here, interrupting Patrick's routine, causing him to remember. He hung his head and tried to hold back the tears that sprang to his eyes, bringing with them all the pain, regret, and guilt he had blocked out. Patrick did not comprehend what was going on and how or why or if the girl had the book, but he was positive of one thing and one thing only. He would not let Amelia down this time. He would get to the bottom of this if it were the last thing he did.

Lobster fact: *Deep-sea lobsters, which live in deep, dark ocean spots, are unable to see, but other lobsters have what are known as compound eyes, which excel at detecting motion and help gather light in dim, underwater conditions.*

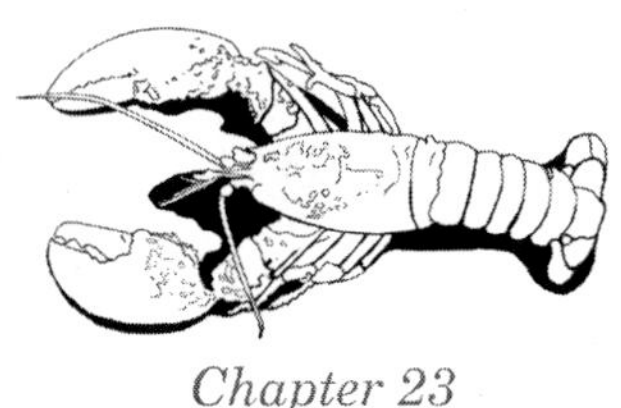

Chapter 23

Sea Shell, Sea Shell by the Seal Shore

Dr. Banke, Ani, and Eliza sat at a table outside enjoying a light supper together. Ani had helped her father prepare one of her favorite summertime meals, mini cheeseburgers with tons of ketchup.

"Ani," her father said, "what number is this? Your fourth or your fifth?"

Ani picked up a juicy cheeseburger and took a huge bite. With her mouth full she tried to answer. "I think this is my fifth, or maybe this is my sixth." She gulped from her bottle of pink lemonade.

"She worked up an appetite today," Eliza said, "chasing Spidey boy around the park in Bar Harbor."

Ani giggled, dribbling ketchup down her chin from another mouthful of cheeseburger. Wiping it away with a napkin, she said, "Dad, you should have seen us today. We chased down the boy who I think might have been following us. He got away, but I was able to grab his license plate from the back of his bike."

"What's this?" asked Dr. Banke.

"Remember, Dad, when we first got here?" Eliza said. "I told you both that I thought I saw Spider-Man in the trees? You didn't believe me, but it has to be true now. I found him circling around us in the park today."

"His name is Roonie," said Ani. "The gardener told me his Aunt Kate works at the big house for Mr. Baxter. Oh, and Eliza, I forgot to tell you. While you were taking a nap upstairs, I think Roonie was watching me from the elm tree, and then he threw a rock at the gardener, who I think was watching me, too."

"Seriously?" Eliza said.

"Seriously right back at you two," said a bewildered Dr. Banke. "What are you girls talking about? Spidey boy, rock throwing, the gardener? It sounds more like your napping is turning into dreaming. I'm glad you're able to get some rest while your poor father has to work from sunup to sundown." He tousled Ani's hair.

"Hey, Dad," said Ani, switching gears. "Any news on what's going on with the lobsters?"

"Yeah, Dad, why are they acting so crazy?"

"No, girls, unfortunately, we don't know what is bringing them to MDI, but we have some general theories that we are testing. We do know that the number of lobsters that normally inhabit these waters appears to have tripled and that the lobsters have almost doubled in size."

"Bigger claws!" said Eliza. "I love lobster claws. Can we get some tomorrow?"

"This is serious, Eliza. Lobsters around the rest of the Atlantic seaboard have decreased at an equally alarming rate. If this pace continues, lobsters in the Northeast would become extinct, except for here, in a matter of a few weeks."

"Wow, Dad, this *is* serious," said Ani.

"What can be done about this?" asked a solemn Eliza.

"That is exactly what I am trying to find out. I have to go back to the lab for an emergency planning meeting. The governor of Maine is due to arrive." Dr. Banke looked at his watch. "In approximately 30 minutes. She wants a full briefing," he said as he got up from the table, "so I need to get going."

"We'll clean up, Dad," Ani said.

"You just go," Eliza said while picking up the plates. "We'll take care of this."

He gave them each a hug and said, "Thank you, girls. This really is disturbing, somewhat a mystery." He sighed. "Stay out of trouble," he yelled before starting his car. The girls watched as their father backed up and headed down the long, winding driveway.

"Let's bring this stuff in and clean up later," suggested Eliza. "All this talk of the ocean has made me want to go swimming!"

"All right," agreed Ani. "Promise you'll rescue me if I need it?"

"Ani, you aren't afraid of a few extra lobsters are you?"

"No, sis," said Ani, letting out a loud burp. "I'm afraid I might sink due to too many cheeseburgers."

The girls cleared the table and set the dishes to soak in the sink. After putting on their bathing suits, they packed towels and water bottles for their swim at Seal Beach in Seal Harbor on the edge of Northeast Harbor.

Eliza opened the refrigerator and stared at the contents. "Nothing fun to bring in here," she said with a sigh.

"We just finished eating. I can't believe you're hungry."

"Well, I didn't eat one hundred mini cheeseburgers like you," Eliza said.

"I'm sorry, you're right. I think there might be some cookies in the pantry. I need to do one more thing before we go. I'll be right back," Ani said and headed upstairs. In their bedroom, Ani removed the deerskin parchment from her backpack along with her notebook and hid them both in the bottom of the clothes hamper in the adjoining bathroom. Then she placed her backpack with the books from the library and Professor Sol and her note cards next to her bed. Last, Ani took her fleece throw blanket from the bottom of her bed and arranged it on top of half of her backpack, allowing the other half to be exposed. She took a few moments to fold the blanket just right so that the small tag was exposed on the right side facing the bedpost. Something that Nancy Drew might do, she thought, and left confidently to join her sister. She wasn't sure why she felt she should do this, but the need to guard her mysterious birthday present was overwhelming. Since discovering the girl in the orb, Ani suspected that somehow her gift was connected to the lobsters. She couldn't imagine how this was possible, but she had this uneasy feeling it was. Her book might have more answers than she originally thought, and she didn't want to run the risk of having the book taken from her when she had only just begun her research.

The girls enjoyed their ride to the beach, which was mostly downhill once they exited the Baxter property and got on the main road through town. Their route followed the coast, and Ani could see the harbor below full of life. Sailboats were returning from a day at sea while others were setting off for a sunset cruise. Ani noticed many lobster boats unloading the day's catch, which at the moment, according to her father, was proving to be quite profitable for the local lobstermen. The sun was glistening off the waves, causing everything to sparkle and look even more like one of the postcards that she had sent to her mother. How she wished she could talk to her mom and let her know what was happening. Unfortunately, she was deep within the Chuska Mountains in New Mexico, and Ani would be unable to speak with her until she came back to Montezuma a few days from now.

Eliza was the first to reach the secluded beach and leapt off her bike, kicked off her sandals, tore off her T-shirt and shorts, and sprinted to the water.

"Last one in is a rotten egg," she yelled back at her sister.

"Eliza," Ani called after her. "You've forgotten something. This is not Massachusetts. The water here is ..."

"Ah! Cold! Cold!" screamed Eliza.

"Freezing," Ani said, finishing her sentence as she met Eliza at the shore. Eliza yanked Ani's towel out of her hand and quickly wrapped herself up. "The normal water temperature here is a cool sixty degrees compared to Woods Hole where the temperature is normally seventy-two degrees."

"Hello, do you think you could have told me this before I made my big plunge?" Eliza said.

Ani dipped her foot in the water and promptly jumped back. "Wow," she exclaimed. "They weren't kidding. This is cold. But it kind of feels good, too," she said and stepped back into the water. "Come on, Eliza, let's swim out to the float," she said, pointing to a small wooden float about fifty feet from shore.

"I don't know if I can." Eliza shivered.

"Oh, you'll be fine. It's no colder than when we swim at the river after hiking in New Hampshire. Besides, we can get to the float and the sun will warm us up."

Eliza agreed, and momentarily the girls were both in the water. After several strokes, Ani felt Eliza pass by and wondered why she was swimming so close to her. Ani gave her a quick shove and pushed her away. Then she treaded water and lifted her head. She was surprised to see that Eliza, who was typically not a fast swimmer, had almost reached the ladder, which was still about fifteen feet away from Ani. Eliza must really be cold to be swimming that quickly, she thought. A few moments later, Ani reached the ladder and climbed out to join her already sunning sister on top of the float.

"Sorry for the shove, Eliza, but you were swimming so close to me I thought you might kick me in the head or something."

"What?" said Eliza.

"The shove, when I shoved you out of the way," continued Ani.

Eliza sat up and looked directly at her sister. "You didn't shove me, Ani."

"Yes, yes I did," Ani argued.

"No, Ani, you didn't."

"You're just teasing me, Eliza."

"No, I'm not, and now you're freaking me out. I want to get back to shore," she said and stood up. "You go first!"

Ani peered over the edge of the float into the water. "I'm sure it's nothing," she said calmly. Then she spotted something in the water. "I see something!"

"Is it a shark?" asked Eliza, closing her eyes.

"No, silly, it's not a shark. These waters are too cold. Man-eating sharks don't like cold water." She looked again. "I think it's a seal," Ani said, shielding her eyes. "Wait, yes, I see two, no, three seals!"

"Hey, I see them, too!" cried Eliza. Just then a large seal popped up right in front of them, waving his head back and forth and barking excitedly at the girls. Soon, other seals appeared behind him also bobbing their heads and barking. "W-A-T, Weird Animal Thing again! I can't take this," said Eliza. "Now I count eight seals. How are we going to get back to shore? Any boats around?" Eliza looked out toward the open water. There was a large yacht in the distance. "Hello, fancy yacht out there. Can you please come and rescue us from the school of seals?"

"Eliza, it's a pod of seals, not a school of seals, and we don't need to be rescued. Seals are normally harmless."

"Normally? Nothing about MDI has been normal since we arrived," Eliza said. "Or have you forgotten about the tiny, little person living in the snow globe up at the Baxter estate, or perhaps the random squirrel that chased me during our first day here, or Spidey boy, or the parade of sea life following us in the Jamison Lab boat, or, hey, let us not leave out the ever-growing lobster population and by growing, I do mean both in number and in size!"

"You're so dramatic," said Ani.

"Dramatic! Dramatic! I'll give you dramatic," quipped Eliza. Something shimmering sparkled brightly across the water.

"What's that?" asked Eliza.

"It's the seal. It's carrying something! Something shiny," Ani shouted. The first seal to approach the girls was in fact balancing something on the edge of his nose. They watched as he ducked under water and disappeared only to reappear moments later closer to the edge of the ladder with the object still resting on his sleek, black nose. The seal stared at the girls and blinked his large black eyes.

"Hey, it looks like … "

Ani finished her sister's sentence: "A sand dollar! A silver sand dollar!" Ani climbed down the ladder.

"What are you doing? Are you nuts?" cried Eliza.

Ani stopped for a second and said, "I've seen this in my book from Mom, but it didn't make sense. Now it does. It was a silver sand dollar! I couldn't figure out why silver would be placed with sand dollar and thought it was just me not translating the Abenaki pictures and words correctly. Don't you see, Eliza? I need to get this silver sand dollar! I just know I do." And with that, Ani jumped in the water and swam toward the seal.

"Ani," yelled Eliza, "wait for me!" She plugged her nose and jumped feet first into the water.

The seals began a game of cat and mouse with the girls. The first seal glided across the water right past Ani, who reached out unsuccessfully for the sand dollar as it went by. Next, the seal passed it to another, smaller seal directly behind Ani. She swam to this seal and once again attempted to grasp the shiny sand dollar, but came up empty-handed as this seal too swam just out of reach and nosed the sand dollar off to another seal with large whiskers.

"Darn it," Ani said, "that was close."

"Let me try," said Eliza. "I just don't want them touching me." Eliza approached the long-whiskered seal, which remained motionless. "I almost got it," she said. As she reached up, the seal dragged both of his front flippers across the water, splashing Eliza in the face.

"Hey, that wasn't nice!" she said, choking and giggling at the same time.

Ani joined her sister, and they were encircled by the seals, who took great delight in swimming close, around, in front of, and behind the girls while splashing and passing the coveted object back and forth. From this strange circle of seals and girls, girls and seals came giggles, squeals, and barks.

"This is a losing battle, Ani," Eliza said. "Can't you ask them nicely to just give it to you? Anytime I get near them I appear to be the one they enjoy splashing in the face. Besides, I can't feel my legs anymore."

"Okay, I'll give it a try," agreed Ani. "Well, this has been really fun playing with all of you, but our skin isn't like yours and we're really feeling the effects of this cold ocean water. So I was wondering, if it wouldn't be too much trouble now, if maybe, you might simply allow me to reach up to whiskers over here and just take this silver sand dollar?" Ani and Eliza waited for some response, but the seals remained still, silently floating in the water. Ani continued, "Again, I want to thank you for the great time we have had today, and I promise you that I will take this silver sand dollar and keep it safe for you for a bit. Promise," she added at the end for good measure.

Whiskers pivoted toward the other seals while the seal who had first approached Ani appeared to nod in his direction as if giving Whiskers permission. Whiskers glided across the water to rest directly in front of Ani. She smiled affectionately. "Thank you," she said softly and then lifted the silver sand dollar off the seal's nose. "Thank you," she said a second time. Whiskers bowed and then all of the seals sank beneath the waves.

"Unbelievable," said Ani.

"Come on," Eliza moaned. "Let's get to shore while we can still kick." Once on land and wrapped in towels, Ani showed the object to Eliza. "Ani, did we not just swim with the seals or am I losing my mind?" Eliza asked.

"We most certainly did swim with the seals, and I know what we need to do next," Ani said as she dried off her wet hair.

"You do?" asked Eliza.

"We need to get back to the girl in the orb. I have some questions about my book, and I think she is just the one to answer them."

"How are we going to accomplish that? I think it was fairly clear that Mr. Baxter had the orb hidden and wouldn't really appreciate us ringing his bell to ask if the girl in the orb could come out and play."

"You got that right," said Ani. "But I have a different plan."

"What's that?"

"I know just the person, or should I say just the Spidey boy, to help us."

* * * *

Barton placed his long-range binoculars on the small table anchored to the floor of his yacht, *The $eaworthy*, presently cruising off the shore of Seal Beach, and took a sip from his freshly squeezed lemonade, brought to him moments before by Sorenson. I have lived here my entire life and never have I ever seen seals swim with children before, he thought to himself, scowling.

"Sorenson," he called out to his butler.

"Sir?"

"Get me Luke and Dave or Lyle and Daniel, or whatever they are called. You know, those guys you mentioned who own Rest from Your Pests. I have a few pests that might be needing a rest."

* * * *

While Dr. Banke was at Jamison Lab trying to provide answers to questions from the governor and her staff, answers that he just did not have, and his daughters were involved in a nontraditional swim with the seals at Seal Cove, Patrick, using the key given to him at the reading of the will, entered the cottage house. He had not been in the house since Barton's thirteenth birthday party. He refused to meet with old Mr. Baxter there, instead choosing to conduct gardening business at the main estate. Patrick took a deep breath and surveyed the surroundings. It was as if time had stood still here, for not much had changed.

He used to enjoy coming here every Friday with his father when he was the head gardener to meet with Mr. Baxter to review important landscaping decisions such as how many bulbs to plant, what bushes needed trimming, or how many additional workers would need to be hired during the blooming season. Many times, Patrick recalled feeling that Mr. Baxter truly looked forward to these conversations with his father since gardening was one of his great passions. And the feeling was certainly mutual. Patrick's father, Michael Timothy O'Leary, respected and appreciated his boss and passed this on to Patrick. Patrick, smiling to himself, remembered how Barton had always been difficult when they were younger and only

Gardener Mike could cause Barton to stop in his tracks. Mr. Baxter had understood that Mike O'Leary was a man of principles, honor, and authority. Patrick was grateful to have been able to witness the relationship between the two great men and had used them both as role models for how he wanted to live his life with integrity, sincerity, and honesty. Patrick believed he had accomplished this goal—that is, until this evening.

Even though he had been named caretaker of the cottage house and given his own key, Patrick knew he had no business standing in the foyer. But he couldn't help it. Not after what happened today under the elm tree. As much as he tried to push his feelings away, he was unable to do so. He may have been old, but he knew he saw that girl with a book much like the one given to him by Mr. Baxter some fifty-five years ago. The book alone might not have prompted so much curiosity, but when Patrick thought about the note cards with those drawings, he knew he wouldn't be able to rest until he figured out what this all meant, which is exactly why he was standing where he was standing.

He took another deep breath and opened the door to Mr. Baxter's study. He was pleased to see that the room had not changed, even after the break-in. Barton, he thought in disgust. It just had to have been him. Barton had been incredibly angry at the reading of the will, and Patrick knew that most of the anger was directed at him. Barton always blamed Patrick for what happened to Amelia even though they both knew it was Barton who knocked the amulets out of Amelia's hand, and it was Barton who grabbed her hair ribbon, and, yes, it was Barton who goaded Amelia into going through the Abenaki door. Oh, that door. Patrick winced at the memory of it all.

He went to the painting behind Mr. Baxter's desk. The painting of Cadillac Mountain had been removed after the robbery since it was too damaged from the explosion. Mrs. Pollinger, Barton's housekeeper, had tried unsuccessfully to replace it. She did manage to find a local artist, Carolyn Allyson, well known in the area for her Acadia images, who created a lovely watercolor view from Jordan Pond House of Bubble Pond and

Bubble Rock. It was only fitting that since the great man was no longer with us, the great picture of Cadillac should also be gone. Patrick also knew from Mrs. Pollinger that the safe had been removed and walled over.

"Nothing was found in the safe, nothing at all," Patrick recalled her saying to him. "We all knew that he didn't keep anything in the safe, so why someone would break into it is a mystery to us all. Townies," she had said disdainfully, even though that was what the summer people called her and the rest of the staff and anyone who wasn't wealthy and had to work for a living. But Patrick knew the truth. He knew it the moment that he first heard about it. It was Barton all right. Barton had wanted his birthday surprise for most of his life, and now, Patrick was certain, he had just what he wanted. He probably had already sold the covenant to some dealer across the globe, anything to increase his wealth, with no regard for anyone but Barton.

Patrick next moved upstairs to the bedrooms. He deduced that the girls must be in the room with the twin beds. He waited at the threshold and surveyed the area. He found what he was looking for in a matter of seconds as Ani's backpack, partially covered by a fleece blanket, was on the floor, resting on the bed-post. The wide pine floorboards creaked under Patrick's weight and his heavy workbooks. He paused and listened, but he could hear nothing but the old grandfather clock ticking away just as it had done for well over a century. Patrick lifted the backpack, and the blanket fell to the ground. He placed it on top of Ani's bed and unzipped it to reveal the contents. Patrick pulled out the note cards, rubber banded together, and a book by Bert Sol. Patrick turned the book over to read the author's bio:

Professor Bert Sol is a foremost leader in Abenaki Indians, their history, culture, and language. He received his undergraduate degree from the University of Maine in Orono and his Ph.D. from Princeton University. Professor Sol teaches at Maine Oceanic College in Bar Harbor, Maine. He also serves as the director of the Abenaki Museum located in Southwest Harbor and on the Governor's Council for Native American Affairs.

The next book was *New England Native Americans: Their Origins and Language Development* by some guy named Merriam.

Patrick opened the outer zipper of the backpack: no parchment. Maybe his eyes were playing tricks on him and he only imagined seeing the deerskin parchment on the girl's lap because the note cards could have easily come from this Abenaki book. He then opened the closet door to find an assortment of flip-flops on the floor and a few articles of clothing hanging from the pole. Next, he opened a few drawers on the side of the closet, but they proved to hold only clothing. Just then the grandfather clock began to chime loudly, interrupting Patrick's unorthodox search. Dong, dong, dong. Patrick looked at his watch. Seven o'clock. Dong, dong, dong rang the clock. Patrick closed the drawers.

What was I thinking to come here and invade these people's privacy? Ridiculous old man is what I have become. Deeply ashamed of his behavior, he placed Ani's books and note cards into her backpack and then returned it to the floor. He was halfway down the stairs when he remembered the fleece blanket. Shoot, he thought, running back upstairs. He snatched the blanket from the floor and carefully arranged it to cover half of the backpack, just as he had found it, or so he thought. Back in the foyer, Patrick looked around one last time before exiting and locking the front door.

Later that evening when all the Bankes were in the house and getting ready for bed, Ani retrieved her present and notebook from beneath the dirty clothes in the hamper. She returned to her room to find Eliza already stretched out on her bed snoring lightly. Ani stared at her backpack and did not like what she saw. The blanket tag was on the opposite side. Someone had moved the blanket! Ani opened her backpack and poured the contents out onto her bed. She swiftly determined that everything was here.

"Eliza, Eliza," Ani cried. "Did you move my blanket?"

Groggily Eliza answered, "Huh?"

"My fleece blanket, this blanket," Ani demanded, holding

it in front of Eliza's face.

"I didn't touch your stupid blanket. Why are you yelling at me? I have my own blanket anyway and I'm sleeping," Eliza whined.

"You promise you didn't move it? I won't be mad."

"Yes, I promise," said an exasperated Eliza. "Now, can I go back to sleep please? The whole seal thing is still creeping me out, and I don't like how you kicked me in the leg when I was telling Dad. Remind me again why we can't tell Dad."

"Remember when we were leaving for the beach, and I told you I had to run upstairs?"

"To check on your precious blankie?"

"No, listen. I went upstairs to hide the parchment in the bottom of the hamper, and I arranged my blanket on top of my backpack with the tag facing the right side." Eliza, who by now had sat up and turned on her bedside light, wrinkled her nose. "After retrieving my notebook and the parchment, I noticed my tag was on the opposite side. Someone had moved it. So I'm asking you again, did you move my fleece blanket?"

"No, I didn't touch anything in the room, I swear," said a more awake Eliza. "Do you think Spidey boy came in while we were swimming? I know I locked the door."

"I don't know, but if I had to place a bet, I would say it's that gardener person, Mr. O'Leary. He was acting fairly strange when I encountered him by the Adirondack chairs this afternoon. He also seemed angry because my cards were blowing around his garden. I think you were right, Eliza."

"Right? Right about what?" asked Eliza.

"He is a creepy old man, and I think we need to be careful around him from here on out. I also think we need to make sure the book is with us or hidden well when not with us because someone appears to be looking for something, and until we know what that is for sure or who is doing the searching, we need to be on alert."

"Don't you want to tell Dad? And why can't we tell him about the seals? You never answered my question."

"Because, Eliza, Dad is so busy right now that the minute

he hears that we think something peculiar is going on, he'll hire someone to babysit us, someone like the person we had last summer who had a fear of the ocean and wouldn't let us put even our big toe in the water unless we had a life jacket on and were covered in sunscreen. Dad will find someone like that, and he will forbid us from exploring on our own. We need more time, Eliza. More time to figure out what is going on before we go to Dad. Agreed?"

"Agreed," said Eliza. "But on one condition."

"What?"

"I won't have to swim with any more mammals."

Lobster fact: *Marine mammals such as seals, unlike lobsters, are very sociable animals. Five species of seals visit the Gulf of Maine in the summer: hooded seals, harp seals, gray seals, ringed seals, and harbor seals. Harbor seals, which are found in Maine year-round, often migrate south for the winter.*

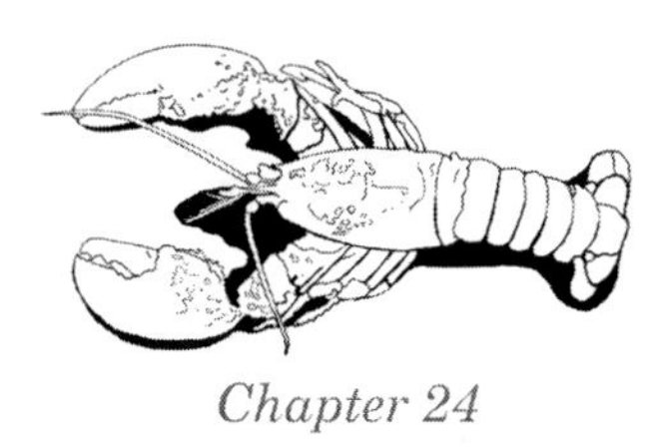

Chapter 24

Roonie and the Orb

"Are you all right, Eliza?" Ani called to her sister.

"Yes, I'm fine." Eliza's voice could be heard from up above. "Unlike you, sister dearest, I'm not afraid of heights."

"Very funny," Ani said. "All set with the plan, right?"

"Got it," said Eliza. "You're going to pretend to sleep under the elm tree while I wait in this neighboring pine tree in order to catch him if he tries to get away through the trees. Is that about right?" She threw a pinecone at her sister, who stared up from the base.

"Hey," Ani cried, "knock it off! And remember to be quiet. For all we know he could be watching us right now and our plan will be ruined."

Ani planted herself in one of the Adirondack chairs to wait. She folded her arms over her chest and closed her eyes. She began to ruminate over all that she had seen and heard since coming to Maine with her father. Ani started with a list of facts, as she always liked to put things in order. Fact number one, the lobsters are migrating to Mount Desert Island and increasing in size and number exponentially. Fact number two, her father and the other scientists have been unsuccessful in determining why this is happening. Fact number three, the tiny girl hidden in the orb may have something to do with my gift from Mom. Question? Who is this girl and how did she get there? Mr. Baxter is involved somehow too. Fact number four, the gardener also might be involved. Question? Did he move my blanket or was it Mr. Baxter or maybe Roonie? Fact number five, W-A-T, as Eliza calls it, appears to be real as evidenced by the trip to Seal Cove. Question? Did we not swim with the seals? Did they not give us the silver sand dollar, which corresponds to one of the drawings in my book? Fact number six, Spidey boy may be key to getting us back to the orb. Question? Will he just make matters worse?

Ani's thoughts were interrupted when Eliza threw another pinecone at her, their signal to indicate that the boy was coming. Ani pretended to be asleep, acting as if she couldn't hear the rustle of the branches above her. She remained silent for a few more moments until all noises from above ceased. Ani did not open her eyes or move her arms as she launched into her much rehearsed speech: "Roonie, please do not go away or be alarmed that we know who you are and that we know that you are up in the tree. If you decide to leave, my sister is in the next tree over and will stop you before you get to the ground, and as you know from our encounter at the park, I am an extremely fast runner and will be able to catch you before you can get away."

Ani paused and listened. She heard nothing. "Now that we have your attention, we need to ask for a favor. We know that your Aunt Kate is employed as a maid for Mr. Baxter, and we found something in his house that we would like to take another look at, something that might be important to us. Do you think you could help us, please, Roonie, please?" Ani sat in the chair with her eyes closed, acting as if she hadn't a care in the world. Nothing happened. No movement and no sounds came from the elm. Ani decided to speak again. "Well, since you're not interested, I guess we will just have to go to our next plan. Too bad, since we really thought we could make it worth your while. Oh well, nice talking with you." And with that, Ani opened her eyes, stood up, and walked away from the circle of chairs.

"Wait, wait a minute," Roonie called from above.

Ani stopped. "It's okay, really. It is clear that you aren't interested in our proposal so no worries. I will be going now."

"I said 'wait a minute,'" Roonie said, this time with urgency in his voice. He swung down to the next lowest branch above the chairs, and the branch swayed up and down with his weight. "Don't go. Wait!" he said.

Ani watched while he let go of the branch over him, put his hands on the branch he was standing on, and swung down feet first before landing in the middle of the chairs.

"What's in it for me?" Roonie asked.

Now that he was on the ground, standing a few feet in front of her, Ani could see that he was in fact wearing a Spider-Man T-shirt. He can't be more than ten or eleven years old, she thought. Ani moved closer and was joined by Eliza, who came up from behind him. "Your bike license plate, Roonie. I'm Ani by the way. Hi. And this is my sister, Eliza."

Eliza smiled. "Hello."

Roonie nodded to Eliza and said, "What else?"

"What else what?" replied Ani.

"What else will I get for my help?"

"Well, that depends."

"On what?"

"How well you can keep a secret."

* * * *

Ani, Eliza, and Roonie ate peanut butter and jelly sandwiches on the patio behind the cottage house. "Now that we are clear on the plan, can I ask you a question?" said Ani.

"Sure, go ahead."

"How come you were following us?"

"Something to do," Roonie replied with a mouthful of sandwich.

Eliza jumped in and asked, "Was that you the first day we moved in here? You were the one who laughed up in the tree?" Roonie grinned back at Eliza.

"I knew it. I knew I saw Spider-Man! At least one mystery is solved around here."

"Roonie, can I ask you something else?" Ani said.

"Shoot."

"Do you always wear Spider-Man shirts?"

"Yup."

"Why, why Spider-Man?" said Eliza.

"Because he is only the greatest hero of all time. Better than Superman, better than Batman, and better than, well, better than all of them, that's why."

"Please tell me you don't really think you're Spider-Man," Eliza said. "There are already enough strange things going on around here." She turned to Ani. "I don't think I'm up for a ten-year-old boy who really thinks he's Spider-Man."

"No, I know I'm not Spider-Man. I'm not stupid!" Roonie said.

"Okay, you guys. Eliza is just being cautious, that's all, Roonie. We have seen a lot of peculiar things since coming to the island. She doesn't mean anything by what she said. We both like Spider-Man, don't we, Eliza?"

"Oh, yeah, sure, we are big Spider-Man fans," Eliza replied sarcastically.

"You're talking about the lobsters, aren't you? That's why you're here, isn't it? Your dad is here to figure out why they're coming."

"Something like that," Ani said, "but that doesn't concern us really and why we need to get into the Baxter mansion. Are you almost finished now? From what you said, we need to get going to see your aunt."

Roonie stuffed the last bite of his sandwich in his mouth and then all three left for the Baxter estate. As agreed upon, Roonie guided the girls back to the stand of trees that bordered the side of the property. He had told them there was a path in the woods that ended up behind the mansion on the ocean side of the estate. His aunt should be in the kitchen at this time, since she would be preparing lunch for the summer workers, and Mr. Baxter would be out, as he usually was not home for lunch. Ani enjoyed the walk, as she was always happiest when out in nature.

Eliza, on the other hand, was on the lookout for anything

out of the ordinary. After the seal incident, she was convinced that something else might happen, something to do with an animal like the squirrels or chipmunks or something larger like a moose or even a bear. Nonetheless, Eliza was determined not to be caught off guard. So far, she hadn't seen a single animal, not even a small bird, and she began to think even this was out of the ordinary. She shared her concern with Ani.

"I have only one word for you," Ani said.

"What's that?"

"Paranoid."

Roonie put his index finger to his lips. "Shh," he whispered, "follow close."

By the time they reached one of the side doors of the Baxter mansion that led directly into the kitchen, all three children were winded but excited. The plan, as devised by Ani with Roonie's assistance, was to have Roonie distract his Aunt Kate and the cook in the kitchen with an offer to help polish the silver, as his aunt was always wanting Roonie to help in exchange for a sweet treat from the cook. Sorenson, as Roonie knew, was always with Mr. Baxter and most likely would be driving him around town or they would be out on his yacht sailing in the harbor and therefore should not be a problem. The rest of the staff should be on a lunch break or would be working in the gardens. This was the best time to get upstairs to Mr. Baxter's study. Roonie hadn't asked what the girls wanted, as Ani had made it clear that he would be told what he needed to be told, and other than that, what the girls wanted to do was none of his business. As a ten-year-old boy obsessed with Spider-Man, he was fine with the arrangement. He was just grateful to be included in anything, even if it meant polishing some old spoons with smelly silver polish.

Roonie pushed open the door and entered the kitchen while the girls crouched in the hallway outside next to the servants' staircase. Roonie was going to say his aunt's name twice loudly, which would be the girls' signal to head upstairs. Lucky for them Roonie was an adventurous boy who knew his way inside and out of the Baxter property. The back staircase would lead to the left side of the mansion. All the girls had to do was pass through the narrow servants' quarters and go through the doorway to work their way to the center of the second floor and to the library. Roonie had been unsure where the vicious Beauregard would be, but Ani had assured him that she would be able to handle the dog, or so she hoped.

"I feel like I need to go to the bathroom," whispered Eliza.

"Eliza, you know that you don't. It's just the excitement," whispered Ani.

Just then the girls heard Roonie exclaim, "Aunt Kate! Aunt Kate! These are the best cookies I have ever eaten."

Ani signaled to Eliza, and they moved silently out of the hallway toward the staircase. Both girls giggled quietly when they heard Aunt Kate say to Roonie, "You know full well that I didn't make those cookies. Are you trying to butter me up? What trouble are you up to now, Roonie?"

Ani and Eliza didn't wait to hear Roonie's reply. They knew their time was limited, and they had to move fast. Once upstairs the girls reached the door to the main hallway quickly. Ani put her ear to the door and listened, holding her hand up to halt Eliza. When she was sure that no one else was upstairs, Ani slowly opened the door and entered the hall. Eliza followed, softly closing the door behind her. After a few steps in the direction of the study, both girls heard the unmistakable sound of a low growl—Beauregard was here! Eliza let out a small scream before stifling herself by putting her hand over her mouth. Beauregard growled louder and deeper, his saliva drooling out of his mouth and landing on the floor. Ani got down on her knees and motioned to Eliza to do the same.

"Well hello, Beau. I was wishing we might see you again. Remember us from last week? I sure hope you do," she said, removing her backpack cautiously. Beauregard snarled his response and this time bared his teeth.

"Not the reaction we were looking for," whispered Eliza.

"Now come on, boy," Ani cajoled, "you don't have to be all tough with us. We're old friends, and friends don't growl at one another, and they definitely don't bare their teeth." Beauregard closed his mouth, but still emitted a low rumble. "That's better," a confident Ani said. "Friends are nice to each other, which is why I've brought you something, see?" She displayed a baggie of small carrots.

"Carrots? Really, Ani? I think this boy would rather have a T-bone."

"Eliza!" Ani snapped, which caused Beauregard to snort at Eliza.

"Sorry. Nice doggie, nice doggie," whispered Eliza.

"Why don't you just come on over here and get your present," Ani said. You know that you want to." Ani bit down hard on a carrot. She chewed. "See, delicious." Beauregard didn't move but also didn't growl.

"What are you waiting for? Get over here now and greet me like a friend is supposed to greet another friend," Ani said. And with that Beau leapt from his spot and landed smack into Ani, knocking her down and covering her face with kisses. Ani giggled under the weight of her new best friend and shoved the carrot in his face. She gave him a good petting and said, "There's my friend, my good boy, there's my Beau." Finally, she stood up and gave him another treat. "Now, take this, boy, and do us a favor. We need to go in Mr. Baxter's study for a bit. Can you be a good boy and watch the door for us? If anyone comes upstairs, why don't you use your beautiful voice and bark real loud to let us know. When we are finished, I'll give you all the carrots in my bag. Okay?"

Beauregard jumped up and licked Ani's face with his big tongue. The girls soon passed through the threshold of the library and closed the door. It took them a few moments to adjust to the darkness, for the curtains in the room were drawn. Ani switched on the desk lamp.

"That was close," said Eliza. "For a minute I thought you had lost your animal touch, and we were both going to wind up ripped to pieces by Psychodog outside."

"'Psychodog' is not nice, Eliza," Ani said. She had already unlocked the cabinet just like she did the other night at dinner, with the secret latch under the hinge. "Here, put my backpack on," she demanded, handing it to Eliza.

"Why am I doing this?"

"Because in case we have to get out of here quickly, I don't want to run the risk of losing it, and I can't keep it on my back while I am standing on this tippy chair. Now, please come over here and hold this steady." Ani rolled the desk chair over to the cabinet. Eliza bent down slightly to hold the chair. Ani opened the doors to the cabinet, and again the shelves appeared completely bare. Ani climbed up on the chair and stood on her tiptoes to reach the top shelf. She wobbled a bit. "Eliza!"

"Sorry," Eliza said. "I thought I heard something."

Ani felt the surface of the shelf, but touched nothing. She called to her sister. "In the side pocket of my backpack is a flashlight. Can you reach it and give it to me?" Eliza let go of the chair, and Ani wobbled again.

"Don't move," Eliza insisted. "I can't hold the chair and get the flashlight at the same time. You're sounding a little bossy, too."

"Not now, Eliza, please. I'm sorry, but could you hurry?"

Eliza found the flashlight and handed it to her sister. Ani swept the shelf with the flashlight and still found nothing, no orb, no tiny person, no nothing. She did another pass with the flashlight, this time freeing a small piece of blue paper that floated slowly down to the top of Barton's desk. Eliza clasped the paper first and read, "*IT'S GONE*," printed neatly in capital letters. Ani took it from her sister's hand and looked for herself.

"Hey, this matches this note pad," Eliza pointed out.

Ani spotted the stack of blue notes on the desk. She was about to speak, but was interrupted by Beau whining outside the door. "It's Beau, and the orb's not here! Mr. Baxter must have moved it, but we have to go." She placed the note down on the desk and closed the cabinet doors behind her. Next Ani pushed the desk chair back in place and ran to join Eliza. By this time Beau was scratching at the door. Ani opened it cautiously and heard Barton at the bottom of the grand staircase barking orders to his housekeeper.

"I am going up to my study, Mrs. Pollinger, and I am not to be disturbed!"

"Yes, of course, sir. May I bring you anything?"

"What? Oh, yes, a cup of hot tea with lemon, but after that I said I don't want any interruptions."

"Yes, sir."

Barton ascended the staircase, which gave him a clear view of the hall the girls needed to scoot across to reach the servants' area and make their escape. Ani whispered in the dog's ear, "Nice job, Beau, now go. I'll find you later and give you your carrots." Beau bounded down the hall and Ani closed the door to the library.

"What to do?" she said. "What to do?"

"Ani, there is no place to hide in here," a frantic Eliza cried.

Ani spied the fireplace and grabbed her sister by the backpack.

"In here!" she said and entered the large fireplace. She shoved Eliza to one corner and pressed her own body against the other. The large vases flanking the fireplace were filled with tall dried ferns, and they might be just what the girls needed to stay hidden from Barton. The door opened at the exact moment Ani noticed the note, the note that now lay on the desk not ten feet from the girls and soon to be only a few feet from Barton, who crossed the room and promptly pulled out his desk chair.

Once seated, he looked around the room before opening the center drawer and removing a stack of papers and several manila folders. Barton retrieved a pen from his inner pocket and hummed softly to himself as he opened the folder on top of the pile.

Ani was so tense she was afraid to breathe. She looked at her sister's face and could tell that Eliza was paralyzed with fear. I can't believe I was so stupid to forget the note, Ani thought. What will happen if he finds it, or worse, what will happen if he finds us? What will he do? What if he locks us up or even tells our father? Dad will be so angry he will never let us finish the search. We will be grounded for the rest of the summer, better yet, for the rest of our lives. Where is Roonie now? Probably left the kitchen when Mr. Baxter showed up. I'm glad someone is going to get away, but he hasn't seen us yet. Maybe he won't notice us. Oh, if only we can be so lucky.

"What's this?" said Barton as he picked up the blue paper. He read the note. Recognizing his own printing, he stood. "Well, well," he said with a smile, "just as I thought. I've had some visitors." He studied the room.

Ani was convinced he could hear her heart beating since it was beating so loudly. Barton walked around the room holding the note. "How did this get here, I wonder? How curious and strange that I could leave this on the top shelf of a locked cabinet and find it on my desk." Ani and Eliza both closed their eyes as if doing so would make them less likely to be seen by Barton. Ani could hear his footsteps getting closer to the fireplace. Of course this would be where he would look. Where else could a person hide in this room?

"Are you in here still?" he asked, opening a closet to the right of the fireplace. "No one in here but us old magazines." Barton laughed while answering his own question. "I've got to get Sorenson to clean these out. Fire hazard for sure and smelly, too," he said, sniffing. "What about the fireplace? Surely, no one would be so stupid as to hide in there?" Barton narrowed his eyes and twiddled his hair.

Ani opened her eyes and saw Eliza looking like she might throw up her peanut butter and jelly sandwich, her face was so pale. A few seconds more and the girls would be caught. Caught with the deerskin parchment in the backpack on Eliza's back, caught without finding the orb and speaking with the girl inside, and caught surely ending their quest before it really even began. Ani held her breath and waited.

"Mr. Baxter, Mr. Baxter!" a voice cried outside of the study door followed by several loud knocks. "Mr. Baxter!" the voice called again.

That sounds like Roonie, thought Ani. Eliza's eyes flew open and she mouthed "Roonie," to her sister.

Barton strode quickly to the door and yelled, "I told you I don't want to be interrupted!" He threw open the door and stopped Roonie mid-knock.

"Oh, hello, Mr. Baxter. Nice to see you again. I'm Roonie and I'm ten. Do you like Spider-Man?"

"What is the meaning of this? Who are you and how did you get here? Mrs. Pollinger! Kate!" he shouted. "Sorenson!" Barton attempted to take hold of Roonie's shirt, but Roonie was speedy and ran in the opposite direction of the servants' quarters hoping Barton would chase him.

Roonie sang, "Spider-Man, Spider-Man, doing all the things a Spider-Man can, cuz he's Spider-Man. Do you like Spider-Man, Mr. Baxter?"

Barton dashed after him down the hall at the same time Aunt Kate came upstairs with a tray of hot tea with lemon. Seeing her crazy nephew run past her followed by her boss, she hurriedly placed the tray on the hall table before joining in the chase. By now Ani and Eliza had left their hiding place and moved carefully out into the hall. Ani caught Roonie's eye at the end of the hall just as he pushed the button on one of his wristbands, causing a tiny white fishing net to spring out of the band and land on top of Barton's head.

"Roonie!" shrieked Aunt Kate while Barton screamed and tugged at the net on his head, making it all the more tangled.

The girls sprinted in the opposite direction, pulled open the door of the servants' quarters and flew down the back staircase and out the side door. They did not stop running until they were upstairs in their own cozy bedroom in the cottage house. Eliza dropped the backpack to the floor and collapsed on her bed.

"I'll second that," Ani said and she too fell to her bed.

* * * *

Meanwhile, back at the Baxter estate, Aunt Kate managed to free Barton from the Spidey web her unruly nephew had shot at him. Later on she would enjoy telling the story to the cook and Sorenson along with some of the other staff, but for now she had to act fast to get Barton calmed down and Roonie out of the house.

"Thank you, sir, for finding my nephew. My brother just called me in a panic because he has been missing since this morning. Roonie hasn't been right since his mother left, and sometimes he forgets to take his medication. Now there," she continued, directing her attention to her nephew, "be a big boy and tell Mr. Baxter you are sorry for bothering him."

"Sorry," said Roonie sheepishly.

Barton shouted, "This is unaccept ..."

But Kate cut him off. "Good, now that this is settled, run along home, Roonie. Your father is just worried sick about you." Roonie looked at his aunt. "You heard me, go!" She gave him a gentle shove, with less emphasis on the gentle and more on the shove. Roonie didn't need to be told again. He galloped down the hall, down the stairs, and out the door.

"Thank you for being so kind and understanding, Mr. Baxter. My brother is lucky to have a friend in you, that's for sure."

A confused Barton replied, "But I don't even know your brother."

"Even better," Kate said. "I always tell everyone how generous and kind you are. People are so jealous that I get to work here for you, and I couldn't agree more, so why don't you let me do my wonderful job and help you enjoy your tea." She escorted her boss back to the library.

Barton soon found himself sitting at his desk, sipping a cup of his favorite tea, Earl Gray, and reversing the blue paper back and forth between his fingers. *IT'S GONE* kept flashing in front of his face. Thank goodness he followed his hunch to move the orb, his beloved Amelia, to a different, more secluded hiding place, he thought. A search of the study had revealed nothing, and Mrs. Pollinger, Sorenson, and Kate had assured him that no one had been in the study since last Wednesday. He knew that he had moved the orb on Thursday morning before going to the club, so someone other than the staff had to have been here, but who and how and when? That Roonie boy most definitely has some sort of mental deficiencies, he thought, so I don't imagine he could have gotten in here, but I wouldn't be surprised to discover those two innocent girls of Dr. Banke's have been snooping. Innocent indeed, he thought, crumpling the paper and tucking it in his front jacket pocket next to a faded blue hair ribbon.

Lobster fact: *Lobsters are not the only sea life that comes up in lobster traps. Among the other animals to have been found are crabs, skate, flounder, cusk, wolfish, "dog fish" (actually small sharks), and sea spiders (Pycnogonida).*

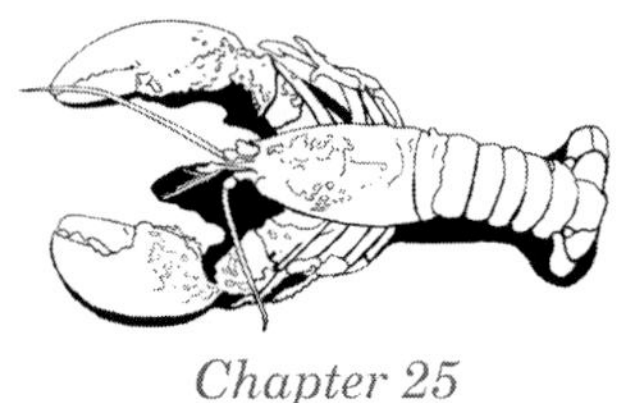

Chapter 25

Mayoral Lobster Meet and Greet

Ani, Eliza, and Dr. Banke went into town to run a few errands. The girls had agreed to help their father with the food shopping, and afterwards they would be able to explore the area on their bikes when Dr. Banke went back to the lab.

As soon as they reached the supermarket, Ani grabbed a cart and the list from her father. "I'll take that, Dad!" she said and scanned the list. "Eliza, get a basket and go to the dairy section. We need eggs, milk, chocolate milk, and cream for Dad's coffee."

"I'm on it," said Eliza.

"Dad," Ani consulted the list, "you go get the meat. I'm not good at picking that out. We need hamburgers, hot dogs, and some already cooked chicken breasts. And I'll go get bread and cereal and meet up with you in the produce section. Sound good?" she asked breathlessly.

"Well, this is a first," said a puzzled Dr. Banke. "You girls must really be in a hurry to investigate the island. I don't think I've seen this much enthusiasm and cooperation from you around food shopping since, well, I guess never. Are you sure you're feeling well?"

"Dad, you're so funny," Ani said, giving him a gentle push. "You're wasting time, and good, here comes Eliza. Go." Dr. Banke grinned at his younger daughter and headed toward the meat counter. Eliza added her dairy items to Ani's carriage.

"What's next and what time are we meeting Roonie?" she

asked.

"We need raisin bran and English muffins and produce," Ani said, "and hurry. He's probably there already."

"Do you think he'll wait for us?"

"What do you think? Of course he'll wait for us. What else would he do?"

"I know, you're right. Tell me again what his note said."

Ani removed a piece of yellow lined paper from her shorts pocket and read, "*I have information. Meet me by the park at Noon. SPD.*"

"What a goof, SPD, Spidey." Eliza chuckled.

"Be kind, Eliza. That Spidey saved our hides yesterday. He and his Spidey web. I can't believe he threw it over Mr. Baxter's head," she said.

The girls didn't notice their father had returned to the cart. "Are you two talking about Spider-Man again? You're slacking, girls. I've gotten the meat while you two are just standing around."

"Sorry, Dad, I'm going to produce," said Eliza and dashed down the aisle.

"Ani, is everything all right?"

"Yeah, Dad, why?" Ani tried to act nonchalant by staring at the grocery list.

"I don't know. You two just seem jumpy."

"We're fine, Dad, really."

"I know what this is all about. I'm feeling it, too."

"You do? You are?"

"Yeah, we're all missing Mom."

Relieved, Ani said, "Yes, Dad, we all miss Mom. That's definitely why we are acting so out of sorts. Definitely why."

Dr. Banke gave Ani a quick hug, and Eliza appeared with fruits and vegetables, a loaf of bread, and raisin bran crowding her little red basket. "Let's check out."

Dr. Banke shook his head in disbelief and headed for the checkout aisle. He unloaded the groceries from the cart onto the conveyer belt. Eliza helped by haphazardly throwing food onto the belt in her hurry to get out of the store. Ani noticed the headline of the local paper, the *Bar Harbor Daily,* and picked it up to read. The front page pictured a local lobsterman, Roy Huston, standing in front of one of his traps stuffed with lobsters. Roy was grinning ear to ear while holding a large lobster in each hand. The headline read, *Lobsteriffic Catch for Huston!* Ani was about to put it back on the rack, but something small on the bottom caught her eye. She read, *Baxter Industries Poised for Profit.* Ani perused the brief story, which explained that Baxter Fisheries was packaging, canning, and shipping the lobsters at a remarkable pace to other parts of the United States and abroad. Early reports predicted tremendous earnings. Ani tapped Eliza on her back and pointed the article out to her.

"Something is fishy about this," she whispered to her sister.

Eliza laughed. "Fishy, get it? You're funny, Ani."

"I'm not trying to be funny, Eliza. I just meant that it seems like too much of a coincidence that Mr. Baxter is now making a huge profit because of the lobsters coming to MDI."

"Sorry. You know how I love a good pun. But you're right, something just doesn't add up with all this," Eliza said. By now Dr. Banke had paid the cashier, and the girls trailed him out of the store. The three loaded the car, lifted the bikes off their carrier, and were about to leave when they heard a male voice calling loudly after them.

"Dr. Banke, hey, Dr. Banke, Dr. Banke! Over here." A large man walked quickly toward the trio. As he neared, Ani recognized him from the other day at the shore, Mayor Peterson. He paused to catch his breath before speaking.

"Dr. Banke." He took a few more deep breaths. "So, so, so glad to see you here." His face was flushed and moist from his brisk movement. Ani gathered that moving fast was not his normal modus operandi.

"Hello, mayor," said Dr. Banke. "Nice to see you. Let me introduce you to my daughters, Ani and Eliza. Girls, this is the mayor of Bar Harbor, Mayor Peterson."

"Hello," the girls said in unison.

"Dr. Banke," the mayor began, "I just wanted to ask you in person what you are doing to stop this disastrous lobster debacle from escalating."

"I, ah, I assure you and everyone else that we are doing all that we can at present. We just need a little more time, and I am sure that we can figure this out. In fact, I am on my way to the lab right now so I'll be saying so long ..." Dr. Banke's voice faded as he opened his car door.

"We are running out of time," the mayor said. "The lobster festival is coming up. We already started the pre-lobster festivities. We can't have all these lobsters showing up on the beach again. It scares off the tourists, and a summer town without tourists is a town without profits. No profits means less money for police, fire, and safety, libraries, snow removal, and schools. We can't have that, Dr. Banke. We just can't." The mayor's red face now matched the color of a boiled lobster.

"I certainly empathize with the predicament, mayor, but as I told the governor, science sometimes takes time, and we need more time," Dr. Banke said.

"I'm not sure if we have that. Have you heard the rumors? People are saying it's because of global warming and ice caps melting, plate tectonics shifts, and a terrorist attack. I even heard someone saying it was aliens at Bay Gulls Bagels this morning at breakfast."

"Aliens?" Ani laughed.

"Did you just say 'bay gulls bagels'? Another great pun." Eliza giggled.

"This is not a laughing matter," the mayor retorted, his full caterpillar eyebrows arching angrily at the sisters. Ani stifled her laugh and cleared her throat.

The mayor resumed speaking. "You know what happens when rumors start flying? Melee and chaos is what happens. This is disastrous for towns, Dr. Banke, absolutely disastrous."

"Please understand, Mayor Peterson, that we are doing everything possible."

"Thank you, Dr. Banke, thank you very much," the mayor said while shaking Dr. Banke's hand. "I believe you're our only hope."

Ani noticed the look on her father's face as Mayor Peterson walked away. It was a look that she had seen only a few times. When he couldn't save the sea turtle caught up in the propeller of a boat and on the day their dog, Calypso, died two years ago. Ani frowned. She knew what it meant. Her father had no idea why the lobsters were coming to the island, and he didn't have any idea how to stop it from happening.

Lobster fact: *The Lobster Conservancy (TLC) works with fishermen and volunteers in the Gulf of Maine region to sustain a thriving lobster fishery through science and community. It tries to involve varied groups in the process of doing science and to disseminate the knowledge obtained from such research back to stakeholders, as well as fisheries managers and scientists.*

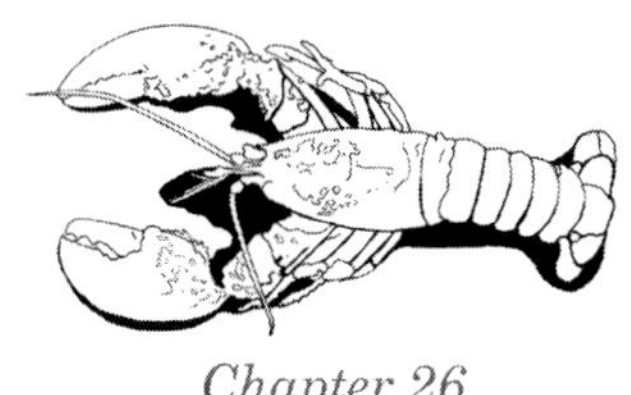

Chapter 26

I See the Violet Moon a'Rising

"Where have you guys been?" Roonie demanded when the girls pulled up to him on their bikes at the park. He glanced at his Spider-Man watch. "It is twelve thirty not twelve."

"We had to help our father," Eliza said. "Relax."

"Don't tell me to relax," Roonie said. "I'm trying to help you guys. Jeesh."

"Hey, hey, knock it off," said Ani. "Roonie, what do you want to show us?"

"We need to hurry; she might be gone." He jumped on his bike. "My grandmother is always on the move."

"Grandma?" Eliza mouthed to Ani. Ani shrugged. The three children pedaled away from thc park and snaked their way through the town of Bar Harbor. They passed several bed and breakfast inns before stopping in front of a lilac Victorian house with white trim with a *No Vacancy* sign hanging out front.

"Your grandmother lives here?" asked Eliza.

"Yeah, cool, huh?" said Roonie. He yelled, "Grandma Violet, it's us, we're here. Sorry for being late. You know girls." He grinned back at Ani and Eliza. The girls leaned their bikes against the front porch and followed their new friend to the front door. Ani noticed the sign overhead that read *Moon Violet Inn, Violet Cyr Proprietor.*

Eliza saw it also. "Your grandmother's name is Moon Violet?"

"That's Lady Moon Violet to you," a loud voice with a thick Maine accent said. Moon Violet stood behind them, dressed in purple from head to toe. Her white hair was braided on either side of her head and then pinned up neatly behind.

"Grandma," said Roonie.

"Come here, child, and give me a big hug," demanded his grandmother, who stretched her arms out wide.

"Maybe later," Roonie said.

"Don't you maybe later me, young boy, or I will have your Aunt Kate tell your father where you were yesterday and whose head you threw a net over."

Roonie ran over to her and gave her a hug. She smiled with the joy of hugging her only grandson and then let him go. "Roonie Jay Cyr! Where are your manners? Aren't you going to introduce me to your friends?"

"I was, Grandma, if you didn't hug me so long and hard, too."

Moon Violet let out a big, infectious laugh.

"Grandma Violet, this is Ani and Eliza Banke. Ani and Eliza, this is Grandma Violet."

"Very special to meet you girls," she said while putting out her hand to shake, her bracelets laden with charms clanking and jangling.

"You, too," said Ani with a smile as she shook Grandma Violet's hand.

"Hello," said Eliza. "Nice to meet you as well." Eliza shook her hand, and Grandma Violet held onto it a bit longer and stared into Eliza's face. "Oh, you are the one with all the humor," she said. "Humor hides the fear, but you are very brave, I see. Braver than you know."

Eliza's eyes widened. "Ah, ah, thank you," she said, unsure of what to do next.

Violet let go of Eliza's hand. "Let's go inside now. I made lunch, and for dessert, we will have a surprise."

"Great, I'm starving," said Roonie.

* * * *

The children finished their Jordan's Red Hot hot dogs, a Maine specialty, and Humpty Dumpty ketchup potato chips, Roonie's must have, and chased it down with blueberry soda. Ani hadn't realized how hungry she was until she started to eat. She even liked the ketchup potato chips, which wasn't too much of a shocker since she liked everything with ketchup. Once she finished, she pushed her plate away and looked around the dining room. The Moon Violet Inn was a bed and breakfast with eight bedrooms, all with separate baths, according to the brochure Ani had found on one of the dining room tables. In addition, four of the bedrooms had working fireplaces, jet tubs, and private balconies. The dining room where they were eating their lunch was where the guests were treated to a home-cooked breakfast from Grandma Violet. Lunch and dinner were not provided, but Grandma Violet always had some chips or dessert or fruit for guests to nibble on in between walks to town, bike rides through Acadia National Park, and visits to other parts of the island.

The interior of the house was immaculate: white painted walls covered with old black and white photographs, white wicker chairs and rockers with crisp white and blue striped pillows. The tall windows that framed the front and side of the house were so clean that Ani had to look twice to make sure there was really glass in them. The entire downstairs projected warmth, light, and beauty—much like Moon Violet. It also smelled faintly of lilacs, one of Ani's favorite scents. Ani could tell that Moon Violet took great pride in the house and thought that her care and attention to detail must make the place very popular with tourists. Just then Grandma Violet came back into the dining room.

"We'll clean up later," she announced good-naturedly. "Let's go into the game room and you can watch me beat Roonie at Scrabble."

"Not this time," Roonie said. "I've been studying my words with that Scrabble book you got me for my birthday." Roonie shoved a few more chips into his mouth and ran into the adjoining room.

The girls joined Roonie at a round wicker table with a glass top. The Scrabble board had been set up ready for play. Bookcases filled with board games and puzzles lined the game room. Several small tables like the one they were sitting at also had games set up and ready to be played. Ani saw checkers, chess, Parcheesi, and backgammon, one of her favorites. She loved board games and was glad Grandma Violet had suggested they play.

Roonie dumped the bag of tiles onto the Scrabble board. "Here," he said, flipping tiles over to hide their letters, "help me flip." Ani and Eliza began flipping the tiles, too.

"Please," Grandma Violet said.

"I mean please," Roonie said.

Once they finished, Roonie, who suddenly became quite bossy, informed everyone to please take seven tiles, and then he passed out the tile holders. He started moving his letters around to form his first word.

"I can go, I can go, Grandma!" he shouted.

"All right, all right, don't get your knickers in a knot," Grandma Violet said. "You can go first." She winked at Ani. "I always let him go first," she whispered to her.

"I can hear you," said Roonie. "But I don't care if you let me go first because I have the best word."

"Let's see it," said Eliza.

"Here it is," said Roonie and he began placing his word in the center of the board. "*B, A, N, N, A N, A*," he said triumphantly.

"Very good," said his grandma while removing one of the middle letter *N*'s. "It's only one *N* there, not two."

Eliza giggled softly. Ani kicked her under the table.

Roonie seemed unfazed by his mistake and counted out his score. "There, I have eighteen points." He handed the pad to Ani to keep score.

The game proceeded with each taking turns, placing words down, and grabbing more tiles. Ani was surprised to see that Roonie wasn't kidding. He had been studying his Scrabble book. Despite the poor start with the misspelling of *banana*, Roonie was leading all of them, even his grandmother, although Ani felt sure she wasn't playing her best. Grandma Violet finished a turn and got up from the table. "I will be right back. Keep playing, folks. I need to put the cookies into the oven."

After she left the room, Ani said, "It's really nice to meet your grandmother."

"Boy, she really wanted to meet you," Roonie said.

"Why?" asked Eliza, putting another word on the board. "Twelve more points for me, Ani." Ani added the score to Eliza's tally.

"You know why," said Roonie. He leaned into the table and spoke quietly. "It's because of the lobsters—oops, I wasn't supposed to tell," he put his hand over his mouth.

"What weren't you supposed to tell us?" Eliza whispered.

"My grandma told me not to bring it up in front of you. Something about she doesn't want you to feel any pressure."

"Pressure?" asked Ani.

"Yeah, pressure," repeated Roonie while looking at the kitchen doorway to see if his grandmother was near. "Pressure about solving the lobster problem."

"Oh, because of our father," said Ani.

"No, not your father," he said even more softly. "You."

Moon Violet entered the room before Ani could ask Roonie what he was talking about. She had a small white timer ticking away. "This is so I don't burn the whoopie pies," she said. "Now, is it my turn again?"

"Yes," Eliza said.

Ani was shocked. What was Roonie talking about?

Grandma Violet hummed a little tune to herself while moving her letters around. She smiled at Ani when she placed her letters on the board. "*L, O*, I'll use the *B* from Roonie's word *beach*, *S, T, E, R*, and *S*. Lobsters," she said. "Fourteen points for me." Just then the timer went off. "Roonie, be a dear and go check the cookies. Eliza, will you go with him and help please."

"Sure," Eliza said.

"Will do, and I don't need any help, Grandma," Roonie said as he left the room.

Grandma Violet eyed Eliza. "Pot holders are in the drawer to the right of the stove. There is another batch on the counter ready to go in, five minutes tops or they'll burn. Thank you."

Eliza nodded and followed Roonie to the kitchen.

"Glad to have you alone, dear," said Grandma Violet. "I will talk quickly because I don't have much time, and I don't have much to say for that matter."

"I don't know what you mean," said Ani. "Maybe we should talk later, and I should help them in the kitchen."

"They don't need any help, but we need yours. When Roonie told me about your visit to Mr. Baxter's house and the note cards and book of yours, I just knew I had to meet you."

"You did?"

"Yes, I did, and I was right. I felt it the moment I shook your hand."

"But 'Eliza, brave with humor.' You didn't say anything to me."

"What I need to share with you right now is for you only. What you do with this information later is your business. Not mine to decide."

"Okay" said Ani.

"You are Kanake-kee."

Ani snapped to attention at the mention of Kanake-kee. "What does that mean?"

"It is an old Indian saying my people taught me long ago."

"Your people?"

"Yes, my Abenaki people. I am three-quarters Abenaki Indian, Acadian tribe. Roonie's father was adopted, so both he and Roonie have Abenaki ancestry only in spirit, not in blood. But that doesn't matter. What matters is you. 'Kanake-kee' is difficult to explain. Suffice it to say, it means great animal spirit keeper." Ani looked perplexed. Grandma Violet continued. "Translated into English it means *one who walks with animals.*"

Ani gasped. "W-A-T."

"What?"

"It's what Eliza calls it when the animals act strangely around me. *W, A, T*, Weird Animal Thing."

"Well, now you know. It's not weird, it's a miracle."

"The girl in the orb, she said 'Kanake-kee.'"

"What girl?" demanded Grandma Violet.

"The girl with the braids that we saw in the orb at Mr. Baxter's. We went back to the house, only she was gone. Maybe we didn't see her at all."

"I knew it," Grandma Violet said. "I knew Barton would be tied up in this, but I never imagined he would go this far. I can't say much, Ani. I just can't or it won't work. I don't want to be responsible for ruining our only chance." Moon Violet rose up and rubbed her forehead. She let out a slow, controlled sigh and said, "Essentially, Ani, your being here is not an accident. The animals are here to assist you, so don't be afraid to ask for their help. Also, beware those who don't want you to succeed. I don't know who they are, but I feel their energy and it is negative. You have feelings, too. Use them and trust in yourself."

"But I'm no one, just a thirteen-year-old from Massachusetts. I'm sure you must be mistaken." Ani pushed back her chair and stood. "I think I'll check on Eliza now."

"Ani, please, do not be frightened," Moon Violet said, gingerly placing her hand on Ani's back. "You know what I am saying is true. I can feel it. You are the special one. Whether you like it or not, you are."

Ani sat back down.

"Now, before they come back, let me tell you a story about an Abenaki covenant made long ago." When Moon Violet finished Ani thought the story incredible, yet at the same time, with what she and Eliza had experienced so far, it all made sense. The covenant was broken, and true to their word, the lobsters were coming back to take over the land.

Roonie entered the room, his face covered in chocolate. "We had to test one just to be sure they were good for your guests."

"Roonie," said Grandma Violet, "it looks more like you

sampled the whole batch. Look at your face. Go and clean yourself up, please."

"All right," he said.

Once he was out of earshot, Moon Violet said, "We can't talk anymore because it is not my story to tell, only yours."

"But I have so many more questions," protested Ani. Moon Violet mimicked zipping her lips shut, yet Ani persisted.

"How are you so sure that I am the one?"

Grandma Violet selected tiles from the Scrabble board, taking an *N* from Roonie's letters. She spelled out Ani's name, *A,N,I,B,A,N,K,E*.

"That's my name," Ani said.

Next, Grandma Violet moved the letters from Ani's name around to form a new word, *A,B,E,N,N,A,K,I*. "Look," she said and then removed the *N*. "Today we know it as this."

Ani read it and gasped. "Abenaki, my name spells Abenaki."

"Kanake-kee," Moon Violet said, "we need you, Kanake-kee."

Lobster fact: *Maine recently named the whoopie pie the Official Maine State Treat, while blueberry pie made with Maine blueberries is the Official Maine State Dessert.*

Whoopie Pies
1 cup sugar
½ cup butter + 1 tablespoon
2 cups sifted flour
1½ teaspoons baking soda
8 tablespoons cocoa
¼ teaspoon of salt
1 teaspoon vanilla
1 egg – beaten
1 cup milk

Cream butter and sugar. Add egg and vanilla. Sift dry ingredients and add to creamed mixture, alternately with milk. Drop by the heaping tablespoon-full on an ungreased cookie sheet about an inch apart. Bake at 425° for 4 to 5 minutes.

Filling
1 cup softened butter
1 cup fluff
1 cup sifted confectioners' sugar
¼ teaspoon salt
1 ½ teaspoons vanilla

Mix filling together. Spread between two cookies and serve.

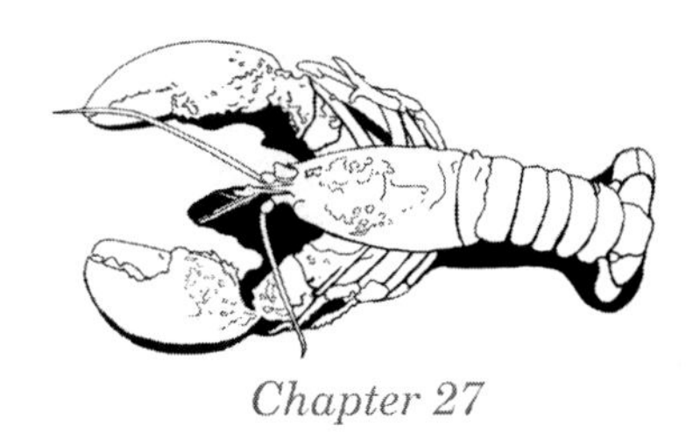

Chapter 27

Ani and the Amulets—The Quest Begins

The grandfather clock struck twelve midnight, but Ani was completely oblivious. She sat propped up on her bed, her flashlight puncturing the darkness in the room while casting eerie shadows on the ceiling. Ani had attempted to go to sleep earlier, but her mind was racing and she just couldn't settle down. By eleven o'clock she had decided not to fight her thoughts any longer and switched on her bedside lamp, but then turned it out in favor of her flashlight because she didn't want to alert her father that she was still awake. Eliza, who usually slept wearing a blindfold, was fast asleep, unaware that her younger sister was wide awake working away. Moon Violet had said that it was Ani's story now, and she alone could decide what to do with it. Ani normally shared everything with her sister, but for now she decided she needed more time to process this new information before consulting Eliza. She would tell her tomorrow.

Kanake-kee, I am Kanake-kee, Ani thought. Grandma Violet was right. I know that I have always had a way with animals. It's as if I can sometimes hear them talking to me. Not in words directly, but more just with a feeling of their needs and desires. Ani smiled, remembering Cottontail at the aquarium. She could sense that he was homesick for his penguin family and that was why he was refusing to eat any fish.

Eliza's snorts brought Ani back to the present. Focus, Ani thought. I need to finish translating Mom's present. She studied the inside cover of the deerskin parchment. The drawing appeared to represent some sort of ceremony between the lobsters and the Abenakis. The lobsters were depicted with a center straight line and two triangles on either side of what Ani guessed to be arms. The Indians were drawn as stick figures much like a small child would sketch today. According to the book from Professor Sol, these drawings stood for both man and lobsters. Grandma Violet said that legend stated that lobsters walked on land with the Indians, and after the tribes agreed that the lobsters would live in the ocean, a covenant was formed to sanctify the treaty. Did this have anything to do with the orb in Mr. Baxter's house? How did the girl end up in the orb? Who was she? Ani added these questions to the growing list she was compiling in her notebook. Moon Violet and other Abenaki members believed that the covenant had been stolen, interrupting the energy surrounding Acadia. This energy was now calling the lobsters back home, a home that had no memory of when they inhabited the land alongside their Abenaki brothers and sisters, a home that was not willing to welcome them back.

The gods are angry, Grandma Violet had informed Ani, and they needed to be appeased with offerings, five to be exact. However, when Ani had pressed Moon Violet for more information, she had said that she was bound by a sacred rule and would not and could not say any more.

Let the animals help you, Grandma Violet had advised. Based on the incident at the beach with the seals, Ani was pretty sure that the silver sand dollar must be one of the objects she needed to find. This reminded Ani of one of her mystery books where the hero, a Navajo Indian, had to survive in the wilderness for one week to be officially welcomed into his tribe. He did this by using the skills he had acquired from his people, but also by embracing the protection provided by objects he wore around his neck, his amulets.

Ani consulted her dictionary. She read, *amulet: a trinket or piece of jewelry usually hung about the neck and thought to be a magical protection against evil or disease.* Maybe I need to find these items from this book, this strange and wonderful birthday present, and offer them up to the gods.

She wrote, *Who are these gods and where do I find them?* in her notebook. She yawned as she reached for her stack of note cards and flipped through them one more time. She stopped at the card that read flame and showed a circle with dashes radiating away from it. Clipped behind this card was another translation and picture copied from the same page of the parchment. Ani read Blueberry Hill and turned the card over to view the drawing she made earlier this evening of an upside down *V* with the tip surrounded by several small circles. Flame and blueberries, she wondered. She consulted the parchment again. "This has to be right," she said out loud.

Eliza coughed, sputtered, and rolled over. In her birthday book the blueberry drawing came after the drawing of the silver sand dollar. Maybe this was a sign that she was supposed to find the amulets, if this is what they were, in a particular order.

Who knows, she thought, but at least it's worth a shot. Ani closed her book and returned her research materials to her backpack, gently placing it on the floor. She turned off her flashlight and closed her eyes. Finally a plan, she thought, comforted by having a place to start. Ani knew where she would be going tomorrow: blueberry picking on Blueberry Hill.

Lobster fact: *Wild blueberries have a special place in Maine's agricultural history. Centuries ago, Native Americans used both fresh and dried blueberries for their flavor, nutrition, and healing qualities. The tiny berries were not harvested commercially until the 1840s, however.*

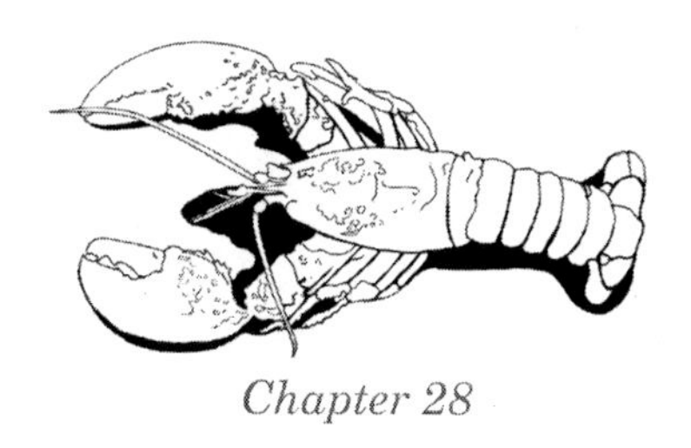

Chapter 28

Lobsters for Professor Sol

As the sun settled over the horizon, Professor Bert Sol decided it was time to begin. He got out of his car and walked around the corner to Beal's Lobster Pier of Southwest Harbor. He had chosen to visit this establishment because Southwest was on the other side of the island from the college and with any luck away from most of his students. Students, he thought with mild irritation. They're always up and in my business. "Hey, Professor Sol, I saw you biking in the park yesterday." Or "Professor Sol, I didn't know you liked walking early in the morning." I can't go anywhere without running into them. They're like middle schoolers with their energy and idealism. How provincial. They think they know it all, and yet, they know nothing, nothing at all.

Professor Sol approached the counter and was pleased not to recognize the college-age kid who greeted him. "Welcome to Beal's. May I help you?"

"Why yes," Professor Sol said, "I would like to obtain some lobsters." He cleared his throat, surprised by how tinny his own voice sounded to his ears. "That is, I would like some lobsters for dinner guests. Larger lobsters, the biggest that you have."

"All right," said the agreeable boy. "We have four- and five-pounders and a six-pounder that just came in this morning. How many do you need?"

"Would you mind," Sol said, craning his neck to look at the enormous lobster tank bubbling behind the counter, "if I, just, well, picked them out myself?"

"No, not allowed, sir. Insurance policy. Some of them can break free of their bands, and their pinch can be quite sharp."

"They wouldn't dare hurt me," Professor Sol grumbled under his breath.

"Excuse me?" said the boy.

"Fine, fine then," Sol said, not bothering to hide his aggravation. "I will take twenty-five of your largest lobsters. And hurry on about it."

"Richard," the boy called, "twenty-five large ones."

A leggy boy wearing fishing waders and rubber boots emerged from the back with a few thick paper bags in his hands. "Got it," Richard said and began weighing lobsters in the large scale adjacent to the tank and placing them in the bags. Other customers approached the counter as Sol fidgeted and muttered. Richard handed the cashier the bill for Sol's order.

"What's with carrot top over there?" Richard said to the cashier in a low voice, nodding to Professor Sol, who was still speaking under his breath in the corner of the room.

"I don't know," the cashier said, "but he sure does have the reddest hair I have ever seen and the rudest personality."

After Professor Sol paid his bill, Richard helped him carry his lobsters to the car. This was no small task, as the load was quite heavy for the two of them, especially with Professor Sol able to use only one hand. As they neared the vehicle, Richard dropped one of the bags.

"Look out, you idiot!" yelled Sol, whose annoyance seemed to cause his fiery hair to stand straight up from the roots. "You can hurt the lobsters!"

"Oh, no," Richard said. "They'll be fine, fine enough to boil that is. Dropping them doesn't hurt."

"How would you know, you insensitive oaf? Give me those," Sol demanded, grabbing the bag Richard dropped and placing it in the trunk of his car. He peeled out of the parking area without so much as a thank you.

"Tourist," Richard said with disdain.

* * * *

Professor Sol stood on one of Maine Oceanic College's docks and peered out over the ocean. He next consulted his watch, which read two in the morning. He yawned and glanced around one more time to see if anyone else, specifically any students, were up at this godforsaken time. The kiddies are all sleeping, he thought, tucked in tightly in their overpriced dorm rooms. They need to have a new recreation and sports complex, yoga, a climbing wall, spinning classes, more dining choices if we are to compete with other colleges and universities. Precious monies devoted to improving facilities, not academics, which are unquestionably the real heart and soul of this college. To think my department had to take a ten percent decrease in order to finish another dorm renovation. Ridiculous.

"How poor are they who have not patience! What wound did ever heal but by degrees," he recited from Shakespeare as he leapt over the dock rail to the beach below. His shoes crunched the rough sand, and the surf roared, rushing in and out along the shoreline. Professor Sol scurried along the beach to where a long forgotten dirt road met the rock bordering the sand, a perfect location to inspect his bounty. He scrambled up the rocks to where his car was parked at the end of the dirt road. He opened the trunk and removed a huge cooler, placing it on the ground. His strength was returning. He could feel it pumping through his body, stretching his muscles, tendons, and ligaments. He felt alive with excitement, with a renewed sense of purpose, a plan, a direction.

He dragged the cooler to the edge of the shore and faced it away from the campus. He removed matches from his pocket and lit the crumpled newspaper and dry sticks he had carefully prepared the previous night. The flame grew, engulfing the kindling. He turned his one arm over the flame and felt the warmth spread through him.

After the fire had caught hold of the split logs piled atop the kindling, Professor Sol focused his attention on the cooler. He lifted the lid to reveal the twenty-five lobsters from Beal's.

Their antennae wriggled and squirmed amid the confusion of legs, claws, and tails. The click-clack of their shells colliding with each other created a constant clamor that seemed in harmony with the crackle of the fire and the ebb and flow of the tide. Sol was giddy as he prepared to investigate his purchases. He grabbed the lobster on the top of the heap and flipped it upside down to expose its underside.

"Are you the one?" he asked. "I was promised you would be coming back." He stepped closer to the blazing fire. He unfurled the body of the lobster ever so gently to scrutinize even more closely the tail.

"Ashemtjo, Ashemtjo," he said, repeating the Abenaki word meaning *friends* several times. "Ashemtjo, ashemtjo?" He shook his head no and threw the lobster into the water. He retrieved another lobster and followed the same steps. "Ashemtjo, ashemtjo," he chanted while checking the backside of the second tail. And, as before, he shook his head no and hurled the lobster into the Atlantic. With lobsters three, four, five, six, seven, eight, his disappointments added up. All of them ending up like their earlier companions, back from whence they came.

Professor Sol's hair became more wiry, fiery, and rigid as he removed his blazer and laid it carefully on the ground. He snatched another lobster and clutched it in his hand. This lobster was noticeably larger than the others, and he could feel how heavy it was as he raised it high above his head, the flames from the fire highlighting the growing barnacle on his left ear.

"Ashemtjo, ashemtjo," he shouted this time and hopped from foot to foot. He circled the fire, waving the lobster, its claws and legs shaking wildly as he sang,

"Retsbol, Retsbol, Retsbol.
Not all agree with you.
Retsbol, Retsbol, Retsbol.
We are not all as one.
Our claws will travel
the ocean floor but never forget
the wooden door.

The tides will change
and we'll return
to stand and walk once more again.
Retsbol, Retsbol, Retsbol."

He finished his dance and song. Sweat poured down his red face. He twirled the lobster upside down and inspected the tail. "Ashemtjo, ah friend, is it true? My kin, ashemtjo?" His beady eyes widened. He couldn't believe what he saw: two darker red lines intersecting like a wavelength underneath the tail, the ancient symbol for Retsbol. The markings were definitely there, faint, but there. He was sure of it. Triumphantly he screamed, "Retsbol!"

Lobster fact: *There is a saying that barnacles on a weather-beaten lobster are a good sign, indicating that the creature hasn't shed its shell in a while.*

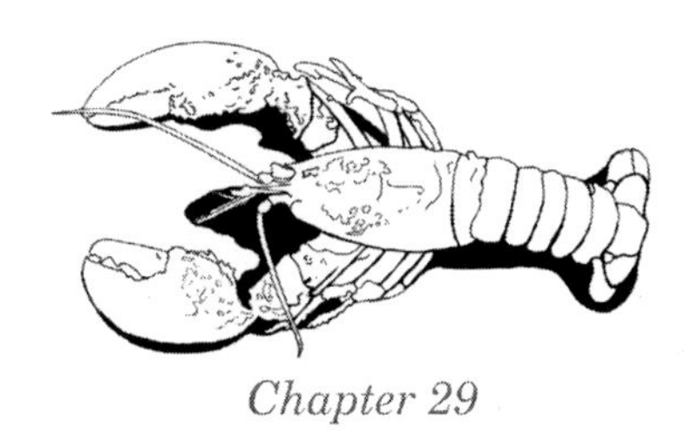

Chapter 29

Barton and His Boys

Sorenson opened the Cadillac door for his employer and waited patiently. The sun was setting over the harbor and reflected off the tin roof covering Baxter Fisheries & More, one of Barton's many businesses. Sorenson fidgeted with his collar. He would have to talk to Mrs. Pollinger about the starch she was using. His neck felt like it had been in a vise grip all day. The combination of the heat and the starch was too much to bear, he thought. Mr. Baxter's insistence that I wear this butler's uniform in the summer is unconstitutional. I really ought to get another job. He sighed. Sorenson's daydream distracted him, and he missed his boss's outstretched hand demanding assistance to get out of the backseat. Exasperated, Barton exited the vehicle unaided.

"Sorenson," he barked, "what are you doing? Sometimes I just don't know about you, really."

"Sorry, sir, sorry," Sorenson said.

Barton removed his sunglasses and glowered. "Where are they?" he said. "You did say seven or am I to be further underwhelmed by your performance and find out you screwed this up as well."

"No, no, no, sir. I was perfectly clear: Seven on the dot."

As Barton was about to get back in his car, a blue van turned into the parking area. Sorenson sighed with relief. "I knew I said seven," he said to his boss.

"Well," Barton said, still frowning. The van with the logo *Rest from Your Pests* on either side, and a large replica of an angry looking wasp attached to the roof, pulled up alongside the Cadillac. "Did they have to show up in this contraption?" Barton asked Sorenson. "Now people are going to think we have insects in the factory."

"I thought this would be just the cover you needed in order for them to be discreet with your special project," Sorenson whispered. "I casually mentioned to Mrs. Pollinger that you were having a routine inspection for insurance purposes both at home and at several of your other properties. No one will be the wiser."

"Very well then, Sorenson, we shall see."

The van doors opened and out stepped the Thibodeau brothers, Daniel and Lyle. The men were in their middle forties and looked nothing alike. Daniel was built like a fireplug with dark curly hair, brown eyes, and sausage-like fingers whereas Lyle was tall and thin, balding, and had mild blue eyes. Lyle didn't say much, and at times it was questionable whether he was rowing with both oars in the water, as is sometimes said in Maine. Perhaps he had inhaled too much of the chemicals the Thibodeaus used to exterminate insects, snakes, rodents, birds, and other home and business owners' annoyances. Daniel was reportedly the brains of the operation. Sorenson had heard that the brothers' services extended beyond pest removal, and he was pleased he had been able to recommend them to Barton.

Daniel extended his hand to Barton. Barton ignored the offer, as he was eager to finish the business at hand and get on with his evening. "Mr. Baxter, pleased to meet you. Your butler informed me of your request, and I'm sure we will be able to fulfill your needs."

In a low monotone, Barton said from behind his dark shades, "I want a daily report via my private line. This also includes pictures."

"No problem. Lyle here is pretty good with the camera. A regular shutterbug. Snapshot shutterbug is what I call him. Old Mr. Click Away, isn't that right, Bro?" Daniel smiled at his brother. Lyle, unresponsive, stared back at Daniel, a vacant look on his face. "It's because of his height. He can get in and get out quickly. Catlike reflexes. Catlike, ain't that right, Lyle?" Lyle didn't move, showing no reflexes, catlike or otherwise.

"As I was saying," continued a skeptical Barton, "I want you to stay out of the way and avoid being seen. No contact whatsoever."

"Incognito, got it," said Daniel. "Lyle is the master of deception and secrecy. Aren't you there, little brother?" Lyle watched a flock of seagulls gliding above the group and hovering, riding the wind, soaring up and down with the breeze. "Lyle. Lyle. LYLE!" Daniel yelled.

"What, wait, what?" Lyle said, acting like an adolescent caught in the hall skipping math class.

"Sorenson!" Barton commanded, unimpressed by the bug brothers.

"Yes, sir?" Sorenson quivered.

"Please handle the details. I've got other business to attend to." Sorenson bowed and Barton entered the factory.

"We look forward to working for you," Daniel said. "And remember, we take care of the pests so you can get your rest!"

Lobster fact: *Lobsters are harvested year-round in Maine, but most are caught between late June and late December when the lobsters are most active.*

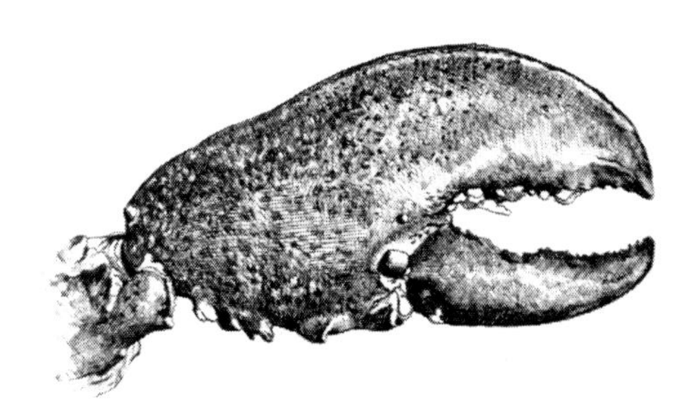

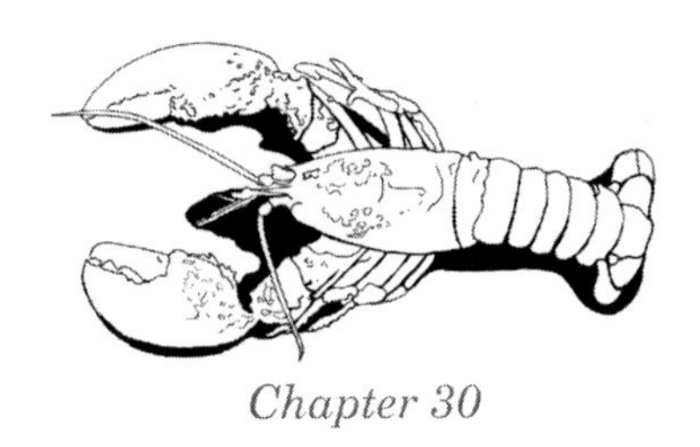

Chapter 30

Barton and Amelia

While Sorenson reviewed the demands laid out by his boss with the Thibodeaus, Barton was searching for the plant manager. Sawyer Ludlow had been born and raised on the island, just like his parents and his grandparents and their parents. He and his family had been involved in fishing these waters forever, and he could not remember any time, real or imagined, when the problem was too much supply instead of not enough. When he was made plant manager the previous spring, Sawyer was thrilled. He was tired of being on a boat, and ever since an inner-ear infection five summers ago, he just couldn't get his sea legs underneath him again. Working at Baxter Fisheries was a good move for him and his family. Sawyer welcomed how the noise from the machines could drown out the ringing in his right ear, which persisted despite the eardrops he used religiously. And he didn't need to worry about being seasick.

Now, with what was going on with the lobsters, the canning machines had been working at full power, morning, noon, and night. It was unfathomable that there could be this many lobsters! And they were getting larger by the week. Sawyer had already had to purchase additional refrigeration units to store the lobsters waiting to be canned. If this kept up, he and all the employees would be receiving very large holiday bonuses. Sawyer was dealing with paperwork when Barton barged into his office.

"Ludlow," he said.

"Mr. Baxter," he said, startled. "Didn't expect to see you this evening."

"Well, yes, I, um, well, if anyone asks, we will be doing pest inspections soon."

"Pest inspections? I was unaware that we had a problem," Sawyer said warily.

"We certainly don't have any pests, and I mean to keep it that way! Last time I checked, I was the president of the company," Barton said as he twirled his hair.

"Is there someone that I can call, Mr. Baxter?"

"No, Ludlow," Barton said. "I've already handled this so you can just go back to the business of canning the lobsters. That is, in fact, why you get paid, am I right?"

"Absolutely, Mr. Baxter," Sawyer said, "absolutely." Sawyer went back to the work on his desk. Barton glanced around, twiddled his hair again, and said nothing. After a few awkward moments of silence, Sawyer felt compelled to speak. "Is there something else that I can help you with, Mr. Baxter?" Barton was lost in his own thoughts. Bravely, Sawyer tried again. "Mr. Baxter?"

Hearing his name a second time brought Barton out of his reverie and back to the present. "What is it now?"

"I was just curious if you needed something else."

"Like what?"

"I don't know, sir, that is why I am checking with you."

"What? Never mind about me. The only one who is to mind about me is me, do you understand?"

Sawyer was now totally baffled by Barton's erratic behavior. Perhaps the old guy was beginning to unravel. Sawyer's father-in-law's mind started to go when he was the same age as Mr. Baxter. "Do you need me to get you some help?" Sawyer cautiously asked. "Sorenson perhaps?"

"No, I don't need Sorenson. What I need is to be left alone. I am going to the top floor, my attic office, for which I am the only one to have the key, and I don't want anyone to pester me. As far as you are concerned, you did not see me nor am I here. Clear?"

"Very."

Barton left Sawyer's office and opened a door to the left, at the back of the factory floor, that led to his attic office and away from the prying eyes of the employees. He needed privacy and time to think. This business with the lobsters and the town in an uproar? Pointless. I have done them all a favor, he thought. The lobsters are not going to hurt the lobster festival one iota. We host the festival because we are the lobster destination for both man and crustacean. He chuckled to himself, and with each ascending stair that he took, his sour mood became sweeter. By the time he reached the top floor, he was filled with excitement just like when he was a boy, a boy celebrating his thirteenth birthday, soon to be given a wonderful surprise, a surprise to share with his special friend.

I wonder if she'll finally speak with me so she can tell me how I might help her, he thought. Barton's brow furrowed, and he hesitated at the door. Amelia was always stubborn, stubborn as a mule. And she never needed or wanted anyone's assistance, especially Barton's.

Barton removed the key from his pocket, feeling its ridged edges momentarily against the softness of the blue hair ribbon, and with it opened the locked door to his attic office. The room smelled musty. It was covered with a thin layer of dust and was sparsely furnished with only a small metal desk, a wobbly wooden chair, and a locked filing cabinet. Barton locked the door behind him and pulled the blinds shut on the windows looking out on the harbor. He placed his ear on the side of the gray filing cabinet before rapping softly a few times. He listened again, and hearing nothing, he gingerly slid out the top drawer and removed a box, which he carefully placed on the desk. His eyes gleamed as he retrieved the orb, or Amelia's Orb as he called it whenever he thought of her, which lately had been nonstop. He hadn't been this eager since, well, he couldn't remember when. He took a deep breath and removed the satin covering. Amelia, tiny Amelia, blinked back at him.

He waited for her to speak. The look on her beautiful face, a face he had never forgotten, high cheekbones, angular but petite nose, dark arching eyebrows framing piercing brown eyes, showed only contempt and outrage. He flinched at her expression, an expression familiar from his youth. No matter how hard he tried—and he had indeed tried to win her favor—she was always agitated with him. Quite so, he recollected, but I did attempt to be a better person, I really did. For you, always for you. And he remembered that before he was old enough to take his proper place within Baxter Industries and the world beyond, when they were young children, they had been good friends.

Carefully he said, "Amelia. Hello, Amelia."

She turned away from him, her braids swinging in tandem behind her back, one still missing the blue ribbon now tucked snugly in Barton's right front pants pocket.

In a hushed voice so soft it resembled a small child's, he said. "Amelia, don't turn from me, please. I don't want to harm you; I want to help you." Amelia stayed immobile, arms crossed defiantly.

"I never would have taken the orb if I had known you were inside. Never," he said. "What am I saying? I would have taken it sooner if I thought I could have rescued you from this, this"—he struggled to find the right words— "this prison."

"Please don't, don't call it that."

"Amelia, thank God, Amelia! You can speak and I can hear you!" he cried pressing his face to the orb, his pale blue eyes looming large at his childhood friend. "I've got to get you out of here! I've got to get you out of here NOW!" Barton surveyed the room. He furiously opened and slammed the drawers of the filing cabinet searching for something, anything, anything at all that he could use to free Amelia from her captivity.

"Empty," he said. Next he explored the metal desk, opening the center drawer and finding nothing. He opened the three drawers on either side, his hands pulling them violently, desperate to find an object sharp, heavy, with the ability to pierce.

"Ugh!" Barton yelled in frustration. "So close, so close, after all these years, and I still can't do anything to help her. Oh, Amelia." His eyes welled with tears, something that Barton hadn't done in the fifty-five years since Amelia vanished through the wooden door. Filled with anguish, rage, and despair, he opened the last drawer. Once again he felt nothing, and he angrily yanked the drawer out completely and slammed it on the desk, causing the liquid surrounding Amelia to swirl murkily.

"Barton," Amelia cried out, but he didn't hear her in his frenzy. He banged the drawer again against the edge of the desk, one, two, three times, as sweat poured down his face. He banged the drawer a fourth and final time on top of the desk and then threw it to the ground, defeated and dejected. He slumped into the chair, saw the center drawer was partly open, and slammed it shut again. This time he heard metal sliding in it. He pulled it all the way open and found a heavy stapler.

"This is it," he said leaping up and grasping the stapler tightly. "This will break the glass!" He raised it high in the air with both hands, preparing to smash it into the orb, so he could claim to be Amelia's rescuer, so he would be the hero. He counted out loud, "One, two, and …"

Amelia put up her hands to shield her face. "No, stop, Barton, please, stop!" Amelia's faint cries reached Barton's hysterical mind. "I will die, Barton. I can't survive outside."

Barton dropped the stapler as if it was a burning hot coal and backed away, shaking, from the desk. He gasped, bracing himself against the windowsill before approaching Amelia. For once, Barton Thuya Baxter III was speechless.

"Barton, I can't come out of here. It is the Abenaki way. I alone broke the rules, and I accept my punishment. I *chibai.* I *chibai.*"

Barton stared back at Amelia. "Chibai?"

"Ghost, to my people, I am ghost now."

"Ghost? Preposterous! But something has to be done! I can do whatever you want me to do. I have money, unlimited resources. Tell me what I can do to get you out of here," he begged, his torment undeniable.

"They care nothing for money, Barton. Material goods are insignificant, something you could never understand as a child and seem still to be unable to understand now."

"If not money, then what is there?" Barton asked, truly puzzled.

"If you are asking this question, then you will never know the answer."

"I don't understand, Amelia."

"Love, humanity, empathy, kindness," Amelia's words floated around the room.

"I have these emotions," he said vehemently. "I have loved you since we were little."

"You didn't love me, Barton. You only thought you loved me because of your jealousy of Patrick."

"Patrick again, it was always Patrick for you," he said bitterly.

"You haven't changed, haven't changed a bit," Amelia said.

"I have changed, Amelia, just let me help you get out of there and I can prove it to you."

"My speaking time is running out, so listen to me carefully."

"What do you mean your speaking time? Who is saying this?" Barton's eyes darted suspiciously around the room. "This is my building here, and I dictate who can and cannot speak."

"Barton, please, stop talking and listen. You have to bring me back to Cadillac Mountain. Removing this orb has angered the gods, disrupted the energy, and broken the covenant, but it is not too late. If you have honestly changed, then prove it to me and return the orb to its sacred resting place. I have accepted my fate, and upon replacing the orb, you must accept your fate, whatever retribution the gods decree."

"I will do no such thing. I am not returning you ever. I am going to find someone to help you. You never did know what was good for you. I was good for you, not Patrick. I could have given you everything you wanted, and still can. There must be a scientist or doctor or someone who can figure out what to do."

"Barton, no, I don't want you to do anything except to return me to my proper place. If you don't, the outcome will be catastrophic for the island. I beg of you, Barton, to put your greed aside and do what I ask." Barton refused to hear a single word that Amelia said. Instead, his mind was busy working on a course of action to get her out.

"Barton, please, listen. I implore you!" Amelia begged. But instead of responding, Barton covered the orb with the satin. "You have been warned," Amelia declared, and at her final muffled words, Barton put the orb back into the cushioned box and stored it in the cabinet, once again hidden away from the world.

Lobster fact: *About once a year, lobsters shed their tough, old shell for a new, bigger shell that hardens over time. These new shell lobsters yield a flavorful meat in a shell that can often be cracked by hand.*

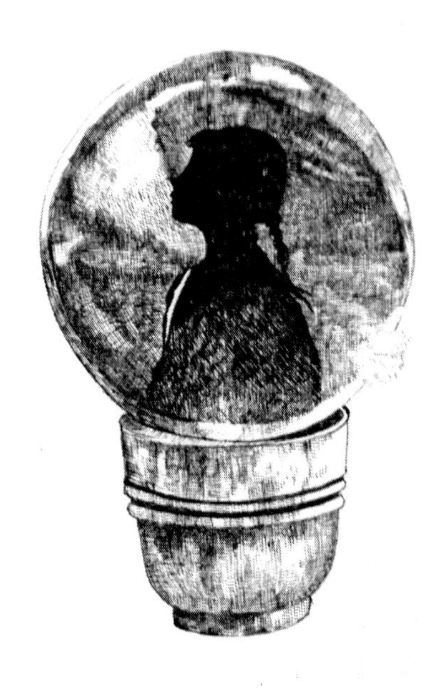

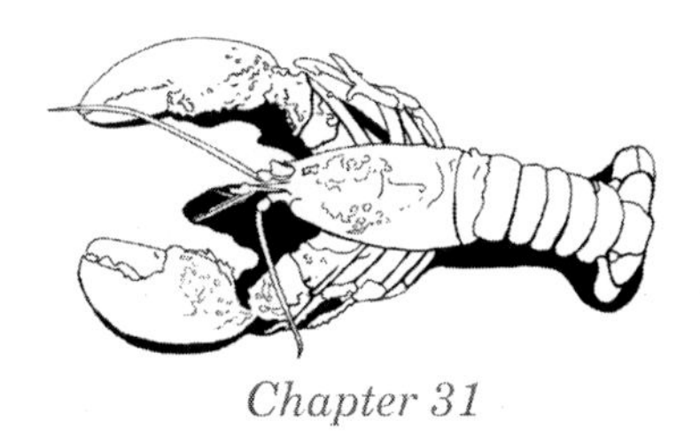

Chapter 31

Blueberries for Eliza

Dad seemed exhausted, thought Ani as she scrutinized the bags under his eyes while he drove the girls to their morning destination. They had told him they had found a delicious blueberry buckle recipe in the Bar Harbor Daily and wanted to pick some blueberries to make it for him so please would he take them on his way to the lab? After the blueberry picking in the morning—everyone knew that morning was the best time to pick berries—the girls told their father they would bike into town.

If Dr. Banke felt like he could get away, he was going to meet them for lunch in Bar Harbor. This business with the lobsters was more challenging than anyone had imagined. He told the girls that Southwest Harbor had had to close a few beaches the previous afternoon. A significant number of lobsters had rushed the beach, much like what happened after their tour on the *JL 73*. Dr. Banke and the rest of the RECI team were convinced that the surge of lobsters on the beach was a onetime occurrence caused by the currents, lobster shedding cycle, and high tides.

Sounds like mumbo jumbo, thought Ani. As far back as she could remember, her father had always been able to solve problems. This was the very first time she had ever felt he was grasping at straws. Again Ani couldn't stop thinking about her mother and wishing that she could be here, especially since her father was so, well, unlike her father. Not surprisingly, Eliza had fallen back asleep, and Ani noticed her head wobble back and forth as their father wove his way around the twists and turns of the drive, which provided intermittent views of the blue Atlantic Ocean and the island's imposing and dramatic cliffs. Ani had read in her guidebook that the cliffs of Mount Desert Island were intrusive igneous rocks, primarily granites. She marveled at the scene despite her growing concern about the amulets, the lobsters, and the mysterious floating girl in the orb.

As the sun rose higher to greet the Bankes, Ani started to tingle with the excitement of what she and Eliza were about to do. According to her research, Blueberry Hill was where they should find the next amulet, something resembling a flame, as was indicated by the parchment, or at least so she thought. This had to be the place, it just had to be. Ani's mind raced with questions. What is it? How can I find a flame? It can't be fire, so what is it instead? Where will it be located? Will it be easy to find? How long has it been on Blueberry Hill, and, last, how did it get there?

"Here you go, girls," said Dr. Banke, disrupting Ani's thoughts.

"Let's go, Eliza, wake up," said Ani shaking her sister's shoulder. "We need to help Dad with the bikes."

"Huh, what? Where are we? I want to go back to sleep." Eliza yawned, yet begrudgingly got out of the car and leaned against the passenger-side door. She shut her eyes and fell back asleep. Dr. Banke tapped her on her backside and said, "Come on, sleepy head. You're the one who was so nuts for the blueberry buckle. I promise to get some vanilla ice cream on the way home tonight, but you two need to get the most important ingredients.

"What?" Eliza yawned deeper and wider.

"He means the blueberries, sleeping beauty," Ani said. "Here's your bike."

"All right, all right, relax, I'm coming. Jeesh, everybody, this is not pick on Eliza morning. Chillax."

"Chillax? Chillax?" Dr. Banke said while handing the girls empty coffee tins.

"Seriously, Dad," Ani said. Eliza raised her eyebrow at

him.

"Oh, *chill* and *relax* combined. Nice, Eliza, very clever," Dr. Banke said.

"What's this?" Eliza asked as if finally waking up enough to notice that she was holding a tin can with a string.

"Patrick gave these to me on our way out this morning. I went to get your bikes from the shed and mentioned to him that you were going blueberry picking. He dug these cans and rakes out for you to use, even though he said it might be too early in the season for blueberries. You put the string over your head like this." He demonstrated by taking Eliza's from her hand and slipping it over her neck. "See, you can rake and then plop the berries into the bucket. Have fun. Hope to see you at lunchtime."

The girls locked their bikes to a park signpost and started climbing up Blueberry Hill. Ani glanced across the fields, a landscape of flat rocks interspersed with shrubs and low-lying blueberry bushes. A soft breeze blew, shaking the bushes gently, beckoning the girls to seek out their blueberry treasures.

Ani tapped Eliza. "Let's look at the clue one more time before we begin." She opened to a page marked by one of her yellow note cards. She held it up for her sister to see. "Here," she said, "look at this again so you know what we're looking for. See both my drawing and the one from the parchment," Ani said as she pointed to the card and then the book.

"I'm not stupid, Ani," Eliza said. "We studied these at length last night. We still don't really know what we're looking for, but if I find something that resembles a circle with angry lines jutting out from it, I'll be sure to yell out and let you know. So please, put your book away and let's just get started."

"I'm sorry, Eliza," Ani said. "I guess we should just get picking first, and once we have these cans filled, we can focus on finding the amulet. That is, if that sounds like an okay plan to you."

"All right," agreed Eliza. "Why don't you start slightly ahead of me, and then I can follow behind so as not to miss any foreign objects in this general area," she said, making a circular motion in front of her. "By the way, what did you tell Roonie? I'm surprised he isn't here bugging us already."

"He said something about having to help his grandmother at her inn today. I think it involved painting the porch," Ani said. She picked up her rake and walked several feet in front of her sister. "Is this far enough?"

"A little more," Eliza said, enjoying the power of bossing her younger, know-it-all sister. Ani walked several feet farther away from Eliza, who yawned and shielded her eyes from the rising sun. Eliza turned her head back to the side of the road. "What the?" she said out loud and read from the side of a van with a very large bug on top of it, "Rest from Your Pests. Hmm." I need a rest from my pest of a sister, she thought, who has us up at the crack of dawn to look for a flame while picking blueberries to make something for Dad's dinner. Eliza forgot about the van and bent down to rake and pick, rake and pick, the blueberries plopping as they hit the bottom of the tin can.

"Kaplunk, kaplink, kaplunk," Eliza said. "Hey," she yelled up to Ani, "I feel like Sal from Robert McCloskey's *Blueberries for Sal*. Remember Mom would read that to us?"

Ani yelled back to Eliza, "What are you yelling about? Did you find something?"

In a better mood now, Eliza said, "I was just asking if you remembered the book Mom used to read to us about the girl and the blueberries she was picking with her mother and then," she stopped, worried. "Oh, no, the bear! The bear was following them!" Eliza dropped her rake and looked nervously around.

"That was just a story, Eliza. There are no bears around here."

"How can you be so sure, Ani? Lobsters, seals, and well, bears are probably next on this freak show animal parade we happen to be a part of."

"Cut it out, Eliza. Let's just keep raking, picking, and looking."

"Looking for what? I am not seeing anything except blueberries."

"I don't think it's blueberries we're looking for."

"No, duh. The Indians couldn't have used a blueberry as an amulet or an offering because they would have gotten all moldy and yucky. Just like that time when Dad left that carton of blueberries in the way back of the fridge and the mold grew all over the green container. It was so gross. And we had to have pancakes without any blueberries, and you know that I can't eat pancakes unless they have blueberries in them. I mean really."

"Liza, concentrate please. Flame," Ani said. She proceeded on ahead of her sister, swinging her rake through the blueberry bushes. As time slowly passed, both girls got into a rhythm of raking and collecting blueberries while looking for the amulet, unaware that the Thibodeau brothers, pretending to be napping in their van on the side of the road, were taking pictures of them and their adventure to share with Barton.

The sun and the temperature rose, and sweat slid down the back of Ani's neck. She was hot, tired, and discouraged. This doesn't make any sense, she thought. We are probably in the wrong place or I translated incorrectly.

Eliza sat on a big rock sifting through the blueberries in her can, discarding a few that did not rank worthy enough to keep for tonight's dessert. Ani frowned. Eliza could be so, so … as she struggled for the right word, she saw a flash from Eliza's hand as she flung another unwanted berry to the ground. The sun's rays hit their mark a second time, casting a momentary dance of light.

"That's it," she yelled and sprinted to her sister. "Eliza! Eliza!" Ani shouted, startling her sister. Eliza knocked the coffee can over, the blueberries she had collected cascading over her and the rock she was sitting on.

"Ani! Look what you made me do!" she cried and held up the empty can.

Ani laughed. "You are simply the best sister in the world," she sang and grabbed Eliza's hand. "You are a genius for wearing this today. Thank you, thank you!"

"What are you talking about? Have you lost your mind? I think the sun has gotten to you."

"No, trust me, I am fine. Now I know what we're seeking and it's all because of you."

"Huh?"

"When I turned around to look at you, I noticed the sun reflect off your ring, your blue sapphire that Mom and Dad gave you for Christmas. Blue sapphire, get it? Blue flame!"

Eliza held up her hand and examined her ring as if for the first time. A smile formed on her lips as she shook her hand, catching the sun and causing a sparkle.

"We are looking for a blue sapphire stone!" Ani said, her enthusiasm for the hunt renewed. "Let's forget about the blueberries for now and look for the stone, okay?"

"Tell me again what you said?" asked an impish Eliza.

"You're the best sister," Ani said.

"In the ...?"

"Eliza Katherine Banke, you are the best sister in the world."

A satisfied Eliza beamed.

"Now let's get to work and find that stone. I'll go ahead as per our original plan."

The girls returned to their quest with a stronger determination. Ani was relieved to have figured out what they were actually searching for while Eliza was feeling smug that it was her ring that helped solve the puzzle.

After an hour or so, Eliza detected a sudden movement out of the corner of her eye. She jumped up, remembering the arrival of the bear from *Blueberries for Sal.* She was relieved to see nothing behind her, nothing eye level that is. She waited and then spotted the bushes rustling. She peered into them to discover a little, furry, gray bunny who had planted herself firmly in front of Eliza, peering back at her with her serious bunny face and looking pensive, as Eliza thought all bunnies did.

In a baby voice, Eliza said, "I'm glad to see only you and not a big black bear. Just you, you little fluffy bunny." The bunny stayed still and stared directly at Eliza. She shrugged and returned to the business of looking for the amulet, working her way up the hill. Her back ached from all the bending, and she was hungry. She noticed a particularly good-looking patch of blueberries on the bush in front of her. She picked several and popped them all into her mouth. She bit down, eager to taste the succulent fruit. "Yuck, sour!" she said, spitting out the disappointing berries behind her. She was surprised to find two more bunnies had joined the gray one. The new bunnies were more beige in color, larger, and sat in front of the little gray bunny. Neither Eliza nor the bunnies moved. After several beats she spoke softly.

"Hello there, you nice bunnies. I am so glad to see you. Not really," she muttered under her breath. "Soon, I am going to turn back around, close my eyes, and count to three. At this time, I am going to ask you bunnies to kindly go and hop away quietly to your little bunny holes or wherever it is that you go, okay? I just don't think I can handle any animal incidents today, so, well, thanks. One, two," she paused here, "three." A seagull squawked overhead, and Eliza looked up. The gull dipped before heading out to the open ocean. Eliza closed her eyes and turned back around, hoping the bunnies had heeded her request. She slowly opened her eyes and yes, she was pleased to see, the bunnies had disappeared.

"Thanks," she said, grateful but not completely convinced that they were gone. Eliza started searching again, but couldn't resist twirling around from time to time to check if her furry friends had returned. She had not a clue to what was actually going on deep within the hidden bunny pathways connecting far and wide throughout the island. The three bunnies had in fact listened to Eliza's request and gone back to where they came from. They went back not to stay, however, but to gather others, as it was looking quite likely that the girls were going to need their assistance. The bunnies were informed to be on guard and give support when necessary, and they were ready, ready and willing to do their part.

As her stomach grumbled, Eliza walked ahead to meet her sister. "Ani, I'm hungry and hot too." She wiped her brow with the back of her hand.

"Eliza, you can't be hungry now," Ani said, facing her sister. "Oh, Eliza!" Ani cried. Eliza spun around and discovered several bunnies, including the three she saw earlier leading the pack.

"Here we go again," Eliza said.

Ani laughed. "Eliza, the bunnies are coming, look!" Bunnies were appearing from all over the hill. From the right, from the left, and from behind the girls, bunnies were soundlessly hopping from every direction.

"Thank goodness it's just bunnies and not bears. Bunnies I can manage," Eliza said. The three lead bunnies inched closer to the girls, and as they did, so did the mass of gathered bunnies. Eliza tried to count them but gave up when still more and more bunnies kept joining the group. "I think there's at least a hundred," she said.

"Amazing," said Ani, who by now was surrounded by bunnies. She put her hand out and the bunnies stopped moving. "I am hoping that you are here to help us find the blue flame. Is this right?" Ani asked timidly. The bunnies remained in place. Only their noses twitched.

"What do we do now?" whispered Eliza.

"I have an idea," Ani whispered back. "Follow me." She climbed up the hill a short way trailed by Eliza and a wall of bunnies hopping soundlessly.

"Freaky," Eliza said. Ani pointed left and they headed in that direction, and again the bunnies followed them. Next Ani moved right, away from the road and toward the ocean.

"That's strange," Eliza said. "They aren't following us now." Ani stopped in her tracks, moved up and to the left, and the bunnies followed again.

"Okay, okay, I think I get your game," Ani said. With a knowing look on her face, she continued on her path, left and up, checking to see if the bunnies were following.

"I get it, I get it, I don't believe it, but I get it," cried Eliza. "This is fun. They really are leading you." She laughed. Ani joined in, giggling at the sight of all these bunnies hopping with them.

They had almost reached the top of the hill, and the view was breathtaking. The sun rippled across the water below. As far as the eye could see, there was just blue sky, blue water, and sparkling sunshine.

Ani cried out, “Blue flame, blue flame!” and she burst into more laughter. Next the bunnies surrounded the girls, brushing their legs as they bounded and hopped past them. As if on cue, the little gray bunny that Eliza first met hopped squarely in front of Ani.

“That’s the first bunny I saw earlier, Ani. I just know it is. She must be the leader!”

Ani bent to get a closer look. The bunny stared back at her and then gracefully hopped aside to reveal a beautiful, sparkling, blue sapphire stone. Ani picked it up; it was about the size of a robin’s egg. The sapphire caught the sun and radiated a magical glow like a blue flame.

“Ah,” said Ani. The bunnies paused for one final moment and then abruptly departed, hopping back down the hill.

“Can you believe that?” Eliza said and struck Ani’s hand, the hand holding the blue sapphire, knocking the stone away.

“No!” screamed Ani.

“Oh, no!” echoed Eliza. “What have I done!”

They watched in horror as the stone flew over the back side of Blueberry Hill to the road below. The girls followed as quickly as they could, but there was no real path and the rocks and dirt and bushes proved too difficult to maneuver around quickly. And the stone proved to be too fast and too round, gathering momentum as it fell, bouncing from one rock to the next, making its way down the hill.

“Stop, stop, stop,” Ani cried, but to no avail. The blue sapphire kept on rolling. Meanwhile, rounding the bend in the road and traveling at a good clip was Bob’s Mini Golf Ball Repair and Cleaning truck. The colorful golf balls that filled the back of the truck had just been washed and glistened in the sun, much like the blue sapphire did in Ani’s hand just moments ago. Ani saw the truck first and yelled, “No!”

Eliza was shocked into silence. The girls, now halfway down the hill, stopped as the precious blue stone rolled even farther away. It bounced off one final rock high into the air, only to come down and land with a “kaplunk” on the mound of golf balls. The truck driver beeped and waved at the girls as he sped past and out of sight.

"Kaplunk, just like in *Blueberries for Sal*," Eliza sighed.

"Kaphuey," corrected Ani, frowning at her sister. "Come on, we've got some mini golfing to do!"

Lobster fact: *Elaine's Blueberry Buckle Recipe*

2 cups blueberries
1/3 cup sugar
¼ teaspoon cinnamon
1 cup sifted "cake" flour
1 teaspoon baking powder
1 teaspoon salt
2/3 cup sugar
1/4 cup butter
1/2 cup milk
1 teaspoon vanilla
1 egg

Heat oven to 350°

1. Lightly grease bottom only of 8-inch square baking pan.
2. Mix berries with 1/3 cup sugar and cinnamon.
3. Cream butter and additional sugar until fluffy, then add egg and beat.
4. Add sifted flour, baking powder, salt, alternately with milk.
5. Put berry mixture in bottom of pan and cover with batter.
6. Bake at 350° for 45 minutes.

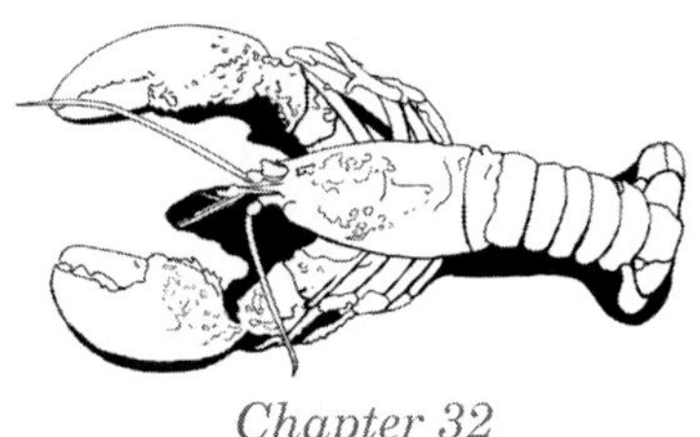

Chapter 32

Blackbeard and the Whispering Pines

The girls scrabbled back up and over the other side of Blueberry Hill with Eliza flailing her arms behind her younger sister all the while yelling, "I'm sorry, I'm so sorry."

Ani didn't want to waste any time or energy turning around and yelling back at her. I will be angry with her this evening, she thought, but right now I have to get that blue flame. Red in the face, the girls hurried to undo their locks, put their helmets on, and jump on their bikes to pursue Bob's Mini Golf Ball truck. Completely forgotten were their coffee cans partially filled with unripe blueberries dropped somewhere on the side of the hill. Dr. Banke would not be getting his blueberry buckle this evening.

Ani and Eliza whizzed past the Thibodeau brothers, who, instead of pretending to be napping in order to take pictures of the girls, were truly napping. Since the early morning when they started spying and then foolishly fell asleep, they had been out of contact with their office manager, Hannah, who had been fielding many calls from irate customers who needed immediate relief from pests. These calls were not like any other calls Hannah Coleman had ever heard tell of in the thirty years she had worked for the brothers and their father before them. People were not complaining about a possum that had climbed into their dishwasher, or squirrels in the attic, or even mice in the cupboards. No, this time the calls were from folks complaining about lobsters in their yards, on their decks, and in their cellars. It was the most ridiculous thing Hannah had ever heard. Lobsters indeed.

She tried reaching her bosses again with the walkie-talkie for what seemed like the hundredth time, and as with her earlier attempts, they did not pick up. Those two nincompoops are probably out fishing, Hannah thought to herself. I guess I will just have to go and investigate some of these calls myself. She flipped the sign on the door to read, *Out on patrol, be back in one hour*. Hannah decided to start with old Mrs. Sullivan because she was the most panicked when she phoned. She insisted that she had several lobsters in her basement that were trying to crawl up the stairs. Mrs. Sullivan reckoned that they crawled in through the bulkhead, which she had left open earlier while she was gardening. Nonsense is what Hannah thought while getting in her old pickup truck and backing out of the driveway. Somebody was playing a wicked joke and laughing right highly at the commotion all those lobsters were causing. Hannah knew that she could get to the bottom of this problem quickly once she had a look at Mrs. Sullivan's basement. Sounds an awful lot like her neighbors, the Mieles. Those children were always up to no good. Why just last week they filled her garden with a hundred plastic forks, which took Hannah most of the morning to dig out. With the Lobster Festival just around the corner, this lobster prank would be sure to make headlines in the *Bar Harbor Daily*.

As Hannah turned the corner leading onto the Park Loop Road, Ani and Eliza passed her racing into town. The girls knew of only one place to play mini-golf, Blackbeard's Cove, and this is where they hoped the clean golf balls along with the blue sapphire were headed after the mishap on Blueberry Hill.

Traffic in town had increased as tourists and townspeople converged on the main street to preview the many lobster-themed events happening in anticipation of the annual lobster festival. Ani and Eliza had to slow to a crawl as they maneuvered their way through the crowds to reach their destination on the other side of town. A large banner hung over the main street, flapping in the wind. Ani read out loud, "*Bar Harbor's*

Lobster Festival, July 14th–21st."

"Where did all these people come from?" asked Eliza.

"Dad said this was a big deal," Ani said, "but I never imagined this many people would turn out for a lobster festival."

"Hey, I like that sweatshirt," Eliza said while riding past a kiosk on the sidewalk with sweatshirts, T-shirts, and hats covered in mini pink lobsters.

"Eliza! Focus! We need to get that sapphire! This is the street that the Moon Violet Inn is on. Let's stop and see if Roonie is free. We could use his help."

Eliza nodded in agreement, and the two girls sped toward the inn, but Roonie was on his bike heading away from his grandmother's. He grinned from ear to ear when he recognized the girls.

"Hey, hello, hi! I was just coming to find you," he shouted.

The girls laughed when they got closer to Roonie. He was covered in lilac paint. He had it on his hands, in his hair, on his white sneakers, and splattered across the front of his Spidey T-shirt.

"Let me guess," said Eliza sarcastically. "You were painting the porch?"

Astonished, Roonie said, "How did you know?"

"She's just teasing you, Roonie," said Ani. "You're covered in lilac paint."

"I am?"

"Never mind that now. We really need your help. We have to get to Blackbeard's Cove and fast. Come on," commanded Ani. "We'll explain on the way."

When they reached Blackbeard's Cove, they parked their bikes out front. True to its name, the mini-golf park looked like the perfect hideaway for Blackbeard's treasures and his pirates. There were waterfalls, treasure chests, walk-the-plank walkways, and ghostly pirate ships with cannons squirting water into a large pond with a fountain featuring a 10-foot-tall green mermaid resting on a clamshell. The pond was littered with coins and multicolored golf balls.

"This is going to be impossible," Eliza whined when she

saw all the golf balls in the pond.

Ani spied Bob's truck backed up against the building. "Hey, look!" she said. Next the truck raised its bed, and the freshly cleaned golf balls tumbled into what Ani could only imagine was some kind of holding pen inside Blackbeard's Cove. The sun glistened off the newly cleaned golf balls as they rolled out of the truck bed and disappeared into the building. The kids were silent as they watched the procession of color, almost willing the sapphire stone to show itself in all of its blue sparkly glory. Ani spotted it first. "I see it; it's there, the blue flame!" she said. "Hurry!" And she led the way to the office.

Once inside, Ani couldn't believe what she saw. The golf balls were being dumped into a glass holding tank connected to a series of clear tubes that twisted, turned, and looped. The balls were shot from the holding pen intermittently to travel through the tubes attached to the perimeter of the room. It truly was a sight to behold.

"Talk about your habitat trails!" Roonie said.

Ani followed the complicated maze to figure out where the balls, once finished with their dance in the tubes, landed. "There," she said, pointing to the center of the room, "they end up in Blackbeard's treasure chest." Squarely in the center of the room was a large replica of Blackbeard's Lost Treasure Chest. Golfers, once they had paid their fee and received their club, were instructed to visit the treasure chest and select a ball to use in the game. The threesome watched as every few moments a different colored golf ball landed with a thunk in the chest.

"Awesome," said Roonie, who surveyed the room, determined to help Ani and Eliza on their quest. "Yellow, pink, green, orange, black, red, blue, pink, pink, orange, and green," he said as the balls flew out of the holding tank and were magically squirted into the tube to start their swirling journey around the room. "There it is, there it is!" Roonie shouted.

Ani and Eliza saw the blue sapphire tumble along the tube just like the golf balls. All three pairs of eyes tracked it through the twists and loops of the maze as Ani approached the treasure chest, eager to retrieve the amulet. They were all so intent on keeping their eyes on the stone that none of them heard the noise of a school bus coming to a halt in the parking lot, followed by the familiar creak of a bus door opening. Within seconds a busload of campers burst into the room and crowded the office. They were wearing matching yellow T-shirts emblazoned with the name Whispering Pines Camp on the left front pocket. There were over fifty kids, ranging in age from five to ten, accompanied by a handful of frazzled looking counselors in training and even more frazzled looking camp counselors. Their enthusiasm and shouts and laughter stunned Ani, Eliza, and Roonie.

"Clearly 'Whispering' was a bad graphic mistake; there is nothing 'Whispering' about these campers," Eliza shouted over the boisterous crowd. Ani was pushed away from the treasure chest by the eager campers, who frenetically grabbed golf clubs, scorecards, and lastly golf balls from the chest. Just as fast as they entered the room, they left to play the game.

"Urgh!" Ani cried. "The treasure chest is empty. The campers have the amulet!" Roonie and Eliza rushed to the chest only to discover that what Ani said was true. The blue sapphire, which just moments before was so close to being in their possession, was now in play on the mini-golf course.

"Thunk," a solitary black golf ball landed on the bottom of the chest.

Eliza was tired at this point and asked, "Can't we just use this one? I mean, it looks blue. It really is a blue black if I had to be more exact."

Ani sighed.

"Kidding," said Eliza.

"Let's play golf!" cheered Roonie.

The kids ran to the counter. "We want to play," Ani said to the attendant with a fake parrot on his shoulder, eye patch, and a blue bandanna tied backwards on his head. He managed to look both bored and awkward at the same time.

He said in a monotone, "You've got to pay if you want to play."

"How much?" asked Roonie, reaching into his pants pocket. The attendant gave him a quizzical look, eying the lilac paint covering him. "I got paid by Grandma Violet," he said to the girls.

The pirate attendant pointed with his plastic sword to the board high on the wall above him outlining the fees. A round of mini-golf, 18 holes, cost twelve dollars. Roonie pulled out a crumpled wad of dollar bills and placed them on the counter.

Sheepishly he said, "I only have eight dollars."

Ani looked at Eliza, who always had money yet could be stingy unless she really really wanted something. Ani was unsure if this would be one of those times. Ani had only two dollars, which she placed on the counter. Eliza looked noncommittal. "Eliza?" said Ani. "Please." Eliza scrunched up her nose, frowned, and then reached for her wallet.

"Seriously, Ani, I only have five dollars. I figured we would meet Dad who would pay for lunch. I was going to ask him for some shopping money then."

Ani gave her sister an I'm-not-sure-I-believe-you look.

"I'm not kidding, Ani. I want to get this amulet as much as you do. Just because you're the one who 'walks with great animal spirit' or whatever the Abenaki Indians call it, doesn't mean that this is all just your search. I saw the girl in the orb, I swam with the seals, and I searched with the bunnies. So here," she said to the pirate worker, "Roonie can play. My sister and I will just watch. Thank you."

The pirate took the money and handed Roonie a golf club. Roonie went to the treasure chest, no longer empty now that a few more golf balls had worked their way through the maze, and selected a red ball, which the girls had learned by now was his favorite color. He headed for the exit and the girls followed him, but the attendant stopped them all.

"You can't go on the course if you don't pay," he said while rubbing his fake patch. Ani couldn't help but notice that every time he spoke, the parrot on his shoulder shook from side to side, making him look even more ridiculous. Eliza did not like to be told what she could and could not do. Ani saw a scowl move across her face.

"Look," she said in her most grown-up voice, "this boy is our cousin, and we are responsible for his well-being. We obviously are not able to play since we have no ball and no clubs. I am hard pressed to see why we are not able to go along with him, making sure that he is safe, safe from harm's way, which I know exists on this course."

The attendant frowned and pointed back up at the sign behind him. "Read this." He tapped at the words dramatically with his sword.

Eliza read out loud, "*No person who has not paid the entrance fee shall be allowed on the course. No exceptions.*"

"You can wait on the benches over there." He gestured again with his silly sword to an area outside.

Ani knew that Eliza was about to argue with him. Mom always said that no one could out argue Eliza when she got started. She also said that Eliza would make a great attorney. Ani thought it more likely that she would just drive people crazy. Ani then saw something off to the right, something that would help them in their search. She tugged at Eliza's arm and whispered, "Don't start with him, Eliza. I have a better plan. Thank him and let's go."

Eliza hesitated and then said, "Thank you," followed by her most fake smile. All three walked away from the pirate employee and huddled by the pathway that led to the course.

"Roonie, you start playing like you normally would, only you are just going to play the first two holes. After that, when pirate boy over there can't see you anymore from the counter, skip the other holes and start looking. If anyone asks what you are doing, say something like you're looking for your sister. Got it?"

"But I haven't got a sister," Roonie said, looking confused.

"Roonie, we know that, just pretend," Eliza said.

"Eliza, follow me out the side exit, where we can wait on the bench until another player comes in and distracts the guy. Just keep smiling and act casual."

All three looked like robot children with frozen grins too

wide and too forced to resemble anything natural. The complacent attendant didn't notice. Once outside, Roonie started the game. The girls sat on the bench and waited. Hole one had a fairly steep uphill putt, followed by another passage that had the ball move over a few hills and between two imitation cannons. It also had two extremely big skeletons dressed in torn pirate costumes propped up against a sizable plastic rock.

When Roonie approached, an automatic voice with a thick pirate brogue called, "Ahoy thar, Matey. Welcome to Blackbeard's Cove." The first skeleton's jaw opened and closed in a rhythm not even close to matching the voice coming out of the speaker attached to the faux grass on the ground.

Skeleton number two added, "Argh, you pirate lad or lass, have fun out there today, and if you see the rogue Blackbeard, tell him we want our cut of the treasure. From the look of us, you can tell we've been waitin' a very, very long time." Both skeletons cackled loudly, and their heads rocked back and forth and then stopped as abruptly as they started. As instructed, Roonie dropped his ball and began the game.

More visitors to Blackbeard's Cove arrived and stood before the counter, blocking the unfriendly attendant's view of what was about to happen.

Ani said, "We've got to move now!"

They approached the skeletons, who began their automated spiel again, "Ahoy thar, Matey ..."

Moments later, when new customers lined up to start at hole one, they, too, were greeted with the welcome, "Ahoy thar, Matey," but this time the two pirate greeters were missing their clothes.

Eliza and Ani ducked behind another fake rock to hastily put their stolen booty on over their own shorts and T-shirts. "Help me with this," said Eliza as she held up a black bandanna. "I can't seem to get it tied." Ani took the bandanna and placed it on her sister's head. She quickly tied the ends.

"There. Turn around." Ani burst into laughter. Eliza joined her sister as she saw how preposterous they looked.

"Ahoy thar, Matey," mimicked Eliza. "What now?"

"Follow me."

"Aye, aye, Captain." Eliza laughed.

The girls crawled noiselessly up the stone stairs that led to the center of the course. They passed several campers on their climb, and Eliza threw out a few "arghs" and "ahoy thars" along the way. At each hole the girls stopped and launched into a pirate routine while secretly looking for the blue sapphire. Unfortunately all they found were golf balls. They also didn't find Roonie, but did notice a stray club lying on the side of the path up past hole four. Ani thought this must be his and he probably dropped it as it got in his way. On their ascent the girls passed more pirate-themed decorations: treasure chests, skeletons, parrots, stockades and jail cages, and a few broken-down dinghies.

"Blackbeard's decorator went a bit overboard," said Eliza, who laughed at her own joke. "Get it? Overboard?"

Ani couldn't help but laugh, especially when looking at her sister in her pirate getup.

The girls entered the passageway to hole nine, which was at the summit of the course. Ani had hoped they would find the amulet early on and then return their borrowed disguises before they were discovered missing. Hole nine and the campers playing it had only golf balls, no blue sapphire stone.

Roonie appeared suddenly from the back of the cave and the waterfall. "I've run up and back twice, and I haven't located it." He paused to catch his breath and bent over and rested his hands on his knees. Ani looked at the lilac paint splattered haphazardly on the top of his head. He continued, "That pond in the center is littered with golf balls. Hole fifteen by far is the trickiest hole on the course. If kids aren't paying attention, swish, into the lake."

"I have seen that pond, and I am definitely not going in. That is a fact," Eliza said.

"We are outnumbered here," said Roonie, his breath slowing down now that he had stopped running. "There are just so many campers."

"That's it!" shouted Ani. "Oh, Roonie, you are brilliant!"

Ani huddled closer to them and whispered her plan.

"Tell me again why I have to do it?" asked Eliza while Ani and Roonie shoved her to the top of the poorly constructed mountainous-type rock overlooking the pond.

"Because you have the loudest voice, and you know that I don't like heights, so it has to be you," Ani said, and then to Roonie she whispered, "and besides you love an audience." Ani smiled. Roonie grinned back at her.

"All right, if you insist," sighed Eliza. Once on top of the rock, she stood tall, fearless, and outlandish in her costume.

"Calling all mates and mateys, all lads and lassies," Eliza began. She repeated herself to make sure the campers stopped their play. "Ahoy thar. Calling all mates and mateys and lads and lassies." Several campers and a few counselors stepped off their greens to see who or what was speaking. In an even louder voice with an even thicker pirate accent, Eliza continued, "Some of our gold has been stolen by Blackbeard's arch enemy, Bluebeard. Luckily, he was discovered and taken to Blackbeard's jail, but the treasure remains here on the course." Eliza waved her arm for dramatic effect. "Bluebeard hid the key to the treasure chest in a bright blue stone that looks just like a mini-golf ball. The first one of you Whispering Pines campers to find the stone gets a free round of mini-golf and, and," Eliza stumbled over what to say next, "and a bag of gold coins for yourself. Now get looking!"

What happened next was complete bedlam. The campers screamed and ran around the course in all directions. They spread the word to those players ahead and behind and soon everyone had stopped playing the game and joined the search. In their frenzy to find the blue stone and win the prize, they abandoned any type of order and took on a mob mentality. Waterfalls turned on and off as someone located the switch, campers were jumping in and out of fake boats, kids were throwing coins out of the treasure chests located throughout the park, while counselors and their CITs blew whistles and tried to gather their campers.

Ani and Eliza ran in and out of all the pandemonium trying to look at every ball. Roonie went back to the office to see if the sapphire was back at the beginning. As an avid mini-golfer, he understood that at hole eighteen, the ball disappeared and miraculously returned to its starting place.

The screams and shrieks of excitement grew louder as the search continued and reached the ears of the pirate attendant, who emerged from the greeting center to witness the chaotic scene on his normally tranquil mini-golf paradise.

"What the heck?" he said while moving far enough away from the office to trigger the automatic pirate welcome at hole one. He instantly noticed that the pirates were naked. "Where are the clothes? Who took the pirate clothes?" he yelled. "I'm calling my boss," he shouted and returned to the front desk.

Ani, Eliza, and Roonie rejoined each other at hole fifteen. This time all three were winded. "Any luck?" Ani asked hopefully. Eliza shook her head.

"Nope," said Roonie.

Pirate boy returned. "You there, you two!" he yelled.

"Time to move it!" shouted Eliza. As they headed toward the end of the course, high above they heard, "I see it, I see it! The blue stone is at hole eighteen!"

Ani, Eliza, Roonie, and the employee all turned toward the voice.

The camper repeated himself: "I see it! I see it! I win!" Ani was able to make out where the noise was coming from. A small boy with a buzz cut had climbed up the mast of a fabricated pirate ship moored in the pond in front of the waterfall.

"Hey, you're not supposed to be up there," yelled the pirate attendant.

Ani, Eliza, and Roonie dashed for the eighteenth hole. They arrived in seconds to witness a cute little girl with golden curls in a *Maine Is for Mainiacs* T-shirt softly tap the blue sapphire stone with her club. The stone rolled slowly down the course, under a cannon, and through the open mouth of a ghoulish skull where it became trapped in a maze of ropes leading to the hole in the center. The girls scrabbled after the stone. Ani was about to snare it as it finally made its way outside of the maze. She stooped to pick it up only to be thwarted by the attendant, who reached her first and roughly grabbed her arm.

"Not so fast, little pirate girl. You've stolen that costume and you're coming with me." Ani glanced quickly at him and then back to the blue flame just as it made its final swirl and disappeared into the hole.

"I almost had it, I almost had it!" Ani said.

The little girl with curls yelled, "A hole in one, a hole in one. I got a hole in one!"

The attendant spotted Eliza and pointed to her as well. Roonie backed away from hole eighteen, but the attendant waved him over. "You there, Spidey with the purple paint." Roonie looked around as if someone else might be wearing a Spider-Man shirt with lilac paint. "Yes, you," the attendant repeated harshly.

A few minutes later, the kids stood in front of the counter again with the pirate clothes removed and folded nicely in front of the attendant. Ani tried to explain what happened with the special stone and how it got lost on Blueberry Hill and then ended up in the golf-ball washing truck and the Whispering Pines campers and on and on. The mini-golf employee was having a hard time understanding what she was saying while Eliza and Roonie added to his confusion with their interjections.

"We're terribly sorry for any problems we might have caused," Ani said and paused to read his nametag for the first time. "Leon. We'll put the clothes back on the mannequins."

From the look on Leon's face, Ani could tell he was still angry and might follow through with his plan to call his boss or, worse yet, the police or, even more horrible, Dad. He will kill us, thought Ani.

Eliza, too, picked up on the seriousness of their situation. She decided to turn it on thick. Ani was amazed to see tears stream down Eliza's cheeks as she made a few audible gasps. "I miss Auntie Ceci so much," wailed Eliza. "So very, very much."

"I miss her, too, Eliza," Ani said.

"She left me her blue stone and I lost, lost, lost it," sobbed Eliza, ducking her head down to use her hair to hide her grin from Leon. Her own drama made her feel like giggling.

But Leon took the bait and started to soften. "Now, now, now, jeesh, don't cry," he said. "Did you check the treasure chest? Maybe Aunt Ceci's stone came back through the tubes."

"Ani, you check. I'm too upset," cried Eliza.

Ani patted her back affectionately and walked over to the chest. Roonie and Leon followed. Only a few balls lay there. Two black, three hot pink, one green, one red, and one orange. No blue flame. Ani and Roonie looked despondent. Even Leon, who had clearly fallen for Eliza's theatrical performance, appeared crestfallen. They all returned to the counter. Eliza, who had grabbed a few tissues, was wiping her face.

KAPLUNK. Everyone heard the noise. Ani rushed to the chest. The blue sapphire rested solidly in the middle, shiny and bright.

"Well look at that," said a surprised Leon, who reached in and plucked up the stone. He held it up as the lighting in the office reflected off the sapphire and cast light throughout the room. "I guess I owe you an apology about the stone." He passed it to Ani who was just about to take it from him when a huge hairy wolfhound leapt out of nowhere and ripped it out of Leon's hand. The dog skidded across the floor, slamming into the wall and then turned around to face the crowd. His big tail wagged back and forth. The dog wanted to play.

"Tiny, not now!" Leon said.

"Tiny?" questioned Eliza.

"Tiny just loves to play with the golf balls. That's why we have to have them cleaned all the time. People don't like to play with slimy golf balls."

Ani started toward Tiny.

"Don't do that!" yelled Leon. "Tiny will just take off, and you'll be chasing him from here to Christmas."

But it was too late. Tiny saw Ani's feet move and he was gone. Gone from the office, out the side door, and just plain gone. He was running full tilt away from Leon, away from Ani,

Roonie, and Eliza. Gone with the blue flame in his mouth.

"Where'd he go?" asked Ani.

"Where he always goes when he thinks someone is chasing him," said Leon.

"Where's that?" Roonie asked.

"To the town park, of course," said Leon and shook his head in dismay.

"Come on, we've got to move and get that stone!" declared Ani.

Lobster fact: *An inexpensive, biodegradable golf ball made almost entirely of lobster shells was recently created by a joint project between the Lobster Institute and the University of Maine. It is intended for use on cruise ships. The balls are made mainly from byproducts of the lobster canning industry that are often just thrown away.*

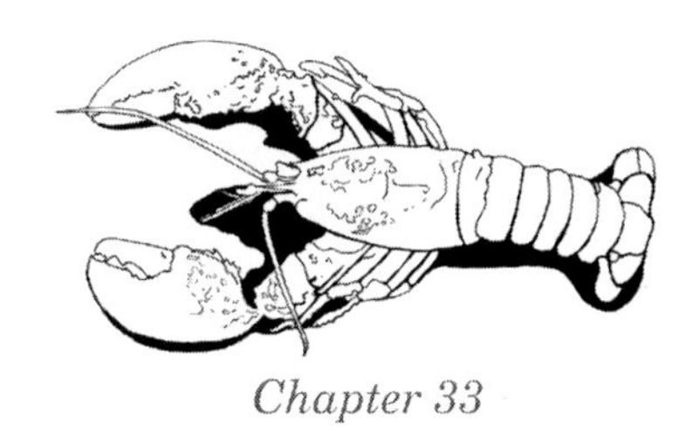

Chapter 33

Hannah and the Lobsters

While the kids were caught up trying to rescue the blue sapphire from becoming one of Blackbeard's permanent treasures, Hannah arrived at her destination. Rachel Sullivan's house was located in Pretty Marsh Cove away from the tourists and the town, tucked cozily between a salt marsh on one side and a small coastal inlet on the other. From the front of her tiny house, she had one of the loveliest views on the island. Her lawn rolled down to a small wall of rocks, beyond which a private beach was shared by only a few other houses farther up the road. The Sullivan family had owned this impressive piece of property for well over 100 years, purchased when no one could have imagined how a scruffy parcel of land in such a remote part of the state of Maine would ever be of any value. Then it was just a place for poor folk, a few lobstermen and fishermen. Now, Hannah couldn't even begin to guess the listing price for old Mrs. Sullivan's place, but she was sure it would be far greater than she could ever imagine.

Hannah parked her truck in front of the house and rang the bell. She waited what seemed like an appropriate amount of time, but Rachel Sullivan did not come to the door. Hannah cupped her hands over her eyes and leaned into the leaded glass on the side of the door to look into the foyer. She didn't see anything. Hannah left the front porch and walked around to the back of the house. Mrs. Sullivan's car was in the driveway, and Hannah figured maybe she was visiting a neighbor.

Knowing Rachel Sullivan wouldn't mind because she had

called to complain not two hours ago about lobsters, Hannah decided to investigate the basement alone. She opened the bulkhead door and pulled on the rope and chain to turn on the light, but nothing happened. She looked up and noticed that the bulb had been broken, not burnt out as she expected, but actually broken as if it had been hit. She pulled her flashlight out of her pocket and headed down the rest of the steps, her feet crunching. The noise caused her to stop and shine the light at her shoes to verify what she already knew were broken bits of light bulb. She waited and listened and heard nothing. The flashlight flickered on and off. She hit it against her hand a few times, but the light grew dimmer and dimmer until finally it gave out completely. Dang it, she thought. Those morons never check their own equipment. She waited again. Pretty quiet, she thought, for a basement filled with lobsters or "abnormally large lobsters," as she remembered Mrs. Sullivan exclaiming on the phone. Perhaps it was time for Mrs. Sullivan to move to an elderly facility—clearly she was losing her marbles. Hannah reached the next to last step and was greeted with cool air that almost seemed to lift from the floor. Her ankles felt damp from moisture. Goose pimples rose on her arms. She paused for a few more moments, but still heard nothing but the beat of her own heart and the distant roar of the waves meeting the shore.

All this lobster talk was making her hungry. Perhaps a nice lobster salad tonight for dinner, she mused. The thought of this delicious meal and the comfort of her own home calmed the nervousness that she was too proud to admit she had been feeling a few seconds earlier. One more step to the bottom, she thought. Won't Daniel and Lyle get a chuckle when I finally get a hold of them and tell them about this visit.

Confidence increasing, Hannah stepped down. She knew in an instant that something was wrong because the cellar floor didn't feel right. It felt like she had just stepped on squishy seaweed, the kind that dotted the Maine coast from here up to the county line.

"Oh, oh, oh," she cried as her left foot slipped, causing her legs to split apart unnaturally. She wobbled uncontrollably and in her effort to right herself, she dropped her broken flashlight to the floor. The impact caused the flashlight to turn on for only a second before the inner light bulb failed and darkness enveloped Hannah again. However, a second was all she needed to see the horror of what was waiting for her in Rachel Sullivan's basement. As she fell she could hear the click-clacking of over 100 lobsters, unimaginably large, converging upon her. The lobsters surrounded her, swiftly and efficiently, and hoisted her upon their backs. As a unified team, they brusquely carried poor Hannah Coleman up the bulkhead, around the side, down the front yard, over the rocks, and into the sea.

Suffice it to say that Hannah Coleman would not be having lobster salad for supper. Quite the opposite would be true. Much like Rachel Sullivan before her, Hannah Coleman would not be eating the main course because, well, because, unfortunately, she had just become the main course!

Lobster fact: *Lobsters were once thought to be scavengers, eating only dead fish, but research has found that they actually eat mussels, crabs, clams, sea urchins, fish, and even other lobsters of the same species!*

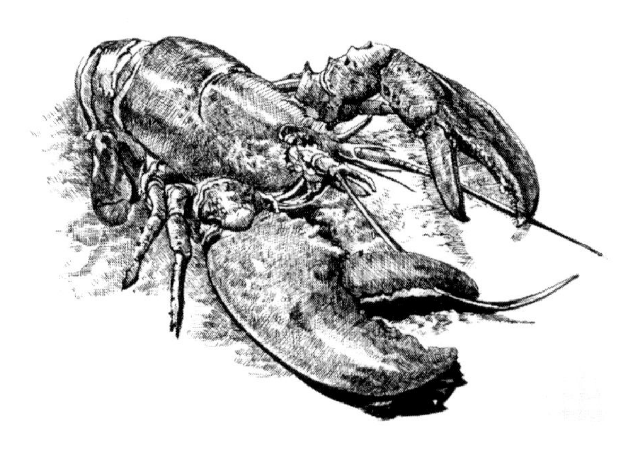

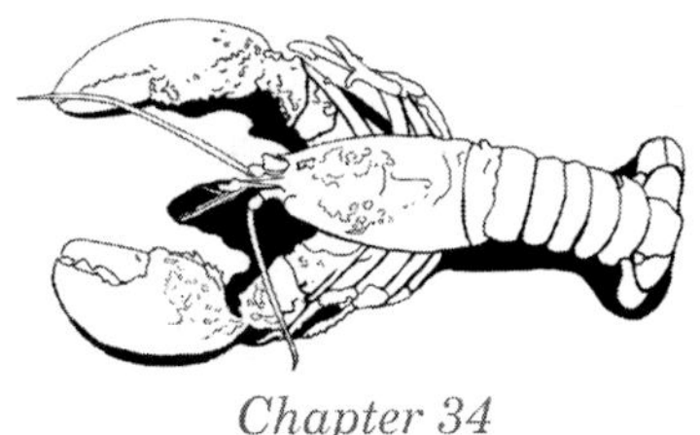

Chapter 34

Lobster Rock

Daniel Thibodeau finally woke up from his lengthy nap, rubbed his eyes, yawned, and looked around. It took him a minute to remember why he was parked next to Blueberry Hill. When he figured it out, he promptly surmised the girls had left. Lyle, with his camera dangling around his neck and his mouth opened ever so slightly, was sound asleep, whistling out of his nose. Daniel removed Lyle's Red Sox cap and whacked him on his head with it.

"Wake up, you idiot!" he barked. "The girls are gone." He started the van, put it into drive and pulled out onto the Park Loop Road. "I sure hope you got some pictures to show Mr. Baxter."

Lyle, slowly coming around, scratched his face and said, "Why do you suppose he wants pictures of those girls blueberry pickin'?"

Daniel hit him again with his hat. "He doesn't pay us to ask why. When Mr. Baxter asks, we just do. Get it?" Lyle nodded. Daniel continued, "Let's go back to the office before we swing by the Baxter estate and see if we can find the girls again. They can't have gotten too far. Besides, we should be in touch with Hannah. You know how angry she gets if we don't check in with her."

* * * *

At the same time the Thibodeau brothers drove back into

town, Ani, Eliza, and Roonie were hot on the trail of Tiny. At the intersection of Main and Firefly Lane, both parties almost collided. Daniel stepped on the brakes suddenly, jerking Lyle so much so that the camera around his neck slammed into the dashboard.

"Watch it!" he bellowed.

"Stupid bikers," yelled Daniel.

Cruising through the intersection, Ani saw the big bug on top of the van. Where had she seen this before, she wondered, but only for a second. She had Tiny and the stone on her mind.

"Hey! It's those girls!" cried Daniel.

"Followed by Spider-Man?" Lyle said.

"This is our lucky day after all, little brother," said Daniel. "Get your camera ready."

"Already on it," replied Lyle, who took a series of rapid-fire pictures, which later showed only the backs of three bikes with tires spinning.

"We won't lose them now," said Daniel, who maneuvered the vehicle down Main Street, but he was shortly stopped by cars, crowds, and concession stands everywhere.

"Oh, no, the pre-—lobster festival festival!" he said. "Lyle, get out and shadow them on foot as best you can."

"What?" Lyle said.

"Out you go. I will find you after I park. Go on, git." He shoved his brother out of the van.

The three kids wove in and out of the street activity on their bikes for a bit farther than the Rest from Your Pests brothers were able to do, but soon realized that the crowds were too great. "It's no good," said Ani as she halted halfway down the street. "Let's lock the bikes up here."

"Good idea," said Roonie. "We'll be quicker on foot. The park is just a block away."

Once the bikes were locked and helmets removed, they tried to move through the mass of pedestrians, strollers, bikers, and merchants. After what seemed like an eternity to Ani, they finally arrived at Tiny's destination, the park. Only this time the park looked more like the inside of the Boston Convention Center and less like a bucolic respite. There were rows and rows of tents with flapping flags and banners advertising items to buy, items to eat, and events to witness. Ani saw spin art, face painting, fried dough, lobster-themed trinkets, and whoopie pies, and this was only right in front of her. The kids could hear band music coming from the gazebo in the center of the park, which was surrounded by onlookers. Normally they would have loved this occasion, but now it only added to their stress as they tried to find Tiny and retrieve the amulet.

"I'm feeling claustrophobic," said Eliza. Roonie giggled.

"You and me both," said Ani. "I think we should split up. Roonie, you go in the center, toward the gazebo and out on the other side. Eliza, you go to the left, the ocean side, and work your way toward Roonie. I'll cover the right." She stood on her tiptoes and tried to look over the crowd. "Eliza, is that a white tent on the other side of the gazebo? Can you see that?"

Eliza stood on her tiptoes, but she too couldn't tell. "Here," she said to Roonie while bending down, "climb up on my shoulders. I'm strong, I can hold you."

Roonie, with Ani's assistance, soon rested solidly on Eliza's shoulders. He surveyed the crowd. Eliza, straining slightly, asked, "Do you see anything?"

"I see the big tent on the other side. It looks like a circus tent. I can see chairs inside. Quick, get me down!" he yelled. "I see Tiny!"

Eliza bent down immediately, causing Roonie to roll off and slam into Lyle, who had his back to him. "Hey, pay attention, you stupid kid," Lyle shouted at Roonie.

"Sorry, sir," a shaken Roonie replied.

Lyle grumbled and walked away, not recognizing that Roonie was with the girls. Lyle bumped into Daniel. "See anything?" Daniel asked, winded from the walk he had to take from the parked van.

"No, just some stupid kid with a Spider-Man T-shirt. He crashed into me by the blueberry pie table. These kids today, I'm telling you."

Daniel grabbed Lyle's hat off his head and hit him again,

this time twice. "Spidey boy is with the girls. Which way?"

* * * *

"He was heading into the big tent," Roonie said to the girls.

"We've got him now," Ani said. They moved past more booths selling lobster-related ware, including lobster claw–shaped ice cream bars and famous freshly squeezed Jordan Pond House lemonade. Eliza was thirsty and looked longingly at the booth but then moved on. They finally arrived at the entrance of the tent and were welcomed by two people dressed in full-size lobster costumes handing out flyers for upcoming events.

"Admission is free, but be sure to come back on Saturday for the fireworks compliments of Baxter Banking and Trust, *Baxter puts the Trust back in Banking,*" cheered the first lobster, handing Roonie a brochure.

"That Baxter guy is everywhere," said Eliza under her breath.

They crossed the threshold and walked past more booths, mostly selling toys. Ani saw a few kids racing each other with their recently purchased jumping lobsters. Squeezing a small pump pushed air through a tube to the lobster, making it jump. She remembered loving the toy when she was younger. Her mother would get the girls one each summer along with a new pair of flip-flops.

"There he is," shouted Eliza, bringing her sister out of her memory. "By the stage."

"I see him!" Roonie said. "He still has the stone in his mouth."

"Tiny," Ani cried. Surprisingly, the dog heard his name despite the noise from the audience and the performers on stage and raised his head and wagged his bushy tail. She called to him again. "Good boy. Stay, stay right there. We don't want to hurt you, buddy, we just want that … "

Tiny responded as if he was being chased again and

whipped around to the right of the stage. The kids bent low and moved among the rows of chairs filled with parents and children. Ani noticed for the first time what was happening on stage. Several clowns with orange hair, red noses, and oversized clown shoes were dancing and singing around a giant lobster pot. A large, costumed lobster clown kept trying to climb out of the pot. Each time the lobster being cooked popped the lid off the top, the crowd of kids would go wild and scream "LOBSTER," alerting the cook clown to pick up the lid and hit the lobster on the head, squishing her back down into the pot. This continued on, loudly, while the kids searched for Tiny. Behind trash cans, under tables, in between rows they looked, but Tiny was nowhere to be found. The kids met at the right side of the stage.

"It doesn't look like they are using that exit point because the flap is down," said Ani, motioning to the back of the big white tent.

"What?" shouted Roonie as the clowns worked the crowd into a frenzy.

"I said," yelled Ani even louder, "I don't think Tiny got past the stage."

"You want us to go on stage?" shouted a confused Roonie.

"We are going on stage?" yelled an excited Eliza.

"You three, finally," said a tall woman with a loud voice dressed as a cowgirl clown. "Where have you been? Jinny has been in that lobster costume for too long. She is about to be cooked from overheating," she said, pushing the threesome up the stairs and onto the corner of the platform. "The band is ready, so just do as we rehearsed. Follow the words on the screen to your left if you can't remember the lyrics." She shoved three red foam lobster hats on their heads and handed Eliza a guitar, Ani a mike, and Roonie a tambourine.

The kids were so befuddled they were oblivious to the audience clapping when the lobster pot clown scene left the stage with the giant lobster "Jinny" finally breaking free and putting the cook clown in the pot to be cooked himself. The floor lights of the stage blinded them and they stood frozen. Cowgirl clown had her own mike. "Next up is a treat: Bar Harbor's own trio of performers singing "Lobster around the Pot" accompanied by Al and his crew from Al's True Value Hardware and bait shop.

"Hit it, Al," the emcee said as she exited the stage. Al's group started playing with gusto while the kids stayed completely still, awestruck. Not surprisingly, they missed their cue to join in the singing.

"Sing, SING, NOW!" demanded Cowgirl. "Follow the screen!" she yelled and pointed excitedly at the karaoke screen scrolling the words to the song. Eliza broke out of her performance stupor and strummed the guitar, as she had had a few lessons last summer at camp, and sang. Roonie next awoke and banged the tambourine a few times on his head to the beat, causing the little kids in the crowd to roar with laughter. Ani couldn't seem to move. It was as if her feet were encased in cement and any motion would cause her legs to break off at the ankles. "Louder!" someone yelled from the audience. "Sing!" another shouted. Ani bounced her knees awkwardly up and down. She did not like to perform, and after heights, being on stage was the next worst and scariest thing imaginable for her. Eliza saw Cowgirl's angry face, so she danced over to her shell-shocked sister. She nodded encouragingly to Ani and faced her toward the screen. Suddenly Tiny appeared on the steps and wagged his tail as if to say to Ani, "You can do it!" Ani bopped her head a few times waiting for her cue to join in, her lobster hat dancing up and down.

Somebody yelled, "That's the way you do it!" Ani smiled and lifted her head up and down more dramatically, her lobster hat flopping more wildly, and the kids cheered her on. Clowns passed out the hats to the audience, compliments of Baxter Banking and Trust, and soon the entire audience was bouncing and singing along. Ani was now on fire from the crowd approval. She sang loudly, jumping and dancing all over the stage. Roonie stuck to his signature move of hitting himself on his lilac-speckled head with his tambourine, not quite following the beat but close, very close. Eliza, too, was in her glory, as she loved to perform. Her camp guitar lessons came back to her like she had played for years, and she sang and strummed away like a pro, sadly unaware that her guitar was not plugged into an amplifier. Tiny, the stone, the girl in the orb, the growing lobsters, none of it mattered for the dedicated trio while they played and sang their hearts out for a clown cowgirl, the crowd, and Al and his band. Ani gave it a big finish with multiple lobster hat head bobs and shakes.

The crowd ate it up and begged for more. Ani couldn't stop bowing, and finally Eliza had to drag her off the stage and shake her out of her fifteen minutes of fame. Just as quickly as Cowgirl had handed out the props, she removed them and scooted them off the stage to usher in the next group of performers. All they had left were their lobster hats.

"Ani? Tiny. Focus in. Remember the stone?" said Eliza, waking Ani from her performance reverie.

"Right, right, Tiny," she said. "He was next to me when I performed."

Roonie yelled from the side of the stage. "There's a side flap here. Do you think he went through?" He pushed on the tent and the flap opened up. The kids exited the tent. Eliza collapsed on the grass, exhausted from the day. Ani's face fell when she realized that Tiny and the stone could be anywhere, anywhere at all.

"Do you want me to climb this tree?" Roonie said, pointing to a large red maple at the edge of the park. "I bet I could see him from there." Roonie felt Ani's disappointment and desperately wanted to help.

"No," sighed Ani, "that's okay. I think we should head back to Blackbeard's Cove."

"I can't do it," Eliza whined. "I'm hungry and tired and besides, we need to see if Dad is meeting us for lunch. You can go back if you want to, but I am heading to Pat's Pizza to wait for Dad."

"Well, fine then, have it that way," Ani said. "We wouldn't be in this mess if you hadn't hit me in the first place. It's your fault we lost the stone."

"Girls," said Roonie.

"Stay out of it," snapped Eliza.

"Just because you're crabby doesn't mean you should yell at Roonie," Ani said. "He's just trying to help!"

"It might have been helpful if you had hung on to the stone tighter when you had it in your hand. Instead of blaming me for what happened, you shouldn't have dropped it. I only tapped your arm!" The girls yelled back and forth, their lobster hats shaking fiercely with each barb thrown. Roonie covered his ears with his hands.

"Ruff." A dog's muffled bark reached them from the tent. The girls stopped arguing. Tiny strutted through the tent flap with the blue sapphire stone tucked firmly in his mouth. "Ruff."

"Tiny," shouted Ani, "we thought we lost you." But she didn't move. Neither did Eliza or Roonie. Any movement could cause Tiny to run, and the three kids were not up for any more chases, not today anyway. Ani knelt slowly to be eye level with Tiny.

In barely a whisper, she said, "You've had your fun, Tiny, and I know that you are tired. You did a good job, boy, a really good job." Tiny stayed perfectly still, his large brown eyes locked into Ani's bright blue ones. "I want to thank you for helping me out on stage. You knew I was afraid to be up there, and just knowing you were there helped me feel better." Tiny wagged his tail back and forth. "Now, I know you just want to give me that stone, and when you do, I promise, I will give you a good scratch and belly rub, just like you love." Tiny cocked his head, listening to Ani's every word, and inched his way toward her outstretched fingers. "That's right, Tiny, come to Ani. There's a good boy. What a good boy."

Tiny moved closer still, his nose within a few inches of Ani's. He panted heavily, and then miraculously, he opened his mouth and let the sapphire roll out onto Ani's palm with stringy saliva stretching from his mouth to the stone.

"Yuck," said Eliza.

"Gross," said Roonie.

"Thank you," said Ani. "Oh, Tiny, I knew you wouldn't let me down. Come here and let me give you a big hug."

Lobster fact: *There are two primary types of lobster found in the United States: the "true" American lobster and the spiny lobster. The American lobster is commonly known as the Maine lobster. Spiny lobsters, also known as rock lobsters, are a family of about forty-five species of crustaceans. Spiny lobsters can be easily distinguished from true lobsters by their very long, thick, spiny antennae and by their complete lack of claws.*

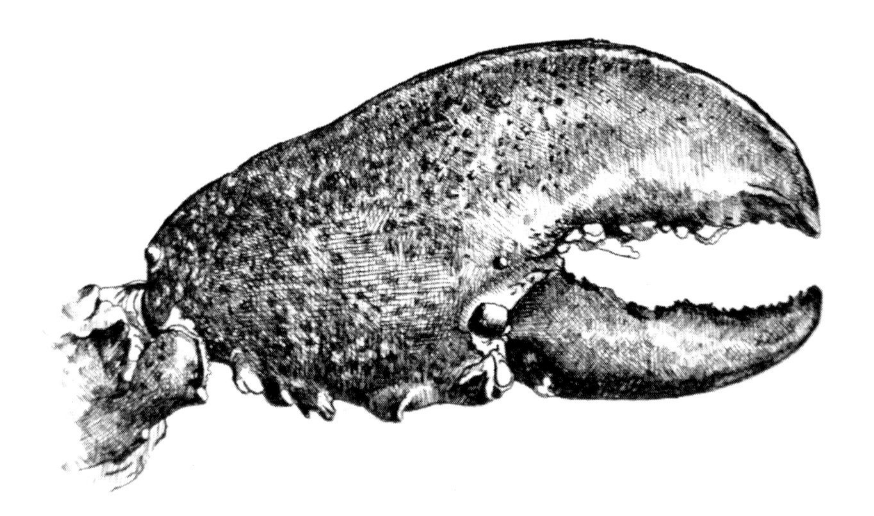

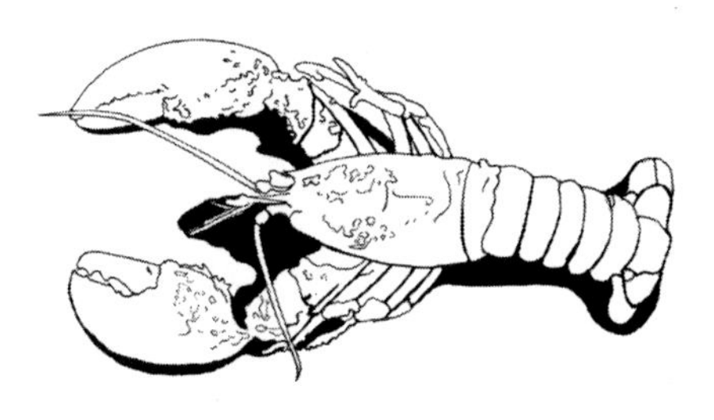

Chapter 35

Oh My, How They Grow

At four in the morning, Captain Andy Gerow had already had his second cup of black coffee. He stood on the dock looking up at the sky, which was just starting to turn a soft pink, as the sun got ready to come up. Andy loved this time in the morning before city folks and tourists overran the harbor. For now, it was just him and the other lobstermen getting ready for what should be a profitable day. Since the lobsters had begun migrating to Mount Desert Island, Andy and his nephew Eli had made a killing. It was only early July, with the lobster festival yet to come, and they had already made double what they made last summer. Andy couldn't believe his good fortune. Now, he thought, his wife, Kimberly, could get the new kitchen she had been clamoring for these past few years. Not bad, Captain Andy, not bad at all. He thought it was ridiculous how everyone was getting so upset about the lobsters. One paper even called it "Lobstergate." He and most of the other lobstermen just wanted to do what they did best: lobstering. Set the traps, collect the lobsters, reset the traps, and sell what you got. Plain and simple, like it was for his father and his father before that.

Where is that boy, he wondered as he checked the time on his watch: four ten. That boy was a lazy son of a gun. If Eli wasn't his sister Jessica's son, he would have thrown his sorry rear end overboard by now. Taking another sip of coffee from his thermos, Andy saw Appleton and Conroy's lobster boats cruise out of the harbor. Looking again for his nephew, he spotted the beat-up silver truck come ripping down the hill, almost as if Eli was driving on two wheels instead of four. Crazy kid, he thought, but at least he was here, well, almost here. Andy climbed on board the *Done Roamin'*, named by his father. The irony of the name did not escape him. A lobsterman was never done. There was always one more trap and one larger lobster to catch. He shrugged as he started up the engine. Lately the lobsters had gotten so big that even Andy was becoming curious—not concerned—but curious as to when big enough was really big enough. Just then Eli jumped on board.

"Sorry, Captain Andy. My alarm didn't go off." His nephew still looked half asleep.

"I think I've heard that one before," Andy said. "Get ready to move."

"Aye, aye, Captain," Eli said and saluted. He untied the thick rope from the side of the dock, shoved off the boat, then jumped and landed safely in the back of the boat. "All clear," he yelled up to Andy.

Andy put the boat into gear and headed out of Northeast Harbor to where the Gerow traps lay two miles due east off the shore of Otter Creek. Two days ago Andy and Eli were amazed at their catch, and Andy was already anticipating what the catch might bring today. Eli joined him up front.

"Last night at Geddy's, Skipper Hall was telling everyone that he heard that down in Pretty Marsh some fella hauled out his trap and the lobster, over two feet in length, was sitting on top of the trap and grabbed hold of his arm with his claw. Skipper said it took two of his crew to pry the thing off of this poor guy. He needed over fifty stitches!"

"How many pints did Skipper have, Eli, is what I want to know."

"He seemed fine to me, Uncle, seriously."

"What about yourself?"

"I was just drinking cokes, Captain; I knew I needed to work today." Eli grinned at his uncle.

"I think both you and Skipper are full of tall tales is what I would say." Andy slowed the boat next to his buoy, orange with a thick white stripe. "Now make yourself useful and pull up that trap, boy."

Eli skillfully caught the buoy in the hook and manually pulled the trap attached underneath. The trap contained several lobsters, again almost double the average in number and size. Andy's smile widened as he helped Eli load the lobsters into the holding tank. Eli replaced the bait and set the trap again before returning it to the ocean water. This process was repeated throughout the morning, Andy driving the boat and Eli doing most of the heavy lifting. They both wanted to move quickly to get back to shore to be the first to offer their catch to the fancy restaurants and wholesale distributors. A few hours passed before Eli thought their tank could hold no more.

"If this continues," he said to his uncle, "you might want to think about buying another holding tank. Skipper Hall said he just ordered two more. A decent price, too."

"Sounds like you and Skipper Hall are right tight now. Thanks for the advice, but I already bought one. You'll need to pick it up from Belcher's later on this afternoon, smarty-pants. Last I checked I'm still the captain of this boat, now, ain't that right?"

"I'll just get back to the traps," Eli said. He methodically hooked the next buoy at the end of the line of Andy's territory as Andy slowed the boat to a stop. Recently the men had moved some of their traps farther away from the shore, just on the edge of their lobstering area. Captain Andy figured that since the lobsters caught closer to shore were getting bigger, it only made sense that the farther out the traps were, the bigger the lobsters would be. So far, he had been right. The last few hauls had indeed been larger. Eli reached for the rope and was surprised by how heavy the load felt. He braced his feet firmly on the edge of the boat and strained with all his might to get the trap up from below.

"Uncle Andy," he yelled, "I'm going to need some help here." Andy put the throttle in neutral and joined his nephew.

"What seems to be the trouble here?" he said, grinning. "Muscles getting tired?"

"No, my muscles are not getting tired. It's just stuck or

something."

"Take the wheel." Andy walked back to the side of the boat and called over his shoulder to his nephew, "Put the boat in low gear and reverse slowly. We'll try to pull the trap loose. It may be some kind of sea junk or trash. Remember last summer when we lost that entire row of traps all on account of some joker deciding to throw his deck chair overboard? Tourists," he said with distain. "Bunch of idiots."

Eli switched the boat into reverse while Andy seized hold of the rope. Eli had youth on his side, but Andy's lifetime of lobstering had made him incredibly strong, and with considerable effort he was able to lift the trap up.

What happened next would go down in the history books for sure, if history books were written by lobstermen, but since that is usually not the case, it would become one of the stories told frequently around the local bars and restaurants, down by the docks and lobster pounds, and among town officials. Eli was sent into such shock by what he witnessed that he hadn't yet been able to get out of BMHI, the Bangor Mental Health Institute. All he could do, when he managed to get back to the dock, was repeat the phrase "Andy gone, lobster took him, Andy gone, lobster took him," to anyone who would listen.

Some wanted to press charges against Eli, but others who knew the pair well knew that Eli Pelletier would never, not in a million years, ever do anything to harm his beloved uncle, Captain Andy Gerow of the *Done Roamin'*. And indeed, Captain Andy was in fact done roaming, God rest his soul.

Lobster fact: *Most lobstermen start taking up their traps for the winter in mid-December, with a goal of having them up by the New Year. Of course, the end of the fishing season is largely driven by how bad the weather is and how good the fishing is. Lobstermen typically start fishing again in April.*

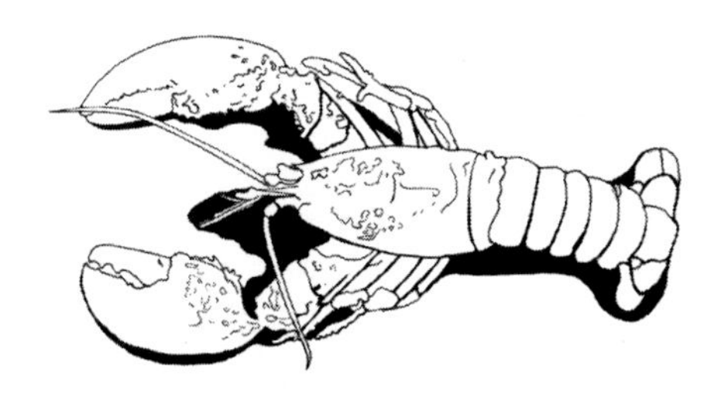

Chapter 36

Thunder Hole

"Where do you think Roonie is?" asked Ani as she craned her head around the booth in the restaurant and looked toward the front door.

"He'll come soon, Ani," Eliza said with her mouth full of blueberry pancakes. "Are you going to finish your bacon?" She jabbed her fork at a piece on Ani's plate. "Roonie was right. These are the best blueberry pancakes in the world!" She slurped her orange juice loudly.

"I wish I had room to finish this," Ani said and pushed her plate away. "The waitress wasn't kidding when she said a single cake was huge. I'm stuffed."

The front door jangled and opened as another customer came into the restaurant famous for its blueberry pancakes and muffins. The wait to get a table had been so long that Ani had had a chance to stop back at Debbah's Gifts while Eliza held a spot in line. Ani had wanted to buy something to keep the amulets in. After the blanket incident, she worried that it wasn't safe to let the treasures out of her sight. She had read that Native Americans often kept amulets in a pouch worn around the neck and had chosen to follow suit. When she had displayed her purchase, Eliza had complained that the brown bundle on a thin leather strap was not the kind of fashion statement she would have made, but Ani wanted to be authentic, and besides, she wasn't planning on traipsing down a catwalk anytime soon.

"Not him," said Ani, checking the entryway. Lyle and

Daniel, the proprietors of Rest from Your Pests, had entered the establishment and eased themselves onto two of the red leather–covered stools that lined the long counter. Lyle spun around a few times like a school boy until Daniel stopped him in mid twirl.

"Just a couple of old men." Ani frowned.

"He'll come. He has nothing else to do," said Eliza.

"It's just that he said something about the tide, and I'm worried we might miss it and not be able to search for the amulet," Ani said.

Eliza finished her orange juice and let out a huge burp. "Sorry." She laughed.

Ani leafed through her note cards hoping beyond hope that by staring at them continually the clue would become clearer and she would feel confident about two things: the first was that they were in fact searching for green tourmaline, a gem found intertwined with quartz, both of which were indigenous to Maine, especially along the coast. After translating the drawing from her book, which was a rudimentary depiction of what Ani thought was a prism with short lines that looked like grass underneath it, Ani concluded that the combination must represent green tourmaline. She had been lucky to find an old book in the garden cottage entitled *Stones, Gems, and Other Jewels of Mid-Coast Maine*, copyright 1935. She learned that green tourmaline was thought to have a strong healing capability. The author, Julie A. Whittemore, had highlighted that the stone was also helpful for healing the earth and aiding the natural kingdom. The more she thought about this, the more she felt it made sense. Obviously Mount Desert Island could use a little earth healing right now, and so she decided, or rather felt, yes felt deep in her heart, that green must be the type of tourmaline they were seeking. And second, Roonie had said they didn't need to do any steep climbing to get to the Thunder Hole area even though they had to climb past Otter Cliff.

The door sounded again. Ani looked out from the booth as Eliza was too busy eating her bacon. Ani whipped her head back and scrunched down in her seat. "Who is it?" whispered

Eliza, registering the concern on her sister's face.

"It's Patrick O'Leary."

"The creepy gardener?"

Ani nodded.

"What's he doing here?" demanded Eliza.

Ani peeked her head out again and whispered, "He's sitting at the counter, probably ordering breakfast." Patrick acknowledged Ani. She responded with a fake smile and ducked back into the booth.

"Oh, no, he just saw me."

"So what," said Eliza. "We are allowed to eat breakfast, and obviously everyone else likes the pancakes here, too." She poured more maple syrup on her pancakes.

Once again, the door jangled. "You look," said Ani.

Eliza popped her head out of the booth and then glanced back at her sister. "You're not going to believe this."

"What? Roonie?"

"No. Professor Sol," she whispered. "And he looks bad."

The professor was talking to a waitress behind the cash register. Ani noticed his hair seemed to be standing up sharper than she remembered from their meeting a few days ago. His clothing also appeared disheveled. His khaki pants were wrinkled, which gave the impression that he had slept in them. His white oxford shirt was partially untucked and buttoned incorrectly, judging by how it hung askew in the front. His movements were jerky, awkward, and uncontrolled. Ani observed him as he approached the take-out counter and then watched him back away a few steps. He repeated this sequence a few times, moving forward and back, as bewildered by what was happening as the waitress, who sighed and looked annoyed.

"You're right, Eliza. He doesn't look well. I wonder what's going on."

The door rattled for the fourth time. "I'm afraid to look," Ani said, but peeked anyway. "It's Roonie! Finally."

Roonie walked down the center of the restaurant, dressed in his usual Spider-Man T-shirt. The girls heard the cooks and waitresses behind the counter shout out as he passed by, "Hey,

Spider boy. How's it going?" and "Roonie, two flapjacks coming right up."

"Hello Max, Sally, Ethan," he said. "I'm starving this morning so flip me an extra cake please."

Ethan, the head cook and co-owner of Jordan's Restaurant of Bar Harbor, grinned. "Nothing but the finest cakes for you, Spidey boy."

Roonie returned the grin and joined the girls in the booth. Ani slid over and Roonie sat down next to her. She was always amazed by how he seemed to know everyone, and she meant everyone, on the island. She felt proud to know him and grateful, too. She and Eliza would never have come this far on their quest if Roonie hadn't been around to help them.

"You were right, Roonie," said Eliza.

"I was?" Roonie said.

"These pancakes are amazing," Eliza said as she put the last bit into her mouth.

"What did you think?" Roonie asked Ani. "Did you like them, too?"

Ani rubbed her stomach. "I'm stuffed, but I would like to come back tomorrow."

Roonie's pancakes arrived, and he spread an enormous amount of butter on them and then nearly a gallon of maple syrup. Ani was impressed by how quickly Roonie finished all three pancakes and two glasses of chocolate milk.

"Click, click, click." The noise of a camera taking a series of pictures got their attention.

"Why is that guy at the counter taking pictures?" Eliza said. "Is he taking them of us?"

"Why would he?" asked Ani, who stared back at the tall man with the camera around his neck. Ani noticed his friend laughing and pushing him back down on his stool.

She overheard him say loudly, "My brother's first day with his new camera, ha, ha, ha. Still trying to figure out what buttons are for what. Now I told you, Lyle," he continued as he directed his comments toward his brother, "that button is for the flash, the one you pushed takes the pictures." Daniel forced another awkward chuckle. The restaurant patrons and employees stopped doing what they were doing to stare curiously at the two men at the counter, but soon lost interest and returned to their own business.

Ani saw Patrick frown behind his coffee cup. Something didn't seem right here, but perhaps it was just her overactive imagination. She also noticed that Professor Sol had left; he too seemed off today. This lobster business must be affecting everyone. She shrugged. "Roonie, do you know those men?"

"Nope," he said.

"It really looked like they were taking our picture," Eliza said, "which is strange and well, unsettling."

"Maybe you're right," said Ani as the door to the restaurant shut again.

Roonie popped up to look and said, "Well, they've left, so let's talk about our plan for Thunder Hole."

They all leaned forward as Roonie pulled out a small booklet containing trail maps of Acadia. They agreed to bike through the national park and leave their bikes at Otter Cliff and then climb over the rocks to Thunder Hole. Roonie said the park rangers wouldn't allow them to enter the Thunder Hole rock formation from the normal viewing platform for safety reasons. Ani looked uneasy.

Roonie saw this and said, "No real heights, Ani, just an easy climb." Ani had read about Thunder Hole and how when the right size wave rolls into the naturally formed inlet, a deep sound like thunder occurs because of the air and water entering the small cavern just beneath the surface. Sometimes water can splash up to 40 feet high from Thunder Hole. Roonie looked at his watch, which not surprisingly had a Spider-Man face. "It's ten, time to move."

Moments later the three rode their bikes to Acadia National Park. Ani was in the rear with Rooney leading and Eliza behind him. Ani had felt apprehensive about their adventure since she woke up that morning and wondered if this feeling meant that they were not following the book correctly. She didn't like hearing Roonie tell her they would have to get past the park rangers, as Ani liked to follow the rules. Her parents had taught the girls to respect authority, be safe, and always obey the park rangers. Yet somehow the girl in the globe and the other happenings here in Maine were definitely not normal, so bending the rules should be the least of her worries. I will just feel better when we have this next amulet secure along with the silver sand dollar and the blue sapphire, she thought, fingering her new pouch.

Ani heard the crashing waves and felt the sea mist on her face before she even saw the deep blue of the Atlantic Ocean. She was in awe of all that lay before her. No wonder the Abenaki people referred to Acadia as *Spem ki Minahan*, Heaven's Island.

Roonie steered his bike over to the side of the road and the girls did the same. All three of them dragged their bikes over the stone boulders that edged the Park Loop, locking them to a stand of birch trees.

Roonie checked his watch again. "Ten thirty. We are about ten minutes from Thunder Hole, and then we will have about forty minutes to find the amulet and get out to beat the tide."

"I hope that's enough time," Ani said.

"It's going to have to be because you can't stop time and tides," Roonie said. Both girls gave him a funny look. "Well, that's what my grandma always says." He shrugged and climbed back to the road. "This way to Thunder Hole."

Roonie led Ani and Eliza to the other side of the road where they found a narrow stone-covered path to Otter Cliff. Roonie said they could climb down the cliff and reach Thunder Hole from the south side. From there they could get to a small beach that could only be reached when the tide was just right. When the tide was coming in, Thunder Hole was awash in seawater slamming into the carved-out rock formation famous for its thunderous sound. Ani had read that Acadia's landscape was the product of thousands of years of glacial ice melting and retreating, exposing the granite that existed today. The combination of crystal quartz and pink feldspar gave the granite a warm pink color. Tidal pools filled with sea water, seaweed, and other sea life were scattered about as the trio hopped from rock to rock, winding their way down toward their destination.

They crossed over the last formation of rocks close to the edge. Ani stared out to sea as the waves slammed into the cliff. The water churned white while it swirled over, around, and between the jagged rock walls. She felt a flutter in her stomach, which she experienced only when she was scared. Right now this adventure was scaring her. Roonie tapped her on the shoulder and motioned for the girls to follow him. He walked to the right and slipped behind a large boulder, disappearing out of sight. Eliza reached the boulder first and said to Ani, "Maybe it would make sense if I, well, just sort of stay up here. This looks tricky."

"I think we should stick together, Liza. That way we can have three people looking for the amulet and be more likely to find it sooner."

"Yeah, I guess that makes sense," a reluctant Eliza said.

Roonie's voice floated up from below. "Let's go. We're wasting precious time." Eliza began the descent while Ani peered around to see if any park rangers with their green hats and brown shirts were in the vicinity. She was relieved to see only a family skipping along the rocks about fifteen yards away. Satisfied that no one was noticing them, Ani climbed down.

* * * *

Lyle removed his lens cap just in time to take a couple of quick shots of Ani as she disappeared beneath the rock slab. Daniel had lost sight of them shortly after they left Jordan's because he couldn't follow too closely without backing up traffic all along the Park Loop. He finally spotted the bikes locked to the birch trees he and Lyle now squatted behind.

"Darn it!" he shouted, slamming his hand on his brother's back. "Did you get anything?"

"Just the younger girl's head and then she disappeared."

Daniel hit Lyle on the head with his cap. "She didn't disappear. She just climbed out of sight, you idiot."

"I know that," said Lyle, "and stop hitting me."

Daniel frowned. "Come on, we need to get closer. We have to meet with Mr. Baxter later today, and I'm afraid we haven't got much to give him. Darn it all," he said again. They lumbered out from behind the trees and crossed over the Park Loop Road to Otter Cliff. "Now where do you suppose those crazy kids are going? There isn't anywhere to go except in the hole. No one is that dumb to go in there, even when the tide is out," said Daniel.

"Dunno," Lyle mumbled.

The two trudged down the same path that Ani, Eliza, and Roonie had taken. When they reached the edge of the cliff and looked over the side, all they could see was the vast Atlantic and farther out, away from the cliffs, the Porcupine Islands, which got their name from the Abenaki Indians who felt their shape resembled the dangerous quills of the porcupine. What the brothers failed to see was the small beach tucked underneath the cliff and known to only a few people who would dare to venture so close to Thunder Hole. The roar of the ocean waves, which would drown out any cries for help, also served to keep the brothers from hearing the conversation between the three children intent on finding another amulet to add to their collection.

Lyle took a few pictures of the islands because at that particular moment he was struck by their size and beauty and by the way the light hit the top of the pine trees, making their branches look emerald green whereas the rest of the trees, those in the shadow, appeared dark forest green or even black. Remarkable, he thought, clicking away and truly enjoying the sound of the whir of his camera. He was so caught up in his beautiful thoughts, thoughts he had never thought before, that he was unaware that his brother was staring at him angrily.

"Lyle!" Daniel barked. "What are you doing? We are not sightseeing here, lest you forget *why* we are here. Let's go back to the van. Perhaps they headed over to Sand Beach, and we can catch them there." Lyle, caught up in the magnificence of the scene, snatched a few more shots before obeying his increasingly ornery brother.

* * * *

Ani was surprised that once she climbed down a few yards and was behind the granite rock the wind diminished. She could hear the waves, albeit from a distance as the tide was out, along with the occasional blast of a foghorn, yet she was struck by the stillness of it all. Roonie had informed the girls that the beach was notorious for pottery shards, sea glass, and Maine tourmaline. Ani made the final leap from the side of the rock and landed with a thud in the wet sand. She looked at her older sister and a smile broke out on her face.

"What's so funny?" Eliza asked.

"It's just your hair." Eliza reached up to touch her hair and Roonie giggled. "It's just so frizzy. You look like you have a big curly wig on."

"Ani, not funny! I hate this misty, humid air. It ruins my flat iron process."

"Girls, girls," soothed Roonie. "My watch says ten-forty, which means we have approximately forty minutes to find this stone and climb back up to the top. You all can discuss hair styles when we are finished."

"Roonie's right. Sorry, Liza. Let's search." Ani, impressed by Roonie's ability to stay on task, reviewed her cards. "From what I learned, the stone might be imbedded on the side of the rock, but likely entwined with the rose quartz or maybe pink tourmaline."

"Oh, the stones are friends. I like that," Eliza said. Roonie shook his head at her in disbelief.

"I will take the edge here where the sand meets the rocks, and if it is all right with you, Eliza," Ani asked, remembering that Eliza responded badly when she was told what to do, "you can work on the right side and Roonie can take the left." All three began in earnest to search for a green prism, a stone that they believed represented healing, among other things, a stone that might be part of the collection of amulets they were gathering, and a stone that, unfortunately, might not even be what they were looking for or be in the location where they were looking. Time passed, and as happens most summer mornings in Acadia, the sun burned off the mist, and the temperature rose. Ani felt the warmth even this close to the water. As she parted more sand with a small pick that she had brought with her and felt around for anything that felt like something, something that might be what they were seeking, she could hear the roar of the waves crashing in and out of the main part of Thunder Hole. It sounded louder to her now than it did even a few moments ago. Ani walked over to Roonie, who was also digging with determination. "What time is it now, Roonie?"

Distractedly he looked at his watch. "Only ten fifty-five. We still have twenty-five minutes left before we have to go."

"Thanks," Ani said and resumed her digging. She sensed they had been there longer than fifteen minutes, but given the stress of what they were doing and the noise of the threatening ocean waves, her judgment might be off.

Eliza hacked in front of her, causing a jumble of rocks to dislodge and spill down the side to land at her feet. "This could be something," she said. "I just know it!" They all sifted through the remains of the small landslide. Something shiny momentarily caught Eliza's eye and she grabbed the stone. "Oh," she shouted. "Oh, oh." She flipped the stone over. "Oh," she now said flatly. "Just mica, no tourmaline."

Ani retreated to her area disappointed. Maybe they should pack up early to figure out where else to look. Perhaps Roonie's grandmother might be helpful or even Professor Sol. She was lost in her thoughts, so much so that she was oblivious to how the thundering of Thunder Hole was getting louder.

Eliza was frustrated that her discovery wasn't what they were looking for. She was also curious about the time and yelled to Roonie, "Hey Spidey boy, what time is it? The beach looks smaller to me. Don't we need to leave soon?"

Once again Roonie stopped what he was doing and checked his watch. "Ten fifty-five" he said. We've still got time." Eliza shrugged, stretched, and struck out again on the rock in front of her.

Ani put down her pick and swept an area of sand with both hands. "Boom!" She jumped from the explosion of the wave slamming into the rock right next to them. She let out a small squeal. "Roonie, what time is it?" she asked urgently, as she observed a small wave coming close to them on a piece of beach that definitely was bigger by a fair margin a few minutes ago.

Roonie also noticed the wave and a flash of panic crossed his face while he consulted the time. "Ten fifty-five," he answered and relaxed.

Ani and Eliza looked equally puzzled. Eliza said, "You told me ten fifty-five what had to have been at least fifteen minutes ago!"

"You told me ten fifty-five when I asked you earlier," Ani said.

Roonie's face went white and he looked at his prized Spider-Man watch. "Still ten fifty-five," he said almost in a whisper.

"Oh, Roonie, your watch is broken!" both girls shouted.

"BOOM! HISS! BOOM!" Thunder Hole thundered louder and spray flew up over the side and covered them as they scrambled up the cliff in front of them. The spray made the rock slippery. Eliza and Roonie fell back to what remained of the ground, now only about twelve inches wide.

Ani climbed higher, but eventually she too slipped and dropped back to the beach. One foot landed on the sand and the other in cold Atlantic water.

"Ani," cried Eliza, "look out!" Ani turned around to face a huge wave headed right for them.

"Hold your breath!" she screamed as the wave's full force caught all three and shook them free from their solid footing. They each popped up at the same time, out of breath and shocked by the frigid water and their dangerous predicament.

"I'm sorry," said Roonie, "really really sorry." Another wave swelled in the distance.

"Duck!" shouted Ani. For a moment the kids disappeared under the froth of the swirling surf.

"Help!" yelled Eliza, who was caught by the current and dragged a few feet from Roonie. He responded quickly, pulling out his spidey net and throwing it in Eliza's direction just like he had thrown it at Mr. Baxter.

"Grab the rope, Eliza," screamed Ani. "The rope!" Eliza obeyed and Roonie pulled her toward him.

"Ani," cried Eliza, "what do we do?"

"I don't know, I don't know," Ani said as they treaded water and looked for the next wave to hit. The ocean appeared momentarily calm.

"As the hole fills up with water, can't we just float up?" Eliza asked.

"No," said Roonie. "The power of the waves can be a gusher and then a crusher, crushing us against the cliff."

"That's not what I wanted to hear, especially not with rhyming. We haven't got much time before the next wave comes. Ani, ask for help," Eliza demanded.

"What?"

"Yeah, that's right," said Roonie. "Ask the animals, ask them quickly!" Another wave rolled into them.

"Hang on to each other," shouted Ani. They grabbed each other and plunged down. Ani asked for help like she had never asked for anything before in her life. Please, please, please, animals, help me, help us, help me find a way out of here. Please, please, please. Ani felt the tug of Roonie's arm above her and the pull of the current below her. Please help, please help, please help, she begged. She rose up and out of the water gasping for air. She was relieved to see that Roonie and Eliza had also broken the surface. Ani's gratitude was quickly replaced by dread as she scanned the horizon for the next wave.

Luckily there was another lull, and the ocean looked peaceful. Ani heard a few gulls squawking above, but she couldn't be distracted even for a moment. What to do? What to do? Suddenly, there was a splash and a large cormorant rose out of the water. His orange bill and brownish black feathers marked him as a double-crested cormorant. He stared at them and then popped down again. Ani could see the ocean swelling in the distance. The bird resurfaced, then dove down, then up and then down. He floated in front of them for a few beats, twisted his black neck toward the growing wave, turned back to the trio, and dramatically dove below the surface.

Ani felt it with the cormorant's final dive. She just knew it or thought she did. But what was the alternative? She had no time to explain to Eliza and Roonie, as the wave was coming in fast. She screamed to be heard above the sound of the roaring ocean. "On my count, take a deep breath and follow me, follow the cormorant!"

Roonie's eyes grew big with fear. Eliza started to open her mouth, but closed it hastily and stared at her sister. Ani counted, "One, two, three!" All three of them dove down, down into the cold Atlantic, down into what they hoped was some kind of a refuge from the fate that surely awaited them if they remained above in the swirling, churning tide coming in for its daily clash with the steadfast rock, the only object to meet the waves with defiance and determination all these years.

Ani spied the single-minded cormorant a few feet in front of her, and she swam with all the force she could muster, unable to check whether Eliza and Roonie were behind her for fear she might lose sight of the bird. Her body was so numb now that all she really knew was that she was cold, scared, and following a cormorant to wherever. A sliver of doubt entered her mind. What if this was just a cormorant out for a swim and not here to help us? What if I made a wrong decision in listening to my voice and this dive, this swim into the cold, dark waters, turned out to be a wild goose chase and we should have stayed and tried to climb up again?

Air, I need air, her lungs screamed. Ani slowed down and the distance between her and the cormorant widened. Cold, it is just so cold, she thought. Maybe we should turn back, she wondered. She could barely make out the cormorant, and she started to panic until she felt a warm current move past her frozen body. This woke her up, and she kicked a little harder. More and more warm water passed over her, and the color shifted from a dark blue to a clearer and lighter hue. She was gaining on the bird, who was just a stroke away, and then it vanished. Ani hoped that this meant only one thing and gave a final push, the final push she had before her lungs would surely explode. Then she was up and out of the water. Her mouth opened automatically and her lungs filled up with air, glorious, glorious air.

She didn't look to see where she had landed, where the cormorant brought her. She dove down again to look for Eliza and Roonie. She spotted Eliza first and pulled on her sister's shirt to help her reach the surface and breathe. Eliza, always dramatic, exploded up and out of the water and took a huge breath. She landed on the edge of an underwater grotto. "Roonie, I lost him," she managed to gasp.

Immediately, Ani plunged into the water to look for their friend. She swam deeper toward where she thought they came from and felt the water grow chillier. She saw a mass of seaweed before her and hesitated. But wait, wait, that's not seaweed, it's white, it's white rope! Spidey's web! Determinedly she kicked and lunged toward the rope and grasped it. She pulled with all her might, and the mass began to move toward her. She was relieved to see that Roonie was attached to the web, but she was worried that he wasn't kicking. I've got to get him out of the water, she thought. After what seemed an eternity, she broke through the water and yelled, "Eliza! Help me. Help me get him out of the water!" Eliza grasped Roonie's shirt, and together they hoisted him up onto solid ground.

"Roonie," Eliza cried, "Roonie, oh no, Roonie."

Ani rolled Roonie to one side. His face was gray and his normally alert brown eyes were closed. She whacked him a few times on his back and yelled, "Roonie. Come on, Roonie. Breathe. Breathe now." Then she whacked him again hard between his shoulder blades. Water sprayed out of his mouth, and he coughed loudly, sputtering and gasping for air.

"Roonie!" both girls cried, relieved to see that he was alive. He reached up and strained at the rope, his own spidey web that entangled him. The more he pulled the tighter it wrapped around him.

"Help, help me, I'm being attacked by a giant squid," he bellowed.

Ani shook his shoulder. "Roonie, you're all right." She lifted the web over his head. "It's not a squid, it's just your web."

"You're fine, Roonie," said Eliza. "Amazingly," she said while looking around her, "we are all fine." Once Roonie stopped struggling, the girls were able to remove the spidey rope. Roonie sat up and the girls were comforted to see his color return to its normal pink shade. "Where do you think we are?" asked Eliza.

The floor of the grotto was covered with shells, pottery shards, and twinkling sea glass. Blue, white, yellow, brown, purple, green, all different shades littered the ground. Light surprisingly filled the area, coming from an unknown source.

"I scooch down and look around and find some pottery, hey!" Eliza sang a familiar little ditty that she and Ani had made up when they were younger and looking for ocean treasures on Cape Cod.

"Too bad we aren't looking for sea glass or pottery shards," said Ani.

Roonie coughed and shakily got to his feet. "My grandfather used to speak about this, but I thought he was just telling a tall tale. He believed that there are underground tunnels that run all through the island. This must be one of them."

"Well, thankfully the cormorant showed us the way," Ani said. "I asked and the cormorant appeared, just like you said, Eliza."

"Now that we're here," Eliza said, "how are we going to get out?"

"We can't go back the way we came," Ani said, looking at the deep water. "The tide is still coming in and that way is not an option. I can hear Thunder Hole, and since it sounds ominous down here, I can only imagine what it is like up above."

Roonie shuddered thinking about what their fate might have been had the brave little cormorant not appeared to rescue the group. Now that he was regaining his strength, he stood up and started moving around. "There has to be a way out of here, based upon what I've heard from my relatives over the years. Let's head away from the roar of the surf."

Another cormorant broke the surface of the water, the splash startling them all.

"Oh my," Eliza cried.

"Hello there," Ani said.

"W-A-T," Eliza said and smiled.

The cormorant regally rose out of the water. This bird was grander than the first, larger in size and with a white throat, a great cormorant rather than a double-crested. Ani watched him shake his body and stretch out his wings to dry them, surveying the area coolly. Once satisfied by what he saw, he joined the other cormorant. Eliza whispered, "Ani, go ahead, go on and ask where the tourmaline is. Use the Abenaki word. Perhaps they will understand Indian better than English." Ani looked at Roonie, who shrugged his shoulders as if to say, why not?

Ani bent down and in her most humble manner asked, "Do you know where the amulet is?" The birds stayed motionless, almost as if they were asleep.

"In Abenaki," urged Eliza.

Ani began again, "I mean, that is, do you know where *skeemitoro* is located?" trying her best to pronounce what is basically unpronounceable to anyone who speaks only English. The smaller of the two birds bowed his head in deference to the larger cormorant. "Please," Ani said, "we would be extremely grateful for your time and your help. *Skeemitoro*, please, just the *skeemitoro*." The trio waited in silence. The boom from Thunder Hole and the intermittent drip of water down the walls of the grotto were the only discernible sounds.

The cormorant opened his bill and squawked loudly. Roonie and Eliza flinched, but Ani remained still. Next, he lifted his wings and flapped a few times, for theatrical effect, as Eliza would argue later when they rehashed the day over ice cream cones at CJ's Big Dipper. Then he strutted to the corner of the grotto. With his rear to them, the cormorant tapped a small circle on the wall that had gone undetected by Ani when she first scanned her whereabouts. Once, twice, thrice, and the circle grew larger. The noise of stone moving on stone made clear that something exciting was happening. Ani felt the hairs on her arms stand up and her breathing and heart rate quicken.

"OMG," whispered Eliza.

"You can say that again," said Roonie.

"Shush," Ani said, putting her index finger to her lips. The shifting stopped and left an opening in the wall, wide enough for Ani to squeeze through. The great cormorant and his companion flew in the hole. "I'll be right back," Ani said, climbing after the birds before Eliza and Roonie could do or say anything. "Oh, ah, oh," Ani's voice echoed from the hole.

"What's happening? What do you see?" cried Eliza who tried to follow, but Ani's back blocked the entrance.

Roonie, right beside her, asked, "Is it in there? Is there any treasure? What's going on, Ani?"

Ani thrust a small green prism through the opening. "This has got to be it! I just know it is," she said flopping out of the hole and sliding to the ground in front of Eliza and Roonie. "Take a look. It's beautiful in there!"

Eliza got to the opening first, but was pushed back by the large cormorant, which squawked and prodded her away. Eliza toppled backward and the cormorant leapt on top of her, followed by the smaller cormorant. "Hey," she cried and sat up in time to see the hole shrink and the wall close up.

"I guess they only wanted Ani to see," said Roonie.

Ani held the object up and twirled the stone, causing light to shimmer over the grotto. "Light!" she squealed. "If there is light in the cave, then there has to be a light source and a way out of here!" And with that declaration, the cormorants dove out of sight.

"Hey," Eliza said. "You can tell us what was in that room later. Let's get out of here. It's creepy now that the birds are gone."

"Is *creepy* the only word you know to describe something strange?" asked Roonie.

"Well, *creepy* is just so creepy and perfect. And everything has been creepy since we got here," Eliza said.

"Thank you," Ani called after the birds. "Thank you for helping, you wonderful, beautiful, useful birds." She placed the green tourmaline into the pouch with the other amulets she now wore around her neck. Roonie took the lead, since he was the only one who had ever heard of these tunnels and caves. Ani felt elated that she had found the third amulet. Two more to go, she thought. Two more and then what? She had no idea, but for now she was pushing that thought out of her mind. She needed to concentrate on getting out of here and getting back to the parchment for amulet number four, which might prove to be the trickiest of them all. After some time, Roonie stopped abruptly.

He gave the girls a jack-o-lantern grin. "I am so smart," he said. "So smart that I remembered the song my grandfather used to sing to me when I was helping with his traps on the dock." He crooned,

"Tide and time remain still,
When down below, below the hill.
Tunnels carved and caves were formed
For passage to hide from mighty storms
Tide and time will remain still
When down below, below the hill."

Both girls look perplexed. "You just follow the tunnel up and above instead of down and below and soon," he said, pointing at roughly carved-out stones that could be used as steps, "ta da!" He sang his grandfather's song again as he climbed away from the girls. Much like they started their adventure, Eliza followed Roonie, and Ani, giving the tunnel one more look, ascended the steps behind her sister.

Lobster fact: *Great cormorants are found mainly in salt water, while double-crested cormorants are found in any open water inhabited by fish.*

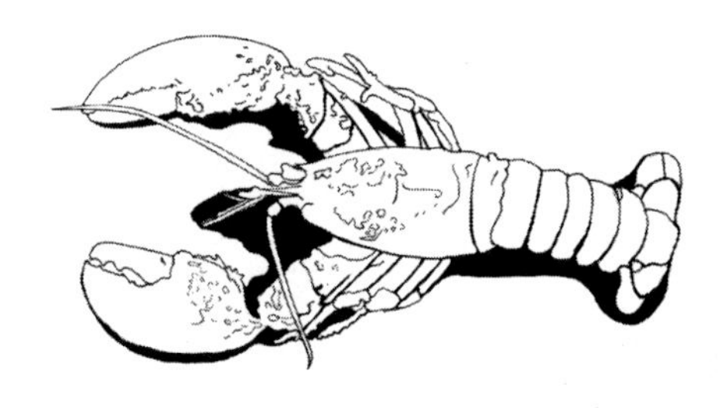

Chapter 37

A Missed Photo-tunity

Lyle and Daniel pulled into a space right in front of the famous Bar Harbor Inn, another acquisition of the Baxter estate. Barton's father purchased the original building after his marriage to Eloise Dyer in 1938. The cedar-shingled hotel was built in 1887 and served as a social club for wealthy New Yorkers. It was sold to the Maine Central Railroad in 1922 and eventually became a hotel. Daniel parked their vehicle and both climbed out of the van. Lyle had a manila folder tucked tightly under his right arm.

"You got the pictures?" asked Daniel.

"Yup," replied Lyle.

"You looked at them already, right?"

Lyle nodded.

"You're sure about this?"

"Sure as the shore is sure," Lyle said, amused by his play on words.

"This is not the time for your silly alliterations. Mr. Baxter is paying us a hefty sum of money, which I should not have to remind you we need. Especially after Mrs. Coleman decided to quit without even so much as a good-bye. She always threatened to up and leave, but I never thought she would actually follow through with it. We have to hire someone else soon, and this new person is probably going to want a bigger salary. Mrs. Coleman hadn't asked for a raise for years."

"What's up with that?" asked Lyle.

"What's up with what?" demanded Daniel.

"Not asking for a raise. Why do you suppose she didn't ask for a raise?"

"What are you running on about Mrs. Coleman and her not asking us for a raise when I already told you we need to focus on Mr. Baxter?"

"Well, you started it," Lyle said.

"I did not!" an exasperated Daniel shouted. "You started it with your silly sure, by the shore, and sure talk. So just stop it."

"Surely." Lyle smiled and ducked his head, anticipating a whack from his brother's hat.

Lyle and Daniel were about to enter the grand foyer when a frantic bellman, who had seen the Rest from Your Pests vehicle parked prominently in front of the hotel, bug and all, met the brothers with his gloved hands outstretched, signaling stop. Once he had their attention, he demanded they get back into their van and park behind the building with the other service vehicles. Lyle and Daniel lumbered back to the van, climbed into the front seat, and chuckled to themselves.

"Gets them every time," Daniel said with a grin.

"Yup," said Lyle.

Once parked in the back, they took the service elevator up to the second floor. Sorenson had instructed them to meet Barton in the Dyer Conference Room. The door was open, and Daniel was hesitant to knock as Barton was standing with his back to them looking out over the gardens and the harbor below. He was holding a black velvet box. Daniel thought he heard him muttering to himself and looked quizzically at Lyle. Lyle shrugged his shoulders.

In fact Barton was talking quietly to Amelia through the special box he had obtained to protect her. He was telling her how his parents got married here and then how his father had bought the hotel. Barton gazed upon the hotel guests enjoying the splendor of the summer garden below. It was rich with color from snapdragons, zinnias, cosmos, and ah, the lovely lupine, Amelia's favorite. The flowers swayed and danced gently in the ever-present ocean breeze.

He peered out further and saw a family emerge from the Cliff Walk, a mile-long path that runs from the hotel in front of the ocean and ends at a park on the edge of Bar Harbor. His own parents had enjoyed a nightly stroll there when he was a lad. They walked arm and arm while Barton skipped ahead, racing back when he felt he had strayed too far from their view. Barton now followed the small boy who also had run ahead on the path, kicking up the tiny stones that lined the trail. Barton patted the top of the box and sighed. He didn't want to go where his mind always took him, but lately he had been too tired and too weak to stop both his memory and his what ifs. He envisioned the picture of his parents on their wedding day that still hung in the morning room of his estate. A wistful Barton imagined how, like his father, he too would get married on the lawn of the hotel. He imagined a band playing below while he whirled his bride around on his arm for all the attendees to see. He closed his eyes and hung his head down. The what ifs took over and the image of the happy newlyweds disappeared. With no defense, Barton allowed the lost possibilities to dominate his mind.

What if he had not taken the ribbon from Amelia that fateful day on his thirteenth birthday? And what if he had just taken the present from his father, the book containing the secret pact created by the Abenakis and the lobsters, and simply said thank you? What if he hadn't been green with envy when Patrick and Amelia were sitting together looking at her treasures, and he hadn't slapped her hand scattering the amulets on the floor when she needed them most, needed the protection from her own ancestry? And finally, what if he hadn't been a braggart and a bully and a brute and teased her into standing by the wooden door, a door so powerful that it was capable of taking Amelia and changing their lives forever? He fingered the frayed hair ribbon in his pocket. A comfort washed over him, and he savored the momentary relief. "Enough," he muttered out loud as if to shake himself from his brooding. Yes, he thought, Amelia would have made a beautiful bride.

Barton was unaware he had an audience that was growing more curious and perplexed by the minute. "Ahem," Daniel cleared his throat and waited for Barton to turn around. Louder this time, Daniel said, "Sir, we're here." Barton turned to greet the Thibodeau brothers.

Daniel was taken aback by Barton's appearance. Lyle gasped at Barton, whose white hair, normally combed down, was tousled and sticking up in several places, making him look like a mad scientist in a secret laboratory. When Barton turned his head slightly, Daniel saw a new bald spot that had not been there during their first meeting. Is he losing his hair, thought Daniel?

Barton's suit jacket was draped haphazardly over one of the leather chairs surrounding the conference table that dominated the room. His blue dress shirt was wrinkled and one of his sleeves was unbuttoned while the other was rolled up to his elbow. His tie hung loosely. Moreover, he looked thinner and smaller than he had at their last meeting, his bony shoulders hunched and protruding almost up to his ears, making his head seem out of place on his tall frame.

But his eyes appeared most changed. The normal intense blue stare showing power, knowledge, and drive had been replaced by eyes that were watery, sunken, and hesitant. You can learn a lot from someone's eyes, thought Daniel, and these eyes were showing desperation.

"Yes?" Barton asked in a sharp, unfriendly voice.

"Mr. Baxter," Daniel said, "we're here for our meeting to review what we've discovered over the last few days about the subjects in question."

"Yes, yes," Barton said, sounding more like his ornery self. "I know why you're here. I called the meeting! What have you got for me?" he demanded gruffly, gingerly placing the velvet box on top of the table. Daniel wondered what was in the box, but he knew better than to ask.

"My brother, Lyle, assures me he has it all on film," Daniel said.

"Well, be quick about it," Barton barked. "I have a meeting that starts …" He looked at his watch. "When I arrive, which, I would say, should be in about five minutes."

"Lyle has done a wonderful, most wonderful job," said Daniel, though he was caught off guard by Barton's demanding voice that belied his disheveled appearance. "As these pictures will show, Sir. Give the pictures to Mr. Baxter, Lyle." Lyle pulled out the envelope and attempted to open the clasp. He fumbled, as he too was shaken by Mr. Baxter's peculiar behavior. "Be quick now, Lyle. Mr. Baxter hasn't got all day." This only caused Lyle to struggle more with the fastener. "Give it to me," demanded Daniel, grabbing the folder from his brother and tearing off the sealed flap. He handed the photos to Barton, who reached for them eagerly. Lyle frowned at his brother, but Daniel smiled, convinced that the pictures would speak for themselves.

And oh how they spoke!

Barton looked at the pictures slowly, first one picture, then the next and the next. With brows furrowed, he flipped to the fourth picture. Daniel's grin faded, as Barton's expression darkened with each picture he viewed. Barton thumbed through the pictures faster and faster, much like one who might be dealing cards in a game of poker, but Barton's face could not be classified as a "poker face." Barton was livid.

Daniel grimaced while Lyle stood there proud as a peacock, completely oblivious to Barton's foul mood. Perhaps he would get out of the bug business once and for all and start his own studio: *Lyle's Luxuries, a photo for every occasion*. Has a nice ring to it, thought Lyle.

"What is the meaning of these?" roared Barton as he threw the photos down on the table. Some slid across the polished surface and floated to the floor. "Is this some kind of a joke? I asked you to get pictures of the girls and report back to me what they were doing!" Lyle stepped back as if Barton physically shoved him. Daniel bent to pick up the photos on the floor and immediately tried to make the best of the situation, a strategy that normally went well with his bug clients.

"Mr. Baxter, please, sir, let me see the other pictures. Perhaps I can clear up any misunderstanding." He retrieved the remaining pictures and rifled through them. "Let's see what we have here. Ah, here we go, sir. This picture," he held one out in front of Barton, "shows the girls blueberry picking on Blueberry Hill, which you can see if you, well, yes, Lyle's finger does make it harder to make out the girls, but they were just blueberry picking. I am sure this is because it was Lyle's first day with his new camera. This next picture will be better," he declared with a bit of hesitation. "This one here shows the girls, well, these next two are black. Again a minor camera issue." He flipped another photo over. "And here's a bunny rabbit, peculiar to be sure." Daniel's hands trembled, shaking the pictures he held. He paged through more photos, giving a brief commentary of what he saw: "A self-portrait of Lyle, a picture of me napping in the van. I can assure you this was only for a few minutes, sir. The kids' bikes tied up in town, the awning at Jordan's Restaurant, blueberry pancakes, blueberry muffins, blueberry syrup, furry little squirrel, a rather ugly seagull, another thumb, several starfishes, nice color here, Lyle." Daniel looked up at his brother.

"Thanks," Lyle said.

"And a large slobbery dog, a kid dressed up like a pirate, several more kids dressed up like pirates. Was this a birthday party, Lyle?" Lyle nodded in the affirmative. "Porcupine Islands, gull, gull, gull, squirrel, squirrel, chipmunk, gull, squirrel, and what's this?" Daniel brought a photo closer to his face and then passed it to Lyle. "Oh, I know, a falcon's wing. Nice angle here, Lyle, but now give us the pictures of the girls. Mr. Baxter has already told us how busy he is, Lyle, so just give him the rest of the pictures and we can get our next assignment. Just do as I ask and put them right there, brother." He tapped on the table. "Then we can get out of Mr. Baxter's hair."

"That's all there is," said Lyle.

Daniel laughed nervously. "You're quite the joker, Lyle, but fun time is definitely over so get the pictures now."

"I'm not joking, Daniel. Those are the pictures. I was surprised myself by the photos because I was sure that I got several shots of the girls and that little Spidey boy nut who follows them around, but when I went to pick them up this is what was in the packet. I don't know what happened."

Barton planted his hands on the conference table. "Out!" he bellowed. "Now!"

"I must apologize for my ..." Daniel started to say, but Barton cut him off.

"I want you both out of my sight and don't come back again until you have something for me, something worthwhile, that is. Find the girls and find out what they are doing! And don't even think of asking for payment. Payment for a bunch of pictures of birds and squirrels. I think not!" Barton grabbed the velvet box and stormed past the stunned brothers, slamming the door behind him.

Daniel took his hat out of his back pocket and hit his brother on the head. "Idiot!"

Lobster fact: *During World War II, the U.S. Navy used the building that is now the Bar Harbor Inn as an observation headquarters. Following a massive town fire in 1947, it was used by the Red Cross to offer aid to those who had been burned out of their homes.*

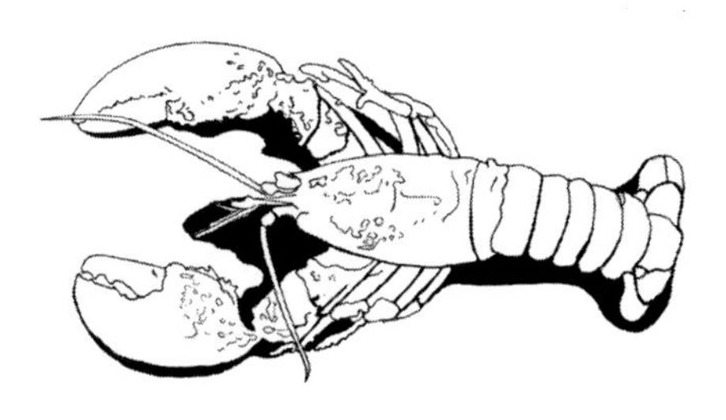

Chapter 38

Town Meeting Gone Awry

Dr. Banke, Dr. Belanger, Dr. Clemens, TJ, Ben, and other members of the RECI team stood in front of a podium in Longfellow Hall, the upstairs meeting room in Bar Harbor's library. Longfellow Hall, in addition to hosting large meetings, also served as the site of weekly adult yoga classes, sewing guild bees, and preschool dance lessons, which, unfortunately had to be canceled today in order to accommodate this emergency town council meeting. Several little girls in tutus waited patiently on metal folding chairs with their mothers. They had been told the meeting would be brief and they hoped to be able to complete their lessons as they were scheduled to perform on the grand stage for the Lobster Festival Follies.

The head librarian, Mrs. Starke, had been displeased when the mayor called demanding, yes, demanding that the room be made available for an emergency town council meeting. Luckily, Dave the custodian was still on duty so he was able to drag the chairs from the back storage area and arrange them according to the mayor's specifications.

Mrs. Starke did not like it when things did not go according to plan; this meeting was definitely not part of the library's plan. She didn't give a fig about some silly lobster problems. Lobsters larger than normal—poppycock! Just a made-up story to attract tourists to the lobster festival. This meeting was probably part of the plan as well, she thought. A couple of reporters, a story in the *Bangor Gazette* and perhaps one all the way down in Portland and voila, instant success of our festival.

Well, she hoped the mayor was correct, and the meeting would be short and sweet, and then her library and the dancers could get back to the order of the day.

"Mrs. Starke," called Officer Sully, a young police officer whom the librarian remembered fondly from when he was a high school student. Helped him with his senior paper on Upton Sinclair and the muckrakers. Lovely paper. Had a tough time with the theme, but finished nonetheless. He even came into the library to show her his grade: B+. Mrs. Starke felt strongly that he had deserved an A.

"Oh, hello there, Timmy," she said. "Nice to see you, but not so nice to have to have this meeting here, especially on such short notice. Lydia's Dance Studio had reserved this room months ago, and their performance is just around the corner. Fiddle dee dee."

"I think it is kind of important, Mrs. Starke. I mean, it would have to be since all the TV stations are setting up outside. I even saw a station from Boston."

"Most unusual," she said. "I think I will head outside and make sure they are not trampling the flowers. As you know, I take great pride in the flowers in the front, Timothy. I remember how you used to help me with the weeding."

"Yes, ma'am," Officer Sully said. He returned to his task of making sure the room was set up as the mayor had requested. Dave wheeled out a large chalkboard. He handed a new package of chalk to Dr. Banke.

"Thank you," said Dr. Banke, looking around the small stage area for any accessories that might aid him in his presentation. He frowned and said to Ben and TJ, "Boys, can you get the chart and place it on top of this chalkboard? I guess this will have to do. We can wheel it to the right of the podium so people will be able to see it from the back."

"Yeah, sure," said TJ.

"On it, boss," said Ben.

"Has anyone seen the green folder?" Dr. Banke asked. People around him paused and a few shook their heads, but most continued with their tasks. He sighed and frowned.

Dr. Banke pulled several more folders out of his canvas briefcase. The other scientists busied themselves with preparations for their presentation. The mayor had visited Jamison Lab earlier in the morning to inform them that due to recent unworldly events, town residents were demanding a report on when this lobster business would be over. He wanted assurances that they had a solution to this tiresome and now potentially deadly problem and that the lobster festival would go on as planned without any complications from the lobsters. When Dr. Banke and the others tried to explain that they were still working on the problem, that science sometimes takes time, and that the town may want to explore canceling the festival, the mayor had marched off in a huff. Dr. Banke had no idea how the meeting would go or even if Mayor Peterson would attend, but he knew he had to at least attempt to answer some questions. This lobster situation had certainly taken a turn for the worse, and he and the RECI team were running out of ideas.

Safety had always been his top priority. In the lab he followed strict rules, but lately nothing seemed to make any sense. There seemed to be no order to anything, especially the ocean. It had always been a consistent and predictable environment for him, but since coming to the island, Dr. Banke had felt like he was in a constant state of confusion. The lobster population was increasing at an alarming rate, their size, too, had multiplied to epic proportions, and new data showed no signs of the lobster migration slowing down. He and other members of the team had collected copious samples and logged countless hours of research, testing, and retesting, yet still they were no closer to a solution. He had heard the rumors in town, as the lobsters were on everyone's mind, and what most residents were talking about was that lobstermen were seeing larger and larger lobsters: two feet, three feet, and even four feet in length, downright prehistoric.

Dr. Banke had been completely blindsided when the mayor had barged into the laboratory and insisted upon an immediate explanation and a presentation at an emergency town council meeting. Peterson had been so agitated that the veins on his neck looked like they might simply explode. Dr. Banke stopped looking through his papers momentarily, thinking about how TJ and Ben had spent the rest of the morning trying to mimic the mayor by holding their breath and straining their necks to make their own veins stick out. This only led to more shenanigans, with TJ humming patriotic tunes while pretending to play his neck muscles. The boys were incredibly hard and dedicated workers, but obviously had no idea how serious the lobster problem was becoming.

Dr. Banke rubbed the back of his head. He felt a major headache coming on. He paused to look out the large windows that framed the meeting room. People missing under odd circumstances, huge lobsters, and lobsters showing up on the beaches, on coastal roads, on docks, and in boats ranging from large fishing vessels to sea kayaks and canoes. The reports streamed in daily to the RECI team, each one more preposterous than the next. He and the others had initially chuckled when reviewing the police blotters each morning, but lately there had been no humor.

Three people possibly dead? Due to crustaceans run amok? Incomprehensible. Nothing he had studied or seen or reviewed or researched had ever prepared him for that. He wished Robin were here. She was always such a good sounding board for him. He had tried to reach her after meeting with the mayor, but was informed that her group would not be back to the base camp for at least a week. He sighed again as several townspeople entered the room. His eyes drifted to the ballerinas in their pink tutus, already restless and fidgeting. Like them, he hoped the meeting wouldn't take too long and everyone could get back to a normal day.

* * * *

Ani, Eliza, and Roonie glided around a corner in town on their bikes. It was all downhill from here, thought a relieved Ani. With the new amulet tucked safely in the pouch around her neck, she could almost feel the healing power already. The trio had decided that it might be time to inform Dr. Banke about what was going on. He was a scientist who relied on facts, and they had evidence that he would not be able to ignore. Ani reviewed the facts in her head: one, the original Abenaki parchment; two, the book from Professor Sol; three, the three amulets already acquired, silver sand dollar, blue sapphire, and now the green tourmaline; four, Roonie's grandmother, Moon Violet, and the Scrabble game where my name spells Abennaki, the original spelling; and five ... Ani stopped her list. She could almost hear her father's words: *These are not facts, but rather fabrications. There is a big difference between the two, Ani, as you are well aware.* Ani squeezed her bike brakes tighter to slow down the momentum she gained from the long hill. And five, she continued, convinced now that her father would never believe that what she was saying held any merit, the girl in the orb. How do I explain that one?

Ani rounded a second corner and put on the brakes. Eliza also skidded to a halt, but Roonie careened past them and rolled up the grassy hill to their right, tumbling off his bike and landing hard on the ground.

"Ouch," he cried.

"Ani, what were you thinking stopping short like that?" Eliza said as she ran to check on Roonie. She now felt protective of him, since his near drowning.

"Roonie, are you all right?" Eliza asked.

"I'm fine," replied a disgruntled Roonie, rising and dusting the dirt off his pants. "No thanks to Ani. What is ..." Roonie stopped as he and Eliza turned simultaneously toward the spectacle in front of the library.

"What is going on?" asked Eliza.

"Yeah, what's all this?" said Roonie.

"That's why I stopped," said Ani. "I didn't want to run into anything."

News vans and trucks of every shape and size crowded the street, reporters with cameramen broadcast on the sidewalk, townspeople and tourists gawked at the commotion, and police tried to maintain order. Cranes rose from the backs of media trucks, while lights, shades, boxes, microphones, cameras, and other equipment were unloaded and set up for action.

A motor home, a regular sight in the summer in Bar Harbor, had unfortunately ventured down the same street as the kids, exactly the wrong place at the wrong time, and was wedged between two news affiliates' vehicles, causing traffic to come to a standstill at both ends of the street. Horns honked, whistles blew, and people yelled. Ani, Eliza, and Roonie locked their bikes to the stop sign and elbowed their way through the crowd.

Ani politely asked an older woman hurrying past her, "Excuse me, Ma'am, do you know what is happening here?"

The woman scowled at Ani, annoyed that she had been interrupted in her desire to get to where she was going. "It's an emergency town council meeting," she said and picked up her pace to pass Ani.

"What about?" yelled Ani, who also sped up and was now hop-running to keep up with the woman.

"Why about the lobsters, of course. I can't talk anymore. I want to make sure and get a seat in Longfellow Hall." And with that the woman ran away from Ani, weaving in and out of the people already in front of her.

"Lobsters? I wonder if Dad is here," Ani said to Eliza and Roonie.

Eliza looked worried. "We should go, Ani, especially if Dad is there. He might need our support."

After some tricky maneuvering, some gentle pushing, and some slipping underneath and between other folks, the kids made it upstairs and squeezed into the meeting room. Ani spied a narrow table along the right side of the room. "Come on," she said, urging the others to follow her. Soon, Ani, Roonie, and Eliza were seated on the table. They had arrived just in the nick of time. A fireman, only about five feet tall and equally as wide from the look of him, barked at the police that the room was at capacity.

"Move back, move back," he commanded to the people

still trying to get in the room. "That's right. Back up here. No more room. You all got to go downstairs."

"Testing, testing." Ani recognized TJ at the front of the room checking the microphone. He blew on it a few times to determine that it was working. He nodded and a petite woman with long, flowing brown hair approached the microphone.

Ani tapped Roonie. "Who's that?"

"Don't know," he said.

"May I have your attention?" the woman started. The crowd quieted down a bit. "May I have your attention PLEASE?" She glowered at the audience and silence prevailed.

An older gentleman, dressed in overalls, boots, and a T-shirt from the Dog and Pony Tavern, Bar Harbor, piped up, "Chairman, I mean Chairwoman Higgins, what is the town planning on doing about them lobsters? I mean, it was great at first what with having the biggest and tastiest lobsters ever seen in these parts, but now with what happened to Captain Andy, I can't get me a crew to go out with me anymore and ..."

"Now, now, Skipper Hall, you know the rules for a town council meeting. I promise we will get to all of your questions in a moment. First, I want to say a few words followed by a brief presentation, and then we will open it up for discussion."

"So that means sit down, Skipper Hall," another voice yelled from the crowd.

A few more shouts and jeers rolled from the audience, "Yeah, sit, Skip, sit" and "Park it, Hall," among them.

"Dad looks nervous," Eliza whispered to her sister. Ani agreed.

Chairwoman Higgins continued, "As all of you are quite aware, we have been having a minor problem with ah, the lobsters."

"Minor?" another person shouted out. "Not according to Eli Pelletier."

"Like I said, what are we going to do about it!" demanded Skipper Hall, rising from his chair this time. Ani noticed a few of the police officers approach from the room's perimeter. Skipper must have seen them as well and reluctantly sat down.

"The town, working in conjunction with Jamison Laboratory, has been investigating this issue and now would like to welcome the scientists, led by Dr. George Banke all the way from Boston, who will update us on what is happening and," Higgins paused and looked directly at Skipper Hall, "what they are going to do about it. Dr. Banke."

He walked hesitantly to the podium and stared out at the crowd, well over 300 strong, and sighed. A line of perspiration appeared at his brow. With a strained smile on his face, he began to talk. His voice sounded thin and small, nothing like his normal presentation style. Ani's throat constricted.

"Thank you, Chairwoman Higgins, and thank you town members for asking me and members of the research team to present at this emergency town meeting." He paged through some of his papers and then nodded to TJ, who placed a large pad of paper on the chalkboard.

"Before explaining our research, I thought I might take a few minutes to review the life cycle of *Homarus americanus,* otherwise known as the American lobster." Ani detected her father's hand shaking as he flipped over the first page to reveal a drawing of the lobster from egg to full size.

From the back row a few lobstermen chuckled and one of them said, "This is a waste of time." Ani felt uncomfortable. Come on, Dad, you can do this, she silently encouraged.

Ani tried to concentrate as he explained, but she had known about the lobster's life cycle since she was a young child, so her eyes wandered. In the background she heard her father's slow and steady voice, thankfully sounding stronger than when he started. She glanced at the other side of the room and recognized Mr. Baxter leaning against the wall. He stared back at her, glaring at her, or so she thought. She tried nonchalantly to look away. A few moments later she turned back to him and found that he had moved and that his spot had been taken by Mr. O'Leary, who returned her gaze directly and nodded.

Barton had spied the Thibodeau brothers he had hired to monitor Ani and Eliza and Roonie. Lyle and Daniel were near the front of the room, unaware their subjects were just off to their right. Barton had moved closer to the imbecile brothers to remind them this was their last chance.

Startled to see the gardener, Ani waved awkwardly and tapped Eliza. "Don't look now, but your friend the creepy gardener is here."

Eliza immediately looked. "I said *not* to look, Eliza," Ani whispered loudly.

"You know I can't help myself when you tell me not to do something," Eliza said. "I feel like we keep seeing him. Do you think he's following us?"

"Where else have you seen him?"

"Today at Jordan's for one and then here. Well, that makes two."

"Eliza, that doesn't mean anything," said Ani.

"And three, he was there when you were working on the cards and Roonie threw a pinecone at him and ..."

"Who's following us?" said Roonie. "Is it the bug guys? I've seen their bug van everywhere lately."

"What are you talking about?" Eliza said. "What big van?"

"Not big van, bug van," Roonie said.

"Shh!" Ani hushed them. "Listen to Dad."

By now the audience was restless, moving their chairs back and forth while speaking softly to their neighbors. Ani pondered what Eliza said about Mr. O'Leary. Her theory about him following them was not so far-fetched. She knew he was responsible for the Baxter estate gardens, but he did seem to be always lingering around, appearing behind trees, corners, and lawn ornaments, now that Ani thought about it. When they had been swimming with the seals and found the first amulet, the silver sand dollar, Ani knew that someone had moved her backpack. Maybe it was the gardener. He did have a key to the place and could come and go as he pleased. But why would he want to follow them? Did he know something about the lobsters, too? Perhaps he was somehow connected to what was happening and had guessed what the kids were up to. But how could he? Ani had always hidden the parchment in different places whenever they left the house, places so clever that if someone was looking for it, it would be hard to find. She had put the parchment inside other books, in board game boxes, under the dirty clothes in the hamper, or where it was right now, beneath the English muffins, bagels, and bread in the bread drawer in the kitchen. Ani also carefully taped the book closed with a piece of Scotch tape. So far, the tape had remained intact whenever they returned from an adventure.

Eliza nudged her sister. "Are you listening to what Dad is saying? I didn't know the problem was this bad."

Dr. Banke cleared his throat and bowed again to TJ, who turned the chart over. This time it revealed a picture of what looked to be an adult lobster. "After five to seven years of molting at least twenty-five times, the lobster is now an adult, weighing approximately one pound and reaching the legal size for harvesting. A one-pound female lobster usually carries over eight thousand eggs that she will carry up to two years before releasing them. From every fifty thousand hatched eggs only two lobsters ever mature enough to be legal harvesting size. That is, until now," he said, pointing to TJ, who flipped the chart once more.

This page depicted a larger lobster next to an enlarged *Anopheles punctipennis,* or spotted-winged mosquito. Dr. Banke had gotten into a rhythm and was more relaxed. He had the attention of the audience again. Ani was relieved.

Skipper Hall shouted out, "Mosquito, the Maine State Bird." The audience laughed.

Dr. Banke smiled and resumed speaking. "According to our research, the life cycle of the lobster has accelerated alarmingly fast. If you factor $x = (1 + i)^n$ for the exponential increase…"

"Speak in English please, Doctor," pleaded the woman whom Ani had spoken to on the street. "What does this all mean?"

"It means that the life cycle has gone from five to seven years to five to seven days."

A unified gasp filled the room.

"Their life cycle now resembles that of a mosquito, and that's not all. The size has increased from roughly one foot to our most recent discovery of four feet long." TJ turned the page to reveal a picture of a lobster on one side and a small child on the other.

This sent the audience into a frenzied state. Cries of "unbelievable" and "how can this be?" and "what is to be done?" echoed throughout the room.

We know what can be done, thought Ani. "We have to tell Dad, Eliza," she mouthed to her sister. Eliza nodded her agreement.

"Unfortunately this rate of growth shows no signs of slowing. While our lobster population increases, lobster populations up and down the Eastern Seaboard have diminished. The lobsters have migrated to Mount Desert Island. We believe this is caused by an unusual underwater current known as *remolino de diablos,* or the devil's whirlpool, a pattern that has not been known to exist for centuries. Why it is happening now is unclear. We need more time to conduct additional experiments."

At this point, Ani spotted Mayor Peterson in the doorway. He had a plastic grin on his face as if he was about to throw out the first pitch of a baseball game instead of listen to the fate of his beloved Bar Harbor.

"Due to these disturbing findings, along with other unsubstantiated yet likely reports of lobsters possibly causing the deaths of three members of this community, we recommend canceling the annual lobster festival and suspending any commercial lobstering until further notice," Dr. Banke said.

"What three deaths? We only know about Captain Andy Gerow," someone in the crowd shouted.

Officer Sully, positioned close to the podium, glanced at the police chief, who was standing by the back door. The chief gave him a curt nod, and Sully stepped to the microphone. "In addition to Captain Gerow's suspicious disappearance, we have had reports of two missing women in which some evidence has pointed to lobster involvement." He stepped away and the crowd piped up again.

"We can't stop lobstering!"

"Cancel the festival! What about the businesses?"

"We won't be able to recover from the loss!"

"This can't be happening!"

The meeting was out of control. Chairwoman Higgins grabbed the gavel and banged the lectern. "Order, order everyone," she demanded, but no one was listening. Several folks leapt from their seats, yelling and demanding better answers.

Mayor Peterson rushed to the front of the room and yanked the microphone away. "Settle down, settle down," he said. "We will not be canceling the lobster festival nor will we have to cancel any lobstering." The attendees stopped screaming and listened to the mayor.

"Mayor Peterson, it is not safe for people to be in the water," Dr. Banke said.

"Now, Dr. Banke, surely you exaggerate here. I am certain that in a matter of days, perhaps after a hard rain, which is predicted for later tomorrow, the lobsters, like all of us, will just get back to routine, and we can proceed with our plans for the festival."

"But I implore you ...," A commotion at the entrance to the hall cut Dr. Banke short. Ani saw a tall, well-dressed woman flanked by two police officers. She turned slightly to whisper to a man behind her clothed in full military attire. Next both approached the podium. Several members of the press followed them, and they clicked their cameras in rapid-fire succession to capture the moment.

"Governor Turner," said Chairwoman Higgins. "I didn't know you would be coming to our meeting." She apologized, visibly shaken by this arrival.

"The governor is here!" Eliza said.

"Wow!" Roonie said.

Francine Maxwell Turner, the Maine state governor, paused and smiled at the audience, and the flashing of cameras accelerated. "Good afternoon. I come here today after receiving several reports from the police regarding the migration and growth of the lobsters. I spoke at length with the director of the Jamison Laboratory, who has kept me informed of Dr. Banke's progress. Furthermore, my office has consulted with the National Marine Institute in Florida, the Australian Marine Conservation Society in Brisbane, and both the Boston Aquarium and the Woods Hole Oceanographic Institution on Cape Cod. I believe that we need to act and to act quickly, as the lobster population has clearly become dangerous.

"To that end, I have developed a two-part plan of action. First, by the powers vested in me as governor of the state of Maine, I have called up the National Guard in order to oversee the plan and maintain order and safety for the citizens of Mount Desert Island. Brigadier General H. Paul Smith, adjutant general of the Central Maine National Guard, will be in charge of the second phase of the plan. I will let him briefly describe it to you now." The governor stepped away from the lectern.

"Thank you, Governor Turner. I will keep this brief," said General Smith, a trim, physically fit man with close-cropped hair. He stared at the audience and cleared his throat loudly, commanding everyone's attention. "At approximately 0100 hours in three days' time we will drop NC 241, a lethal low-sinking gas that will destroy the crustacean population. We will target the areas one hundred yards from each of the main harbors on the island: Bar Harbor, Northeast Harbor, and Southwest Harbor. Additional canisters will be detonated at various locations selected according to the current lobster population as determined by the RECI team from Jamison Laboratory. The governor has issued a state of emergency and has ordered that all fishing, including lobstering, cease and desist twenty-four hours before detonation." The general stepped back from the lectern. The audience was stunned.

"The governor will now be available to answer a few questions," Chairwoman Higgins said.

Several people raised their hands and shouted out questions: "How safe is this? What about the other sea life? When can we get back to fishing?"

"What about the festival?" said the mayor.

The governor did her best to answer as many questions as possible while Dr. Banke and the other scientists processed the shocking announcement. From what little knowledge he had about the gas, NC 241 was deadly. It would definitely kill the lobsters, but it might also kill all the other sea life in a wide radius and that was just in the first twenty-four hours. No one was completely sure of the shelf life of the gas. It was supposed to dissolve within the first twenty-four to forty-eight hours of release, but these studies took place in a laboratory, a controlled environment, not in an actual live ocean with colder water and a thriving and abundant sea population.

He raised his hand and shouted, "Governor Turner, Governor Turner."

"Yes, Dr. Banke?" the governor said.

"I am deeply concerned about the potential aftereffects of …"

The governor glanced at her watch and smiled. "Sorry to cut this short, but I have to meet with the National Guard. I understand the concerns, but am willing to take the risk in order to prevent any further catastrophes. Brigadier General Smith will be available to answer any further questions. Thank you and God bless us all." And with that, the governor exited the room to both cheers and jeers from the audience.

"TJ and Ben," Dr. Banke shouted. "Pack up the materials here and take the van back with the rest of the crew to the lab. Dr. Belanger, Dr. Clemens, and I will use my car, which is thankfully parked a few blocks from here, to get to the lab sooner. We need to switch gears and investigate NC 241. I don't believe the state is aware just how deadly this gas will be, and I aim to get the facts and report back to the governor immediately."

Ani, Eliza, and Roonie fought their way through the crowd to get to Dr. Banke. Ani was the first to reach him. "Dad, Dad," she cried out, her voice barely able to be heard over the noise. "I know what is going on!"

"Ani," he said, reaching a hand out to pull her to him.

"What did you say?"

"I know what is going on. It's all about the book, my present from Mom. I decoded it, Dad, with the help of Professor Sol and his book, and something has been stolen, actually an orb, and it disrupted the energy around Cadillac Mountain and signaled to the lobsters that they needed to come back to take over the land. And I need to find the amulets to offer up somehow and somewhere when I collect them all. I'm not really sure about this part, but I know with your help I can figure it out. But that doesn't matter right now. What matters is that I have three of the five amulets already, and I have a pretty good idea where to find the fourth one because I am the one to do it. The girl—oh yeah, this one is going to be hard for you—there is a girl in the orb, and I am Kanake-kee and then Roonie's grandmother, Moon Violet, confirmed it because my name, A-N-I-B-A-N-K-E, spells Abenaki. Well, actually the old spelling which had two *N*'s, A-B-E-N-N-A-K-I."

Ani's father stared at her, as he had never looked at his daughter before, as if she were a complete stranger.

She continued, aware of how crazy she sounded, but she just had to make her father understand, she just had to. "Dad, don't look at me like that. I know it sounds silly and childish and ridiculous, but it is all true. I promise."

Eliza and Roonie made it through the melee and joined them.

"It is all real, Dad, honest," Eliza said.

Roonie nodded his head up and down in solidarity.

"Really? Orb? Girl in the orb? Lobsters and Indians? I don't have the time for this foolishness," he said as his jaw tightened. "Did you not just hear what Brigadier General Smith and the governor said? They are going to drop canisters in less than three days and kill all the lobsters and perhaps all the sea life in a hundred-mile radius. This area will need years to recover, if it ever does, and you believe you have the answer from the book Mom gave you? Really? Ani, really?"

Ani opened her mouth to protest, but closed it quickly as her father scowled at her. Eliza pursed her lips tight. Roonie stared at his feet awkwardly, wishing he were somewhere else, anywhere but here listening to Ani go on and on and dig herself into a deeper hole with each word that came out of her mouth.

Dr. Banke looked around and sighed. He put a hand on the shoulder of each girl and leaned in toward them. "I don't know what you're rambling on about or what game you three children are playing, but this is not the place nor the time for playing games, do you understand?"

Both girls nodded. Ani tried hard to hold back the tears she felt prickling her eyes.

"I have to go back to the lab to run some more tests and look into this NC 241. I'm not sure when I will be back, so I need for you to be good, behave, and be careful. I can't be worrying about you and your antics while there is so much at stake here, so please, no more adventures, stay in and around town or at the house, and by all means don't go in the water. Clear?"

The girls nodded again. Roonie silently started to walk away. "That goes for you, too, young man," Dr. Banke called out to him.

Ben interrupted. "We are ready to move to the van, Dr. Banke. See you back at the lab."

"Great, Ben, and remember, don't say anything to the press outside."

"Yes, sir," he said as he headed toward the entryway, arms laden with charts and files.

Dr. Banke reached into his wallet, removed some money, and handed it to Eliza. "Here, take this and use this for food and incidentals. If you need me, you can call me at the lab. Now, promise me no more talk about orbs and Indians, okay?" He kissed both the girls and joined Dr. Belanger and Dr. Clemens.

Ani walked away from Eliza and Roonie and wiped the tears she had successfully hidden from her father away with the back of her hand. How could she have been so foolish? She had rehearsed what she was going to say to him, and then when she had the chance, she blew it. Even when she was speaking she knew she sounded like a lunatic. Of course her father couldn't listen to her now, not after what just happened. The National Guard, the noxious gas, the sea life in danger! She wiped her nose with the bottom of her T-shirt and breathed deep. She was the chosen one. She was Kanake-kee, one who walks with animals, and she was the one who was going to stop the lobsters. She faced Eliza and Roonie.

"Well," her voice sounding remarkably confident despite the situation, "I know what we have to do, and we have to do it fast."

"You do?" Eliza asked, surprised by her sister's sureness.

"We have to simply locate the other two amulets, find out where we bring them, and voila, lobster problem is solved."

"What are you talking about?" Roonie said. "Your father said we can't have any more adventures, and we can't go anywhere or go near the water."

"He's right," Eliza said. "He did."

"What he actually said," Ani said with a mischievous smile, "is no more adventures, stay in and around town or at the house, and by all means don't go in the water."

"And?" asked Eliza.

"And," Ani said, "finding the amulets is not an adventure; it is a necessity. And we will stay in and around town, but he didn't say specifically what town so that means the entire island. And finally, from the clues that I have deciphered about the next amulets, I don't think we need to go in the water, so actually, we are following Dad's rules."

"Why, Ani," declared Eliza, "you sound more like me every day." Ani smiled and Roonie looked relieved.

"We need to get going," Ani said. "We can't waste any time. We have less than seventy-two hours, so we don't have a minute to spare."

Ani, Eliza, and Roonie left Longfellow Hall more determined than ever to finish what they had started. Ani knew, or hoped she knew, where they had to go next, some nearby island. But she needed to do more research to figure out which island. Her eagerness to start helped to lighten her mood. When they reached the bottom of the stairs, she had already formulated a plan and felt better about the exchange with her father. She didn't really like to break the rules but felt justified stretching them because of the special circumstances.

She heard a low rumble from above and peered at the sky. Like many afternoons in the summer, heavy storm clouds rolled in off the coast. Sometimes it rained and sometimes it didn't. The sun poked through the tangle of clouds. Ani doubted it would rain. A large seagull was perched atop a mailbox near the stop sign they had tied their bikes to. He squawked loudly and then flew over them before veering to the sea. Ani sensed he had been guarding their bikes, making sure they were okay and would be there when they returned. She noticed a gathering of two chipmunks, one squirrel, and one tiny gray bunny disperse and scamper behind the rock wall that lined the sidewalk. Kanake-kee, she said to herself, Kanake-kee.

* * * *

Her father wasn't the only one taken aback by what Ani had said after the town meeting. Patrick O'Leary, who recently had been feeling that something big was going to happen and that somehow he was going to be included, had woken up that very morning and knew today was the day to act.

His knees, which normally were stiff and uncooperative upon rising, felt young and fresh. Instead of making himself his normal breakfast of oatmeal and anadama toast with the cook's homemade strawberry jelly, he decided to work for a few hours and then head into town to eat breakfast. Lately his sleep had been disrupted by dreams of Amelia and Barton and himself when they were young and hadn't a care in the world. But then the dream took a bad turn and always ended the same way, by the garden door and with the black mist, the menacing awful black mist, and then Amelia gone. However, last night he dreamed only of Amelia and the two of them running in the garden, away from the door, and among the lupines.

Patrick had felt refreshed and eager to get outside to his beloved plants. He dressed and went directly to the beds on the south side of the main estate. The dahlias and the foxglove needed to be staked, and Patrick wanted to do the job before the heat of the day made it too uncomfortable to work outside. For the first hour he worked without interruption and without much thought. He got into the rhythm of cultivating around the plant, placing the wooden dowel next to the base of the intended target, and then using the green twine attached to his belt to coax the plant to grow straight and tall along the dowel.

When he was done, he noticed two bunnies, one beige and larger than the other gray one, resting under a stand of red cypress trees about fifteen feet from the edge of the flowerbed. Patrick got up slowly and dusted the dirt from his pants. He walked closer to the rabbits, who stared directly at him without blinking. Unusual, he thought. He had never seen rabbits stay so still before. Cautiously he advanced closer, and again they stayed put. As he got even closer, he spied something on the ground in front of the larger rabbit's paws. The hair on his arms rose. He couldn't believe what he saw. When he was just two feet from the bunnies, the larger one blinked twice and both hopped away. Patrick bent to pick up a frayed blue hair ribbon, just like the one Amelia wore so many years ago. "Amelia?" he said out loud.

He watched the bunnies hop to the edge of the trees and duck behind the enormous mountain laurels and rhododendrons that outlined the area. He shook his head to clear it and tucked the ribbon into his pants pocket. He cleaned up and headed into town to eat his breakfast and figure out what he should do next, again with the overwhelming feeling that he had to be a part of whatever was going on. Was Amelia urging him on? Was this her blue ribbon? It couldn't be a coincidence, it just couldn't be, he thought to himself as he backed out of the garage and drove the old red pickup truck into Bar Harbor.

Upon entering Jordan's he was surprised to see the Banke girls and that Roonie kid. After he ordered his breakfast, a double stack of blueberry pancakes with blueberry syrup, he saw Lyle Thibodeau stand up and take a few pictures with his camera. While Daniel had said for all to hear it was a new camera and Lyle was just trying it out, Patrick believed that Lyle was actually taking pictures of the kids while they sat in the booth. He lowered the brim of his sun hat and pretended to read his *Bangor Gazette* while listening to the brothers. He did not like what he overheard. Something about getting paid to take pictures and figure out what the kids were doing. He learned that they had already observed the kids picking blueberries, playing mini golf, and running around the park with a large, slobbery dog. Patrick also heard them mention Barton's name a few times. Why would Barton want to know what the kids were doing? This made no sense, but made perfect sense at the same time. Wherever there was trouble, it took very little digging before Barton Thuya Baxter III surfaced. Patrick made it a point to pay Barton a long overdue visit and find out what was going on and why he wanted the kids followed.

When Patrick first heard about the lobsters migrating to Bar Harbor, his immediate reaction was, good for the local lobstermen. Like most folks, he blamed it on global warming or strange wind patterns, much like with dolphins that sometimes beach themselves or end up in shallow water for no apparent reason. But now, he wasn't so sure that someone, someone like Barton, might not be responsible for the migration and ensuing problems. As much as he found the ancient Abenaki story implausible, Patrick had no doubt that it was Barton who broke into the cottage. Even though nothing was reported stolen, Patrick knew that the safe had been blown open and reckoned that Barton had finally gotten his birthday book, which had been taken away from him years before. Did Barton use the book to locate and disturb the covenant? Did he steal it and sell it on the open market like he had intended when he was thirteen? Could he be culpable for the lobsters being on the move?

Patrick had waited for the kids to leave the restaurant, and as he expected, the Thibodeau brothers followed them in their van. Curious, he thought. Patrick paid his bill and decided to pursue the brothers. If they were stalking the children, then Patrick would follow them and find out why. It was on his way out of the diner that Patrick heard about the emergency town meeting at two in the afternoon. He knew this was going to be an eventful day.

Like most members of the audience, he had been astonished to learn how severe the lobster problem had become. Staying up at the Baxter estate, Patrick had chosen to keep to himself most of the time, preferring to avoid others as much as possible. Lately, however, he had changed his solitary viewpoint and sought out excuses to drive to town to pick up supplies or do some other odd job or even run an errand for Cook. There was a buzz of excitement in the air, and he wanted to be involved, to be helpful, and to maybe make amends.

Three people missing? Their bodies never found? The National Guard and poison gas? But what he overheard Ani announce to her father was even more unbelievable. Patrick had been standing behind the screen covered in clouds and seagulls the ballerinas were going to use as a backdrop. Lucky for him he had elected to step out of the fray and wait for the attendees to disperse before leaving the hall. He had heard Ani's declaration in its entirety. Orb? Girl in the orb? Could this be the covenant? Could Amelia be the girl in the orb? His pulse increased as he felt a surge of excitement in the pit of his stomach.

Like Ani, he too knew what he needed to do. He needed to find Barton, find the orb, and if she was the girl in question, rescue his beloved Amelia.

Lobster fact: *After humans, cod are probably the lobster's main enemy, followed by other bottom-dwelling fishes. Raccoons have even been known to raid coastal lobster pounds at low tide.*

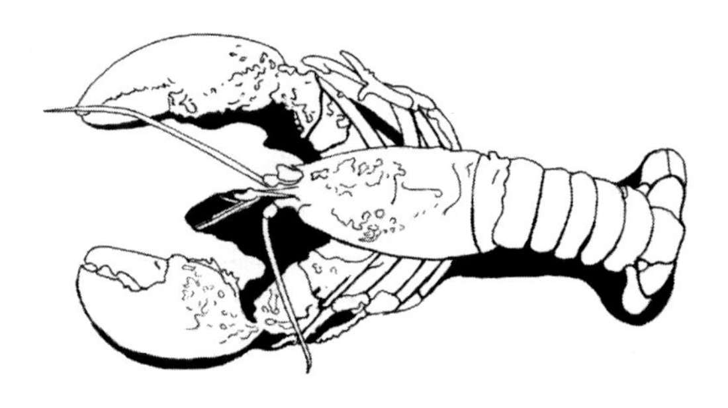

Chapter 39

The Eagle Has Landed, Sort of

The kids decided to bike to the garden cottage to revisit the book and review Ani's note cards. After the fiasco at the town meeting, Ani needed the ride to clear her head and get her mind ready for the next amulet quest. She was not upset anymore with her father. How could she be with all that he had going on back at the lab? She sighed, thinking about her Mom and how much she would like to see her now. Ani could almost feel her mom brush back her hair from her eyes and tuck it behind her ears, something she had done since she was little, and tell her everything would be all right. She imagined her mother saying, You know your father, Ani, he thinks like a scientist. Always has and always will, honey. You can't expect him to believe what is really going on, Ani, he just can't. His mind is unable to comprehend the implausible, especially now with the threat to the ocean imminent. Please be patient with him, and don't forget, he loves you very much.

She cringed, remembering how she just blurted out the whole crazy story to her father, sounding even more outlandish and bizarre as the tale catapulted out of her mouth. She pedaled a little faster, trying to put distance between herself and what just happened at the library. She needed to stay focused and follow the path established by the Abenakis so many years ago. The book had not let the three of them down yet and she hoped it would not disappoint them now.

Searching for the amulets had been exhilarating, something fun and clever and different to pursue while spending a magical summer in Maine. She certainly believed in what they were doing, but even after seeing the girl in the orb, meeting Roonie's grandmother, and having the animals assist her, Ani had still felt she was playacting and that her fantasy would end when her father and the rest of the Jamison Lab folks unearthed the scientific explanation. But today was a game changer. Even before they had gone to the town meeting, Ani understood that the stakes were higher, especially after Roonie almost drowned trying to find the green tourmaline. Their quest no longer felt like a game. The fate of the island was in their hands and their hands alone.

Roonie sped ahead of the girls and glided up the long driveway to the wooden door marking the entranceway to the cottage grounds. He threw his bike down and with some effort pushed open the heavy door to the path leading to the Bankes' borrowed house. Eliza followed Roonie, panting slightly as she had tried to keep up with him. She didn't want to let him out of her sight and take the risk that he might get hurt again. Ani arrived and studied the carvings in the door, her fingers caressing the many shapes and indentations. She could make out the fox with his long and bushy tail, the seagull with its familiar beak and rounded body, the deer with its regal stance. She traced other images down and along the bottom of the door: raccoon, skunk, rabbit, elk, bear, robin, cardinal, snake, chipmunk, and owl. These were easily recognizable, but several drawings didn't make any sense to her.

"Come on, Ani," called Eliza. "You're the one who said we have to get moving. Roonie and I are starving. I'm going to make some grilled cheese sandwiches and you can plan where we have to go next."

After they had eaten their sandwiches, which were slightly burnt on one side, a mishap Eliza blamed on the old pan she had to use, the kids went to the side porch to discuss their next steps. Ani had been able to figure out that the Abenaki drawing of a solitary circle meant *island*, but the problem was which island? Mount Desert Island was itself an island, but also was surrounded by several smaller islands. Why would they hide an amulet somewhere away from Mount Desert? It just didn't make sense. Fortunately, Ani had determined they needed a feather, a bald eagle feather. The drawing in her book was of a feather, which would have been obvious to anyone even without Professor Sol's book, but it had a half circle on top of it, which for the Abenakis meant bald eagle. Ani had read that several Indian tribes believed that birds were spiritual messengers between humans and the gods, and others believed the eagle represented peace for all mankind, so it made sense to her that a feather would be selected as an amulet.

Ani had already discovered that bald eagles nested in and around Mount Desert, as she had been lucky enough to see a few flying impressively overhead while touring the island. She always felt such joy to spy one and was quick to call out to Eliza and Roonie whenever she did. Eliza had read that bald eagles were mean-spirited birds that took food from other nests. She called them the "bullies of the sky" and felt they should not have been chosen as the national emblem. Many times Ani had tried to explain to Eliza that they were at the top of their food chain and that their role as a predator was just to do what they needed to survive. She reminded Eliza that eagles were fortunate to be alive given that humans shot at them, or electrocuted them, or poisoned them. But Eliza would hear none of this. She did not like them and nothing would make her change her mind. She argued that even Benjamin Franklin felt them to be scoundrels. This argument continued anew until Roonie pointed out to them they were wasting time and could argue later.

"Roonie," said Ani, "I might need your island expertise."

"Sure," he said with a mouth full of cookies. "I think I need some milk first," he said and got up and went to the kitchen.

"Drink it inside," Ani said. "I don't want to take the chance of spilling something on the parchment. The pages are very fragile."

"Okay," Roonie yelled from the kitchen. Within a few minutes he rejoined the girls at the table. "What do you need?"

Ani pushed the book to Roonie. "See here: this feather

with the half circle on the top is a bald eagle feather."

"Harrumph," said Eliza.

Ani glared at her and continued, "And this single circle means island. What I don't understand is what this straight line sticking out to the left before the circle represents. It kind of looks like it's connected to this oddly shaped diamond that I think represents MDI in its entirety."

Roonie stared at it for a minute. He turned the book sideways, and then upside down, and then back to the right side.

"Easy," he said nonchalantly while scratching his face.

"Easy!" both girls cried together.

"Yeah, easy. Bar Island. This stick must be the sandbar that connects MDI to Bar Island. And there are several eagles known to be nesting there."

Ani stared at the picture. It was so simple yet so perfect, she thought. "Roonie!" she said, "You're magnificent, absolutely magnificent!" Eliza ruffled his hair and Roonie beamed.

After consulting the tide chart extensively and not wanting to repeat their earlier broken-watch-and-tide debacle, they concluded they would not be able to get onto Bar Island until the tide was on its way out. They figured they would be able to cross over about an hour before low tide and have approximately two hours to find the eagle feather. But low tide was happening then, and they would not be able to bike to the sandbar in time. The next low tide was at three fifty-nine in the morning; it would be too dark to search for a feather then. That meant they would have to be ready for the next low tide at four ten in the afternoon, almost twenty-four hours from now, to make it across the sandbar, search the island, find the amulet, and get back to the mainland. Roonie had agreed to help his father pull his lobster traps out of the water early in the morning, but he promised he would be able to meet them tomorrow afternoon.

The girls were exhausted and went to bed early. Their father had come home from the lab very late to take a shower and check in with them. He saw that they were tucked into bed and asleep before he left again to head back to the lab. Ani had only pretended to be sleeping, and as soon as she heard his car drive away, she leapt out of bed and returned to the parchment.

Ani wanted to waste no time deciphering the final amulet location. She felt even greater urgency because her father had been evasive when she asked him what he knew about NC 241. She could sense that he was lying to her and Eliza, but what else could he do? He wasn't going to tell the girls anything that was going to cause them to worry more. Ani had done her own research but was unable to find anything definitive about the gas, yet she felt the real results were being hidden by the government agency responsible for NC 241. How could something that was going to kill the lobsters not affect other sea life? Reportedly it was a dense gas that once discharged would settle to the ocean floor and obliterate the lobster population. It had a limited shelf life and after it destroyed the lobsters and their eggs, which should take less than thirty minutes, the gas supposedly would naturally break down and dissipate, neutralized by mixing with the sodium in the water.

Ani didn't buy it. Not for one minute. Her father would have known about this gas, as he already had been given top security clearance when he worked on several major oil spills and other ocean catastrophes. And if her father believed the gas did dissolve as purported, he would have already suggested that NC 241 might be a viable solution to the lobster problem. It wasn't and he hadn't. That was enough for Ani.

The search for the green tourmaline had not been easy. Roonie could have been seriously hurt or even worse. Ani shuddered thinking about what might have happened. She bent her head down and stared at the parchment. Again, another circle, which meant an island, but this one had a zigzag on top of it, which she thought represented the Porcupine Islands. There were three islands surrounding MDI that were called the Porcupine Islands. Could they really want her to search all three? She hoped not. However, the zigzag shape also represented two other words, or so she thought. Professor Sol did mention that the Abenakis frequently used one drawing to stand for several objects. Sometimes the objects were connected to each other, but many times they were completely unrelated. Like baby and apple or seaweed and stream. Ani found decoding the first few amulets to be relatively easy. As she progressed, however, the translating and interpreting proved more challenging.

Her neck muscles hurt and her eyelids were heavy. She yawned and stood up to stretch and get a drink of water. She walked to her father's bedroom and lay down on his bed. It felt good to rest. Ani gazed out the open bedroom window. The moon was almost full and the night breeze gently caressed her tired face. She sighed and closed her eyes. She heard nothing. The evening was still. She could do this, she told herself. They will simply go to Bar Island and get the bald eagle feather. They have a plan, and they just need to follow it through. Easy. Easy. She sighed again and the doubt came rushing in. What if they couldn't find any bald eagles? What if the eagles knew what was going on and decided to fly the coop and go somewhere else, somewhere safe, somewhere far away from NC 241 and the lobsters? What if she wasn't able to figure out the next clue? What if, what if, what if?

The very faint but distinguishable sound of an owl hooting in the night interrupted her worries. Ani opened her eyes and listened. Seconds passed and she heard it again, this time a little stronger and a little longer. He's moving closer, she thought. She sat up and tiptoed to the window. The moon shone down on her, enclosing her small frame in pale golden light. She lifted back the sheer white curtains and peered out into the night.

"Who, who," the owl hooted.

Ani whispered, "I am here. I am Kanake-kee."

The owl answered her call with his own. "Who, who," and again "who, who."

"Thank you," Ani whispered back. The owl was perched on the branch of a pine tree. His eyes were dark, piercing, and all knowing. Ani stared back at him and bowed her head slightly. She returned to her father's bed and covered herself with the throw blanket. She was not afraid anymore.

* * * *

Since the word had gotten out about the NC 241, the entire island was in an uproar. Environmental groups, pro-lobster groups, anti-lobster groups, anti-government groups, pro-military groups, and just about any group that perceived it had an issue with the gas solution appeared overnight and took up residence on the island. While the National Guard had secured the entrance to the island by land, folks managed to find a way to reach the island by ocean. This too eventually was restricted and secured by the Coast Guard, but by the time that operation was in full gear, the island had already been inundated with people clamoring, arguing, videotaping, and, much to Mayor Peterson's delight, purchasing.

Sequestered away on the Baxter estate, the sisters had no idea what bedlam was going on in town. Journalists from all over the globe had arrived to report on the lobster catastrophe that was now making international headlines. Trenton, the last mainland town before the bridge to Mount Desert Island, was clogged with traffic coming on and off the island.

The mayor had gotten over his despair at having to cancel the lobster festival, as Bar Harbor was at capacity with all the extra visitors. He was slightly concerned about the gas canisters being dropped in the harbor, but he was confident the officials knew what they were doing and he simply trusted that soon all would go back to the way it was before. Never one to shy away from the cameras, the mayor had planted himself in the center of town. Eating his favorite sandwich, a lobster roll, he bounced from reporter to reporter, telling his own story of how he was the one who originally discovered the lobsters were migrating to MDI and other such tall tales for the eager audience hungry for any news, truthful or not.

Ani and Eliza rode their bikes to town. The streets were overcrowded with cars, mostly filled with tourists evacuating the island. What visitors had hoped would be a relaxing and memorable vacation was certainly memorable, but certainly not relaxing. The girls had to abandon their bikes a few blocks from the library and proceed on foot. Ani wanted to do some research on the bald eagle. She wanted to be clear what their feathers looked like. As much as the sea and all the creatures of the deep intrigued her, she wasn't much of an ornithologist. Most feathers looked alike to Ani, save the obvious variations in color, but she wanted to be sure she knew what they would be seeking on Bar Island.

Mrs. Starke was seated at the front desk when the girls arrived. As usual, her gray hair was pulled tightly back into a bun, yet the dark circles under her eyes made her look like she hadn't slept in a week. Ani remembered how upset she had been with the upheaval caused by the impromptu town meeting, but this morning she kindly directed the girls to an area where they could find several books on the American bald eagle.

Eliza picked up the latest beauty magazine and refused to cooperate in any investigation that centered on the eagle. Her dislike only increased when Ani showed her pictures of them, pictures that depicted them soaring after their prey or, more often than not, stealing prey from another bird.

"I told you they let others work for them," she said, thumbing through her magazine. "What do you think of this hair style?" She showed Ani a picture of a girl with long, curly blonde hair.

"Wouldn't work for you," Ani said and quickly resumed her research.

"I think I would look good as a blonde," Eliza said, pulling her long ponytail in front and staring at the ends.

"Eliza, really?"

Eliza frowned.

"Here, this is a good picture of the feathers. Have you seen a copier anywhere?"

Eliza didn't look up but pointed behind the circulation desk.

"I'll be right back," said Ani, grabbing a few of the books on the table. Luckily she had stuffed some change in her pocket before they had left the cottage. Ani waited while the picture of the eagle's wing slid out from the copier. This one showed in detail what a feather looked like. I hope this helps, she thought and headed back to retrieve her sister.

When she got back to their table, Eliza was nowhere to be seen. Her magazine was on the ground, but no Eliza. That's strange, thought Ani. She knows we need to go soon. Frustration and anger welled up inside her. Eliza could be so difficult sometimes, especially when she got in one of her moods. This was one of those times. Ani took a deep breath and looked around. Where is she? We need to go home to get some supplies before meeting Roonie.

"Psst, psst." Ani turned toward the noise coming from behind her, near the staircase. "Psst, psst." The noise repeated. Ani could hear it but was unsure where it was coming from or where to go next. Before she had time to react, she was grabbed from the back and pulled into a corner behind the stacks.

"Hey," Ani cried, but a hand covered her mouth muffling the sound. Ani's eyes grew wide, but she relaxed when she recognized Eliza's voice whispering in her ear.

"It's those weird guys, the ones from the restaurant yesterday morning. The tall one has his camera, and he was taking pictures of you while you were making copies. I went to get another magazine and saw them!" Ani tried to speak but her words came out garbled. Eliza removed her hand. "Sorry," Eliza said.

"Where are they now?" Ani whispered.

Eliza took a large book, opened it wide and placed it on the shelf they were hiding behind. It shielded their heads when they stood. Eliza motioned to a seating area to the left of the circulation desk. The men were seated in comfortable leather chairs hiding their faces behind newspapers. Ani noticed the taller guy was holding his paper upside down and higher than the other man, exposing the camera dangling around his neck.

"Why are they following us?" asked Eliza.

"I don't have any idea."

"I bet they're connected to the creepy gardener somehow, and he's asked them to keep an eye on us. They were all at Jordan's Restaurant yesterday!"

"But why?" Ani said. "It just doesn't make any sense."

"They could work for the government or something and are on to us and what we are doing."

"The upside-down newspaper the camera guy is pretending to read leads me to believe they are not professionals."

Eliza peered out from behind the book and giggled softly. "I see what you mean, Ani."

"Your theory about the gardener could be correct. He has been strange around us and always seems to be popping up wherever we are. When we saw him at the cottage, I figured it was because he was the gardener and needed to be everywhere to supervise the other workers. But now I'm not so sure. You haven't seen him here have you, Eliza?"

"No, not yet anyway. But that's probably why he sent these guys, the bug guys, as Roonie called them yesterday. He doesn't want us to see him for fear we would figure out what he's up to. They're here to check up on us and report back to him. No tourist would be taking pictures in a library," Eliza said.

"Uh oh," whispered Ani. "The bug guys are getting restless. The small one just stood up and hit the other one with his hat."

"Most likely because he noticed the paper." Eliza chuckled. "Time for us to exit."

"I have what I need," said Ani, tucking her copies into her back pocket.

* * * *

Eliza had been correct. Daniel had noticed that Lyle was pretending to read a newspaper upside down and yes, he had hit him with his hat as a result. Daniel wondered what was taking that girl so long at the copier. Their stuff was still strewn about the table, but he felt uneasy that the girls hadn't returned. He and Lyle couldn't afford to mess up again with Barton. They had to report to Sorenson later this afternoon, and Daniel wanted to be sure to have something to report. Nearly fifteen minutes had passed since Lyle photographed the girl making copies. Daniel resumed pretending to read his paper but found an article that caught his attention. *Missing woman's glasses found. Hannah Coleman's glasses were found on the basement floor of Mrs. Rachel Sullivan's house, the second woman to go missing in the past few days.* Daniel read on, concerned by what he was reading. *Police suspect foul play was behind both women's disappearance. Police discovered a freshly baked blueberry pie on the counter in Mrs. Sullivan's kitchen with clean laundry hanging from the line."Not something you normally see if someone was planning on taking her own life or running away," declared Bar Harbor Police Detective Randy Rayhill.*

The article continued, *Moreover, Daniel Thibodeau, co-owner of Rest from Your Pests with his brother, Lyle Thibodeau, had recently reported to the police that Mrs. Coleman had showed up for work earlier in the week and left a note for the brothers that she was going out on a pest call and that she would return soon. She did not return, however, and has not been heard from since. Her optician, Gina DeStefano, verified that the glasses found on the Sullivan premises earlier this morning were Hannah Coleman's. Why and how the glasses ended up in the basement is unclear. The other mystery is the inordinate amount of seaweed that was reported found on the basement floor along with a few lobster legs. This is puzzling to be sure, as the area surrounding the Sullivan residence has not experienced any tidal surges as of late. Several local people believe that the recent influx of lobsters, both in population and size, might have something to do with the disappearance of the two women. Police are asking anyone with any information regarding this case to please contact the station.*

Daniel put the paper down in shock and disbelief. Hannah killed by lobsters? Could this be true? No, it can't be. Hannah just got fed up with us is all and she probably took a trip to visit her sister out to Brandy Pond. These reporters are most likely in cahoots with the town officials, trying to drum up business for the festival. At least the reporter had gotten the name of the business right. Once when he had taken an ad out to promote a new monthly special—ants, fleas, and silverfish treatment 20 percent off—the paper had made a typo and instead of Rest from Your Pests, it read Test for Your Pests. Who wants a test for their pests? Lyle had thought this was hilarious, but Daniel had been angry. The idiot at the newspaper had simply said, "sorry" and offered to rerun the ad for free. It still made him mad to think about it. The staff at Jordan's had had quite a good time making fun of him and Lyle every time they entered the restaurant. They pretended to be bugs and asked them test questions such as, "If a silverfish travels by train from California to Maine while an ant travels by plane from Maine to California, what time do the fleas arrive?"

Lyle crumpled Daniel's newspaper. "I think we lost them again, Daniel."

"What?"

"The girls. I checked the entire library. They're not here."

Daniel hit Lyle with his hat for the umpteenth time. "Mr. Baxter is going to throttle us. Lyle, how could you let this happen?"

"Me?"

"Stop standing there with your mouth open. Go get the van and meet me out front. We have to find them and find them quickly."

As Lyle exited out the back to the parking lot, Daniel raced out the front door of the library. He looked up and down the street, but didn't see the girls anywhere. Main Street had become even more crowded than when he and Lyle entered the library about an hour ago. How was he going to find the girls now? Daniel walked down the granite stairs and to the corner to wait for Lyle.

But then Daniel spied a small boy on a red bike weaving his way through the crowd of people and heading right toward him and the library. As the boy drew closer, Daniel recognized the Spider-Man T-shirt. Roonie locked eyes with Daniel as he sped past the library and smiled.

Daniel thought to himself, where Spider-Man goes the girls are sure to follow. "Lyle," he hollered to his brother as Lyle rounded the corner, "we've got a spider to pursue!" Daniel made Lyle shove over so he could drive. "I'm in your web, spider boy," Daniel muttered, "and I don't think you're going to like it." He chuckled to himself and banged the side of the van.

* * * *

Patrick had spent the morning deadheading the annuals, as he liked to do this time of year. He appreciated the vibrant colors and the diversity of the petals that some of his favorite annuals demonstrated in July: the coral of the snapdragons, the intricacies of the folds of the cut and come again zinnias, and the fragility of the slender stock. Patrick loved these plants much like a teacher loves his students. Both gardener and teacher soon learn that with support, tenderness, and encouragement mixed with plenty of sunshine and fresh air, plants and pupils will grow and bloom. But this was not the case today. Patrick pretended to weed the bed closest to the wooden door in hopes of catching Ani and Eliza as they left the property. He felt the need, a protective need he had not felt since Amelia vanished, to follow the girls to see what they were doing and to determine if the Thibodeau brothers were pursuing them.

At about ten in the morning, the girls had bounded out through the cottage door and leapt on their bicycles. Patrick had hid behind the grouping of mountain laurels unseen by the sisters. He overheard the older one mention the library. He waited an appropriate amount of time before jumping into his pickup and driving to town. Surprised by all the hubbub, he elected to park in Don's Stop and Shop parking lot and walk the few blocks to the side entrance of the library.

When he reached his destination, he recognized the Rest from Your Pests vehicle in the back. These guys have got to get a different van, he thought. You can spot that bug a mile away. Patrick snickered to himself and opened the heavy glass door to the library. He lowered his straw hat to cover his face, but really, whom was he kidding? Green Dickies, a blue denim shirt, and work boots had been his uniform for as long as he and anyone else in this town could remember. If he ran into the girls, he could mention that he was doing research on a new perennial or something like that. He didn't like to lie, never had, and never would, but these strange times called for strange behavior.

Patrick walked the perimeter of the library and glimpsed the girls at one of the large tables. They seemed busy and didn't notice Patrick at all. He decided to search the back for Lyle and Daniel. He found them in the next alcove, both sitting behind newspapers. Lyle's paper was upside down. These two were definitely not the sharpest tools in the shed, an expression his father liked to use when Patrick was younger. Patrick moved to a point halfway between the girls and the Thibodeau brothers. He opened a book and waited. He had all day if necessary.

During this time Patrick observed Ani head to the copy machine and Eliza get another magazine. He next saw Eliza discover Lyle and Daniel and quickly inform Ani. The two left via the same side door that Patrick had come through while Lyle and Daniel continued to wait. Hey dummies, Patrick wanted to shout, they went that a way. He decided to leave as well and to see if he could follow the girls. Lyle and Daniel could do no harm sitting in the library.

Once Patrick walked back to Don's food store and retrieved his truck, he backtracked to the library and saw Daniel on the street pointing to that Roonie kid on his bike. Like the brothers, Patrick knew that Roonie had been hanging around the girls since they had arrived. As he couldn't see the girls anywhere he looked, he too reckoned that following Roonie would lead him to the sisters.

* * * *

Roonie was no fool. Using his bike mirror, he quickly knew the bug guys and the gardener were shadowing him. His suspicions had been right, and he felt downright smug, thinking Ani and Eliza would think him so clever when he unveiled his plan. He had been specific with them yesterday about what they needed to bring, and where and when they were to meet him before their journey to Bar Island.

Let's bring these gentlemen on a joy ride through the Park Loop, he thought, passing the gate to Acadia National Park. The park rangers waved him by, as he really did know just about everyone on the island. Roonie was disheartened to read that the Cadillac Mountain Summit Road would be closed to all traffic, foot, bike, or car at sunset tonight. It really is happening, he thought, but he felt better knowing that he was part of the solution to everyone's problem. Roonie coasted downhill, picking up speed as he rounded the corner. He loved this part of the Park Loop Road: mountain on one side, ocean on the other. Where the mountains meet the sea, his father always said to describe the beauty of Acadia. Roonie hadn't been to too many places in his young life, but figured that Mount Desert Island had to be one of the most beautiful in the world. He checked his bike mirror and was pleased to see that, sure enough, both vehicles were hot on his trail.

* * * *

The girls had arrived home, winded and hungry. Eliza swiftly made them lunch, cucumber sandwiches with sliced tomatoes and chips. They were running low on food since Dad hadn't been around to shop or sleep much, for that matter. Ani tore around the cottage looking for the items on Roonie's list: picnic basket, extra-long pants and sweatshirt for both girls, two hats, preferably sun and not baseball cap, beach blanket, water bottles, marker, crackers, and golf umbrella. He had called very early this morning excited about a plan he had and made Ani promise to do as he instructed. Ani had been able to find everything except for their hats. She rummaged around a few closets downstairs and was grateful to find one fishing hat and one old Red Sox hat. It would have to do. She didn't know why Roonie needed her to bring these things, but she appreciated his help.

Eliza was still in her funk, and Ani was looking forward to meeting up with Roonie. He had a way of making Eliza laugh and reducing the tension. Both girls had been stressed over the lobster situation and equally worried about their father. This summer vacation had turned into a whole lot more than what they bargained for. Ani was drained, and the expression "vacation from my vacation" kept popping into her mind.

After they had eaten and cleaned up their dishes, the girls put the long pants, sweatshirts, and hats on as directed by Roonie. Eliza complained that the baseball hat would mess up her hair, so Ani offered to give her the tan fishing hat. Then she argued that the fishing hat was too ugly, so she changed her mind and kept the baseball hat instead. The girls loaded the other supplies into the picnic basket with some snacks for Eliza, note cards, a blanket, and the pictures of the eagle feathers. Ani strapped the basket to the back of her bike while Eliza placed the umbrella across her handlebars and they were off. Roonie had wanted them to arrive at two in the afternoon, lock their bikes around the corner by the Rock Shop Café, and set up the blanket like they were having a summer picnic.

"Okay, this is bizarre," Eliza said. "All these lobstermen are pulling their boats out of the water, the tourists are leaving, the National Guard is moving in, and others are wandering around in a fog while we are having a picnic." Ani shrugged and sat down on the plaid blanket to wait. Her long pants and sweatshirt made her warm, and she rolled up her sleeves. Eliza scratched her head a few times under the oversized hat. She really hated wearing hats.

"Hi, guys." A smiling Roonie landed in the center of the blanket, flinging his rucksack next to the picnic basket. His Spider-Man T-shirt was clinging to his back with visible sweat stains. "Do you have any water?" He panted. Eliza handed him a bottle from the basket. He grabbed it, twisted open the cap, and gulped it down.

"Roonie," said Ani, "are you okay? What have you been

doing?"

Roonie detailed, while downing another water bottle, his bike ride through the park and how both the bug brothers and the gardener followed him.

"I knew it," said Eliza. "I knew the gardener was involved with this somehow."

"I biked by the library about the time you two left there, and soon I was being pursued by the ugly bug van and then bam, the gardener showed up, too. For the last hour, I have been touring them around the park roads and," he added while dropping his voice to a whisper, "don't look, but I would guess that all three of them will be here soon." Eliza looked up immediately.

"Eliza, don't look," said Ani.

Eliza bowed her head and murmured, "I can't help it. When someone says 'don't,' I just have to do."

"I know," said Ani, exaggerating the *know*.

"They must all have something to do with the lobsters, and that is why they are chasing us. They know what we are doing and they want to stop us," Eliza said.

"I'm not so sure about that," Ani said.

"Why?" asked Eliza.

"Yeah, why?" said Roonie.

"Because if they really wanted to stop us, they could have simply stopped us, taken our bikes, kidnapped us, and locked us up, or worse, told Dad that we were traipsing all over MDI."

"Maybe," replied an unconvinced Eliza, "but something is up with them because don't look now, they're here."

Both Roonie and Ani glanced up to see the bug brothers sitting on a park bench behind them and the gardener on a bench on the opposite side eating an apple. "See, it's hard not to look up when someone tells you not to," Eliza said and smiled.

"Roonie, what do you have in mind? We have all the stuff so now what? We need to start over to Bar Island soon," Ani said.

"We're going to create a little diversion in order to guarantee that we're not followed as we find the next amulet."

Roonie explained to the girls his plan, which, Ani had to admit, was pretty darn good. As instructed, Ani opened the golf umbrellas—Roonie had brought one as well—and placed them side by side. This created a nice protective cover so neither Daniel, Lyle, nor the gardener could see what they were doing. The kids took off their outer layers of sweatshirts and jeans and an extra Spider-Man T-shirt for Roonie.

"Okay," Roonie said, clearly enjoying being in charge for a change, "before we go to part two of my plan, each of us should stick our head out with our hats and make sure they see us before ducking back down behind the umbrellas. Got it?"

Eliza went first, peeking out with the overly large Red Sox hat, yawning ostentatiously, stretching her arms over her head, and sitting back down. Next up was Ani who grabbed a few crackers from the basket and ate them while in plain view of the three men.

"Hey, don't eat those," Roonie said. "We need them for part two!"

"Sorry," said Ani and crouched back down behind the umbrellas.

Roonie then emerged with a red knit hat pulled tightly down on his head and paused before disappearing from view. He reached into his rucksack and pulled out a package of balloons. He handed round ones to the girls and said, "Here, take these and blow them up. I will do the long ones."

"Huh?" asked Eliza.

"See," he said blowing a few puffs into his long red balloon, the kind normally used for making balloon animals at birthday parties and other special occasions. "We can use these ones for the legs and arms." He blew some more. "And the round ones we can use for our heads."

"Our heads?" asked Eliza letting the air out of her balloon.

"Oh, I get it, Roonie. Ingenious," said Ani. "We're making decoys of ourselves to fool our stalkers."

"What if we blow away?" asked Eliza. "It is kind of windy out."

"We'll use these," Roonie said, flourishing short gardening stakes. "I hope you don't mind a few holes in your clothes."

"Roonie, this is fantastic!" Eliza said.

"Yeah, Roonie, great idea," Ani said. "But how are we going to leave without them seeing us?"

"Part three of my plan is foolproof. Let's finish this and I'll show you." The girls did as instructed and blew up their balloon heads. They each stuffed their own clothes with the balloons and attached the pants and sweatshirts together with twine, safety pins, and packing tape. Roonie took a marker and drew a big smiley face on his balloon with a winking eye.

"Nice touch," said Eliza.

Close up, it looked like an elementary school art project gone bad. But from a distance, it did look like three people enjoying a summer day having a picnic in the park. They put their supplies for Bar Island into Roonie's bag. Ani checked her newly purchased watch. She wasn't taking any chances after what happened at Thunder Hole. Three o'clock: time to get going, she thought and felt a twinge of apprehension.

"Ready?" asked Roonie with a mischievous grin planted squarely on his freckled face. Both girls nodded. Eliza giggled nervously.

"When I say run, you run low and fast down the hill and left to the bikes, okay?"

"Yes, sir," said Eliza, saluting as if in the military.

"Roger," Ani said.

Roonie was pleased to see a large crowd of people, reporters, military personnel, and a few locals, walking on the sidewalk about twenty feet in front of them.

"Perfect," said Roonie as he stuck his hand back into the basket and pulled out the box of crackers he had asked Ani to bring. He took out the four full sleeves and began crunching them up with his fingers. His hands moved quickly as they squeezed and pressed and squished the crackers until he was satisfied that they were mashed into crumbs. He ripped open the tops of each sleeve and carefully placed them on the edge of the grass by the blanket. "Get ready to run on my command," he said to the girls. Next, he crawled forward, still mindful to remain hidden behind the umbrellas, and picked up the sealed end of the sleeves. Then he flung the bags toward the crowd, and the cracker crumbs flew out in all directions. In a flash, gulls swooped down upon the area eager to feed. People yelled and shooed the squawking birds away.

"Run," commanded Roonie, "Run!" And they did just that. They ran down the hill and around the corner. They reached their bikes out of breath and excited.

"Are they coming?" Ani asked.

Roonie, already on his bike, looked behind him. "I don't see them. Hurry!"

The girls followed him to Bridge Street, which led to the water's edge and the sandbar, when it was visible, to Bar Island. The kids hid their bikes underneath a clump of thick juniper bushes. Ani was anxious to get started, but unfortunately the sandbar was barely apparent, as the tide was still receding. There was nothing they could do but wait for the path to the island to connect once the tide had gone out farther. Several signs, which had to have been newly planted, dotted the landscape. They read,

BEACHES CLOSED UNTIL FURTHER NOTICE
NO SWIMMING, WADING, OR BOATING
PER ORDER OF THE TOWN OF BAR HARBOR

Roonie picked up a rock and hurled it into the water and then jumped back when a few good-sized lobsters sprung out of the water to capture whatever had interrupted their swimming below the surface. Both girls screamed.

"Leaping lobsters!" cried Roonie.

"You're not kidding," Ani said.

"I think I want to go back home," Eliza said.

"What are you kids doing?" a man in uniform said, causing all three to jump again and turn away from the water. He was a reservist sent to watch the area and keep civilians from crossing over to Bar Island. No one answered.

He repeated himself sternly this time. "I said, what are you doing here?"

All three spoke at once. "Nothing, not anything, nothing at all."

"You're not supposed to be here so get along home now."

"But we need to get over to Bar Island, sir," Ani said.

"Well, I'm afraid that won't be possible, little lady."

"Tony?" said Roonie. "Tony Seymour? It's me, Roonie, Roonie Jay Cyr. You were our paper boy, 43 James Street, remember?"

"Roonie! Wow, it is you. You've really grown up. I barely recognized you. Who are your friends?"

Roonie introduced Ani and Eliza. The girls said hello. Ani was impatient to get to the island as she could see the sandbar emerging from the receding water and getting larger. Soon they would be able to cross over and then the clock would really begin to tick because the sandbar wouldn't last forever. Ani nudged Roonie and gave him a hurry-up-and-convince-this-guy-to-let-us-go look.

Eliza grinned. "Isn't it funny that Roonie would know you? He just seems to know everybody and everything on MDI. Isn't that right, Ani?"

Ani matched Eliza's grin with her own. "Yes it is. In fact, ever since we got here a few weeks ago, Roonie has been an excellent tour guide."

"Excellent," Eliza said.

"That's right, I have been," Roonie said.

"He was going to take us over to Bar Island. That's why we're here," Eliza said. "We were so hoping that Roonie would be able to take us there. I just love a sandbar, don't you?"

"Love it, yeah," said Ani. Tony frowned.

"What do you say, Tony? I mean Captain Seymour?"

"I'm not a captain, Roonie," Tony said. "Only a sergeant."

"I'm sure you'll be a captain soon," Roonie said. "Do you think I can take the girls over there real quick? I promise we will come right back." Tony hesitated and stared at the kids.

"We so want to see the island. We can be really, really, really speedy," Ani said.

"I could get in trouble, big trouble."

"You won't get into any trouble because we will be back before you know it. Please?" Roonie said.

"All right, but you need to wait until I walk over to the other corner, okay?"

"Thanks, Sergeant Seymour." Tony smiled and moved away from them. After a few strides, he turned back to ask Roonie to say hello to his parents for him, but the kids had already run off and were halfway across the sandbar.

Roonie was in the lead, next Ani, and then Eliza. Finally they were doing something, Ani thought. Maybe they would get lucky and just find a feather lying on the ground, ready to be picked up and put in with the other amulets. Ani had hidden the parchment in the freezer behind the vanilla ice cream and waffles. She was glad that she had taken the time to hide her treasured Abenaki book, even more so now that they knew the gardener was also spying on them. He could go into the cottage house whenever he wanted and probably did when she and Eliza left the property. I bet it was him who moved my backpack the first time I hid the book, she thought. I wonder if they have figured out that we're not picnicking? Ani broke into a grin thinking about the gardener and the bug guys sitting on the bench back at the park. She had to hand it to Roonie. His plan had been incredible.

Ani leapt onto the edge of the island from the sandbar and hurried to catch up to Roonie, who had already taken the path that he had said wound around to the more desolate part of the island. He had explained that it was on this part of Bar Island he had seen an eagle's nest when out on the boat with his father. Consulting her watch, which she was relieved to see was working correctly, Ani called to Eliza, "We will have only about two hours to find the feather so ..."

"So I know, hurry up, Eliza. I'm coming, I'm coming," Eliza said. "I just need to catch my breath." She reached her sister and put her hand on her shoulder, bending over and trying to gulp in more oxygen.

"We haven't got time to rest. The sandbar is larger and soon the tide will change. Look," Ani said and pointed back to the mainland, the sandbar widening almost before their eyes.

"Oh my, well look at that. You could drive a car over now!" Eliza said.

Roonie yelled from the path, "Come on. Quit your gabbing and let's go."

"We're coming," said Ani.

The path through the woods narrowed and the foliage thickened as they moved deeper into the island. The sunlight, once bright and warm, had become intermittent and at times completely blocked by the tall pines, cedar, and birch trees. Low-lying shrubs and ground plants became denser and prickl-ier, slowing down the kids as they tried to bend the branches back out of their way and then hold on to them to avoid whack-ing the person walking behind. The air smelled woodsy mixed with a pungent low-tide aroma. Maine, thought Ani affection-ately.

The mosquitoes also increased. Ani had been bitten sev-eral times and small welts had emerged on both her calves and forearms. The burn and itch was uncomfortable, but she did not complain. Eliza, on the other hand, had enough complaints for everyone. She was hot, she was tired, she was hungry, she was getting scratched, the bugs were bad, and on and on. Over the years, Ani had learned to tune her out and not say any-thing, as responding to her always made the situation worse. Roonie, however, had not grown up with Eliza and had reached his limit.

"Eliza! Please stop."

"What?"

"What? Seriously? What?"

"Yeah, seriously, what?" she mimicked him.

"You're complaining. I really can't take it." Roonie looked for confirmation from Ani. Ani looked up at the trees and pre-tended to whistle.

"Complaining? I'm not complaining! I'm just saying out loud what everyone else is feeling. The island should be called

Bad Island, not Bar Island. It is just all bad. We haven't even come close to seeing anything that resembles a feather. If we were looking for mosquitoes, we would be all set."

Wisely, Ani ignored her, but Roonie sighed heavily and barked, "I'm not feeling anything that you're saying out loud. All I am feeling is that I can't listen to you yelling at the stupid bushes and the stupid mosquitoes and the stupid plants and the stupid this and the stupid that!"

"Well they're all stupid!"

While Eliza and Roonie bickered, Ani forged ahead and discovered that the path came to an end at the beach on the far side of the island. Ani scanned the tree line with her binoculars. If there was a nest, it was hidden well. She checked the time again. A little more than an hour left before they had to leave, and they were no closer to finding the feather. Roonie and Eliza continued to argue as they approached her. She had to take charge. There was no more time to mess around.

"You two can finish your argument later, but right now we need to find a nest. I can't see anything because the trees are too close together. Anyone up for a climb?"

Roonie and Eliza jumped at the chance to get up in the trees. They shared a love of heights. Each found a pine tree and climbed up, up, up. Ani followed them with the binoculars. Thirty, forty, fifty feet up in the air she saw them climb. Ani's stomach flipped over. Seeing them so high caused her to feel dizzy and lightheaded. She yelled at them from the ground, "Do you see anything?"

Both yelled down, "Nooo."

Not good, not good at all, Ani thought. Ten more minutes passed, and the climbers got still higher. Not finding a nest, Roonie and Eliza eventually climbed back down.

"Now what?" asked Roonie. A shadow crossed over their heads, and all three looked up.

"An eagle, an eagle!" they cried.

"Chase him!" shouted Ani. "He might be going to his nest!"

The eagle glided in toward the trees and then out over the ocean. Please go to your nest and not back out to sea, thought

Ani. The eagle took another big loop over their heads before soaring back to the trees and eventually landing in a tall pine close to the shore. The eagle perched alongside his nest, resting from his flight. "Wow," Ani said, lowering the binoculars. "Now that I know where he is, I can easily see the nest. Do you see it?"

With her hand Eliza shaded her eyes from the sun, as her too large Red Sox cap was atop a balloon back in town. "I see it, I see it. He's in the taller tree, about one, two, three trees back from the edge."

"Where? I can't see him. What tree?"

Ani moved Roonie's head and pointed. "There, up there."

"Oh, now I see it. Thanks. Now what?"

"Now you and Eliza climb up and get a feather. There must be one just lying around in the nest. Roonie, you climb the tree to the right since it looks like the nest overlaps with that tree. And Eliza, you climb the tree he is in. Okay?"

"We can't go while he is in the nest," Eliza said. "He'll attack us. I haven't forgotten the picture of the talons."

"He won't attack you two because you're too big. He'll fly away as you get closer, and then you'll be able to search."

"Sounds good," said Roonie.

Eliza frowned. "I hope you're right."

* * * *

Patrick's own snoring startled him awake and caused his hat to fall off and land on the ground in front of him. He picked it up and placed it back on his head. His watch indicated that he had been asleep for only about fifteen minutes. It took him a second to remember where he was and what he was doing. He hadn't slept very well lately and right now he felt each one of his sixty-eight years of age. He noticed that Daniel was still sitting on the bench, but Lyle had left. Scanning the area, he saw Lyle walking back up the hill in the center of the park with a large chocolate ice cream cone. The kids' umbrellas were still there, and he could see the boy's leg sticking out. Perhaps they also had fallen asleep, but he doubted that. When he was their age, he could go all day without being tired.

Patrick watched as Lyle took a few licks of his cone and moved even closer to the kids. He stood up, feeling that protective emotion again. He decided to stroll down the side of the park just to be nearer to the kids in case, well, in case he was needed. He could see that Daniel also had gotten up and was moving toward the blanket. Now Lyle was only a couple of yards away when he dropped his cone to the ground and lunged for Roonie's leg, which he lifted high over his head, causing both umbrellas to flip back and land upside down.

Lyle shouted to his brother. "They're gone! The children are gone!"

Daniel had reached Lyle at the kids' blanket. "What do you mean gone?"

Lyle grabbed another figure and handed it to his brother. The fishing hat fell off, revealing a peach colored balloon. A smiley face with one of the eyes closed to look like a wink stared at the brothers mockingly.

"They used balloons!" said Lyle. "They stuffed balloons into their clothes."

"I can see that," Daniel said, hitting his brother on the head with the winking face balloon. Patrick stopped on the sidewalk and pretended to tie his shoe. He could hear everything the brothers were saying.

"Mr. Baxter is going to throttle us, and worse, we won't get paid. We have no idea what they were doing, what they have been doing, and where they are doing whatever it is we don't know about! This is disastrous."

"Huh?" said Lyle.

"It doesn't matter. What matters is that we have to find the girls and that boy and find them quick. Mr. Baxter wants us to meet him later on tonight with new information and photos of their whereabouts, and we have nothing to show him. Let's get the van and drive around. We might get lucky."

When they were out of sight, Patrick examined the scene.

"Clever," he said, "very clever indeed." Obviously the kids

knew the Thibodeau brothers were spying on them, but did that mean they knew he was following them, too? And what does Barton have to do with all of this? Why in the world would he want to know what three children were doing? He despises children. All people for that matter. Patrick folded up the umbrellas and jumped on the clothes to pop the balloons. He collected the other belongings and headed back to his truck. It might be time for me to visit my oldest friend, and see if I can figure out what he is up to. Whatever it is, Patrick thought, it can't be good. *Good* and *Barton* are two words that never go together. Never have and never will.

* * * *

Roonie was a good climber, but Eliza, at her age and with her height, was faster. Despite being more of a girlie girl, Eliza was strong and determined when it came to climbing and gained more confidence the higher she went.

Ani, using the binoculars, could see Eliza's tree sway slightly because of her weight and noted she was still about eight feet from the nest. More important, the eagle was still there, seemingly unaware that he was about to get company. Roonie was only a few feet lower than Eliza. My goodness, they are both so high up, Ani thought, feeling that queasiness come over her once more. She rested her head against a tree, and when she looked at Eliza again Ani was surprised that she hadn't made any progress. What's wrong, she wondered? The higher branches looked solid. Why isn't she climbing up? Why is she waving her hand around?

"Oh no!" Ani exclaimed. "What are those birds doing?" She tightened her grip on the binoculars and squinted to get a better focus. Birds of all varieties were flying around Eliza. Seagulls, falcons, cormorants, terns, petrels, and puffins flapped their wings, squawked loudly, and, "Oh no!" Ani cried again. The birds were pooping on Eliza. "Oh, gross, gross, gross, gross!" But Ani got it. She knew the second she spied the first bird. She knew it before she had instructed, no demanded, that

Eliza and Roonie climb the trees because of her fear of heights. It was not supposed to be Eliza and Roonie who found the amulets. It was supposed to be her, Ani, Kanake-kee.

Ani reached the base of the tree and yelled, "Eliza, Eliza, come down. They'll leave you alone once you climb down. I'm so sorry. So very sorry. Roonie, you, too. Come down before they attack you as well." But Ani didn't need to tell him anything. He was already on his way down hoping to avoid the same fate as Eliza. By the time Eliza landed, she was a mess. Her arms and legs were scraped by her scramble to reach the ground. Her shorts and shirt were torn and covered in sap, and bird poop clung to her hair, her back, and her calves. Eliza stood as if frozen to the ground, whimpering slightly.

"Roonie, go grab a few water bottles and a bandanna from my bag. Hurry!" She pulled a few clumps of pine needles from the side of Eliza's face. Ani whispered, "I'm sorry, Eliza, truly I am."

Roonie came back from the beach, and both kids gingerly cleaned up Eliza. They all knew she just couldn't jump into the water to wash off. The lobsters might be too big and too powerful, and they didn't want to find out. Ani's father had been adamant: *Don't go in the water, whatever you do!*

Eliza came out of her stupor. "Yuck, yuck, yuck," she moaned. "I think I'm going to puke!"

"Now you've got something legitimate to complain about," said Roonie, trying to lighten the mood. It didn't work.

Eliza cried while removing her outer T-shirt to reveal her tank top. "You're just lucky that I'm such a better climber than you, or you would've been the one they attacked."

"I know, I know," said Roonie, handing Eliza another wet bandanna.

Ani looked at her watch again: five-thirty. Alarm spread throughout her body. They needed to leave the island by six to make it across the sandbar. They already had one near mishap due to the tides when they were at Thunder Hole. She did not want to have another one. "Here, Roonie," she said, "help hoist me up to this limb. I have to get started if we want to make it back around the island and to the sandbar."

Ani pulled herself up on to the first limb. "Don't look down," said Roonie.

"Thanks," she said, trying hard to sound confident, but the crack in her voice let them know it was an act. Don't look down, don't look down, Ani repeated to herself. She would be fine if she didn't look down. This is what her parents always said to her when they were climbing together. I need to distract myself and remain calm. She climbed a few more feet. Suddenly, a poem that her favorite third grade teacher, Mrs. Multer, taught her came to mind.

Tis Bald Eagle, majestic and proud
Who soars above the trees so high
Tis Bald Eagle, majestic and proud
Wings aloft to help him fly
Tis Bald Eagle, majestic and proud
Talons strong so others flee
Tis Bald Eagle, majestic and proud
Bird for America, land of the free.

Repeating this made Ani feel a little better. Well, except for the part about the talons and the fleeing bit. Maybe by the time she reached the nest, her original hope would come true and the eagle would have departed and left a feather or two lying about.

She wanted to see how far she had come, but she knew if she did look down it would all be over. She was high enough now that she could feel the ocean breeze pick up force and make the tree sway, ever so slightly. She paused and then climbed higher. She was most struck by the stillness. Save for the wind, it felt as if someone had put the world on mute.

The silence reminded her of the time she went hang gliding with her mother. Her mother thought it would be cool for the two of them to glide over the Black Hills of South Dakota, where she was directing a dig hoping to uncover artifacts from the ancient Lakota tribe, who were early craftsmen in the area. Ani had been terrified by the prospect of being so high, but the beauty, along with the silence, eased her fear. She wondered what her mother was doing now. She wondered how she would react if she knew what her daughters were up to. She was fairly certain her mother wouldn't be pleased about them climbing without telling an adult. She probably wouldn't like them swimming with seals or cormorants or being chased by the creepy gardener and men who drove around with a large insect on their van. Good thing she isn't here, Ani thought, climbing higher.

At this height, Ani could see the bottom of the eagle's nest resting snugly between two limbs that formed an *X* near the tree's trunk. Twigs were connected in a haphazard yet unified manner. Impressive, thought Ani. I hope the eagle decided it was time to get some dinner and has flown off to hunt fish or something. She glanced out over the harbor still congested with the traffic of boat owners pulling their property out before the NC 241 was detonated. Despite the activity, from this height it all looked peaceful. Ani wondered what was actually going on beneath the surface. Were all the lobsters large or just some of them? What would the lobstermen do for a living once the lobster population was eradicated?

Her mind was filled with questions and worry. She reached for the next branch with her right hand and simultaneously moved her left foot to a bare limb. She hoisted herself up and raised her right foot to reach the next branch, but something terribly wrong happened. The branch supporting her left foot gave way and snapped free, tumbling down and bouncing on other limbs on its way to the ground. For a few unbelievably long moments Ani was hanging on to two limbs about three feet apart while her feet struggled to find something to stand on. When they finally landed on the same branch, Ani's entire body was awash with fear. She made her next mistake and looked down and saw only branches jutting out from the trunk of the tree. Paralyzed with fright, she was now unwilling to move up or down. Her breathing became rapid. Sweat poured into her eyes. Her palms were slippery around the branches she was gripping with all her might. She rested her forehead against the trunk and sighed. She recited the poem again, but this time out loud:"Tis Bald Eagle, majestic and proud/Who soars above the trees so high."

A breeze blew around her, cooling her almost instantly. She continued, "Tis Bald Eagle, majestic and proud/Wings aloft to help him fly."

Her heart rate slowed and her legs felt sturdier.

"Tis Bald Eagle, majestic and proud/Talons strong so others flee." She still didn't like this part of the poem.

"Tis Bald Eagle, majestic and proud/Bird for America, land of the free." She finished reciting, her voice stronger than when she started. "I have to do this. I simply have to do this," she said.

Slowly, Ani uncurled her right hand and extended it straight up to grab the higher branch. Next she bent her right knee and placed her foot securely on the next branch up. She climbed higher. With each step she believed more strongly she would reach the top. The bottom of the nest was only about three feet away. Ani was amazed by both its size and depth and tried to imagine how long it took for the bird to build his home. She climbed higher still, and the nest was within her reach. She scanned the structure: no luck, no feather sticking out.

Again, the wind picked up and the tree swayed. Ani noticed a string waving from the side of the nest. She shimmied closer and discovered that it was not a string, but a ribbon, a pale blue hair ribbon, nearly translucent from exposure to the elements. How did that get here? Then she remembered. The girl in the orb! The girl in the orb had her hair in braids, but one braid was missing a ribbon, a blue ribbon!

The ribbon was a sign. It had to be! Without hesitation she climbed up on the limb next to the nest. Fear had completely left her body until she faced the enormous bald eagle stoically awaiting her arrival. Ani gasped. The eagle stared at her with his steely yellow eyes. His talons were more frightening in person than the book from the library portrayed. For a few moments eagle and girl simply stared at each other.

Finally, Ani spoke. Her voice came out as a whisper. "I'm very sorry to disturb you, sir." The eagle blinked twice. "You see, I need to have a feather, a bald eagle feather to be exact, to stop the lobsters from taking over the town and also from being destroyed by the military." She paused as the eagle inched closer, his talons looking ever more scary and sharp. "So I was wondering, if it wasn't too much of a problem, if I, or if you would allow me to take one of your feathers, eagle, sir?" Ani finished her request and bowed.

The eagle turned his white head to the right, then left, and then right again, and then it happened. Roonie particularly loved this part of the story, and made Ani tell it over and over again. The eagle lifted his wings and extended them both full out, brushing Ani lightly in the face in the process. The wingspan had to be at least seven feet. He stood there, majestic and proud, wings aloft to help him fly, and swoosh, he lifted off. Talons strong so others flee, Ani thought, only Ani didn't flee. She stayed put. And the bald eagle, majestic and proud, dropped a feather into her hand before departing into the sky. A beautiful, golden feather from the bird for America, land of the free.

Lobster fact: *Not everyone agreed with the choice of the American bald eagle as the country's national symbol. In fact, Benjamin Franklin argued that the turkey would have been a more appropriate symbol.*

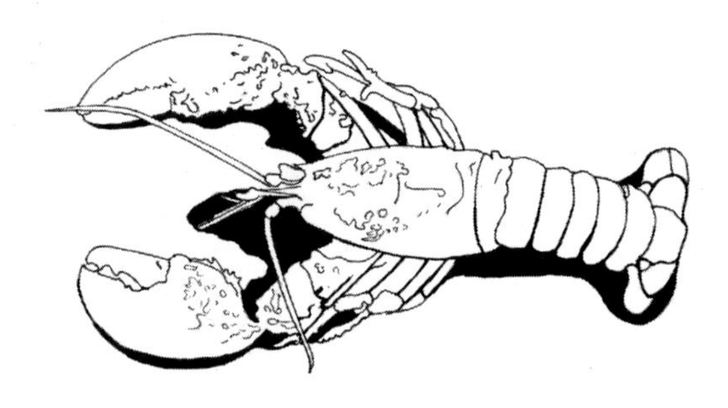

Chapter 40

Leaping Lobsters!

Although Ani had a difficult time getting up the towering pine, she had no problem getting down. "I got it!" she exclaimed as she dropped to the ground and held up the feather.

"Great job!" shouted Roonie as he grabbed his rucksack.

"Yeah, nice job, Ani," said Eliza, looking better after recovering from the attack of the birds.

"Thanks," Ani said. "I'll tell you all about it when we get back. Right now we've got to boogie. It's five forty-five. That means we've got fifteen minutes to get to the sandbar and reach the other side."

"Fifteen minutes!" bellowed Eliza. "We'll never make it."

"We've got no choice. If we don't, we're here for another twelve hours and we still have to get the final amulet."

"I know a short cut," Roonie said, and he took off. Roonie was a fast runner, but the girls kept his red Spider-Man shirt in sight as he moved in and out of the trees. Ani's chest tightened as she ran and her limbs grew heavy. Her slip seventy-five feet up in the pine tree had taken its toll. Her muscles ached all over, but she forged ahead, despite the pain, knowing she had to keep moving. Eliza, once again, lagged behind. As much as Ani did not like heights, Eliza detested running. Ani yelled to her sister, "Come on, Eliza, keep up. We can't get too far behind Roonie." Eliza grunted and scowled.

Roonie vaulted over a downed birch tree directly in their path. Ani copied him and easily jumped over the obstacle. Eliza, on the other hand, already tired from her trek, leaped as if she were running hurdles, cleared the log with her left foot, but caught it squarely with her right one.

She screamed. And Ani turned in time to see her sister somersault in mid-air and crash into a juniper bush. "Ouch. Dang it!"

Ani ran to her. "Eliza, are you okay?"

"Do I look like I'm okay?" said Eliza, who resembled an old man rubbing his backside. Several broken branches stuck out of her hair, reminding Ani of the time her mother had dressed them up as trees for a Halloween party. No store-bought costumes for the Banke children. They had hated that costume. Ani hid her grin. Eliza was fine.

"I can't see Roonie, can you?" she asked. Eliza rotated around in a semicircle and shook her head.

"Roonie, Rooooniiieee," cried Eliza.

The girls waited but heard nothing except for the occasional chickadee chirping chicka dee dee dee.

"Which way?" said Eliza.

"I'm not sure," said Ani.

"I'm a little disoriented," Eliza said.

Ani twisted to the right, then the left, and then back to the right again. Dismayed, she didn't have a clue. "I have no idea."

"I know one thing," said Eliza. "We are not going to make it off this island in time."

"We can't give up yet. We just need a little help."

"A little help? We need a search and rescue team is what we need," said Eliza as she pulled another branch from her hair. "Nice," she said, throwing it to the ground. Ani heard a rustle in the bushes and out scampered a raccoon and a skunk. "This is perfect," Eliza said. "This is just when we need the W-A-T to happen. Now we can be attacked by Rocky the rabid raccoon and then his pal stinky can spray us. This is ending up a perfect day!"

Ani smiled at the pair and spoke softly in a singsong voice. "I don't think they're here to hurt us, Eliza. They're here to help us."

"Of course, that makes wonderful sense. When in need, send in the skunk and raccoon. They always know what to do in a crisis."

The skunk, as if understanding Eliza's tone and message, arched her back and lifted her tail. Eliza immediately stepped back. "Sorry," she whispered. "Just kidding," she added in an attempt to strengthen her apology.

Ani bent her head. "Hello there." She cleared her throat. "I mean to say, so nice to see you. Can you show us how to get to the sandbar?"

The animals walked past the girls and into the trees. As if for effect, the skunk kept her tail up the entire time and stayed particularly close to Eliza. Eliza bowed in submission.

"Let's go," said Ani and took Eliza's hand.

"Hope they know a shortcut, too," said Eliza. They did, and when the girls arrived at the shore, Roonie burst through the trees as the raccoon and skunk headed back into the woods.

"Well, look at that," he said. "I thought I lost you two, but obviously you were in good hands. Or should I say paws?" Roonie laughed.

"You're hilarious, Roonie, a regular riot," quipped Eliza. Roonie tapped Ani and raised his eyes questioningly.

"She had another little mishap with a fallen birch tree, and let's just say the tree won. Very cranky."

"I can hear you," Eliza said.

"Time factor?" asked Roonie as the trio ran down the path leading to the sandbar.

"It's going to be close, real close," Ani said.

They were astonished to see how drastically the landscape had changed from when they first arrived. Where there once was an area large enough for a highway, now there was only a tiny strip measured in inches, not feet.

"No time to waste, girls," said Roonie, who kicked off his sneakers, placed them in his rucksack, and sprang onto the sand.

The girls tied their sneakers around their necks and,

with trepidation, ventured onto the sandbar. Roonie, never tired from any cardiovascular activity, sprinted ahead. Ani, seeing the sandbar get even narrower right before her eyes, felt a rush of adrenaline pump through her and ran to catch up to Roonie.

Eliza, beaten up by the birds and the birch tree, had lost all of her steam and slowly began the trek to reach the other side. The first few yards were easy, as the sand was intact and wide enough for a tired teenager to cross. However, twenty feet away from Bar Island with still about sixty feet to cover to get to Bar Harbor, the tide surged in and the strip of sand swiftly disintegrated into tiny islands much like stepping stones through a summer garden. Only this was no summer garden. This was a tide rolling in faster and deeper with each passing moment and loaded with lobsters, large, lurking, lethal lobsters.

Eliza, understanding the urgency, catapulted herself into the air to reach the next mound of sand. She landed in the center. This is easy, she thought, and leaped again to the next spot. Again and again, she leaped, landed, and coiled herself to leap again. But tide and time do not stand still, as the old saying goes, and today tide and time seemed to be on their fifth cup of coffee. Eliza was so focused on reaching the next mound, she neglected to look further toward the shore. By now Roonie had reached Bar Harbor and was promptly joined by Ani. Both pivoted around to look for Eliza, who much to their horror was standing about halfway on the one and only remaining patch of land on the sandbar. This was not Eliza's day.

"Eliza!" screamed Ani. "Stop!" Ani watched as Eliza prepared for her next leap, which would land her in the water.

"Ani," Eliza screamed back. "I'm stuck."

Roonie, whose bravery continued to impress Ani, ran toward Eliza and into the water. The ocean covered his feet and reached mid-calf. "I'm coming, Eliza. Stay put."

Eliza yelled back, "No need to tell me twice."

Ani could tell by the look on her face that Eliza was terrified. Roonie waded in only a few yards when they all heard a loud splash from Eliza's left. Eliza screamed and Roonie stopped moving.

"What was that?" he called.

The water between Roonie and Eliza erupted as two sizable lobsters, four feet or more in length, careened out of the rising water, battling each other, and then fell back, creating a huge spray, much like a seal show at the Boston Aquarium except this was not a fun, interesting show to tell friends about. The kids felt no joy in the knowledge that two alien-sized crustaceans created the splash.

"Roonie, get back. Hurry!" Ani said. He retreated as soon as his legs could catch up to his brain. The lobsters, hearing the sound of his limbs sloshing to the shore, untangled themselves and turned toward the noise. Their tails bobbed up and down in the water, which barely covered their hard, mottled-green bodies. But Roonie made it to shore.

"Ani, did you see that? They're huge! How are we going to get Eliza?"

Ani spied a piece of driftwood lying on a mound of seaweed. She picked it up and entered the water. The lobsters hovered in place, their antennae twitching.

"It's like they're crocodiles, and we're standing at the edge of the Nile River," Roonie said. "You can't go in there."

"I can. Just watch me." Ani yelled, "I am Kanake-kee." She rushed into the water, now reaching her knees.

"Ani, hurry. I'm running out of room," shouted Eliza. Wobbling on one leg, she looked like she was practicing an ancient dance, hopping from foot to foot with her arms outstretched for balance.

"Get back, get back," Ani commanded the giant lobsters and poked the surface of the water with the driftwood. "Get back, I tell you!" She ventured further still, each step getting her closer to her stranded sister, but deeper in the rising tide. The lobster nearest to her submerged, his long antennae sticking out of the water, the only way to determine his location. Leading with the stick, Ani marched carefully toward Eliza's shrinking platform. The second lobster, apparently responding to Ani's movement, crawled toward her. She jabbed the driftwood at the approaching crustacean. "I'm talking to you, Mister Lobster, or are you hard of hearing? I'm losing it. I know they don't have ears, she muttered under her breath. The lobster retreated. Ani sighed, temporarily relieved, one lobster moving back and the other still visible in the water, ten yards from Eliza. So far so good. She took two more steps closer and the lobsters stayed where they were.

"Ani, hurry. Please," pleaded Eliza.

I hope these creatures are the only ones swimming near us, Ani thought as she jabbed at the water. She ventured forward. The water now covered her knees, and the current was pulling her away from the shore. She was only a few feet from her sister, almost able to reach her with the wood, and then the unthinkable occurred. The retreating lobster had backed away, but instead of heading out into the harbor, he swam behind Eliza, where the water was deeper. He crawled up on the edge of the remaining sand, his right claw as huge as a dinner platter, clicking loudly. Ani gasped in disbelief. She lunged toward Eliza and pulled her behind her so that her own body stood between the lobster and Eliza. The lobster lashed out with his pinching claw. Both girls screamed and hopped in and out of the water from the smidgen of sand that had diminished to the size of a Frisbee, not nearly big enough for both of them to stand on.

Ani turned to the shore to shout for help, but Roonie was gone. "Where is he?" Ani said.

"What do we do?" cried Eliza.

"Stay close to me and stop moving," she said, poking, jabbing, and stabbing her driftwood at the threatening lobsters as Mr. Antennae had joined his earlier enemy, both now united in stalking their prey. "Most deep-sea lobsters are blind," Ani said.

"Most?" asked Eliza.

"Most, and let's hope these two are the deep-sea kind. It might be our only chance to get out of here."

"Hope? I hope they don't have any friends."

"That, too," said Ani. The girls stood back to back, each watching a would-be attacker.

"I thought lobsters were vegetarians. Why are they after us?"

"They eat plants but also small fish, crab, and starfish. But who knows what these jumbo species eat," Ani said.

"Did you see the claw on that one? These guys are humungous. They look like they will eat anything they get their hands or claws on. I'm thinking the NC 241 might not be enough. I say we should drop the A-bomb. These lobsters mean business."

"Eliza, not now," scolded Ani. Then she whispered, "We're going to have to make a run for it. There's no other option." The shoreline seemed impossibly far away as the ocean worked to take back its territory.

"I'm scared," Eliza said, her voice shaky and tearful.

"Me too," said Ani. "Listen, when I count to three, you throw both of your sneakers as far as you can in opposite directions. When the lobsters swim after the noise, we book it to shore, okay?" Eliza didn't answer. She was numb with fear, her mind unable to comprehend the simple command dictated by her sister.

"Eliza," Ani whispered louder. "Eliza! You have to snap out of it! No choice, we have no choice but to make a break for it. You with me?"

"Yes, I guess so," Eliza said in a timid, almost inaudible voice.

"That's my sister." Ani started the countdown: "1, 2 …" Eliza raised her right arm to throw the first sneaker. "3!" Eliza hurled her shoe, and it splashed about a dozen feet away. Mr. Antennae pivoted toward the sound, his enormous claw breaking the surface of the water, his tail lifting, and all his legs scurrying to move his massive body.

Eliza threw the other sneaker, but this one didn't go as far, only seven feet to the right of the girls. The second lobster submerged, and they hoped that he, too, was headed for Eliza's other shoe. Ani knew they didn't have time to wait around and find out.

She yelled, “Go!” and shoved Eliza into the water. Both girls moved as best they could, pushing against the rising tide and moving current, fighting hard with each step. To the girls’ horror, one of the lobsters glided past them and planted himself strategically between them and the shore. Ani pointed her driftwood at him. “Go away,” she ordered. The lobster ignored Ani’s command and instead hovered in place, twitching forward and back, legs, claws, tail, and head working in unison, creating rippling splashes with each jerky movement. Ani used to love seeing the lobsters in the glass tank at the grocery store when she was little. Her mother would leave her there to gaze at the crustaceans, all clambering on top of each other, constantly in motion, but making no noticeable progress. Ani would count the legs, the claws, the antennae, fascinated by their very presence, leaving only after her mother dragged her away with promises of a return visit when next they needed to shop for food. These mutant lobsters up close and personal made Ani yearn to be back at the store with her mother and with a glass tank separating her from all sea life.

“Where’s the other one? Do you see it?” Eliza asked.

“No,” said Ani. “Do you?” A loud splash behind them answered their question. Eliza jumped, and Ani twirled around and jabbed at the air with her stick. They were in serious trouble. “Well, not the answer I was hoping for, but an answer nonetheless.” She waved the driftwood again.

Again the lobsters were positioned on opposite sides with the girls stuck smack in the middle. “Talk about your lobster sandwich” Eliza said. “Now I know how they must feel.”

The tide had continued to rise, and the water was now up to the girls’ waists. “I’m going to throw the stick. It’s the only thing left to distract their attention away from us.”

“Oh, Ani,” said Eliza, and feeling the need to confess added, “You’ve been a great sister. Sorry that I took your tan flip-flops and accidentally lost one at Daisy’s birthday slumber party last summer.”

“I knew it! You said you had no idea where they were and I looked everywhere!”

"I'm sorry, really I am."

"We will discuss this later when we are on shore. On my count again," said Ani. "One, two, three!" she shouted and threw their only defense as hard and far as she could. The lobsters whirled around, their attention on the girls sidetracked by the smack of the driftwood hitting the water's surface. Ani cried, "Now!" and grabbed Eliza's hand. The girls swam-walked as best as they could, but the current was too powerful, sabotaging their efforts.

The lobsters, discovering that driftwood was not something to eat, swam back toward the girls. "They're coming, Eliza, they're coming back!" Ani screamed.

"Ani! Oh, Ani!" Eliza's cries matched her sister's in intensity, volume, and alarm. The girls plunged into the frigid Maine water and kicked with all their might, still hoping they could outswim their predators.

Ani was the first to feel the creature brush up against her. She screamed, her cries muffled by the water that filled her mouth. The water was salty and gritty with sand. She kicked hard to the right, waiting for the imagined pain of the lobster's giant claw clamping down on her calf, but it never came. She was promptly bumped on the left side and twisted her head expecting to see the orange-green sheen of the crustacean's shell, but instead saw only black, a glistening black shape, like a long tire inner tube, swimming alongside her.

"Ani! Ani!" she heard Eliza's cries. But these cries were shouts of joy, not fear.

Ani felt another bump behind her and then underneath her, lifting her tired body further up, up to the surface. Everywhere she looked she saw black. Eliza too was surrounded by long, sleek, beautiful, brave, black seals. Ani stared into the eyes of Whiskers, the seal from Seal Beach, who had helped the girls find the silver sand dollar, their first unexpected amulet. "Whiskers!" Ani shouted. "Oh Whiskers, thank you, thank you!"

Whiskers responded with the only sound he could: "Ort, ort!"

The girls' slippery seal escorts glided to the shore and

rolled to one side, allowing Ani and Eliza to slide off into the sand. Roonie sprinted from around the corner, his hands full of heavy stones.

"What happened?" he asked, dropping them to the ground. "Are you guys okay? I ran to collect these to throw at the lobsters, but it looks like you got all the help you needed." Roonie stared at the black seals on the shore and bobbing in the water. "There has to be at least fifty of them!"

Ani rose and found her friend Whiskers. "Thank you," she said again. "Thank you to every one of you." She kissed Whiskers on his wet seal cheek. He barked and clapped his flippers. Ani noticed that the lobsters were nowhere to be seen, chased off by the presence and number of seals that had converged upon the area. Whiskers barked one last time, and as swiftly as they arrived, the pod retreated and disappeared into the cold Maine waters.

Lobster fact: *According to research conducted at the Marine Fish Division of the Department of Fisheries and Oceans (DFO) in Dartmouth, Nova Scotia, if seals eat lobster at all, it is only a minor part of their diet. Harbor seals, which are the predominant species in Maine, tend to change their diet with the seasons.*

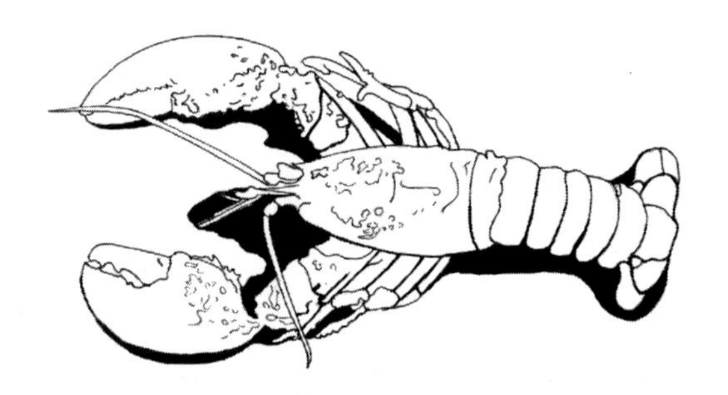

Chapter 41

Reunion

Patrick placed the kids' belongings on the passenger seat of his truck and slammed the door shut. Then he crossed Main Street and walked the familiar two blocks to Baxter Banking and Trust, a bank started by Barton's great-great-grandfather. Money begets money, he thought, but money doesn't buy you happiness; he could hear Amelia's words in his head. She always knew what Patrick was too embarrassed to admit to himself and especially to her. When they were kids, Patrick was jealous of Barton's wealth, the estate, the businesses, and all the other properties. He believed, like most young people who haven't had time to settle in their own skins much less understand the ways of the world, that having money and lots of it was the ultimate goal.

Amelia, always an individual, never wanted any of Barton's money or anyone else's for that matter. She felt that all humans were connected on a spiritual level and that the purpose of life was already predetermined before we uttered our first newborn cry. Like her ancestors before her, Amelia accepted her fate or position in life, even at the young age of thirteen. She believed the earth had enough natural resources to provide for her and people all over the world. For Patrick it took her disappearance and many hard years of soul-searching to understand what she meant. Patrick, although never a wealthy man, had a roof over his head, beautiful gardens to keep him busy and contented throughout the year, and savings for a rainy day. Yes, he thought, he wouldn't trade places with

Barton for all the tea in China. He had everything he needed, everything except Amelia.

He sighed, his heart sinking as he allowed himself to remember, if only for a moment, her friendly smile and beautiful brown eyes. But, he thought, I must push her out of my mind. I'm not strong enough to handle these memories, and he shook his head as if that would clear his past away. His eyes filled with tears and he swiped at them, relying on his Yankee stubbornness to squash their presence.

Patrick opened the heavy glass door and entered the bank lobby. The cool air was a welcome relief from the heat of the day. The bank's interior resembled the decor of Barton's library in the main house, dark with heavy furniture and shiny tiled black floors, polished so clean Patrick could almost see his own reflection as he approached the only available teller behind the long, dark green, granite counter.

The teller, a petite older woman with tight curly hair and a kind face, greeted him cheerily. "Hello, Patrick, what can I do for you?"

"Well hello there, Pamela. I desire to speak to your boss. Is he here today?" As Barton was owner/director/president/CEO of several local businesses, he could be a number of places on any given day. He used to enjoy informing Patrick that having offices scattered about his various establishments kept his employees on their toes because they never knew where and when he might show up. More likely he kept them constantly on edge, Patrick surmised. When Barton's father became too old to supervise Patrick, Barton used to do the same thing to Patrick, showing up at random times throughout the day to ask him why he was mulching here or why he was putting fertilizer there. It just about drove Patrick crazy, but experience had taught him that it was better to answer Barton calmly and never let him know how incensed he felt and how irritating it was for him to have to answer to Barton. Keep your emotions tight inside; don't ever let someone know how you are truly feeling. Those were the words Patrick chose to live by, a motto for life and one he had followed since he was a lad. Barton soon deduced that Patrick was the rare employee he couldn't rattle with his inquiries, and so he tired of "surprising" Patrick and mostly left him alone. Patrick was the most well thought of and respected gardener on Mount Desert Island, something that did not go unnoticed by Barton. Underappreciated, definitely, but not unnoticed. Barton was all about appearances, and owning one of the largest estates with the most beautiful, elegant, and well-cared for gardens had always been a source of pride and accomplishment for him. Patrick's and Barton's awe of the glorious gardens was perhaps the only thing the two men had in common. That and the love of a young girl with pale blue ribbons in her hair who disappeared on a birthday never to be forgotten.

Pamela leaned in conspiratorially, and Patrick did the same. Her voice dropped to a whisper and she said, "Yes, he's in. He came in a few hours ago and asked not to be disturbed. He was acting very, very strange." Pamela glanced up quickly to make sure no one was listening. Once convinced the coast was clear, she lowered her head again and bent in even closer. "Stranger than normal." She pursed her lips and bobbed her head up and down to further prove her point.

"You don't say."

"I do say, and I'm not the only one who has noticed. Ever since those lobsters have gotten bigger, he has gotten more peculiar and more persnickety, too."

"Thank you for the tip, Pamela. I best be on my way."

"Good luck," she said, "and don't say I didn't warn you."

Patrick waved good-bye and walked to the elevator at the rear of the building. Memories of earlier visits to the bank, far too numerous to count, rushed through his mind and took him away to happier times. Coming into town with Cook after finishing his summer gardening chores with his father proved to be a highlight of his youth. He, Barton, and Amelia were allowed to run free, frequenting all of their favorite haunts. Amelia loved to press her face up against the glass of the sweet shop—she loved peanut butter fudge loaded with peanuts—and watch the sweet confection being made from scratch.

"Can you smell it?" she asked, smiling widely and not really waiting for a response. Patrick liked to visit the rock and tumble shop with its precious gemstones from around the island. He and his father uncovered many when digging up the gardens to plant the annual fall bulbs. Barton, on the other hand, adored coming to his father's bank.

"Someday this will be mine, all mine," he said, opening the door as if he already was president. Patrick remembered how the entire bank staff bowed in deference to Master Barton, who might or might not acknowledge their presence depending upon his mood, which, more often than not, was sour.

Mr. Baxter was always elated to see his only child and his young friends. He stopped what he was doing even if he was in a meeting and whisked them into his private office. He had a jar of peppermints on his desk that he practically forced upon them. I can almost taste them now, Patrick thought, recalling how the refreshing, minty flavor would melt in his hot mouth, cooling him in an instant.

Routinely Mr. Baxter offered more treats, but Patrick and Amelia had been raised to accept only one so as not to appear greedy. Next, he would introduce the children to his colleagues and allow them to play around the big conference table, not caring if they shrieked or laughed or yelled. He then doled out money to Barton to treat them all to an ice cream cone at Cronin's Creamery on the corner. A few times Barton even followed through with his father's wish and purchased them a cone, a small one, of course, but mostly he just kept the money for himself. Patrick's mother used to say Barton was difficult because he was grieving over the death of his own mother and that he had too much idle time on his hands. She was sure that Barton needed a project, something to feel that he was useful and had a real purpose in life. He did not, however, need to be coddled by everyone in the household just for breathing the air. It's a shame, his mother would add, Mrs. Baxter had been a sincerely delightful woman.

The elevator dinged, signaling its arrival, and Patrick floated back to the present, entered, and selected the top floor.

He leaned back against the cool, sleek interior and closed his eyes, filled with dread about meeting with Barton. He had barely spoken to him since the reading of the will, when Barton discovered that Patrick, not himself, had been bequeathed the rights to the small cottage. Patrick was now more convinced than ever that Barton had been the one to break into the cottage and steal the Abenaki book before the staff had removed his father's personal items. He was positive that Mr. Baxter would have ordered that the treasured parchment be returned to the tribe. Mr. Baxter, always a generous and thoughtful individual, must have accounted for it in his will. Patrick had been privy only to the part of the will that involved him and he didn't know other details. But Mr. Baxter was no fool. Surely he would have recognized how critical it was for Barton not to claim ownership of the book. Alas, thought Patrick, it didn't matter. Barton won in the end. He always did, with limitless money and power to back him up. But not this time, Patrick vowed, especially if Barton's scheme involved harming the Banke girls.

The elevator reached its destination and again the ding of its arrival disrupted Patrick's ruminations. The doors opened and to Patrick's surprise, Daniel and Lyle Thibodeau stood outside in the hall. Patrick did not move.

"Coming out?" asked Daniel.

"Ah, no, not exactly," stammered Patrick. Both men gave him a quizzical glance. "I guess I pushed the wrong button," Patrick said. "I'm going down."

"Well all righty then," Daniel said, and he and his brother entered the elevator. Patrick pressed himself against the back wall and lowered his head. He hoped the two men would disclose something that might shed light on why they were tailing the kids. He wished he had been quick enough to hit a few buttons to other floors, lengthening their time together, but it was too late. The doors closed and Daniel pressed *L* for lobby. Lyle noticed his shoelaces were untied and bent over to fix them. Fortunately for Patrick, Lyle's backside rubbed up against the buttons and inadvertently pushed them, causing a few to light up as if requested by the passengers.

"You idiot," said Daniel, "look what you did!"

"What?" asked Lyle, standing upright and leaning on a few more floor numbers.

"You did it again. You pushed all these extra buttons, and now we're going to be even later to complete our tasks."

"What tasks? We don't have any pest jobs today. What are you talking about?"

Daniel tilted his head and raised his eyebrows up and down. Lyle, not surprisingly, didn't comprehend that his brother's actions were meant to keep him quiet since someone else was riding in the elevator.

Daniel whispered, "You know, the job, Mr. Baxter."

Lyle wrinkled his forehead. After a few seconds, he broke into a smile. "Right," he said, "right, the job following and photographing the girls and their Spidey boyfriend so Mr. Baxter can figure out what they are up to, especially if they have any contact with the lobsters, large or small. Isn't that what he just yelled at us about?" Lyle's face returned to its perpetual look of confusion.

Daniel hit him several times with his hat. Patrick pretended not to hear anything, but his hearing was just fine and he understood every word that nincompoop just repeated. Bingo, he said to himself. Confirmation validated. Baxter was enmeshed with the lobsters.

As Lyle and Daniel persisted in debating what was said and by whom while someone was trying to tell someone that he should keep his stupid mouth shut and that someone still didn't know what someone meant and on and on, Patrick grew angry. As the elevator car proceeded down, stopping at nearly every floor because of Lyle's button blunder, Patrick's mind stewed.

Barton definitely had broken into the cottage and stolen his long ago intended birthday present. He must have figured out the Abenaki writings or paid someone to do it for him and then discovered where the covenant was buried. Exactly what his father didn't want him to do some fifty-odd years ago, Barton did! He and he alone was responsible for desecrating the sacred treaty and causing the lobsters to run amok and converge upon the island.

The elevator finally reached the lobby. The brothers exited the car still arguing heatedly. Patrick was relieved to have the elevator to himself. The doors closed, and he punched the top number for the second time today. He was clear about his mission. He was going to find the covenant, that is, if Barton hadn't already sold it, and make Barton return it to its rightful place at the base of Cadillac Mountain.

Barton had stepped away from his office, but his secretary let Patrick in and instructed him to have a seat. Patrick chose a worn brown leather chair that rested across from Barton's father's desk, which was now Barton's. Patrick, taking in the room, was surprised that not much had changed from when last he visited, only two days before Barton's thirteenth birthday party.

As painful as it was for him, he remembered. Amelia, Barton, and Patrick were supposed to meet Mr. Baxter at four-thirty sharp because he was going to take us on a boat ride through the harbor on his new cabin cruiser. Amelia and Patrick had arrived promptly at four-thirty after being earlier separated from Barton who didn't feel it was his job to help Cook carry her purchases to her automobile. During this time, time alone without Barton, Mr. Baxter hinted that during Barton's birthday party, a special gift would be unveiled not only for Barton but also for Amelia and Patrick. When Amelia and Patrick implored him to tell them more, he became tight lipped. Amelia and Patrick could think of nothing else during their boat ride later that afternoon and on the subsequent drive home. They talked about it all the following day, speculating what it might be and how lucky they were to be singled out by Mr. Baxter. Patrick thought, how excited and naive we were about the special present.

And then the worst thing imaginable happened, all because of Barton's greed. He had every material object money could buy, but it wasn't enough to satisfy him. Barton always wanted more and demonstrated this on his birthday. His father's disappointment in his only son, his only child, was enormous. Mr. Baxter had done the only thing he could do; he had rescinded the gift. Barton's greed and jealousy were at the root of Amelia's vanishing, but now he had taken it too far by stealing the parchment and possibly the covenant and sending those fools to chase after the Banke girls.

Patrick's heart beat fast, and his impatience and ire swelled. He marched over to the beverage cart and poured himself a glass of water to quench his thirst. He peered out the open window at the harbor below and watched the hustle and bustle of folks pulling out their boats, both big and small, some fancy and others beaten up by the sea. Police officers and soldiers blew whistles to get people's attention, waved them through or stopped them with hand gestures (some not so friendly), and barked orders through bullhorns. Patrick noticed several reporters and TV camera operators dispersed amid the chaos. What a mess. This entire disaster engineered by Barton's selfishness, self-centeredness, and self-indulgence! Patrick massaged his right shoulder, feeling the strain of his anger settle in his muscles.

Without warning, a gust of misty ocean air blew in and scattered the papers on Barton's desk throughout the room. Patrick, even as upset as he was, sprang into action, retrieving papers from the floor and returning them to their proper place. While tidying up, he noticed a copy of the *Bar Harbor Daily* lying haphazardly atop a velvet box on Barton's desk chair. The box was about a foot wide and a foot high. That's peculiar, thought Patrick. What would Barton be doing with that? He certainly wasn't giving it away as a present because he never gave anything to anyone ever. He just takes, and takes, and takes. Patrick lifted the paper and let it slide to the floor. His mouth opened in bewilderment. He stared at the box for a few minutes and was startled when it shifted ever so slightly to the left.

"What the devil?" Patrick exclaimed and rubbed his eyes. He leaned in closer and waited, convinced his old eyes were playing tricks on him. Nothing happened. I am really losing it here, he thought, but then, shockingly, the box moved again, this time with more force, causing the lid to open a tad. Slowly he wheeled the chair out from behind the desk, completely revealing the box. Cautiously and with misgivings, Patrick lifted the top, impressed by how soft the material felt on his fingers, only to discover a piece of satin resting on top of what appeared to be a dome-shaped object. Could this be the covenant? The rose quartz covenant created centuries ago by Abenaki craftsmen? Patrick froze with the reality before him. Placing the lid gingerly on top of Barton's desk, he reached for the satin wrapper.

Just then, Barton burst into the room from the side entrance, catching Patrick about to unveil his precious orb, and lunged with all the force he could muster, shoving Patrick out of the way.

"No, no, no!" Barton cried as Patrick slammed into the conference table. "That's mine!" Swiftly, Barton grabbed the lid and placed it on the box, securing it tightly before locking it in a file cabinet behind the desk. Next he punched a button on his phone and said, "Security immediately to my office. I have a visitor who needs to be removed, now!" Patrick, bruised and shaken by the surprise attack, winced and cradled his left elbow while he struggled to straighten himself.

"You!" shouted Barton. "Get out of my office! You have no business being here and touching my, my," he searched for the right word, "my personal possessions." Patrick was used to hearing the indignant tone, but the person behind the voice had changed dramatically. Barton looked frail, like he hadn't slept in weeks. Moreover, the color of his skin, normally tan and healthy, was sallow and sickly. Barton twitched his head and revealed a tiny bald spot above his right ear. Patrick knew that Barton always played with his hair in this very spot when he was anxious, and it looked as if he had twiddled his hair away. But Patrick felt no concern for his longtime employer, only disgust.

"Your personal belongings?" cried Patrick, matching his

foe in fury. "I think not! It was you! You broke into your father's garden cottage and stole the Abenaki book."

"Don't be ridiculous," shouted Barton. "I did no such thing. Where is that security? Security," he bellowed.

"You did and then you figured out where the covenant was hidden and you took it. That's what is in the box. You probably have sellers lined up all over the world. Shame on you, you greedy, horrible, sinful old fool! Look at the chaos you've created," Patrick cried and waved at the harbor. "Your parents must be rolling in their graves watching what you've done." Spittle flew from Patrick's mouth, his wrath unleashed after years of being buried deep within. "And it's all your fault, you soulless, disgraceful excuse for a human being. You are the one and only one responsible for Amelia's death!"

Barton gasped at the mention of his beloved Amelia's name. "It's not true! Don't say that, Patrick, don't say it!" His body trembling, he glanced at the locked cabinet.

Patrick stood face to face with Barton, pointing his finger at him. "You stole her hair ribbon to get us to chase you. You teased and tormented her about being Abenaki. You challenged her to go in that door, and you knew she would never pass up a challenge. It was what we both loved about her." Tears cascaded down Patrick's cheeks, but he didn't care. He had wanted to say this to Barton for years, and he couldn't stop.

With each word Patrick uttered, Barton shrank, his frame stooping as if Patrick's words were physical punches. He knew Patrick was right, and there was not a thing he could do about it. Barton's own tears flowed. "No. Stop. It wasn't my fault," he whimpered. "No, no."

"And you never really loved her because you don't know what love is! You only wanted her because you wanted to own her, just like one of your other prized possessions, and because you knew she didn't love you. She loved me! She loved me and you couldn't stand it!" Patrick's voice broke and he gasped for air.

Barton collapsed in his chair, as if Patrick's words knocked him down. "No, no, no," he repeated softly through his tears. "I loved her," he said. "I love her." And then sobs wracked his body.

Security Officer Scotty Walter exploded through the door and pointed his gun at Patrick. "Stop. Put your hands in the air where I can see them," he shouted, stunned to find the two old men in tears.

Patrick raised both hands in surrender. "No need for the gun, Scotty. I haven't come to rob the bank. I'll go peacefully."

Patrick walked toward Walter, who carefully took his right arm and holstered his gun.

Patrick stopped and turned toward Barton. "And if what you said is true, and somewhere in that cold, wretched heart of yours, you find you have any kind of empathy, you know what you need to do. Return the covenant to its rightful place and stop this madness. And leave the Banke girls and that Roonie boy alone. Call off the Thibodeaus, and let them be. They're just kids doing kid things and don't need an old coot like you spying on their every move."

Walter guided Patrick through the doorway. Patrick, regaining some of his strength, stopped again and said, "Redeem yourself. It's your only hope. It's what she would have wanted." He paused. "No, it's what she would have demanded from you, and it's what she deserves." And with those final words, Patrick left the office, exhausted but satisfied that he had finally said what he had rehearsed in his head ever since Barton's birthday party on July 25, 1957.

Barton slumped over in his chair, speechless and defeated. He was a shell of his former self, unable to move or think of what to do next. Numbly he rose and unlocked the cabinet. He removed the orb from its protective box and gently slid the cover off. Amelia, curled up in a tight ball, with her tiny head buried in her knees, refused to look at him. Barton wrapped his tired arms tightly around her prison, the orb, in a desperate embrace, and wept.

Lobster fact: *Lobsters show no obvious signs of aging. They typically don't slow down or become weaker or more susceptible to disease. They don't get infertile. In fact, older lobsters are actually more fertile than younger ones. Most lobsters seem to die because of something inflicted upon them rather than because a body part has failed.*

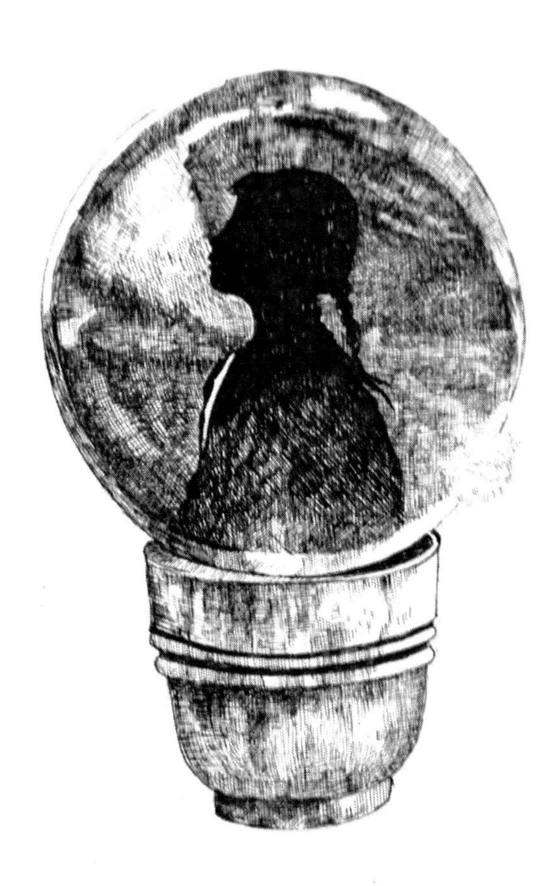

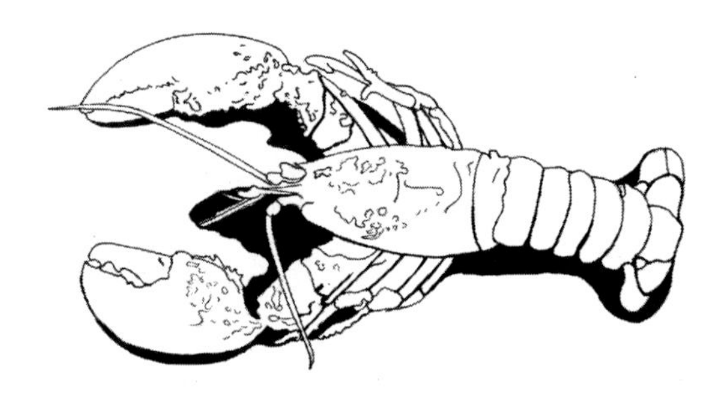

Chapter 42

Spilled Milk!

Moon Violet brought the wooden spoon to her lips and blew on the steaming liquid before taking a sip. Cautiously, she swirled the hot liquid around her mouth and nodded approvingly. She placed the spoon in her white ceramic sink and turned the stovetop burner to low. Good, she thought, this will be perfect by the evening. She ran through a mental checklist: linens changed and bathrooms cleaned, candles, water, wine, firewood. It will be a hot night to have a fire, but they can move the pit a little farther from the barn. She ticked off the other items on her list: towels, paint, lavender, and watermelon. She pursed her lips, looking at the tough rind of the watermelon. I will have to ask Cousin Reggie to cut this when he arrives, she thought. Now where is that knife of mine?

She felt anxious, excited, fearful, and scattered. Her mind raced between listing what supplies she needed for the gathering and wondering if the Abenakis would band together and bring about a solution more peaceful than detonating gas bombs to the problem of absurdly large lobsters overrunning the island. She took a fully stuffed tote bag, opened the back door and stepped outside. The humidity combined with the heat made the air feel murky and heavy. She walked a few yards, stopping to watch a yellow butterfly hover over the orange calendula that lined her walkway.

Moon Violet closed her eyes. Yes, she knew the ancestors were here. She had felt their presence for weeks now, but today she awoke knowing they were all around her. In the stillness she could hear them, whispering, praying, chanting, and dancing, sending the land, the people, and even the lobsters positive energy of light, life, and love. She smiled at the power of their essence, strong yet also tender, like the wings of a butterfly. The Abenakis were going to need everyone, young and old, living and deceased, to unite as one voice, one prayer, and one spirit. Whew, she thought, so much to do and so little time.

It took all her strength to wedge open the barn gate. The wheels on the rusty track emitted a low creak as she slid the heavy, black wooden door. The sunlight poured into the room, illuminating the empty space. The familiar smells of hay, dirt, dust, and grain wafted out of the narrow opening, flooding Moon Violet with memories of her childhood when this was a working barn filled with horses. Misty was her very own. Oh, how she loved her. She was a white pony, perfect for Moon Violet when she was little. Her mother had made her a special outfit befitting an Abenaki princess that she wore at tribal events and other special gatherings. Blue, white, turquoise, and purple beads created patterns of ancient symbols on the traditional Abenaki dress. Moon Violet especially admired the white leather boots with the matching hat. She never felt prouder to be Abenaki than when she and her family rode together, all of them wearing their unique and distinctive "show" outfits. The horses too were groomed meticulously before an event, their manes and tails braided with special ribbons that coordinated with their riders. Misty's ribbons were always purple, Moon Violet's favorite color. "We need your help too," she said to the vacant barn, asking the spirits of the animals to be present and in harmony with the dancers.

She set her tote bag down and glanced around until her eyes found what she was looking for—the broom. I'll have Roonie sweep this out when he arrives later this morning. Darn it, the scones! The blueberry scones were still in the oven and might be burning. "Where is my head?" she muttered to herself.

Moon Violet hurried out of the barn and dashed back to the kitchen in hopes of rescuing Roonie's late morning snack. The barn remained silent, sunlight still streaming in through the open door. If Moon Violet had remained in place and allowed her mind to rest, she might have discerned the faint outline of a pony standing at attention, ready to answer her call, long passed these fifty years, but never far, never far from her beloved Moon Violet.

Thankfully she arrived in time to hear the timer buzz. She opened the oven door and took out the scones. Something I am doing right today, she thought. Moon Violet hummed a little song as she lifted the scones with a spatula from the baking sheet and placed them on a wire rack to cool. She hadn't been able to eat her normal breakfast of toast with marmalade this morning as her stomach was topsy-turvy with excitement about tonight's activities, but the smell of the warm scones, blueberry with a dash of cinnamon, made her stomach growl, and she decided to sit and have a bite and a sip of tea.

Moon Violet retrieved the butter from the refrigerator, walked over to her kitchen table, and sat. She studied a small, framed photo of her mother on a shelf opposite her as she nibbled on the delicious scone. Her mother, Little Bird, had passed only five years ago at the age of ninety. Her blueberry scone recipe Moon Violet had used this very morning along with her healing broth instructions. Moon Violet liked looking at her mother's distinctive handwriting with its tiny print and curling letters. The scone melted in her mouth and filled her empty belly. She sighed and thought back to when she danced with her mother and her uncle, Raven's Wing, right after Amelia had disappeared. She was only fifteen, and it had been her first protective dance experience. She remembered that it was conducted with a heavy heart under the watchful eye of the full July moon. It was then that her uncle, elder tribal member and name presenter, had awarded Violet her Abenaki name, Moon Violet. Funny, she thought, how one event always connected and led to another, and on and on it continued. The Abenaki saying was *cheree ma to jupes*, which meant one acts and others react. Amelia, disturbing the sanctity of the door, spurred the gods to take her against her will, which prompted Violet and her family to dance under the moon, which resulted in Violet's name being changed to Moon Violet. Moon Violet, thus named, acquired the skills to utilize the healing properties of the moon and channel the restorative power of herbs and plants. Her curative abilities had led to many successful treatments for Abenakis and others. "*Cheree ma to jupes*," she repeated, hoping the saying would hold true for them tonight, eager that their dancing would lead to the desired outcome: stopping the lobsters and stopping the NC 241.

Moon Violet heard the front door jingle and Roonie's footsteps pounding through the hallway toward the kitchen. He entered the room with a huge frown on his face. Moon Violet noticed his cheeks looked stained as if he had been crying. He slumped down into the chair next to his grandmother and folded his arms across his chest. Moon Violet got up and put a warm scone on a plate and placed it in front of Roonie. He pushed it away and said, "I don't understand girls. One minute, it's 'Roonie, you're so clever, what a brilliant plan,' and the next it is 'Oh, Roonie, you're such a klutz, you ruined everything.'"

"What happened?" asked Moon Violet.

"Before I came here, I biked over to meet with Eliza and Ani to see if I could help them figure out the next clue, you know, for the amulet. Ani needs me, Grandma, and you said I was to assist them whenever I could. I have been a tremendous help. Ani even said so yesterday. More than once!" he added.

"Go on," said Moon Violet.

"When I got there the girls had just finished their breakfast and were sitting out on the porch."

"Right, so then what?" Moon Violet said taking a sip of her tea.

"Ani asked me if I wanted to make up a plate for myself as they had some leftovers on the stove in the kitchen. Eliza made scrambled eggs, and let's just say she isn't too good as a chef, so I decided to just have some chocolate milk."

"You do love your chocolate milk."

"Ani was looking at her special book, and I'm not sure what happened, but I guess I might have, well, accidentally of course, knocked over my milk and it poured all over the table," he said in a small voice, his face crestfallen.

"There's no use in crying over spilled milk," said Roonie's grandmother, trying to sound positive.

"There is if it pours over the last few pages of the book and ruins them so Ani can't figure out the final amulet, and now we'll never stop the lobsters, and I've ruined the island, forever!"

"Oh, Roonie, that's terrible," cried Moon Violet, more strongly than she intended, but what he just told her made it impossible for her to contain her own distress.

"That's how come I went from brilliant to moron and idiot. We got into a big fight, and I stormed out of there. Girls, to heck with them is what I say. I didn't do it on purpose, honest, Grandma Violet."

"I'm sure you didn't, Roonie, but it doesn't change the fact that it happened. What to do, what to do?" Moon Violet murmured, tapping her chin with her index finger.

"I know what I'm going to do," Roonie said.

"What's that?"

"Never talk to those girls again. They are ungrateful, unappreciative, and unforgiving and, and …"

Moon Violet interrupted him. "Ronaldo Jay Cyr. You stop this crazy talk this instance. You hear me?" Roonie had learned over the years that when his grandmother spoke to him in that voice, he had better just do what she said. "You need to finish this scone—and quick—and march yourself right over to their house and apologize for spilling your milk. They need your support, not your aggravation. And this is certainly not the time to let your pride and stubbornness get in the way of you helping them. We all need to work together, now more than ever."

"I don't care," Roonie said. "And besides, they don't want me. They both made that clear when they told me to leave and go home. I'm going to the barn to sweep!" He ran out of the kitchen, crashing the door.

Moon Violet shook her head. Sweeping will be good for him she thought. He needs to cool down and then I'll go out and speak with him again. I know I'm not supposed to interfere, as only Kanake-kee can be the solver of the puzzle, but it might be time for me to call on a certain gardener I know. He was there when Amelia went through the door and he might just hold the key to the missing clue that the girls need.

* * * *

Unfortunately, Roonie had been telling the truth about his mishap with the chocolate milk earlier that morning. What he had neglected to tell his grandmother was that Ani, once again, had specifically requested that he drink his milk in the kitchen because she didn't want any liquids near her treasured parchment. He hadn't listened to her, and that resulted in the chocolate milk disaster. And, yes, tensions had been high as all three erupted, the girls at Roonie, and Roonie at the girls for yelling at him for something that was clearly an accident. Eliza had hurried to get paper towels to try to soak up the liquid, but this had only caused the pages to meld into the towels, speeding the ruin of the parchment. Ani had been able to save the first pages, but the last few were gone with no chance of salvation. They simply dissolved into a sticky clump, like the paste from a jar used in elementary school. Roonie stormed out in a fit of anger while Ani wept silently. Eliza too had felt tears pool in her eyes.

It was over, Ani thought now, and she had failed. She had failed the Abenakis, the island, and most of all, the girl in the orb who had asked for her help. Ani couldn't believe how far they had come, to be so close yet unable to proceed any further. The girls had moved into the kitchen. Eliza did the dishes while Ani leaned against the counter.

"If only I had made copies," Ani lamented to Eliza. "I was so afraid of taking the book out in public because it might get stolen or ruined that I never copied the pages."

"What about your note cards, your colored note cards? Didn't you copy down all of the pictures while you were translating?" she asked, wiping her hands on the dishtowel.

"I did for most of them, but not for this last one. I only

drew the first picture." She held up a yellow card depicting three shapes that each looked like the letter *V*.

"Well, that's good," Eliza said, trying to sound more hopeful than she felt.

"Not really. I think it means 'animal tooth,' but there was more to the drawing, and I don't know what kind of a tooth."

The girls stared at the remains of the last pages, now separated from the parchment and rolled up into a ball of white goo on the table.

"Do you remember what the remaining pictures looked like? Here," Eliza said, handing some cards to Ani, "take these blank note cards and close your eyes and think. You have a good memory. I'm sure it will come to you, I'm just sure of it."

Ani wrinkled her nose, letting Eliza know without words that she hadn't any recollection of the few remaining pictures. Her frustration with Roonie but also with herself was almost unbearable. Ani's mind was blank. All she felt was dread and despair.

Eliza once again rose to the occasion as cheerleader, a role Ani normally played. "I know, Ani," she said, "let's go visit the weird Professor Sol. Perhaps he might be able to shed some light on the subject. I have a feeling he knows more Abenaki info than he originally told us. What do you think? It's worth a try."

When Ani didn't budge, Eliza slid a chair over to her sister. She leaned in to get close to Ani's face. "Ani, I know you. You're no quitter, and now is not the time to become one. So you're going to listen to me and listen good." Eliza reached for a napkin and handed it to her sister. "Wipe your face, stand up, get your book, and follow me. We're going to Maine Oceanic College to meet with the wacky, wild, and certainly weird professor. He might not have the answers for us, but it's a place to start. Okay?" Ani didn't answer, her head hung low.

Eliza repeated, "I said, okay?"

"Okay," said Ani, in a soft voice. Eliza gave her a stern look and Ani replied again, this time louder, "Okay." Ani pushed her chair back, stood and said, "Thanks, Eliza, thanks for not letting me give up." She gave her sister a quick hug. Eliza beamed, glad to be able to help and glad Ani was ready to move.

* * * *

Moon Violet added a pinch of salt to the pot simmering on the stove. At sunset the fasting would begin and the dancers would be allowed only water and the *wimta,* the special healing broth. Moon Violet was grateful to have a few deer bones in her downstairs freezer. Her son Robert, *Summer Sun*, had killed the buck over the winter. The proper way for making the *wimta*, by bow and arrow. I guess I knew even then that it might be necessary to make a batch, Moon Violet mused. She picked up the recipe, written in Abenaki with an English translation on the side, which had been handed down from her mother and her grandmother before her. It was really very simple. The bones of a deer, boiled for a solid day, adding well water throughout the process, two sweet onions, parsley, and salt. Other ingredients varied depending upon the situation. For this, Moon Violet had to rely on her own instincts. This evening's ritual was the most sacred in Moon Violet's memory. She added cumin and rosemary, both thought to soothe the soul and restore energy. She stirred the liquid a few times before covering it with the copper lid. Next, she left Roonie a note letting him know that she had to run out for a quick errand. Perhaps when she returned, he would have succeeded in sweeping out his sour mood along with the barn.

* * * *

Moon Violet was not surprised to find Patrick on his knees, trowel in hand, weeding around a patch of lupines. Amelia's favorites, she thought, sighing deeply. For years now she had wanted to speak to Patrick about her, but instinctively knowing the subject was too painful for him, she never did. Today, however, was different. It was time she intervened. The girls needed his help.

Moon Violet looked around the beautifully manicured gardens. She used to frolic here as a child. She was only two years older than Amelia and sometimes was included in the play with Barton, Patrick, and other children of similar ages. They played hide-and-seek and kick-the-can. Amelia was the best at these games. She was a fierce competitor, and she was fast as lightning. Moon Violet hadn't been here since the night she danced with her mother and uncle a long, long time ago. Even now, after all these years, the flowers still awed her. It is ironic, she thought, that some place so pleasing to the eye could also be the location of such devastation. She glanced farther down the path, looking for the door, but she couldn't see it. It was completely overgrown with thick bushes, tangled together to form a natural barrier, shielding it from visitors. But Moon Violet and Patrick and Barton, too, for that matter, would never forget where it stood and the awesome powers behind it.

It was well known that Mr. Baxter had demanded that Patrick's father replace the door after Amelia's disappearance, but Barton would not hear of it. He protested vehemently and was convinced that if they removed it, Amelia would not be able to find her way home. Barton made his father promise to leave it alone. For weeks after the incident, Barton kept a daily vigil by the door, hoping it would open and Amelia would be there, ready to play and willing to forgive him. Patrick, however, responded in the exact opposite manner. He was afraid to go near it and avoided that section of the garden for years.

In the mornings when Barton arrived to sit and wait for his beloved to appear, he found another branch had grown across the door. This distressed Barton because he worried that it might block Amelia's ability to pass through. Barton had taken to bringing his own small ax to chop away at the encroaching vine, only to find the next day that the branch had reappeared, along with a few more. Gardener Mike had offered to help Barton clear them away, but this had only made Barton angry. He had to do it himself; it was his job alone.

Each day his task became more difficult and took more time to accomplish, his small frame using all of his strength to hack away at the branches. And each morning, the branches, as if mocking Barton, had grown back thicker, longer, and harder to clear. This cycle repeated itself until one day Barton couldn't find the door. The branches had grown so dense, he simply couldn't see it.

Gardener Mike had discovered Barton, screaming, cursing, and crying until he collapsed in a heap on the ground, exhausted from his efforts and overwhelmed by his inability to clear the branches away. Mike had scooped him up in his arms and brought him to his father, who was in his cottage house office. Barton had been rushed to Bar Harbor Hospital and afterwards he and his father had gone on a European trip for the remainder of the summer. When Barton came back, he never visited the door and never spoke about Amelia again. He also returned meaner than ever. His grief combined with his failure to save Amelia had destroyed any hint of compassion or empathy, replacing them with heartlessness and cruelty.

Moon Violet cleared her throat. Patrick didn't look up and carried on with his digging, "Violet," he said.

"Patrick, it is time we spoke. The ancestors are asking for your support."

"I don't know what you're rattling on about, and I'm not interested in any of your Abenaki malarkey, so you can just turn around and go about your business," he said.

Moon Violet understood his sentiment and didn't really blame him. Patrick was convinced that it was the Abenakis' fault that Amelia had vanished and as a result he distrusted anyone who was Abenaki. "Patrick, you old fool, why is everyone being so difficult today of all days? The girls need you."

Patrick shrugged and gave her his best attempt at acting like he didn't know what she was talking about.

"You know what girls I'm referring to. The Banke girls and in particular Ani." He put down his trowel at the mention of Ani's name. "I can feel you know more than you're willing to admit. Let me speak my peace and then you can choose what, if anything, you want to do."

Patrick rose and peeled off his gloves to rub his chin. "All right. Speak."

"I am not allowed to interfere, as I have not been chosen

to do so, nor am I looking for any confirmation from you. In fact, I would rather you say nothing, so as to be certain that I don't anger the gods any more than they already are." Patrick frowned at this, but Moon Violet ignored him. "I believe you are in possession of a certain treasured Abenaki manuscript." Patrick raised an eyebrow. "This manuscript could prove to be invaluable to one thirteen-year-old who is working hard to find the offerings to appease the gods and ..." Moon Violet stopped herself, recognizing that she was possibly saying too much. She would get an earful from the elders tonight if she persisted, and this was something she definitely wanted to avoid. "And, well, I guess that's all. But given what my grandson Roonie told me recently," she paused, hoping to read something from Patrick's face. Empathy? Concern? Kindness? No, nothing, his face was void of emotion. "Suffice it to say, Ani could use some assistance. The manuscript was bestowed upon you, and therefore only you may determine what to do with it."

Patrick said nothing. Instead, he put his gloves back on and crouched down to finish his digging. "So be it," said Moon Violet. "But I will leave you with this."

"What?"

"Superheroes or superhero wannabees might come in handy locating the girls. Spider-Man's in my barn."

And with that, Moon Violet said good-bye to Patrick and hurried back home to finish her preparations for the night. She wasn't sure if anything she said to him had made a difference, but she was pleased that she had at least attempted to intercede on Ani's behalf. She was fairly certain that she could persuade Roonie to change his mind and find the girls and apologize. Whoever said that it was no use crying over spilled milk didn't understand how the milk might be the one thing that could destroy an entire harbor and all the creatures in it.

Lobster fact: *The literal translation of Abenaki is "dawn land people," or "easterners."*

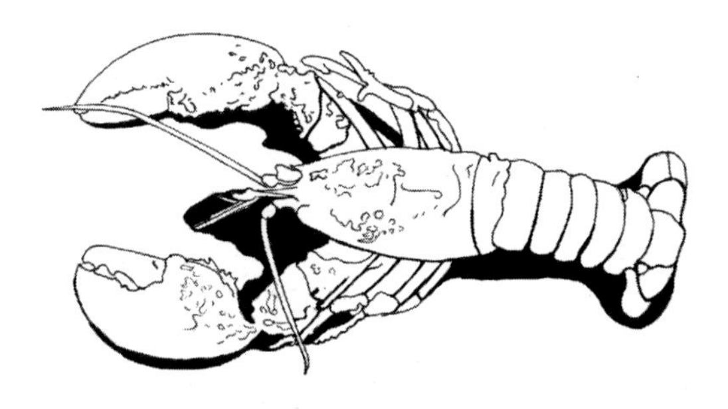

Chapter 43

Most Bizarre

Ani and Eliza biked under the archway marking the entrance to Maine Oceanic College. It had been only a short while since their first visit with Professor Sol yet the college already appeared different. The gatehouse was empty. There was a handwritten sign taped on the door that read, For Security Questions, Please Call 207-555-1000. The girls pedaled slower and both were struck by the quiet of the campus. Where last time it had been a vibrant, bustling community with summer students, professors, groundskeepers, and campus visitors, it now was a ghost town: silent, deserted, and spooky. The parking lot was almost empty. The few cars remaining looked like they had simply been abandoned, left to fend for themselves depending upon the outcome from the NC 241, scheduled to detonate at one in the morning tomorrow. Ani shivered, thinking about the military discharging the noxious gas into the harbor. Then she thought of Roonie and the chocolate milk, and despair filled the pit of her stomach. I let everyone down, everyone, Ani thought, steering her bike toward the Department of Native American Studies.

"I hope he hasn't evacuated like the rest of the campus," Ani said.

"I hope," Eliza said, stressing the word *hope*, "that he isn't as bizarre as the last time we saw him at the blueberry pancake place when he kept making those random, jerky movements. Freaky."

"Be kind, Eliza. You were the one saying we should come

here."

"I know, but being back here reminds me of just how strange he is. Remember that awful sweater-vest?"

"Eliza," Ani said with a hint of agitation.

The girls arrived in front of the Rowe Building and leaned their bikes against the stone wall that lined the walkway. Ani and Eliza climbed the granite steps and went through the front door. They entered the professor's outer office. The same bored girl, Sophie, was seated at the desk, her head bent into a book opened on her lap. She was so engrossed in her reading that she didn't even look up. Eliza whispered to Ani, "I think she might be asleep."

"Excuse me," said Ani. Sophie remained still. "Excuse me," Ani repeated even louder. Startled, the girl's head snapped up and her eyes popped open. Ani noticed a thin line of spit spilling down the left side of her chin. "Oh, wha, what?" she managed to croak.

"Sorry to disturb you. Sophie, right?" Ani asked. Sophie nodded, awake but not fully. "We are here to see Professor Sol. Is he in his office?"

"Letmecheck," Sophie said, stringing her words together. Bleary-eyed, she yawned and rolled her head from side to side a few times before leaving her desk.

"She's certainly a real live wire, huh?" Eliza said. Ani smiled.

When Sophie returned, she handed Ani a piece of paper with a note in Professor Sol's cramped handwriting. Ani read it while Sophie explained in a monotone, "He says he went to the pier hoping to catch up on his mail. Strange place to read mail with the wind and all. He also says he is not to be disturbed unless it is an emergency. Is this an emergency?"

Ani opened her mouth and started, "Well, not exact …"

"Yes! Definitely, it's definitely an emergency!" Eliza blurted, not allowing Ani to finish. "Which way to the pier?"

Sophie, not surprisingly, was completely uninterested in what the emergency might be that would warrant interrupting the professor. She said, "Just follow the main road through the campus. The pier is at the end. Most likely you will find him in the gazebo working at a picnic table on the edge of the water."

"Thanks," Eliza said.

"Yes, thank you," said Ani.

"Oh," Sophie said, stopping both girls in their tracks, "I don't think he has been feeling all that well lately."

"Really?" asked Ani. "What's wrong?"

"I certainly don't know." She yawned again. "He just seems a little off." Sophie looked at her watch. "I guess I need to be going now, so if you don't mind, I need to lock up the office. The college is officially closing at noon."

"Sorry to keep you," said Ani. Sophie followed the girls outside. When she was out of earshot Eliza said, "Well, that was random. She takes bored to a whole new level."

Ani climbed onto her bike. "I'll say. What do you think she meant by 'off'?"

"I told you he was off, way off, when we saw him at breakfast," Eliza said. "The question is, how much more off can he be?"

"We'll soon find out," Ani said.

"Do you know what you want to ask him?"

"Sort of, I guess," Ani said. When they arrived at the end of the road and the pier, Ani could see the water behind the gazebo located squarely in the middle of the dock. She could discern a figure seated at the picnic table underneath. "Looks like he's still here," she said softly to her sister. The girls laid their bikes down on the grass. Ani reached the wharf first and within seconds of her sandal making contact with the wooden dock, a voice shouted at her from the gazebo, a voice that sounded familiar but higher and more squeaky.

"What brings, brings the Banke girls to Maine Maine Oceanic College today? More questions, questions about the Abenakis perhaps, haps?"

Eliza raised an eyebrow at her sister. She whispered "off" and twirled her right index finger by her ear, making the universal sign for crazy.

Ani grinned at Eliza. "Hello, Professor Sol. You're right,

it's Ani and Eliza Banke," she said and walked up the stairs to the gazebo. "I hope we're not disturbing your work ..." Her voice trailed off as she noticed the picnic table was littered with seaweed and empty crab, clam, and mussel shells. The smell was nauseating, a blend of raw fish, wet seaweed, and damp leaves. Ani wrinkled her nose.

The professor was dressed in loose, light-colored clothing, quite a contrast to the neat attire he wore when they first met him in his office. He had large, dark sunglasses so big that they almost covered his entire face, and a floppy hiking hat, the kind they sell at all the gift shops in the national park. Next to him sat a pile of books. Ani could just make out the titles: *A Lobster, a Lighthouse, and You, How You Can Protect the Lobster Population Now and Forever,* Homarus americanus*: The American Lobster and Its Impact on the New England Economy*, and *Lobster Wars: A Serious Business*.

Strange, thought Ani, what is the man known for being an authority on the Native American population doing with all these books on the American lobster? Eliza and Sophie were right: there is something left of center about the professor.

"No, no, no," he repeated, his voice sounding even shriller, "I am taking a break, break, from my re, re, research. Just doing some pleasure reading," he said, obviously aware that Ani was staring at the titles. "Lob, lob, lobsters are a most interesting species. Would, wouldn't you agree, Ani, daughter of Dr. George Banke, leading expert on *Homarus americanus*. A species changing right before our very eyes," he said, waving his hand awkwardly at the water. A small piece of skin dangled from his palm and flapped in the breeze. He appeared to be peeling severely, more severely than Ani had ever seen anyone peel before. He must have gotten a horrific sunburn, or maybe he has a skin disorder, Ani wondered. His waving intensified, as if he were frantically trying to shake off the dead skin, temporarily forgetting that he had company. The skin finally broke free and floated lazily in the wind before disappearing out of sight. For a second Ani thought the skin might land on her or worse, Eliza. That would have sent Eliza over the edge, even more so than a plaid sweater-vest would have. Professor Sol retracted his arm and rested his hand on his lap. The exposed skin was pink and shiny.

"Where, where were we?" he asked, moving his head rapidly between Ani and Eliza. "Alliteration, alliteration, Alice asks the aardvark's advice yet the aardvark's answers aren't appreciated," he recited and finished with a cackle.

Eliza whispered, "Let's go."

"No, no, no, need to depart, my dear ones. My diction only, only deserves a re, re, response. How about you try this one on, on, on for size? Sally sells seashells by the seashore." He grinned an unnaturally wide grin and repeated the childhood poem, faster and louder, "Sallysellsseashellsbytheseashore, kind of catch, catch, catchy, don't you think?" He scratched his forehead and another piece of dead skin came loose and fell into his lap. "Hot, hot, hot," he pronounced and stood laboriously. "Hot, so hot, hot, hot." He clumsily exited the gazebo, teetering on the edge of the dock.

Ani flew to his side. "Professor Sol, are you feeling all right?" She grabbed his wrist to help stabilize him. He jerked his arm back, dislodging another large piece of skin that stuck to Ani's fingers. She shuddered in disgust and hastily shook her hand to remove it.

"So long sis, sis, sisters. Seems silly not to swim, swim, swim while at the sunny summer seaside." He leaped into the ocean, the spray soaking Ani.

Eliza ran to the edge of the dock and peered into the water. "He's gone," she cried. "I can't see him. Should we call someone or go in after him?"

"Look!" Ani exclaimed and pointed several yards out. "I see him! He's by that red and blue buoy. I can't believe how fast he swims, especially missing an arm."

"He's missing a lot more than an arm," noted Eliza. "Try chunks of skin, and let's see, ah, his mind. He's bonkers."

"Yeah, yuck!" Ani wiped the hand that had had his skin attached to it on her shorts. "Let's go home," she said. "Professor Sol is not going to be able to help figure out the final clue."

"You, you, you, can say, say, that again." Eliza giggled. "Batty Bert Sol's behavior is blatantly bizarre."

Lobster fact: *Adult lobsters molt three or four times a year; this is the only way they can increase their size. In preparation, the lobster lays down a new, soft shell underneath its old hard one. If it finds itself unable to squirm out of its old shell, the lobster may amputate its leg or claw to release itself. Within several hours after molting, the lobster regains its bigger size and the new shell begins to harden.*

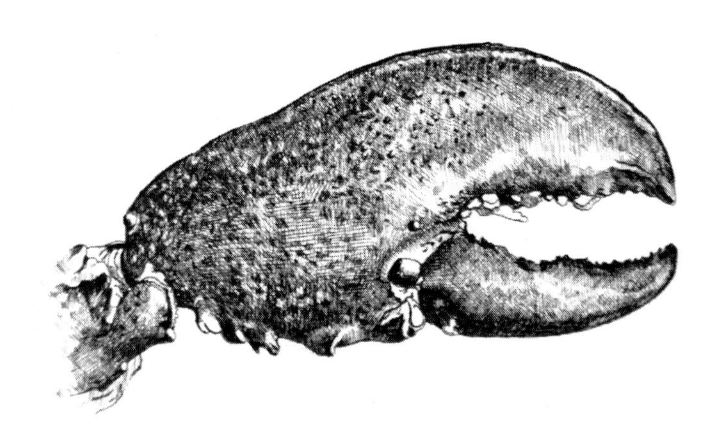

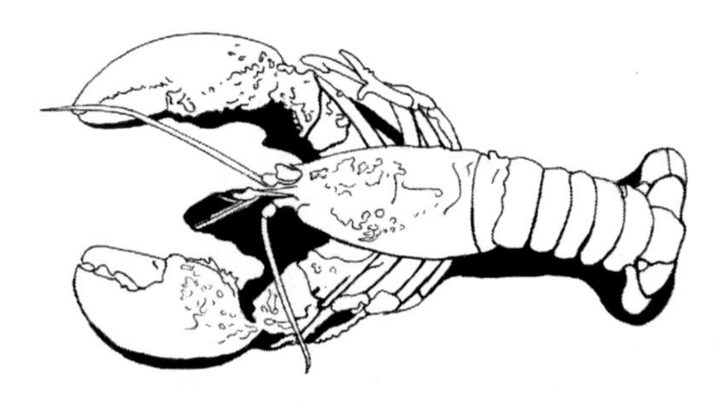

Chapter 44

Moon Violet Dances Again

Abenakis from all over the island descended upon the Moon Violet Inn throughout the afternoon. With each knock on the door, Moon Violet was reminded of a childhood song she used to jump rope to, Doctors, Lawyers, Indian Chief. Only today she found herself adding teachers, factory workers, accountants, and retail clerks. Abenakis are abundant on Mount Desert Island and represent many professions. She found it amusing to greet people at the door looking like just regular island folks only to see them later completely transformed in full Abenaki dress. As much as it was an extremely serious situation that had brought them together, Abenakis are joyous people by nature and try to find pleasure in all that they do. Tonight was no exception. Friends, neighbors, distant relatives, and new acquaintances were welcoming and receiving one another with handshakes, hugs, and kisses.

Moon Violet lit a match and placed it under the pile of logs arranged earlier by some of the dancers. The kindling wood ignited, creating a line of gray smoke followed by a tiny flame. Onto the center of the flame, she then tossed a mixture of dried herbs selected for their healing capabilities: mint, for purity and calming of the soul; lupine petals, for endurance for the dancers; mustard seed, for clarity; and lavender, to sweeten the air. She watched as the fire fluctuated from bright yellow to green and then dark purple. Perfect, she thought and breathed in the many scents emanating from the flame.

She bowed to the elder of the group, Mother Tall Lynx,

who removed the ceremonial Abenaki blanket draped over her shoulders. The blanket was woven many, many years ago and was always worn by the eldest female in the tribe. Tall Lynx was adorned in Abenaki celebratory dress from head to toe. Her silvery white hair hung in a solitary braid down her back and contrasted in color with her gown of royal blue embellished with ribbons, beads, and feathers and almost reaching the ground. Her feet were bare, but around her ankles, wrists, and waist she had tied strings of tiny seashells that tinkled with each deliberate movement she made. She raised her arms and held them open wide to the sky. She sang, her voice ragged from age yet full of hope.

"Kanake-kee, Kanake-kee pa ra
Gatay, dante, wa gatay
Kanake-kee, Kanake-kee
Matum, dante, wa Matum
Kanake-kee, Kanake-kee pa ra
Sa, ma, ta, gi, sa, Cadillac
Sa, ma, ta, gi, so lo"

As Mother Tall Lynx finished, several of the elderly tribesmen kept the rhythm of the song going and banged softly on drums hand-carved from birch trees and covered with deerskin. The Abenakis believed the drums housed ancestral spirits who were called to serve when the drums were played continually. Tall Lynx repeated the song, this time joined by others in the audience who added hand gestures and dance steps, circling around the growing fire.

"Kanake-kee, Kanake-kee, pa ra." One Who Walks with Animals, we call to you, Ani, for help and to receive our help, Moon Violet translated into English, trying hard to remember the Abenaki language. "Gatay, dante, wa gatay." Pray, dance, we pray, asking to bring our ancestors together. "Kanake-kee, Kanake-kee, pa, ra." One Who Walks with Animals, again, calling on Ani. "Matum, dante, wa Matum," Peace, dance, we call for peace, peace among us and the lobsters. "Kanake-kee,

Kanake-kee, pa ra." Calling for Ani to receive us for the third time. "Sa, ma, ta, gi, sa, Cadillac." Gods of Cadillac Mountain, we are your children, offer your protection for our souls.

All the Abenakis took up the chant and danced around the fire. They would continue throughout the evening, ending at the exact time the NC 241 was scheduled for detonation. When Tall Lynx became tired, the next eldest woman would take over and so on until every female had a chance to lead the chant. Likewise, the eldest man would keep the tempo with the drums until he tired and this was passed on to the next eldest man. The broth was used sparingly to replenish the weary revelers.

When the sun took its final bow of the day, Moon Violet would dance again along with her Abenaki brothers and sisters, united in a common purpose for peace and harmony for both human and lobsterkind.

Lobster fact: *Before contact with Europeans, there may have been about 40,000 Abenaki in North America, but after the American Revolution, that number dipped to under 1,000. There are now approximately 12,000 Abenaki living in northern New England and the Canadian Maritime Provinces.*

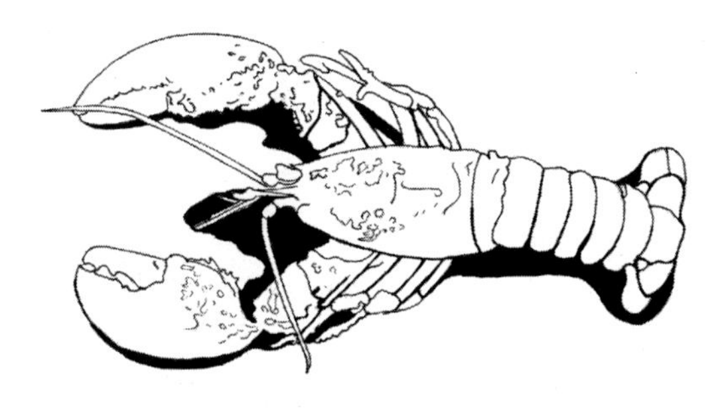

Chapter 45

A New Mexico Seagull

The heat index was high that day in New Mexico, so high in fact that the team would probably finish early and rest in the camps in the afternoon. Dr. Robin Banke used her gloved hand to wipe away the sweat pouring down her face and into her blue eyes. She knew she probably just rubbed dirt all over her forehead, but she didn't care. A dirty face indicated a productive dig, and by the look of the members of her team, this dig was very productive. The area that she was excavating was small, about four feet by three feet. She surmised that the Sandia tribe of New Mexico had used the spot to store their pots and other vessels. She had already uncovered several large pottery shards and what she thought were remnants of rudimentary tools most likely used for food preparation, a highly successful morning for the dig overall, given that it was common to spend many days digging to unearth only a single shard.

She took a long, slow drink of water from her canteen, purposely allowing some of it to pour down her chin and onto her shirt. Her dirty blonde hair was wet with sweat and clung to the back of her neck. It would feel good to jump in the ocean right about now, she mused. I wonder if the girls are swimming? It had been such a long time since she had reached them. The last time she had spoken to her husband, George, the connection was frustratingly poor, and she could barely understand him. She got a sense that his research wasn't going well, but they both knew that research results weren't always predictable. Despite this, he had seemed more discouraged than usual. How bad could it be there? Larger lobsters sounded like a delicious problem, especially to her when she was miles away from any ocean. She missed the girls. She hoped they were doing all right in Maine. George had a tendency to become ultra-focused when he was involved in a research project. She was thankful they had raised the girls to be independent and responsible, but still, she worried about them.

"Dr. Banke," a voice called to her from above. She recognized Carl, her top graduate student, this time leading his own site excavation.

"Hey there, Carl. Find anything interesting?" she asked while setting down her brush.

"No, nothing, unfortunately."

Robin climbed up the makeshift ladder to get out of the dig. "I'm sure you'll find something soon."

"I know," he said. "Like you always say, patience isn't a virtue, it's a necessity on a dig."

"Exactly."

"We might need to close up shop for a few hours," he said, looking up at the clear blue sky and a full-on sun.

"I was just thinking the same thing," Robin said. She also squinted up at the sky, and what followed resulted in her swift and sudden departure and Carl's immediate promotion to site director.

She spotted a flock of seagulls flying into view, squawking and cawing loudly. "This is unusual," she said.

"I didn't think they would come this far from water," Carl said.

"They don't," Robin said. The gulls hovered over them, their loud cries enveloping the area. Soon others from the dig stopped doing what they were doing and joined Robin and Carl, perplexed and amused by the spectacle. After a few minutes, the gulls flew up into the sky, high and almost out of sight, and then abruptly turned around, as if on a specific mission, and dove straight down toward the crew. Chaos ensued as everyone scattered for cover, hoping to avoid being hit by the birds, everyone except for Robin.

Fear, excitement, and wonder pulsed through her. She knew deep down that the gulls wouldn't hurt her, she knew before they reached her, before they all flew over her, each dropping a solitary feather as they passed, on her head, her shoulders, her chest, her back. Feathers gently cascading over her entire being, cleansing her, calling her, pleading with her to go. *Go*, she felt them say to her. *Go, go to Ani. She needs you. They all need you*. Tears poured down her face, mixing with the dirt and the dust and yes, the feathers. She knew, oh, how she knew.

"Thank you, thank you all," she called to the gulls who cried back to her, loud, joyful, and hopeful, before disappearing into the bright blue sky.

Lobster fact: *The seagull is perhaps best known for being a scavenger. It is most often seen in large, noisy flocks wherever food is available, such as hanging out around fishing boats, picnic grounds, parking lots, and garbage dumps. Many people consider gulls a nuisance, but they actually perform a very valuable service by scavenging dead animals and organic litter that could pose a health threat to humans.*

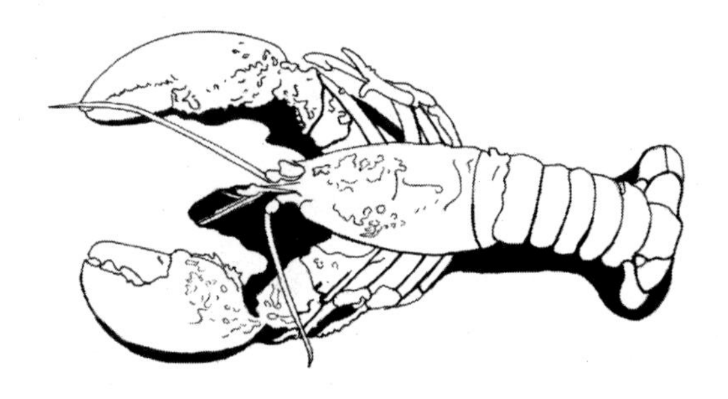

Chapter 46

The Door Holds the Key

The girls returned to the cottage, tired, hot, and defeated. Especially Ani. She had barely spoken on the ride back and went upstairs to their room as soon as they got home. Eliza made peanut butter and jelly sandwiches, about the only thing left to eat in the house since their father was at the lab and the girls had been too distracted to think about buying food. Eliza heard Ani's footsteps on the stairs and looked up, hopeful that Ani's mood had changed.

"I've made us some sandwiches, Ani. Come and eat with me."

"I'm not hungry. I think I'll go outside and get some air."

"Do you want some company?"

"No, no thanks." And she was gone.

Ani was a mix of emotions. She felt her body throb with rage and regret. An uncomfortable feeling settled in her stomach when she thought about her fight with Roonie. She knew he didn't mean to spill the chocolate milk, but of all times to be klutzy. Her anger was not solely directed at Roonie anymore, but at herself as well.

Why did I let Roonie, or really any of us, have drinks around the book? I didn't do my job. I was selected to protect the book, to protect the animals, to help the girl in the orb, and I failed. Tomorrow the lobsters will be destroyed, but so will all the sea life in and around the harbor. Acadia will be ruined. It will take years for this beautiful and sacred place to recover. And I thought I was so clever. I'm Kanake-kee. I can solve the puzzle and save the island. But I was wrong, and the Abenakis were wrong to place their faith in me. I didn't solve anything, and the only thing I offered was false hope.

Ani fought back tears and decided to take a walk through the garden, too upset to stay still. She left the porch and took a few steps on the crushed stone path that led to the center of the main garden. She felt something soft brush past her cheek. She swatted at her face and walked on, thinking she might have walked into a spider's web hanging from a nearby bush. Then something landed on top of her head. She reached up and felt a feather. She brought it to her face and determined by its vibrant red color that it was a cardinal's feather, her mother's favorite bird. Curious, she thought. She took a few more steps down the path holding the beautiful feather. Several feet in front of her, she spied another red feather. She picked it up. Coincidence? she wondered.

Ani looked around and waited. She heard the cardinal's song, something Mom taught her and Eliza to recognize when they were little. Sure enough, another feather dropped from above and landed farther down the path. This time, Ani ran to it, her mood lightening. The game continued with Ani pursuing the feathers throughout the garden, turning this way and that along the path, stopping to listen to the cardinal's song serenading her, beckoning her to keep moving. After a time, she found herself standing in back of the wooden door with all the carvings that served as the opening to grounds surrounding the cottage.

Ani was energized. Her body tingled with anticipation. She opened the door a few inches, expecting to find another feather, but saw nothing. The sun had rounded the back of the house and the rays illuminated the door's surface. That's strange, she thought, why would I be directed to the back of the door? Ani had never looked at it closely before. In fact, like most visitors to the cottage, she had focused only on the etchings in the front, but the back also had carvings, a narrow border running along the perimeter. She ran her hand over them. Her fingers slid in and out of various shapes, swirls, and lines, trying to discover a pattern if one existed. Standing on tiptoes, Ani stretched up and traced the edge with the tips of her fingers as far up as she could manage. At five feet four, with the door being at least seven feet high, Ani needed a stepladder to reach them all.

She raced to the garden shed behind the cottage. Ani had seen the gardener carrying a stepladder before, presumably to aid him in pruning trees. Perhaps he stored it in the shed. She hesitated and then knocked tentatively. No response. She looked around and called out softly, "Mr. O'Leary?" She waited briefly and hearing nothing, she entered. The shed was dark, with only a small window directly across from the door. It smelled earthy, a blend of mulch, grass clippings, and manure. Ani blinked a few times to help her eyes adjust to the diminished light. The room contained gardening tools arranged on shelves and hooks on each wall. She spotted the stepladder hanging to the right of the window. Beneath the window, on top of a workbench, lay a trowel, a pair of worn gloves, and a small watering can. Her eyes moved to the window ledge. She saw a bud vase with a solitary pink flower. Lupine, she thought, and moved closer.

"What's this?" she said out loud as she cautiously removed a musty old book entitled, *A Gardener's Glory: A Gardener's How To for the Northeast* by Mandy Randall, from the bench. A blue hair ribbon was tucked inside. Ani gently tugged on the stained ribbon, which was frayed at the edges. Just like the ribbon at the eagle's nest! This can't be a coincidence. It has to be a clue from the girl in the orb. But why does Mr. O'Leary have one, too? Ani opened the book to where the hair ribbon was resting. A curling black and white photograph was inserted between the pages. She picked it up and studied the picture. A girl with two braids with little bows at the end stared back at her. For some strange reason, the picture seemed vaguely familiar. She knew she had seen a similar picture before, but where? She flipped it over and struggled to decipher the inscription. The script was tiny and faded. Ani turned to the light of the window.

"*A, m, e,* and something, and *i,* and *r* or is that *a*?" she read aloud. "America? No, it has to be Amelia! Amelia, 1957."

"What are you doing in here?" demanded Patrick, whose harsh voice shocked even him. "Give me that," he shouted, ripping the photo from Ani's hands.

"I'm sorry," she stammered. "I, I only came in here to borrow a stepladder."

"What do you need a ladder for? You should have come to find me, and I would have gotten it for you. It's not safe in here for kids. These tools can be dangerous if used incorrectly." He swiftly slipped the picture inside his front pocket. "I don't like people snooping around my stuff."

"I don't know what to say," Ani said. "It won't happen again. I promise."

Patrick reached toward her, and for a moment Ani thought he might strike her, but he grabbed the stepladder from behind her and lowered it down from its hook.

"Here," he said, thrusting the ladder toward her. "When you're finished, put it in front of the shed. I'll put it away. And stay out of here."

"Yes, sir," she said and left. Patrick slammed the door behind her.

Ani, relieved to be out of the shed and away from Mr. O'Leary, headed back to the wooden door. Amelia, Amelia, who is Amelia? Why would he be so upset when he found me with the picture? I'm going to have to tell Eliza about this encounter. This will rate high on her creepdar rating scale. Was the blue ribbon Amelia's hair ribbon? If so, then the blue ribbon that I found on the eagle's nest and the blue ribbon I found in the shed could be from the same girl. The picture was so old and worn it was impossible to really identify the girl's features, but if she could, Ani felt that they would be identical to those of the girl in the orb. The girl in the orb and the girl in the old photograph were one and the same: Amelia! It just had to be true. And somehow Mr. O'Leary was connected to her. Why else would he have that picture and ribbon secreted away in a book?

Once back at the door, Ani opened the stepladder and climbed up. She forced herself to stop thinking about the gardener and the girl in the orb, or rather Amelia, and centered her attention on the door. On her tiptoes, she braced herself against the door. At least at this height she wasn't afraid, remembering yesterday's pine tree incident and the eagle feather. Was the cardinal leading her to a clue now that her book was ruined and Professor Sol was, well, was out of his head?

She took a deep breath, something her mom always told her and Eliza to do when they were worried, and let her lungs fill with air. She let it out slowly and examined the border at the top. Her eyes were nearly level with the shapes. These markings look familiar, she thought. Each shape or series of shapes appeared to be separated by two solid short lines. The pattern repeated itself after every fifth series of shapes. The first one was a circle encompassing a star, followed by a circle surrounded by lines, then a prism with lines below it, then a feather topped by a half circle, and finally a what? Could this be what I think it is? Could it really have been here all this time? Ani retraced the patterns until she was satisfied with her findings. "Thank you, thank you, thank you, Mr. Cardinal!" she cried and leaped off the stepladder. She ran full tilt to the cottage and bounded up the stairs to her room. Eliza had just gotten out of the shower and was resting on her bed, her wet hair wrapped in a towel.

"Eliza! Eliza! I figured it out. The cardinal showed me the way, and I figured it out. I need a piece of sketch paper from your book and one of your charcoal pencils."

"What are you talking about, Ani? What did you figure out?"

"Follow me! Oh Eliza, it is so wonderful, and clever, and oh, just perfect." Ani ran back down the stairs. Eliza, excited by her sister's enthusiasm, followed Ani, wet hair and all, back to the wooden door.

"Hold these, please." Ani gave the sketch paper and pencil to Eliza. "I'm just going to get up here," she said and climbed back up on the stepladder. "Now first hand me the paper."

"Okay." Eliza passed the paper to her, bewildered by what Ani was doing. Ani placed it on top of a series of markings at the top of the door.

"Now the pencil," she called down, and Eliza dutifully handed it to her. "Remember when we did this near Plimoth Plantation on the annual third grade field trip? Grave rubbings."

"Don't tell me the Pilgrims are involved with the Abenaki Indians and the lobsters. I can't take it. Hey, didn't they have lobsters for Thanksgiving?"

"This hasn't got anything to do with the Pilgrims," said Ani, who by now had finished with her sketching and jumped down next to her sister.

"When I came outside to think, a red cardinal feather floated down across my face. I found other feathers that eventually led me here. I explored the back of the door and discovered this border."

"I never even looked at the back before," said Eliza, noticing the border for the first time.

"Precisely," said Ani. "I borrowed this stepladder from Mr. O'Leary. Remind me to tell you about what happened in the shed."

"What? What happened, Ani?"

"I said remind me to tell you, not now. This is too important. Can you hold the paper? Walk with me, and I will explain everything to you." Ani handed the paper to her sister and hopped-skipped down the path to the shed despite carrying the ladder in front of her. Eliza stared at the shading on the paper. "Eliza," Ani said, "hurry. Hurry. We're wasting time!" Eliza ran to catch up with her sister.

By the time they returned the stepladder to the shed, where Ani was most thankful not to run into Mr. O'Leary, and gone back to their bedroom, Ani had told her sister about her discovery.

"So the sequence of shapes on the door matches the sequence of shapes in the parchment?"

Ani nodded while flipping through the pages of Professor

Sol's book.

"So all you need to do is figure out this fifth shape, and this will lead us to the fifth and final amulet, right?"

"I certainly hope so because we're running out of time."

"Well, before Roonie ..." Eliza stopped. "He really is sorry, Ani." Ani made no response to this and kept looking in the book. "Before he ruined the page with the fifth amulet on it, you were fairly confident that we were looking for some kind of an animal's tooth, correct?"

"Yes," said Ani. "According to Professor Sol's book, three V shapes together is the Abenaki word for tooth."

"How big a tooth are we talking about?"

"I'm not sure yet, but I think I have a good idea of where we're going."

"You do?"

"Yeah, come look."

Eliza walked over to the desk.

"This circle shape by itself means island," Ani said, pointing to the symbol in Professor Sol's book.

"I can't go back to Bar Island again. Honestly, I just can't do it. It just was so, so gross. I can't wash my hair enough."

"No, Eliza, not Bar Island. Check out this shape. It is an oval with a series of ridges on the back."

"It looks like a rhinoceros, kind of," Eliza said.

"Think smaller."

"Huh?"

"Porcupine. The shape means porcupine."

"Porcupine Islands?" asked Eliza. Ani smiled at her sister. "How do we know which one?"

Ani flipped open *Mount Desert Island, a History* by Chris Murphy. "This book reports that only one island, the largest of the three, has animal inhabitants."

"But again, Sherlock Holmes, whose tooth are we seeking?"

"I'm working on that," Ani said and switched back to Professor Sol's book and then to the etchings from the door. Her eyes widened and her mouth dropped open. "Uh-oh. Oh, no," she said.

"What is it? Do you know?"

Ani grimaced.

"Chipmunk? Rabbit? Squirrel?" asked Eliza while Ani shook her head no to each new inquiry.

"Skunk? It has to be a skunk. Somebody has a pretty sick sense of humor. How are we going to get a skunk's tooth? Do they even have teeth?"

"If only it was a skunk," said Ani in a slightly quaking voice.

"Okay, now you're completely freaking me out, Ani. What is it? What type of tooth do we need to find?"

Ani turned to a page in the Mount Desert Island book and held it up for Eliza to see.

"A Maine Black Bear," Eliza said. "Oh my!"

Lobster fact: *Black Bears are the smallest and most commonly encountered bears in North America. They are the only species of bear found in the eastern United States. They can run up to 25 miles an hour and are great climbers. Adult males typically weigh between 250 and 600 pounds, while females average 100 to 400 pounds. Unlike grizzly bears, however, black bears rarely attack humans. Maine Black Bear is also the name of a popular flavor of ice cream consisting of vanilla ice cream with swirls of black raspberry syrup and chocolate candies filled with liquid black raspberry.*

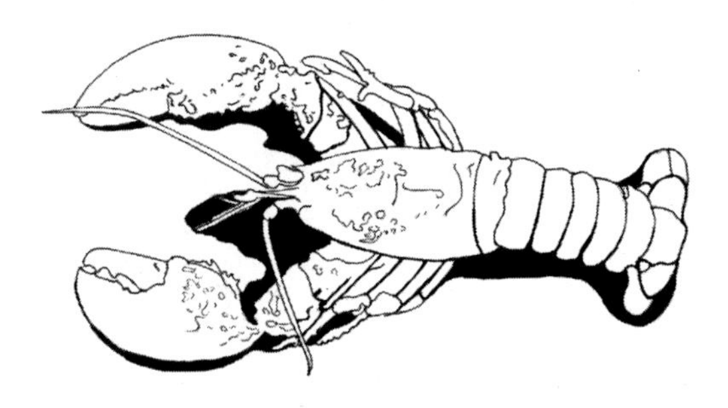

Chapter 47

My, What Big Teeth You Have

"Bears." exclaimed Eliza. "Are you sure, Ani, are you really sure? Boy, these Abenakis ask too much. How are we going to get a bear to give us his tooth?"

"I don't know, Eliza, but we have to try."

"I'm thinking I might need to stay back here and wait for Dad. He might come home and need, need a peanut butter sandwich or something." Eliza knew full well that Ani wouldn't buy her hedge.

"Eliza, you were the one who told me Dad had called when I was outside and said he wasn't coming home and that if we needed him, we could come to the lab. So no excuses, I need you to come with me."

"I thought swimming with the lobsters was bad, but a Maine black bear?"

"Maine black bears are not grizzly bears, Eliza. They like to eat blueberries and fish and well, normally are frightened of humans."

"I don't like how you said 'normally' since nothing that we have experienced in the last few days or really since we first came to the island has been normal."

The grandfather clock in the hall chimed loudly. "Eliza, we can't argue about this now. We have to go if we are going to make it to Porcupine Island."

"How are we getting there?"

"The sunset cruise of the *Martha Thomas*. It's the tall ship that sails to and from the first Porcupine Island every night at sunset. Tonight is the last one for a while, and the ship will mostly be filled with reporters and scientists."

"Well, how are we going to get on then since we are neither?"

"If you had paid attention when we first went out on the *JL 73,* you would have remembered TJ saying that he worked selling tickets for the ship every night after finishing with his duties at the lab. He will just have to give us some tickets since Dad is basically his boss."

"What if he isn't working?" Eliza said. "What if he has to stay at the lab and prepare for the recovery after the NC 241 is released?"

"There's only one way to find out."

Quickly Ani collected supplies including flashlights, water bottles, bug spray, and crackers (for Eliza to snack on) and headed to the porch to wait for her sister. Eliza wanted to change into jeans to protect her legs from the bear's claws or something ridiculous like that. Ani knew better than to argue the point that if the bear wanted to attack Eliza, the jeans would not prevent him from doing so. She needed Eliza's help, especially now that Roonie was out of the picture, so she wisely chose to keep her mouth shut. Outside Ani thought she saw someone step back from the path and hide behind one of the tall cedar trees. She promptly bent down and pretended to tie her sneaker while secretly spying on the intruder. Ani pursed her lips together once she recognized the brim of Mr. O'Leary's straw hat.

Why would he be spying on us? she wondered. Could this prove he is mixed up in this mystery? And if so, why and how?

About the only thing Ani knew for certain was that she didn't want him following them to the *Martha Thomas*. They couldn't run the risk of him getting in their way and ruining their plan.

Just then Eliza bounded out the door and practically bumped into Ani. "Why aren't you at the bikes? I thought you said we were in a hur ..." Ani put a finger to her lips and hushed Eliza.

Ani whispered, "The creepy gardener is lurking around the corner. We don't want him to hear what we're doing or where we're going. Quick, make up something about where we are headed and talk loudly. We can try and shake him if he follows us."

"Why me?" Eliza asked.

"Because you're a better liar."

Eliza's eyes widened.

"I mean you're more creative. Please."

Eliza scowled but did as she was asked. At full volume she said, "Hey, I'm beat. I'm going to take a nap and you can cook dinner. Then we can play a long slow game of Monopoly."

"TMI, too much information."

"What?" Eliza said.

Standing, Ani said in an equally loud but less affected voice, "Sounds like a good plan, Eliza. Let's go in the house now." She placed a hand on Eliza's shoulder, and they went back in the house. Ani threw her backpack down and ran upstairs to her father's room. She crawled on her hands and knees to make her way across the floor to the window and peeked behind the curtain. She had a perfect view of Patrick, who rested against the cedar and stared at the cottage. "Come on, come on, old timer, leave, just leave. We're not going anywhere, so you can go back to doing your creepy thing somewhere else."

Eliza stood in the doorway. "Who are you talking to?"

Ani ignored her. "There you go, Mr. O'Leary, that's right, head away from the cottage." Satisfied that he had finally departed, she turned to Eliza. "Don't just stand there. We have to move. Let's go out the kitchen door and hope he hasn't looped back around the path."

The girls were soon on their bikes speeding on the road toward the dock of the *Martha Thomas*. Fortunately, the ship now departed from Northeast Harbor, not Bar Harbor, which had already been completely shut down. The girls arrived at their destination exhilarated and breathless from their ride. They ran down the plank, pushing past the crowd of ticket holders as politely as possible despite their urgency to get to the ticket booth. I hope beyond hope that TJ is in that booth, thought Ani as they approached. But luck was not on their side. It was not TJ who greeted them. Instead it was an old man with a scruffy beard. Ani's heart sank.

"Tickets are all sold out, ladies, and besides," the man added, "this trip is only for reporters and scientists, which I'm thinking by the looks of you, you ain't neither."

Ani pivoted as if to leave, already trying to devise a plan B when Eliza pushed past her and slapped down her and her sister's official badge from Jamison Lab, the badges they made before they went on the *JL 73*. Their dad had thought it would be fun for them to have their own Lab badges when he was getting his credentials. The girls weren't too impressed at the time, complaining that occasionally their father acted like they were in elementary school, but they did each make one anyway to please him. Eliza must have taken them when I was upstairs checking out the gardener, Ani thought, grateful for her sister's quick thinking.

"As you can see from these badges, we are affiliated with Jamison Lab as our father, Dr. George Banke, is in charge of the research. He specifically requested that we be on the *Martha Thomas* to take water and other samples." Eliza's act was much better here than it was back at the cottage.

The old man looked puzzled. "What about them other scientists from Jamison Lab? Aren't they already here for the samples, untainted by gasoline emissions from a speedboat, so they prefer to be on a sailboat, powered by the wind and all?"

Eliza's skills were now in full swing. She glanced around conspiratorially and leaned in closer to the man. Speaking softly and slowly, she said, "My father believes there are infiltrators within the Jamison Lab community. He is afraid they might falsify their findings in order to," she stumbled here to find the right words to say but only for an instant, as she noticed the man sported a Foster's Lobster Pound logo on the pocket of his shirt. She continued confidently, "in order to prevent the common man, common lobster and fisherman for that matter, to prevent them from harvesting these waters surrounding the harbors of MDI." This last line seemed to do the trick because the old man appeared angry. He might even have been a lobsterman himself, many of whom believed that this lobster thing was something cooked up by government officials to regulate the system and take over the fishing industry.

He bought it hook, line, and sinker, thought Ani. Way to go, Eliza, way to go.

* * * *

Patrick paced around the garden shed, not wanting to go home but not wanting to go too close to the cottage. He did hear the girls say they weren't going anywhere, but he wasn't convinced they were telling the truth. They must have seen him hiding behind the tree. He wasn't cut out for all this sneaking around. He was also angry with himself for yelling at the younger Banke girl earlier today. He had just been so shocked to find her in his shed and with Amelia's picture no less. It was too much for him, and so he yelled. He walked over to the potting table and picked up the picture of Amelia. His Amelia smiled back at him, his last picture of her before she disappeared. He removed the hair ribbon from the pages of the book and stared at it. Amelia's? How could this be? Next, he lifted the tools and then the tarp off the old trunk under the potting bench, extracted the key from his pocket, undid the lock, and reverently unwrapped the trash bag to slide out the ancient Abenaki parchment. This thing has caused more trouble than good he thought, but he was compelled to open it. Shaking his head, he rifled through the drawings that had once brought him such a feeling of pride. Mr. Baxter had chosen him, Patrick Sean O'Leary, son of Michael Sean O'Leary, an Irish immigrant and gardener to one of the most important men on the island, to receive this precious document. What a fool I was back then, he thought. He sighed and closed the book.

"I'm ridiculous," Patrick said out loud, and after tucking the parchment under his arm, he exited the shed. He strode down the path that circled around to the front of the cottage house. He felt like a trespasser even though he had been made caretaker of the property! Ridiculous, he thought again. I'm just going to go up to the house and knock on the door and make sure they're okay. I'll make up some kind of story about their father and how he had spoken with me and wanted me to check on them. But what if they call their father and he tells them that he never did ask me to check on them? Then I would just be some strange old man knocking on the door. He took a few more steps. Moon Violet did tell me I should assist the girls. I'm going to show them the book and tell them about the Lobster Tale. Violet said it was my choice, and, well, I'm choosing to help. Yes, this is the right thing to do.

By the time he reached the cottage, he hesitated, but only for a few seconds, and then knocked on the door. No answer. He knocked again, and still no answer. He peered through the side windowpane and saw nothing. The lights were on and he could hear the radio playing in the kitchen. Maybe the older one was indeed napping, and the other one was cooking dinner. He went around to the back of the house and knocked on the kitchen door. No one answered. Slowly he turned the door handle and found it unlocked. "Hello," Patrick called out. "Hello. Is anyone home?" He looked into the hallway. It was eerily quiet despite the radio hum from the other room. "Hello?" This was the second time he had been in the house since the Bankes' arrival, the second time he was there uninvited. He truly had lost all sense of decency, he thought, but found that once inside the cottage, he needed to explore. He swiftly headed upstairs, announcing his arrival but receiving no response.

Convinced the girls were gone and feeling deflated that they had tricked him, he decided to hunt around for a clue as to their whereabouts. He learned nothing from his search upstairs, as the girls' desk was bare. He checked the kitchen and living room tables again and came up empty-handed. He was about to leave when he heard a bump coming from Mr. Baxter's library and office. Silently he opened the door to the study and flicked the overhead light on, throwing a yellow glow into the room. He stood in the doorway, his frame completely blocking any escape.

"Who's in here?" he called in the harshest voice he could muster. "I know you're in there, so if you want to save me from calling the police, come out and show yourself to me." He waited, but the only sound he could hear was the tick, tick of the old grandfather clock in the foyer. He was about to leave when he glimpsed something shiny underneath the great mahogany desk. Softly he said, "I guess I must be hearing things." He turned off the light and closed the door, but instead of leaving, he stayed put, sure that the culprit would show himself once he believed the coast was clear.

Roonie came out from under the desk and slammed directly into Patrick, who yelled, "Gotcha ya!" and grabbed him by the back of his red Spider-Man shirt.

"Letmego, letmego," hollered Roonie.

"What are you doing here? Where are the girls?" Patrick demanded, switching on the light. "Roonie?"

Roonie attempted to swipe at Patrick's arms and shouted, "What do you mean 'Where are the girls?' I want to know what *you* did with them. You probably kidnapped them. I should call the police. Always snooping around and following them. Along with those wacky bug guys." Roonie squirmed under Patrick's grip, but Patrick's many years of gardening had made him strong and definitely strong enough to keep a ten-year-old at bay. Roonie, noticing what Patrick held in his other hand, cried, "Hey, that's Ani's book, her special book. What are you doing with it? Give it to me." He kicked Patrick in the shin. Patrick dropped the book and released his hold on Roonie's shirt to grab his leg.

"Ouch! You little brat, don't kick me!" Roonie dove for the book, but Patrick was too quick for him and lifted it up before Roonie could get it.

"I said," Roonie shouted, "that's Ani's book. She's using it to find the amulets to appease the gods of Cadillac who will make the lobsters go back to, back to, well," Roonie wasn't sure where they came from so he finished his statement with, "well, wherever they came from."

"Ani's book? Ani's book? This is my book, my book given to me by Barton's father, Mr. Baxter. Amelia's book told about the amulets and the offerings to the gods."

Roonie, curious and exhausted from his struggle, stopped hitting Patrick and asked, "Who's Amelia?"

"Amelia is or Amelia was ..." Patrick couldn't find the words to answer Roonie's question. "Just someone I used to know is all."

"Oh," said Roonie, sensing from Patrick's more serious tone that he shouldn't ask any further questions.

"Ani has a book like this?" Patrick said. Roonie nodded his head yes. "Do you know where she got it?"

"I don't know," he said, standing up. "I think she said something about her mom gave it to her on her birthday."

"She recently had a birthday?"

"Yeah, right before they came to the island," Roonie said.

"She wouldn't have just turned thirteen?" Patrick asked, his voice slowing down, not really needing a reply from Roonie.

"Yeah, she did. Eliza keeps telling me how they're teenagers and I'm only ten. It's annoying."

Patrick just stared at Roonie, his eyes feeling moist. The Abenakis, he thought. Moon Violet was right. They must be involved with Ani. And I must help her.

"Roonie," he said, forcing himself to push aside his emotions, "I have not hurt the girls. I am trying to help them. I realized the Thibodeau brothers were following them, and I was trying to figure out why and what they were up to."

"Did you? What do they want with the girls?"

"I'm not really sure, but I think it has something to do with the lobsters. Do you really have no idea where the girls went? You three have been inseparable."

"Well," Roonie said, looking sheepishly at his feet, "we sort of had a fight, and I sort of spilled milk on the last part of her book and ruined the pages with the final clue. I came over to say I was sorry, but they weren't here."

"Did Ani have any idea as to where the clue might be?"

"No, she didn't. She was working on that when the milk

spilled."

"They can't have gotten too far on their bikes," said Patrick.

"I did find this on the desk in here," Roonie said, his face lighting up as he removed a piece of crumpled paper from his shorts pocket.

Patrick eagerly took it from him and smoothed out the wrinkles. He read it out loud, "*M Thomas, 7 P.M.* Hmmm."

"I don't think the girls know any Mr. Thomas," Roonie said.

Patrick smiled. "I got it! It's not Mr. Thomas, Roonie. It's the *Martha Thomas*, the schooner. She sets sail every night for Porcupine Island and back. I bet that's where they're going. Come on, superhero. I need your help navigating."

"How are we going to get there? We'll never make the boat now."

"We are going to borrow Barton's whaler," Patrick said. "I know where he keeps the keys."

* * * *

The girls headed to the bow of the *Martha Thomas*, a unique 151-foot four-masted schooner with bright red sails recognizable from vantage points all over the island, and waited apprehensively for the ship to sail. Normally the sunset cruise was filled with tourists who came not only to view the remarkable sunsets, but also to hear the lively music and enjoy the humor of the jovial crew. Tonight was different. The mood was somber and passengers and crew were subdued. Some, most likely reporters or photographers, took pictures of the harbor. Ani assumed this was a before and after kind of record keeping. Others stared glassy-eyed into the bay as if forcing themselves to remember what it was like to be here prior to the discharge of NC 241. The captain rang the bell signaling the crew to cast off lines from the dock. The *Martha Thomas* was off. The girls observed a few passengers bow their heads as if in prayer, understanding the significance of this final expedition to Porcupine Island.

Ani heard the sails billowing in the wind and looked up at the sky, which was still warm and inviting, a sharp contrast to the chaos simmering below the water's surface. The sunlight danced upon the water, producing tiny bursts of glistening silver flashes sprinkled over the rolling waves. Ani was reminded of the first amulet they discovered, the silver sand dollar, when she and Eliza swam with the seals. She wondered where Whiskers and his friends were that night. Would they be safe? Would they know to stay away from the harbors? She was afraid for them and all the other sea creatures that lived in and around Mount Desert Island. Music swelled up from the stern. Ani recognized the violin. Perhaps a crewmember had elected to serenade the passengers. The music was soft, the tune melancholy. She welcomed the sound and the cool breeze blowing against her cheeks, her heart heavy with sadness and concern. It was unbelievable to imagine that this harbor, along with Southwest and Bar Harbor, would be destroyed in the early hours of the morning.

Eliza, never one to pass up the offer of free snacks, headed to the center of the schooner to nibble on cheese and crackers. The old man had said the ship was at capacity, and Eliza found it difficult to avoid bumping into people as she maneuvered herself in front of the small appetizer and beverage station. "Thank you," she said while taking a glass of cool ginger ale from the crewmember behind the table. Abruptly the *Martha Thomas* shifted, and Eliza was knocked off balance by another passenger and spilled her soda onto the tray of crackers. "Sorry," she said wincing. "I'm so sorry." She turned to see who hit her and was shocked to recognize the tall bug guy wearing a fake mustache and beard.

"Ah, sorry, Miss," Lyle muttered. "Wave got the better of me." He chuckled.

Eliza kept her head down and said, "No problem." She departed quickly to find her sister. She slid next to Ani and whispered in her ear, "They're here, the bug guys!" Ani's eyes widened. She had forgotten them. "The tall one rudely bumped into me, and I spilled my soda. He has a disguise on, or should

I say an attempt at one anyway. A fake mustache and beard, but it was unmistakably him. I'm sure his brother is here, too. They're always together."

"What do you suppose they want? They couldn't possibly know what we're doing."

"I can't imagine how they would," Eliza said. "We don't even really know what we're doing ourselves."

"We have to lose them when we dock on the island. We can't run the risk of them taking the amulets." Ani felt for the pouch now strung securely around her neck and tucked underneath her shirt. "We just can't."

"I wish Roonie was here," Eliza said. "We could always count on him to create a diversion."

"I know. Me, too."

As the ship sailed into Frenchman Bay, the Porcupine Islands came into view. The islands looked liked the quills on a porcupine's back, as seen from the summit of Cadillac Mountain. They were known for their gentle slopes on the north side and dramatic drops on the south, carved, like much of Acadia National Park, by retreating glaciers. The *Martha Thomas* sailed to the closest of the islands, Bald Porcupine, which served as a home to many species of wildlife and as a natural protective barrier of the harbor. As the distance between the ship and Northeast Harbor increased, Ani's anxiety grew. Forget about the tooth for a moment, what if she couldn't find the bear? And if she did find him, how was she supposed to get his tooth? What if they couldn't escape the bug guys, and they were really after the amulets as she imagined they were?

Eliza nudged her arm. "Ani, look," she said, pointing toward Bar Harbor. "That barge with the enormous crane must be a military vessel and that must be how they're placing the gas canisters on the ocean floor."

Ani frowned. "Do you think Dad is there?"

"If I know Dad, he's still working at the lab trying to find a harmless solution to the lobster problem and a way to stop NC 241."

Eventually, the Porcupine Islands, in the shadow of

Mount Desert Island as the sun set in the west, loomed large as the *Martha Thomas* approached the pier. The ship's passengers and crew were silent except for the violinist, who continued to play his haunting melody.

"We have reached our destination," the captain said. "Please wait for the crew to attach the plank securely before departing. You will have approximately sixty minutes to complete your research and explore the area. Two shots from the flare gun will be your only warning to return to the ship. Thank you."

Eliza spied the other bug brother, also sporting a false moustache and dark glasses, a few feet behind Ani as the passengers prepared to depart. While the crew tied up the *Martha Thomas*, Eliza and Ani tried desperately to be the first to exit. Their size and agility were on their side, and within a few moments both girls had finagled their way to the front of the line. Ani glanced over her shoulder and saw the taller brother, now several people back, point in their general direction as he waved at his brother, who had been pushed farther behind. Ani, relieved to discover they were distant from their stalkers, whispered to Eliza, "Good, they seem to be caught in the crowd of people. We need to hit the ground running and head for the far right, toward the most northern path. The south side's landscape might be too severe for bears to thrive. I'm thinking our wisest strategy is to head to where the easiest fishing would be for them and hope for the best. If we come up empty-handed, we can always circle back to the center path."

"You can be sure that I'm hoping for the best," Eliza said, biting the inside of her lip, "which would be to simply skip down the trail and find a bear tooth laying in the path with a note that says *bear tooth, take me.*" Ani giggled despite the butterflies in her stomach.

The plank secured, a crewmember offered his arm to Ani. She took it while Eliza ran past. "Thanks," said Ani, following her sister's lead. Sprinting, the girls reached the path quickly and disappeared into the trees. They ran side by side until the path narrowed, and then Eliza fell back behind Ani. Eliza saw no evidence the bug brothers were following them. Panting, she called to Ani, "I don't see them, so can we stop for a second to catch our breath?" Ani paused and waited for Eliza to reach her.

"Can you tell me how we're going to find the bear?" Eliza asked.

Ani looked down the path. "In the summertime, bears usually eat fish and small mammals."

"I like the sound of 'small,'" Eliza said.

"Small mammals, berries, fruits, and nuts," Ani said. "They also prefer to use the forests for protection and safety."

"And?"

"And I mashed up this mixture of berries, nuts, apples, and birdseed," which she pulled out of her backpack, "and once we are far enough into the woods, I'm going to spread it all over and call the bear to dinner."

"Dinner? That's your plan?"

"What? What's wrong with that? You have a better idea?"

"No, not really. I just don't like to mix the words *bear* and *dinner* together. It gives me the willies."

Ani consulted her watch. "We need to move," she said.

"What time is it when a bear sits on your car?" asked Eliza.

"What?"

"You heard me," she said. "What time is it when a bear sits on your car?"

"I don't know, Eliza, you tell me."

"Time to get a new car," Eliza said and grinned.

"I think the correct question involves elephants," Ani said. "And it's time to go find the bear and stop telling stupid jokes."

"I'm just trying to lighten the mood here."

The girls walked for twenty minutes, the fading sunlight filtering through the trees. When they reached a clearing with a few large boulders surrounded by hardwood trees, Ani said, "This is a good spot," and opened the bag of food and spread it around the clearing. "Hello, Mr. Bear. I'm Kanake-kee, and I've brought some din." She stopped herself. "I've brought some snacks to share with you." She motioned to Eliza to follow her behind a sizable boulder.

"Now what?" Eliza asked.

"We wait," Ani said.

The sun's rays dipped lower as dusk arrived. Soon they would need flashlights to find their way back to the pier. Ani listened for movement, but all she could hear was Eliza breathing hard behind her.

"Liza," she whispered, "breathe softer."

"I can't," she said. "I'm too freaked out by what we're doing. And I need to pee, badly."

"Not now, Eliza," said Ani.

"I can't help it. You know I always have to go when I'm scared."

"Well hurry back. I don't want to be here alone if the bear comes."

"I will," she said and scooted off to find a more private spot.

Eliza's footsteps faded, and Ani resumed listening for a bear's approach. Her heart was beating so loudly she was convinced the crewmembers on the ship could hear it. Come on, bear, please hurry. I don't want to miss the boat back to the harbor. She soon heard Eliza returning to their hiding spot. Since they were little, Eliza had never managed to be quiet while walking in the woods. When they went bird watching with Dad, he used to say she could single-handedly scare away all the birds in a hundred-mile radius with her heavy footsteps. Ani felt her sister's breath on the back of her neck and softly said, "I'm glad you're back. I didn't hear or see anything, did you?" Eliza didn't respond. Ani spoke a little louder. "If the bear doesn't come soon, I'm afraid we're going to have to go back to the ship and come up with another plan of action."

Again, Eliza gave no response. Annoyed, Ani spoke in an even louder whisper. "Eliza, cut it out. Answer me!"

"Why are you yelling at me?" Eliza called to Ani, her voice coming from about ten feet away to the right of where Ani was standing. If Eliza was over there, Ani thought, then who was behind me? Panicked, Ani twisted her body completely around and discovered a male black bear had been the one breathing in her ear!

"Ahhhhh," she screamed, horrified to be nose to nose with the bear.

The bear matched Ani's surprised scream with his own roar and stood up on his back paws. His deep black fur stuck straight up, and he stood at least six feet tall and weighed in at more than 300 pounds.

Ani crept back slowly from the bear and was promptly joined by Eliza, who was trembling all over.

The bear dropped back down on all fours and appeared less menacing. He swung his large body from side to side as if pacing, and never let his eyes leave Ani's face.

"What do we do? What do we do?" Eliza said, her voice filled with terror.

Ani was unable to respond. She was consumed with fear, a fear deeper than she had ever experienced before, greater than when she almost fell climbing the pine tree for the eagle feather or when they were trapped by the lobsters at Bar Island. The bear's massive size and growl were too much for Ani, whose concern about the Abenakis, the lobsters, the amulets, and Amelia vanished when the bear first opened his mouth and roared.

"Ani, do something," said Eliza. "You're Kayakee-key or whatever the Abenakis call you. Ask for the tooth. Or should we tuck and play dead like Mom taught us to do when we were hiking in Yellowstone National Park?"

Shakily Ani opened her mouth and tried to speak. "I, I, I," she stuttered. "I ..." The bear, as if angered by her voice, rose to his full height again, front paws stretched high and spread wide to reveal spear-like claws. He roared for a third time, this one more powerful and frightening than his earlier cries. Ani flinched and pressed herself against Eliza. The two clung to each other, waiting for the bear to pounce, imagining his claws ripping and tearing their flesh. But seconds passed and nothing happened. The bear lowered itself again. Restless and pensive, he lumbered back and forth, back and forth, flaring his nostrils and emitting low growls and rumbles. The ground shook with each paw he planted heavily on the forest floor.

The bear seemed calmer now, and Ani attempted to talk

again. "I am Ani Banke, Kanake-kee. I am here to ask, most humbly, for the honor of your tooth for the Abenakis." She paused here, listening to loud, crackling noises that sounded like tree branches being broken. Eliza turned around to look for the source of the noise, but Ani stayed completely still, not daring to divert her attention from the bear, who jerked his huge head upwards, obviously aroused by the sound. The noise grew louder as whatever was making it moved closer to Ani, Eliza, and the bear, who were straining to hear and see what was approaching.

Ani could make out voices. "I can't see anything so stop yelling at me," said one. "Remind me to quit when we get back home," said the other.

"The bug guys," whispered Eliza.

The bear heard their voices, too. Up he rose, blocking any remaining light and casting a dark shadow over the girls, adding to their fright. The Thibodeau brothers broke into the clearing and were thrilled to find the Banke girls huddled together. But their joy was swiftly replaced with outright horror when they discovered the Maine black bear looming tall over Ani and Eliza.

"Ba, ba, ba, ba," stammered Lyle.

"Ah, ah, ah, ah," Daniel stuttered.

The bear, clearly agitated by the intruders, came down again onto all four paws, huffing and snorting. The girls clung more tightly to one another and scrunched their bodies low, trying to disappear into the ground away from the bug brothers and away from the terrifying bear. The bear roared, a long, low, furious roar.

Daniel jumped into Lyle's arms and sobbed, "Oh no, oh no, don't let him get me, don't let him get me."

At this, the bear sprang up once again on his hind paws. He opened his mouth even wider than before, sucked air deeply into his lungs, and then roared again so powerfully that it dislodged a gigantic front tooth, which flipped and spun and hit Eliza soundly in the forehead before bouncing off into Ani's right hand.

Lyle, horrified by what he witnessed, dropped his brother and ran in the opposite direction. Daniel crawled backward, sobbing, before rolling over and following after his younger brother.

The bear fell on all fours and licked his face with his long, pink tongue. Then he lunged up and over the girls, clearing them by several feet and landing solidly on the ground behind them. He spun his head and roared a final farewell, showing a black hole where his tooth had been, and bounded after Lyle and Daniel.

The girls barely had time to recover before they heard the two shots from the *Martha Thomas* and saw the red flares illuminating the skyline indicating that it was time to set sail.

"We're never going to make it back in time," Eliza said.

Ani tucked the bear tooth in the amulet pouch with the other treasured items. "We might if we run!" She handed a flashlight to Eliza and took one from her backpack for herself. The girls switched them on and sped back along the path to the dock and the *Martha Thomas*. As usual Ani sprinted ahead, but Eliza, still filled with adrenaline from the bear encounter, did a superb job keeping up with her faster, younger sister. The girls broke through the tree line only to see the distant outline of the *Martha Thomas*, its red sails mocking them, cruising back to port.

Eliza bent over in dismay. "Too late," she cried. "We were so close, but too late."

"Of all the rotten luck!" Ani said. "We can't possibly swim back because of the lobsters."

"Lobsters?" said Eliza. "Not just the lobsters, Ani, but the distance. We would never make it."

"I know, you're right." Ani sighed. "We've worked so hard and come so far, it doesn't seem possible we should fail now."

"It doesn't," agreed Eliza.

Ani stared up at the night sky, the stars filling her view. "We need to get to the top of Cadillac before the canisters are detonated at high tide. That's only a few hours from now. There has to be a way. Let's look for something to get us off the island."

The girls shone their flashlights around, looking over and under the dock. Eliza extracted a large piece of floating Styrofoam wedged between the metal frame of the pier and the edge of the island, and Ani found two long pieces of thick rope. She also found a sweatshirt and a broken flip-flop. The girls placed their discoveries on top of the dock, briefly proud to have accomplished something but quickly realizing they still couldn't get back to the mainland.

Ani tied one end of the rope to the piece of Styrofoam and climbed on top. "I can use this flip-flop as a paddle," she said to Eliza.

"No, no way. You're not doing this. I can't let you."

"You can't stop me, Eliza. I'm going and that's final."

"Are you nuts? I think the bear blew away all your common sense."

"No, I'm not nuts," Ani said. "I just have to get these amulets over to Cadillac. Everyone is counting on me."

"This float can't hold you. The only thing people will be able to count will be how many seconds it takes for you to drown once you fall off this ramshackle boat."

Ani ignored her sister and, dragging the chunk of Styrofoam by the rope, rushed to the end of the dock. Eliza hurried after her and hurled herself on top of the float to stop her sister. The rope broke free.

"Eliza," screamed Ani. "Look what you've done!" She held up the frayed rope for Eliza to see.

"Good," Eliza said.

"Get off," Ani demanded. "I said get off!" Eliza planted herself even more firmly on the foam, clearly demonstrating to Ani that she had no intention of budging.

Ani used both hands to try to shove her sister off, but Eliza was heavier and wouldn't be moved. "Eliza, off! I am ordering you off!"

"Ordering? You're ordering me? Who do you think you are? You're not the boss, Ani, even though you're Kayake-kee."

"It's not Kayak, you moron, it's Kanake-kee."

"Whatever. You've been ordering me around since we first arrived on this disaster of a vacation, and I'm sick of it. Sick of it, do you hear me?"

"Enough, Eliza. Get off now!" Using all her strength, Ani jumped on her sister, hoping to roll her off the float. The girls struggled against each other to gain the upper hand. They were so consumed with fighting they did not recognize the sound of a motor coming toward them over the water. Suddenly, Ani saw the boat's floodlight and heaved Eliza off of her. "Look, Eliza, a light! I think it's a boat."

Eliza sprang up and peered out toward the light. "I see it! I see it, too. We're going to be rescued! Yay!"

Ani jumped up and down, waved her arms, and shouted, "Hey, we're here, over here! We're stranded and we need to get back."

"Help us, help us!" Eliza called.

The girls hugged each other quickly, pleased to have a way off the island and slightly embarrassed by their childish fight.

The Boston Whaler slowed her motor as she neared the dock. Ani and Eliza rushed to meet their rescuer, eager to welcome him and depart Bald Porcupine Island. Eliza shone her flashlight onto the water next to the pier providing the operator a clearer path to the dock. Ani thought she saw movement in the water, but was so overjoyed with the appearance of the boat she chose not to look deeper.

Eliza's cheerful voice called, "Ahoy there, Captain. We're so glad to see you. We missed the *Martha Thomas* and need a way back to the mainland."

The back end of the boat swung around, and Eliza's light shone on the person at the helm. To the girls' dismay, Mr. O'Leary stared back at them.

"Ahoy there yourself," he said to Eliza.

Eliza dropped the flashlight and it rolled into the water. She stumbled backward, and tripped over the piece of foam. "Ouch," she yelled.

Ani, upon hearing the gardener's gruff voice, shoved the boat away from the dock. She grabbed Eliza by the shoulder and lifted her to her feet. "Run!" she cried. "Eliza, run!"

A thump reverberated through the pier as Roonie sprang onto the dock.

"Never fear, ladies, Spider-Man and the gardener are here!"

"Roonie!" both girls shouted and ran to him.

"Did he kidnap you?" demanded Eliza. "Why are you with this creepy man?"

"No, no, and he's not creepy. He's here to help us."

"He is?" asked Ani.

"I am," said Patrick.

"You have to believe him and me, too. I know we haven't got much time left," said Roonie. "Did you find what you were looking for?"

"Yes, yes we did!" said Ani.

"And then some," said Eliza.

"Great, said Roonie. "Get in the boat, and we can talk about it on the way back to shore."

The girls hopped on board, and the boat raced to the mainland. Ani glanced at the pile of odds and ends that she had been planning to use for a raft and felt a great sense of relief and gratitude for Roonie. She didn't understand why the gardener was helping them, but at this point, she was willing to take any assistance offered.

Roonie handed the girls water bottles and Ani took a long drink. She shifted to the back of the boat, feeling exhausted, and plopped down and closed her eyes. It had been a difficult and tiring day, and it still wasn't over. Getting to Cadillac and finding where they were to offer up the amulets loomed ahead. The remaining pages of her book might have instructed her where to go, but those pages were gone to a milky grave. Her head felt heavy, and she rested it on the back of the seat. She gazed up at the stars brilliantly dotting the night sky and wondered how they could look so peaceful when the water below was in so much turmoil. Soon, the motion of the boat speeding across the waves lulled her into a deep sleep.

In their haste to depart Bald Porcupine Island, Roonie had forgotten to pull in one of the mooring lines that now trailed a boat's length behind the Whaler. Weaving and winding its way through the water, the knotted rope created ripples on the surface of the ocean. Ordinarily this disturbance would have no great effect on anything living below, but these were not ordinary times. While Ani was taking her well-deserved nap, a particularly large, fast, and curious crustacean shot out of the water and clasped the end of the rope in its right pinching claw. Swiftly, unbeknown to the late night boaters, the lobster crawled his way up the rope toward the moving vessel.

Eliza, sitting closest to the stern, spotted it first and screamed, "Lobster, lobster, lobster!"

Roonie and Patrick pivoted in their seats and were appalled by what they saw. A lobster, his dark body wet and glistening, hung onto the rope with his many legs and left claw. His enormous right claw, at least three feet long, opened wide to reveal its inner row of sharp teeth and was preparing to clamp down on Ani's head! The smell of the lobster, a mix of rotten fish, seaweed, and decay, was pungent and overpowering. Eliza gagged and pinched her nose.

"Ani, move!" Roonie shouted and lunged for her, grabbing her T-shirt and hoisting her up and out of her seat. Ani twisted around to see what was the matter and found herself standing face-to-face with the mutant lobster.

She shrieked.

"Roonie," Patrick ordered, "take the wheel!" He freed the wooden oar housed neatly along the side of the boat. "Get back, get back," Patrick screamed at the lobster while smacking it on the head and claws repeatedly. But the determined lobster clung to the rope, his long, spindly antennae revolving wildly. The oar landed in the lobster's huge claw, which instantly shut and split the oar in half as if it were a toothpick. Patrick gasped but beat the lobster with the remaining piece of oar. Eliza, recovered slightly from the sickening smell, removed the second oar from the opposite side of the boat and joined Patrick in his fight against the lobster.

Roonie yelled to Ani, "Here, Ani, you drive!"

"I don't know how!" she shouted but moved next to him.

"Just stay straight and keep the speed up," he said.

Roonie knelt down between Patrick and Eliza. He pulled out his Spider-Man jackknife and flipped open the sharp blade.

"Cover me," he shouted to them. Roonie slid to the metal clamp the line was attached to and sawed the rope as fast as he could.

A loud crack of splitting wood resounded in the night. The lobster had halved Eliza's oar as well. "This isn't working!" she screamed.

"Keep hitting him," yelled Patrick. "Don't stop. He can't hang on forever." But the lobster showed no signs of letting go. Snap, the lobster's menacing, stronger than strong right claw bit off another part of Patrick's oar. The lobster crawled even further up the line, his head, upper body, and claws looming straight up over the end of the boat, his tail and legs tightly wrapped around the rope.

"Look!" Eliza cried as she whacked away at the lobster, "there are two more lobsters hanging onto the rope!"

"Hit harder. Go for the head," said Patrick.

Roonie sawed faster and faster, but his Spider-Man knife split only tiny threads with each pass back and forth.

Crack. This time another piece of Eliza's oar was broken off, leaving her with only a foot remaining of the oar. Speedily the lobster destroyed this as well, crushing it into splinters. Eliza grabbed at anything she could find, seat cushions, life jackets, a tackle box. All were swiftly obliterated by the lobster's crushing claw. With nothing left to fend him off, Eliza cried, "Roonie, give me your net, your Spidey net." Roonie reached into his pocket and threw it to Eliza and went back to sawing the tough rope with his little knife.

"I can see the shore!" screamed Ani, "Should I slow down?"

"No!" Patrick and Roonie yelled in unison, understanding that if the boat slowed, the lobsters would climb in and they all would be doomed.

Sweat poured off Patrick's face, yet he persisted. Again and again, he beat at the lobster, mindful not to be caught in its thrusting claw, clicking and clacking violently in the air. Eliza ripped open the net and attempted to throw it over the entire lobster, but her toss was not high enough and it landed on Roonie instead.

"The shore is getting even closer!" shouted a concerned

Ani.

"Liza," Roonie screamed, unable to move with the net on his head and hands.

"Sorry," she said, and untangling the net from Roonie's head, she threw it up into the air again, and miraculously it settled on top of the lobster, covering him from gigantic claw to tail.

This slowed the lobster for only a few seconds, but that was all the time needed for Patrick to call to Roonie, "Switch," and hand off the remaining piece of the oar to Roonie while seizing the knife. While the lobster worked fiercely to free itself from the white Spider-Man net, Patrick sawed the rope with all the force he could muster.

"Shore is closer and closer!" Ani shrieked, but Patrick knew this was their only chance.

"Another lobster joined the rope!" exclaimed Eliza.

"I think I need to slow down, soon," shouted Ani.

"Almost have it, almost have it, stay steady, Ani, steady," hollered Patrick.

"Hurry, hurry, he's almost free, Mr. O'Leary, the lobster is almost free!" screamed Eliza. Roonie twisted to see the approaching shoreline. He knew they had only a few seconds before he had to take over the wheel and slow the boat down or they would crash into the dock.

"I'm going to need some help," cried Ani, her voice heavy with alarm.

"Oh, no, he's free, he's free," shouted Eliza, who bounded to the front of the boat. She screamed when she saw how close they were to land. Patrick felt fragments of the Spider-Man net drop on top of him.

"Break, come on, break!" Patrick yelled at the rope.

"Faster, faster, Patrick," urged Roonie, who was still beating away with the piece of oar. "Another lobster is crawling on top of this Lobzilla."

"Roonie!" screamed both Ani and Eliza, now thirty feet from shore.

"Go," shouted Patrick. "I almost have it."

Roonie hit the lobster one last time, momentarily knocking its colossal head to the left, and ran to relieve Ani at the wheel. "Oh, no," he cried, seeing firsthand their proximity to the dock. Roonie slowed the motor down with his right hand and spun the wheel with his left hand sharply to the left, turning the boat violently but keeping them from crashing into the dock and throwing the other lobsters off the line, but the first tenacious lobster remained on the rope.

"Mr. O'Leary, look out," Ani shouted as the lobster's right claw dropped down and opened wide to close around his neck. Patrick looked up at the same time his final thrust of Roonie's knife severed the remaining fibers, and the rope broke free. The lobster, still clinging to the rope, flew up and away from the boat and landed with a giant splash in the dark ocean water.

Ani jumped down to the gardener and hugged him tightly around the neck, forgetting her earlier dislike of him. "Thank you, thank you, thank you!" she exclaimed. "You saved us from the lobsters."

Patrick, typically not comfortable with affection from anyone, welcomed the warm embrace. "You're welcome and thank you," he said softly, feeling appreciated for the first time in years. "Thank you," he repeated, grateful for choosing to help and grateful to be a part of the solution.

Lobster fact: *A lobster recently caught in Maine weighed twenty-seven pounds and had claws strong enough to break a man's arm. Maine law, however, forbids fishermen from keeping any lobsters that measure more than five inches from the eye to the start of the tail.*

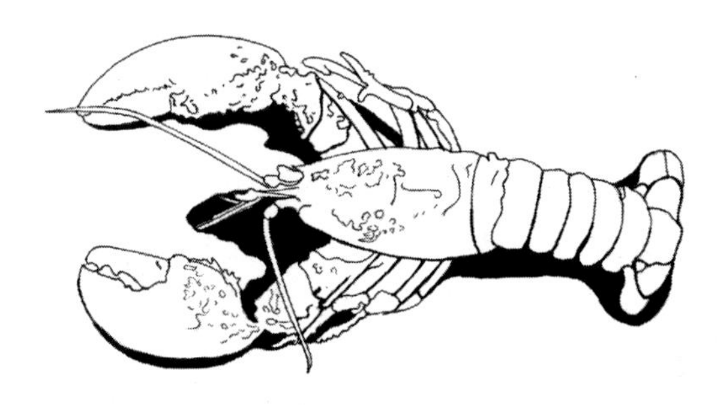

Chapter 48

The Climb to Cadillac

Roonie maneuvered the boat expertly next to the dock, and Patrick jumped out and tied it in place. Ani and Eliza leaped over the side to the dock, eager to be on land and safely away from the water and the maniacal lobsters.

Ani glanced at her watch. "It's ten. We have three hours until high tide. Dad told us the NC 241 would be detonated at one past one. We need to get up to the top of Cadillac and fast. Mr. O'Leary, do you have your truck? Can we drive up?" Ani asked as she zipped up her backpack.

"Can't," said Roonie.

Ani frowned.

"Yeah, they closed the road," Patrick said. "They don't want the protesters or other curiosity seekers causing a disturbance up on top. We're going to have to climb."

"Climb?" said Ani, trepidation in her voice.

"It isn't too much of a climb," said Patrick, picking up on her fear. "Really more like a steep hike."

"Ani doesn't like to hear *steep* and *climb* together," Eliza said.

"That's not true," Ani said, trying to convince herself while remembering her climb up the pine tree. "I'll be fine." But the butterflies fluttering in her stomach told a different story.

"I'll drive us to the start of the trail," said Patrick. "Do you know what you're looking for?"

"No," said Ani. She smiled softly at Roonie to let him know she forgave him. "I don't have the last few pages of my book."

Patrick reached into the back seat and retrieved his own ancient parchment. He took it out of a plastic shopping bag and handed it to Ani. "Here, I remember seeing something about Cadillac in the back of my book as well. Why don't you take a peek?"

Ani's mouth dropped open in astonishment. "You have one of these, too?"

"Isn't it neat?" Roonie said. "When we were at your house, I thought he was stealing your book, but Mr. O'Leary had his own book. Given to him on Mr. Baxter's thirteenth birthday. Just like you, Ani. Weird, huh?"

"I'll say," said Eliza.

Ani turned on her flashlight and looked curiously at Mr. O'Leary before carefully opening the Abenaki artifact. The book was similar in size to her own parchment, but the drawings were completely different. Patrick's pictures depicted more plant-like images with leaves, stems, and roots.

"I don't understand," she said. "How did you get this book?"

"I'll explain on our hike. It's a long story."

"Ani, I have an idea," Eliza said. "Since we have our bikes, I think Roonie and I should bike over and find Dad at the lab. I'm sure you and Mr. O'Leary will be able to get to the top in time. In the meantime, I'll tell Dad about the Abenakis and the amulets with Roonie's help, of course." Roonie grinned and Eliza continued. "I'll simply have to convince him the story is true and explain to him your Kanake-kee status [she finally got it right], and how the lobsters will go back once the gods of Cadillac are appeased. I know he's a scientist and all, but he usually believes us, and I'm hoping he just might be desperate enough to listen and stop the gas bombs."

"Sounds reasonable to me," said Patrick. "Tell him I didn't believe either." He looked at Ani, "and it took you kids to help me finally recognize that the spirit of the Abenakis and their legacy, both good and evil, is calling on us to stop the lobsters and the poisonous gas from destroying the island we love. Put your bikes in the back of the truck. I can drop you on our way to Cadillac."

The kids did as instructed and soon they were on their way to the final destination of Ani's strange quest. Ani felt comforted having Mr. O'Leary involved in their adventure. Sitting in the truck, she realized how tired she was, and it felt good to have someone older take over, if only for a little bit. Ani wished she had brought Professor Sol's translation guide, as it might have helped her decipher some of the drawings at the end of Patrick's book. However, she did recognize a few of them, such as the large upside down *V*, which she had translated earlier from her own book as the symbol representing Cadillac, the highest peak on Mount Desert Island. There were several other random drawings, mostly of plants, she guessed, and then a grouping of three circles around an *X* shape in the middle she remembered as similar to an image in her own book. But Ani had no idea what this symbol meant or whether it represented blueberries or stones or shells or wildlife.

Worry washed over her body, and she felt the familiar fear in the pit of her belly. At least with Mr. O'Leary's book, they stood a better chance of locating where they were supposed to offer the amulets, but she wasn't even sure if the drawings in his book were connected to the amulets. Her thoughts wandered to her father. Could Eliza do it? Could she persuade him to believe the story and stop the detonation of the gas until she accomplished her mission?

Patrick pulled the truck over to the side of the road and got out to help Roonie and Eliza unload the bikes. Roonie had to lower the seat on Ani's bike to better fit his smaller frame, and while he did so, Ani approached her sister. "Thanks, Eliza. I couldn't have gotten this far without your help."

"Well, duh," she said. "Now you just work your W-A-T, weird animal thing magic, and finish the job soon. I know you can do it, Ani."

"Thanks," Ani said.

"Let's go," shouted Roonie. "I know a short cut!"

"He always does," said Eliza, and they were off. Ani stared as Eliza's bike light faded into darkness.

"We can drive a little closer to the trail," Patrick said as he headed back to the driver's side of the truck. Ani scrambled in next to him and slammed the door. Patrick opened his glove box and said, "I've got some water and extra flashlights here. Why don't you put them in your backpack?"

Ani did so, and shortly Patrick pulled the truck over a second time and parked in the Sieur de Monts parking lot. He turned off the ignition, got out of the cab, and strode to the truck bed. Ani followed him and watched as he opened the truck storage bin and pulled out a blue backpack with hiking gear dangling from the straps. "Honored member of the Acadia National Park Hiking Club since 1954 when I completed my first climb of Cadillac with my father. One of my proudest moments," he recalled. "And I always like to be prepared."

"Lucky for us," said Ani, identifying several of the climbing accessories, ropes, a daisy chain, and a nylon sling, as well as a compass and a pair of binoculars. Ani also noticed a pair of hedge clippers and pointed to them.

"Hedge clippers?"

"I was given the book as a way to take care of the area. I might have hidden it away, but I never forgot that I was charged with protecting the land. Besides the hiking club, I am a member of the Historical Trail Preservation Society. Most Sundays we hike the trails and help the park rangers clear the paths of downed trees and loose boulders."

"Makes sense."

He pulled out a bottle of insect repellant and opened the lid. He handed it to Ani. "Here, you'll want to cover yourself with this, especially your neck, face, and behind your ears. The mosquitoes are vicious during the first part of the climb and even worse in the evening."

Ani grabbed the bottle. "Thanks," she said, generously applying the lotion. The smell was terrible and the lotion made her already sweaty skin feel sticky and tight. Mosquitoes loved her, more so than any other member of her family. Her mother used to say it was because she was so sweet. Dad said different body chemistries are more attractive to biting insects. Dad, always the scientist, but maybe tonight he'll look at the situation differently, she hoped.

"I think we should follow the Gorge Trail, which runs between Cadillac and Dorr Mountain," Patrick said. "It may be slippery at times because of the Kebo Stream and natural condensation, but I think it will be the most direct route. When we get to the notch, we can veer off to the right. We'll be less than half a mile to the summit of Cadillac." Patrick placed his own Abenaki book back in the plastic bag and then in his backpack. He zipped it up and then hoisted his backpack over his shoulder. He pointed his flashlight in the direction of the trail and started walking. Ani followed him.

"Sounds good, Mr. O'Leary."

"Please, call me Patrick."

"Will do, Patrick," Ani said.

"The hike is rated moderate to strenuous. I understand you have an aversion to heights, but there's only one dangerous section above the tree line when we will be on the upper part of the mountain. Fortunately the trail has iron rungs and ladders for hikers to use. We shouldn't need any ropes."

"Okay," said Ani, not really liking to hear about this section of the hike. "Let's go, and while we walk, you can tell me the story of how you received your own Abenaki manuscript."

As Patrick recalled the day he was given his "special surprise" from Mr. Baxter, the two wound their way through the Gorge Trail. The forest consisted mostly of spruce and thick pine trees. Patrick led and routinely pointed out the trail markers, bright blue rectangular splotches of paint scattered intermittently along the trail, and instructed Ani to keep her eye out for them. Thank goodness they each had bright flashlights as the denseness of the trees made it almost impossible for any light from the night sky to get through. The air smelled of pine and felt cool and refreshing. For the next several minutes Patrick explained the situation that led up to Amelia's disappearance from Barton's birthday party.

He hadn't spoken of the incident to anyone for over fifty years, and he was amazed how good he felt unburdening his mind from this painful memory. He told Ani the whole story, keeping only his personal feelings about Amelia to himself. He didn't believe it was information Ani needed to know. But who am I kidding, he thought, as he outlined the sequence of events in as straightforward a manner as he could manage, sticking to the facts. She may be a young kid, but she is certainly wise or the Abenakis wouldn't have chosen her to save the island.

Ani indeed sensed the depth of Patrick's feelings and easily detected the sadness underlying his matter-of-fact recollection of the infamous birthday party. She chose not to interrupt him until he was finished speaking, even though her mind was racing with questions.

Patrick started with Mr. Baxter's buildup about Barton's birthday party and the promise of the surprise. Then he explained how Amelia decided to share her own precious amulets with Patrick and how honored he had felt sitting next to her while she reviewed each one, recalled who bestowed it on her, and described the unique powers each individual amulet possessed. He told how Barton had slapped Amelia's hand, scattering the amulets pell-mell across the floor and under chairs and sofas, and how he and Amelia had been unable to retrieve them before meeting with Mr. Baxter. Then he related to Ani the history behind the three books and how angry and disappointed Mr. Baxter had been when Barton immediately said he planned to locate and subsequently sell the rose quartz orb, the sacred Abenaki lobster covenant.

At this point, Patrick's voice became shaky and low, but he continued, not breaking his pace or the seriousness of his tone. "And so Barton tore the blue hair ribbon from one of her braids and Amelia, never one to look the other way, sped after him as fast as she could down the path to the forbidden Abenaki door. Barton made fun of the Abenakis and their 'silly' traditions and bullied her into opening the door. Amelia defended her Abenaki ancestors and defied my own pleadings to turn back and forget about Barton. But then the padlock opened and fell off the door."

Ani pictured the scene clearly. Amelia, strong and determined, running to retrieve her hair ribbon while Barton, smug and pompous, challenged and cajoled her to walk through the door. I would have done the same thing, thought Ani.

Patrick's voice hitched. "And so, as Amelia stood there, a yellow mist came through the door and enveloped her. Then it changed to black, and within seconds it surrounded her and lifted her up and off the ground." Patrick gasped and took a deep breath. "And the mist dragged her through the opening, taking Amelia away from me—I mean us—and the door slammed shut and locked, shutting us out and making it impossible to help her. Oh, we tried to break open the door, but it was powerful, too powerful for two scared and shocked thirteen-year olds."

Ani, hesitant to divulge what she suspected to be true, cautiously said, "Mr. O'Leary?"

"Patrick," he said.

"I mean, Patrick?"

"Yes." He turned his head slightly to look at Ani.

"I'm not sure about this, but I think I know what happened to Amelia."

"What?" He stared at her in disbelief.

"When Dad, Eliza, and I were having dinner with Mr. Baxter, his dog, Beauregard, chased Eliza and me upstairs and into his study. We discovered something hidden up high on one of his shelves."

"Go on," Patrick said, his eagerness evident.

"And we opened it and found, we found—this is hard to describe so I'm just going to say it—we found a pink-colored, egg-shaped object with a small girl with two long braids trapped inside. She was missing a hair ribbon."

"Amelia!" he cried. Patrick stopped on the path and grabbed Ani by the shoulders. "I knew it! The other day I felt as if she was near and she was."

"You saw her too?"

"Not exactly. But I did see a big velvet box when I went to see Barton. I knew he broke into the cottage house after the death of his father, who had left the house to me. Barton was furious, and although I can't prove it, I'm sure he stole his birthday present, his Abenaki book, from his father's safe. He did exactly as he said he would when he turned thirteen. He used the map to figure out where the covenant was buried at the base of Cadillac Mountain and removed it from its sacred resting place. I should have taken that box from his office and run when I had the chance." Tears pooled in Patrick's eyes but he persisted. "What did she look like? Did she say how we could get her out? Was she okay?"

"I think she looked just like the picture I found of her in the garden shed."

Patrick was now unable to control his emotions, and tears flowed down his cheeks. He removed his hands from Ani's shoulders and wiped his eyes with the back of his right hand. He cleared his throat. "Did she ask about me?"

With as much empathy and kindness as she could muster, Ani said, "We didn't have much time to talk as Mr. Baxter was approaching. She told me that I was Kanake-kee and that I should use my present—or her book—and to beware of the lobsters, or Retsbol."

"I see," said Patrick, incapable of masking his disappointment.

"But she did look good." She paused. "I mean, good in the sense that she was, or hasn't, or I mean, she's the same as you remember her." Ani's voice softened. "Only smaller."

Patrick nodded and started hiking again with Ani close behind. She waited a few minutes, allowing Patrick time to let her confirmation about Amelia being stuck in the orb sink in, before asking, "So what you've told me is all true, I mean, as you know it to be?"

"Yes. I've included some other facts about the Indian legend and the time when man and lobster walked side by side on Mount Desert Island until the island got too overpopulated. As you probably have figured out, I'm not much of a talker. Being a listener has its merits, and I've learned quite a bit from sitting quietly and keeping my ears opened."

"Then my book must be the one given to Amelia before

she disappeared through the Abenaki door."

"I think so," said Patrick, holding his hand out to Ani and pulling her up onto a large boulder marked with the telltale blue rectangle.

"I wonder how the book made it to New Mexico."

"Huh?"

"My mother sent it to me for my thirteenth birthday. She's an archaeologist and is leading a dig in New Mexico. She wrote me saying that she found it in an antiques shop in Montezuma where they were getting supplies for their camp."

"I'm learning, kind of late, that the Abenakis work in mysterious ways," Patrick said.

They walked in silence. Patrick was right: the mosquitoes were downright vicious. The buzzing by Ani's ears was constant, and she itched where they bit her. She found it incredibly hard to slap at her neck while holding a flashlight. The intensity of the buzzing kept increasing, and Ani continually swatted and slapped at the mosquitoes as they attacked her body. She accidentally hit herself with the flashlight and was grateful Patrick hadn't seemed to notice.

The trail became steeper with less vegetation and more challenging rocks. When they passed the tree line, Ani grew anxious about the more treacherous part of the climb ahead. She peered at her watch: ten forty-five, only two hours and sixteen minutes left before the NC 241 was detonated. She sighed and looked up at the sky. The night was calm and the sky was clear, the stars and the full moon shining brightly, helping to illuminate the path. Ani occasionally heard the hoot of an owl and wondered if it was the same owl that had perched outside her father's window, urging her to finish her journey, the journey to save Mount Desert Island.

Patrick offered his hand again, and Ani accepted it, appreciating his assistance. Her limbs ached and her feet felt as if she were lifting cement blocks with each step. The day's activities had clearly caught up with her, and Patrick seemed to understand her fatigue and increased his support, staying close and describing the steps in front of her. *Stay left here*, he said, and *watch out, this part is tricky*; or *big step up here, Ani*; just like her father used to do when she was little. She wondered if Eliza and Roonie had found him, and if so, had they persuaded him to believe the Abenaki lobster tale?

Ani heard running water. "Patrick," she called, "what's that noise?"

"That's the stream that originates on this side of the mountain. The trail parallels it so watch your step, as the water running down the rocks can make for some slippery spots."

They strode farther up the trail, the rush of the water becoming louder. Soon Ani could feel the moisture in the air and the temperature dipping. Goosebumps crawled up and down her arms. She was chilled and blew on her hands to warm them up. Patrick noticed and stopped. He pulled an old flannel shirt out of his backpack and gave it to Ani. "Here, put this on."

She took it, put it on, and promptly felt warmer, the flannel soft against her cold and clammy skin even though it smelled like the garden shed. Amazing to think that only a few hours ago, Eliza and I thought he was just some creepy old guy, she thought. Creepy and mean, she corrected herself, remembering their confrontation in the garden shed. No wonder he was so upset with me. I had found his picture of Amelia.

"Ani, you need to stick close to me here," Patrick said, shouting to make himself heard over the roar of the stream. He tied a short rope to a back loop on his pants. "Hold on to this rope and I can help steady you. This part of the trail is wetter than I expected. Stay to the left of the water, and keep your light directly on the ground in front of you, and we should be fine. This is not a very long stretch, and soon we will veer away from the stream."

"Okay," she said, once again grateful for his presence and familiarity with the area. She might call the water cascading down the rock more of a rushing brook, but she did as Patrick requested, taking the rope in her right hand and holding the flashlight with her left.

Patrick's pace was slower than before, and he often paused to check his footing before proceeding. He was wearing a pair of heavy treaded work boots, appropriate for this type of a climb. Ani, on the other hand, was wearing tennis sneakers, and with each careful step she took, her foot slid on the water-soaked rocks, the surface resembling an ice rink. Several times she skidded and relied on the rope to keep her upright. Patrick waited patiently until Ani told him she was ready to move on. She hoped he had been correct about how short this part of the walk was. She didn't dare take her eyes off the ground to look at her watch. She guessed that another fifteen or twenty minutes had gone by. Her worry and anxiety had reached a peak. We have to move faster, we just have to, she thought.

"Ani, watch out!" Patrick cried before he fell back into her, knocking them both sideways. "Ani, let go of the rope," he yelled, realizing that he was slipping to the side of the trail, the part where the water ran the heaviest. But his weight had already pulled Ani next to him and within seconds both of them were sliding down the face of the smooth rock. Ani let go of the rope, but managed to hang on to her flashlight as she tumbled and flipped, down, down, down. She tried to reach out and grab anything that might help her stop falling farther away from the summit, but all she felt was wet, slippery rock. Patrick, heavier by at least seventy-five pounds, rolled faster and farther than Ani and miraculously succeeded in rolling off to the other side of the stream. He shone his flashlight upward and saw Ani tumbling in his direction. Patrick quickly threw the rope still attached to his belt loop toward her and yelled, "Ani, grab the rope."

But Ani was too disoriented by what was happening, and by the time her brain could make sense of what he was yelling, it was too late. She missed the rope completely and glided into the darkness below. Helpless, Patrick watched as she somersaulted out of sight. "Ani!" he cried after her as she fell even farther away.

Ani plummeted another fifty feet before she hurled herself to the other side of the stream, almost back where they had begun the climb. Luckily she had felt something scratchy brush across her leg, and she had blindly reached for it, hoping the plant would be strong enough to hold her weight. She seized the branch and then flung her legs up and over to move her body away from the rockslide. She landed with a thud onto the ground, which was covered with pine needles and leaves, softening her fall. But her right shoulder crashed into something sharp, piercing her with pain and causing her head to shoot forward and then slam back into a heap of smaller rocks.

"Ouch," Ani cried out before blackness took over and she lost consciousness. The flashlight fell from her hand, flickered a few times, and then went dark.

Patrick, paying no attention to his own aches, pains, cuts, and bruises, headed back down the trail that paralleled the gorge, on the side opposite from where Ani lay. Pointing his flashlight in front of him, he ran as fast as he could, his wet boots sloshing loudly. "Ani," he called. "Ani, where are you?" But he got no reply, as Ani remained knocked out, oblivious to Patrick's cries. He continued running and calling out, becoming more frantic with each unanswered shout. His chest felt heavy and sweat poured down his water-soaked back, and he knew he had to catch his breath. He clutched hold of a birch tree and flexed his leg muscles, which were cramping up from the climb and the running.

"Ani," he yelled again. "Ani!" His voice resonated with a mix of fear and despair. Please, please, answer me, Ani, he thought, but all he could hear was the sound of the running water and his own breathing.

An owl hooted, startling Patrick, who was unable to see anything but the branches of the dense pine and spruce trees. He journeyed downward, hoping and praying he would find Ani, momentarily forgetting about the Abenakis. He needed to locate Ani and make sure she was safe.

* * * *

While Ani lay unconscious on the forest floor and Patrick scrambled down the mountain trying to find her, Roonie and Eliza approached the security gate of Jamison Laboratory. The area was ablaze with lights as the community prepared for the detonation of NC 241. Their father had told the girls that once the gas was released, the Jamison Lab underwater vessel, the *Sea Mouse*, would be deployed to take samples and assess the aftereffects on the lobster population and any other damage in the immediate area. He and other members of the RECI team would be coordinating the research. He had also informed the girls that the Jamison Lab emergency medical animal services, EMAS, would be ready and waiting on the *Jamison Lab 2*, one of the largest ships in the fleet and a complete working marine mammal hospital. Neither of them had asked their father if the hospital would be needed, but from his somber voice, Ani and Eliza knew he was anticipating the worst.

The security guard, a portly man in a too-tight ugly brown uniform with buttons gaping, strutted out of the gatehouse when he saw the kids on their bikes. "Halt," he cried, holding his white-gloved hand out. "No civilians allowed near the Jamison Lab facilities. We are in operation search and rescue level 4 and therefore," he cleared his throat, "therefore, no unauthorized personnel are permitted upon the premises."

Roonie smirked and looked down at his feet. Eliza, shrewdly surmising that she was going to have to lay it on thick to convince this rent-a-cop that she and Roonie should be allowed in to see her father, decided to go the "teenager in distress route" versus the "I demand to see my father now" approach.

She sighed. "Oh, Commander Myers," she said, playing off the name on his ill-fitting shirt, "Commander, Officer, Sir, my name is Eliza Banke and this is my cousin Roonie Jay Cyr. My father, Dr. Banke, is one of the lead scientists for Jamison Laboratory, and he, he," she faltered here, and Myers's lips curled, but she recovered. "And he, or I, need his help and need to see him immediately," she said, wiping her forehead with the back of her hand.

"Well, little lady, that won't be possible, as your name," Myers said glancing at his clipboard, "is not on my sheet and that means," his speech slowed as if he were talking to a toddler, "that you and your cousin need to bike on home and find someone else to help you, because I don't care who you say you are, and what in tarnation you are doing out so late at night, but you are for sure not coming onto the Jamison Laboratory compound." He pointed his finger away from the entrance and tapped his gun holster with his clipboard a few times.

Eliza, shocked by his uncooperative manner, was uncharacteristically speechless. Roonie, sizing up the situation, attempted to jump in and persuade him to let them by.

"Oh, please, sir," he said, "I'm the reason we need to see Dr. Banke. I mean my Uncle Robert." Eliza kicked him in the foot. "Ouch, why did you go and do that, Liza?" he demanded, forgetting he was about to launch into some ridiculous story about why they needed to be there.

Myers was swifter than his appearance hinted. "She kicked you because Dr. Banke's first name is George, not Robert. Like I said before, you need to leave now or I will be forced to call the police officers waiting just inside the fence." He tipped his head toward the police car, lights on, parked on the other side of the gate. "They will personally deposit you two home. Don't you know there's a curfew tonight for all areas less than 500 feet from the water? Now get out of here," he yelled, more animated and angrier than before.

Roonie raised his eyebrows at Eliza. She returned the glance with a worried grimace and shrugged as if to say I don't know what to do next. "I said move!" Myers shouted, repeating his instructions. "That means now!" he barked and shoved Eliza, who bumped into Roonie, who stumbled into his bike causing it to crash loudly to the ground.

"Hey," cried Eliza. "There's no need to get physical. He's just a ten-year-old boy!"

"I don't care what age this Spidey fellow is, you two need to go now!" And with that, he reached into his pocket and pulled out his whistle, smugly proclaiming, "You asked for it. I'm going to blow my whistle three short bursts that signify S.O.S., which will alert the police and you two will be in big, big, trouble!"

Security Guard Myers placed the whistle between his pouting lips, but before he could manage his first blast, a horde of possums, in a variety of sizes, scurried in from every direction and leaped, crawled, dove, jumped, and climbed all over his body. They clung to his shoes, his pants, his shirt, and his hands, hanging off his fingers, his neck, his shoulders, and his stringy hair. Every inch of his body was covered with tan-colored, furry balls scuttling and scampering up and down, over and around, clicking, hissing, and growling. Myers dropped the whistle in the chaos, and Eliza giggled as she watched a large possum run into the woods with its tail wrapped tightly around the string dragging the whistle behind. Myers tried to shake the possums off, but they became angrier, screeching louder, and clinging more tightly to him. Myers opened his mouth to scream, but a baby possum, climbing out of her mother's pouch, dove into his mouth, silencing him completely. His eyes widened in alarm as his body jerked from the force of the attacking marsupials.

"He should drop and play possum," Roonie said.

"W-A-T and without Ani, too," Eliza said. "Let's go and find my Dad."

The kids jumped on their bikes and rode down the drive to the lab. Once inside, they sprinted down the hall and ran into TJ and Ben.

"Whoa, whoa," TJ said.

"Where's the fire?" added Ben.

"I need to find my father," Eliza said. "I know how to stop the lobsters without NC 241!"

"It's Ani. She's the one. You have to take us to him, please," Roonie said.

"Okay," said Ben.

"Anything to stop the poisonous gas," said TJ. "I'll take us. I've got my jeep out back. He's at the military base site for the detonation. He and Dr. Belanger were attempting to persuade the military to postpone the discharge of NC 241 until we had collected more data."

"He really didn't believe he was going to be successful,"

Ben said, "so any help you might be able to provide couldn't hurt. Let's go!"

Eliza and Roonie rode in the back seat of TJ's jeep as TJ explained that the headquarters of the Operation Crustacean Extermination was on a Coast Guard vessel docked in the harbor. Several smaller Coast Guard ships were scattered throughout the harbor along with the EMAS on the *Jamison Lab 2*. TJ brought the car to a screeching stop in front of the pier where the headquarters vessel was tied up. He and Ben were allowed entrance to the area because of their Jamison Lab ID and security clearance. Dr. Banke had made sure that everyone involved in the RECI team had full access to the base operations zone. While TJ and Ben were showing their IDs, Eliza and Roonie hid behind the jeep waiting for Ben and TJ's signal.

"Here we go," whispered Eliza after Ben dropped his ID on the ground. The two Coast Guard officers reached down to help retrieve the ID and Ben crashed his head into theirs. TJ waved and the kids crouched low and moved silently and swiftly up the ramp onto the ship. Fortunately no one was on the dock side of the ship, and Eliza and Roonie stopped to review their plan.

"Ben said that he thought Dad would be at the command headquarters located behind the bridge," Eliza said. On the ride to the dock, Ben and TJ had told them the military would be monitoring the activity of the lobsters using thermal heat sensing, cameras, and radar. "I think we should hug the edge of the ship and then cut in and try to find Dad."

"Roger that," said Roonie and saluted Eliza.

She rolled her eyes and tugged on his shirt. "Enough of that already." They crept cautiously forward but soon heard footsteps from around the corner.

"Hide," Eliza whispered and they dove behind a raft tucked under a stairwell.

"We are forty minutes to go time," the kids heard one officer say.

"Forty minutes," mouthed Eliza. "Time to take one for the

team because we need to find Dad now!" She pushed Roonie out directly into the path of the approaching officer.

"Hey, Eliza," Roonie shouted as he landed hard on the floor.

"What the?" said the first officer.

"Stop," shouted the second and lifted Roonie up.

Eliza popped out from her hiding place. "You got us," she said, trying to put her most angelic and innocent face on. "I'm Eliza Banke, Dr. Banke's daughter, and this is my friend Roonie. I forced him to come with me, sirs. I wanted to be with my Dad during this historic and monumental event for the," she paused as she stared at the young man's uniform, "for the great U.S. Coast Guard." The second officer lowered Roonie to the deck.

Eliza smiled sweetly. "I'm going to be a sophomore in high school, and I am seriously considering the Coast Guard Academy. My father is planning on taking me on a tour when the business with the lobsters is over. Won't you please take me to him?"

The two looked at each other. One said to the other, "We need to take them to the commander and let him decide what to do."

"Thank you," said Eliza meekly. Now Roonie rolled his eyes at her.

The door to the command center slid open and Eliza and Roonie were ushered in. "Dad," Eliza exclaimed but the first officer stopped her from rushing to her father.

He looked up from a large table in the center of the room covered with a detailed map of the ocean floor. His face changed from disbelief to relief to anger as he moved to embrace his daughter. "It's all right. She's my daughter and this is her friend."

The commander nodded to the officer, who stepped aside, allowing Eliza to run into her father's arms. "Dad!"

"What are you two kids doing here? Is everything okay? Where's Ani? And why is she not with you?"

"Ani's safe. She's with Mr. O'Leary," Roonie said.

"Mr. O'Leary? The gardener?"

"Can we go outside? We need to talk," Eliza said, noticing that everyone in the room was looking at them. She lowered her voice. "Privately."

The commander cleared his throat and motioned to a timer next to a radar screen that beeped with each sweep of the underwater area. Eliza tapped Roonie and pointed to the screen. She mouthed the word *lobsters,* and Roonie's eyes widened. The timer flashed 35:07.

"Get to work, people, five minutes to final systems check."

The captain replied, "Yes, sir," and everyone returned to their tasks.

Dr. Banke passed through the hatch with Eliza and Roonie. "What is going on with you two? How did you get here and where is Ani?"

"Dad, Dad," Eliza said, "you need to stop talking and listen, really listen to what I am about to say. Don't interrupt. We haven't got time. Do you understand?"

"Yes, but," he said.

"No, Dad, seriously, I am begging you, the fate of the harbor is at stake here."

"Okay," he said skeptically. "I'm listening."

Eliza took a deep breath and said, "Ani is Kanake-kee, an Abenaki word that means *one who walks with animals.* We figured out the purpose of her ancient book with the help of the librarian, Mrs. Starke, and Professor Sol from Maine Oceanic College, and from Roonie's grandmother, Moon Violet." Roonie smiled at the mention of his grandmother's name. "Moon Violet told Ani about the history of when lobsters and man both walked on land, but eventually it got too crowded and the lobsters agreed to go live in the water and allow the Abenakis to stay on the land. They formed a covenant that was buried at the base of Cadillac Mountain, but somehow this got stolen and disrupted the energy and well, it sort of called the lobsters back to MDI, bigger and stronger, just like they were before, when they lived with the Abenaki Indians. Only now they are angry, large and angry."

“Definitely really, really angry,” Roonie said, remembering the boat incident.

“Moon Violet showed Ani on the Scrabble board that her name, Ani Banke, spells Abennaki, with two *n*’s, the original spelling. Mr. O’Leary is also helping us as he has his own ancient Abenaki book.”

“He has his own book? How did he get his?”

“Dad,” Eliza said, “I don’t know how he got the book, but that’s not important. He and Ani are climbing up Cadillac Mountain right now to find the exact place to offer the amulets that we have collected over the last several days, the amulets outlined in Ani’s special birthday present. And as you know, Mom found her book in New Mexico, an Abenaki book that somehow was waiting in an antiques shop near Mom’s dig site. Coincidence? I don’t think so. The book outlines the amulets that Ani needed to find in order to pacify the gods of Cadillac Mountain and restore peace and harmony to the island, signaling to the lobsters that everything is okay and they can go back to the ocean and return to their normal size.”

Dr. Banke looked dubious, but he listened intently.

“You know the animal connection is true, Dad. I know you do. Ani has always had a way with animals, wherever she goes, always. You’ve seen it yourself, but have never been able to come up with a scientific reason as to why animals were drawn to her. And most recently, remember when we were on the *JL 73* and all the animals ended up following the boat? They were following Ani because she is Kanake-kee. The animals know this and have been assisting with finding the amulets. And the reason for this is that it has nothing to do with science and everything to do with light, energy, spirituality, and love. Leave your head for a moment and feel with your heart, something Mom always says to you. Trust Ani, Dad, you have to trust her. She has the power to stop this catastrophe, but she needs more time.”

He stared at his elder daughter with his mouth open in amazement. Images flashed before his eyes, images of Ani and her many interactions with animals. “This goes against everything I believe in as a scientist, everything. But I never imagined encountering freakishly large lobsters either. And I can't for the life of me figure out why this is happening, even with all the tests we've conducted."

"Dad, you never were going to be able to find out the 'why' no matter how hard you tried."

"I think I see that now," he admitted. And then he scooped Eliza in his arms and hugged her tight.

"Yes, yes, Eliza, you're right. It doesn't make sense, none of it does, but then again, it makes perfect sense." Eliza smiled, tears falling down her own cheeks. "Come on," he said. "Let's stop this NC 241."

They hurried back into the command center and Dr. Banke loudly announced, "Can I have your attention please?" Everyone stopped what they were doing and looked at him, Eliza, and Roonie. The digital countdown screen flashed 28:16. "We need to abort this mission now!" he demanded.

"What are you talking about?" asked the commander, an imposing man whose voice matched Dr. Banke's in urgency. He beckoned and three officers moved toward them.

Dr. Banke held his hand up as if to ward off their approach. "I know the reason behind the lobsters. It's because of the Abenaki Indians when they used to share the land together with the lobsters. The covenant got stolen and messed everything up. My other daughter, Ani, is Kanake-kee and has collected all the necessary amulets and right now she is on top of Cadillac looking for the special place to offer them to the gods of Cadillac and …" His voice trailed off. Roonie slapped his forehead in disbelief while Eliza looked devastated.

"He's talking too much," whispered Roonie, "much too much." Eliza frowned and nodded in agreement.

The three were hastily forced out of the command center and placed in a holding cell on the lower level. Dr. Banke had protested emphatically that he wasn't insane and tried to explain in even greater detail about Ani's name and Moon Violet. With each utterance, he sounded crazier and crazier. The door closed tightly behind them and each heard the latch click securely.

Roonie ran to the door and tried in vain to open it. "It's locked, all right. Now what?"

Dr. Banke rubbed his face with his hands. "I should have just burst in there and hit the stop mechanism."

"The what?" asked Eliza.

"The termination switch," he said. "If pressed, it immediately halts the countdown and prevents the detonation."

"Well, we need to get out of here!" said Eliza, pulling vigorously at the door.

Dr. Banke glanced around the sparse room, which had only a tiny sink and a cot attached to the wall. Roonie grinned and reached into his shorts pocket. "Spider-Man to the rescue," he said with glee. He held up his multi-tool jackknife with the Spider-Man logo emblazoned on the side and slid out a tiny nail file.

"Roonie," cried Eliza, "thank you and thank Spider-Man."

* * * *

Ani felt something tickle her nose. She tried to move her arm to swat away whatever was tickling her, but her arm was unresponsive. It was as if she were lying in wet cement, her body heavy and immobile. The tickling continued, but now the gentle sensation, like a damp washcloth on her skin, had moved to her eyes and then her ears. She tried to open her eyes, but like her limbs, they were indifferent to her simple commands. The tickles turned into a nudge, and something pushed her injured shoulder, causing sharp pain to shoot through her.

"Ah," she cried out loud, as she slowly came to and recognized that she was being licked awake by an animal. But instead of anxiety, Ani felt relief. She attempted to raise her head, but the throbbing was too intense and she chose to take stock from the ground. The pain radiating from her right shoulder and arm was excruciating, so she used her left hand to feel for the amulet pouch. To her delight, it was still intact, safely around her neck inside her shirt. The licking ceased as the animal sensed she was alert. Ani could hear its breathing, shallow and quick.

"Hello there," she managed to croak out, her throat dry and scratchy. Cautiously she strained to sit up, feeling her head pound and the deep pain in her shoulder. She looked down at her legs and noticed that one of her sneakers had fallen off in her tumble. Great, she thought, how will I ever climb back up barefoot? Where is Patrick? I hope he is okay. Her mind wandered. She was confused. She forgot an animal had awakened her. The animal carefully approached Ani and covered her face with its tongue. It felt rough and wet and interrupted her musings. She looked up and discovered a small deer with soft butter and red colored fur that must have been responsible for rousing her.

"Hello," Ani said. "Thank you for waking me up." The deer tilted her head. Ani made an effort to stand, but she was too dizzy and decided to wait before moving. Her mind drifted again. I wonder where my sneaker is?

The deer prodded her back and pushed Ani out of her reverie. Concentrate, she thought. I need to get up and find Patrick and hike back up the mountain. With incredible effort, Ani hoisted herself up onto her shaky legs. A warm trickle inched down the front of her left calf. She inspected her shin and saw she had a large cut oozing with blood and covered with dirt and pine needles. She bent over carefully and used the front of her T-shirt to wipe it away. Mom would not be pleased to see the stain on this shirt, she thought and laughed a little thinking about this. Come on, she commanded her brain, which seemed to be acting without direction at the moment. Did a deer just lick my face?

Standing steadier now, Ani listened intently. She heard nothing but the running water. "Patrick," she yelled, "where are you?" No response. "I guess I'm going to have to move without him," she said. Ani took one step forward and wobbled. "Whoa, whoa," she said as the deer trotted to her side to keep her from falling. She leaned on the deer's back to stabilize herself. "Thanks," she said. The deer's fur was warm to her touch.

Ani shivered involuntarily as her shock began to diminish. She was cold, wet, tired, missing a shoe, suffering from a mild concussion, bleeding, and lost. "At least I can stand," she said. She tried to make her brain come up with a plan, but she couldn't think of anything. The deer poked her from behind, gently shoving her toward a boulder resting next to a cluster of birch trees. Ani warily placed her shoeless foot forward. I can rest when I reach it, but I just need to reach it first, she thought. She took a few more steps, inching herself closer.

And to think I was most worried about the part of the trail with the rungs and ladders, not ever imagining that I would be taken down by slippery, water-soaked rocks, she thought. With each step, her head throbbed, matching the pain in her shoulder, but the dizziness had faded and her brain was less fuzzy. She leaned on the waist-high boulder and took a few deep breaths. She checked the time, but was disheartened to see that her watch face was cracked and filled with water.

"Seriously? My watch is broken, too?"

Tears welled in her eyes, spilling over onto her cheeks. She felt helpless, alone, and defeated. The deer bumped against her as if trying to provide comfort. Ani stroked her fur and said, "Thanks for the company, pretty lady. If only you could help me find Patrick and get us to the top of Cadillac Mountain."

The deer unexpectedly made an explosive whoosh followed by two short grunts that startled Ani. Is the deer trying to tell me something? Next the deer dug at the ground with her front hooves and then turned in a circle a few times before raising her head up and down excitedly.

"What is it? What are you trying to tell me?" Ani asked.

The deer grunted again and bowed her head low. Then she moved behind Ani and pushed her head between Ani's legs. Ani chuckled from the feel of the fur against her skin. It was ticklish.

"Hey, hey," she said, "what does this mean?"

The deer backed up and repeated her actions and then blinked her large doe eyes.

Puzzled, Ani scrunched up her face and asked, "Are you

trying to tell me to get on top of you? Do you want me to ride you like a horse?"

The deer whooshed, louder than before.

"Amazing," Ani said and climbed on the boulder. "I can get on top of you easier from here," she told the persistent deer. Ani grabbed the fur at the back of the deer's head and lifted one leg over her back and sprang off the rock. "How's this?" Ani asked, once astride the deer.

The deer snorted gently and forged ahead. Ani hung on tightly despite the piercing pain emanating from her shoulder while amused by the very idea that she was actually riding a deer. *Let the animals guide you*, she could hear Moon Violet's voice saying. But I wonder if she meant let me ride them, she thought, and what would Eliza say if she saw her now. W-A-T happens again! Soon the deer reached the gorge and the running water. Without hesitation she stepped up onto the rocks now glistening in the moonlight and confidently strode across the path to the other side. Ani tightened her hold on the deer, bracing herself for the fall that she was sure was about to happen, but to her great relief, the deer effortlessly maneuvered them through the water and crossed safely to the trail.

"Thank you, oh, thank you," Ani said. The deer, now on more stable ground, picked up her pace. Ani squeezed her legs firmly around the deer and bent her head low to avoid being thwacked in the face by branches they passed. Before long Ani heard her name faintly from a distance. It's Patrick! He's okay. Oh thank goodness he's all right.

"Patrick, Patrick, I'm here! It's Ani!" she shouted.

Ani heard her name again, louder this time, "A-n-i-i-i! Where are you?" The deer sprinted even faster. Suddenly, Ani and the deer burst through a clearing and found Patrick, wet and disheveled, leaning against a thick pine tree with a large buck standing pensively in front of him.

"Patrick, I was worried. I'm so glad you're okay."

"Ani?" he said, astonished to see his young friend riding a deer. "What the blazes?"

Ani interrupted him. "The buck is here to give you a ride.

Trust me and climb on top. They will take us to the summit. I just know they will."

The buck snorted defiantly as if to say, *I told you so, you old fool.*

"Well, this is most unusual, but so is being attacked by an overgrown lobster, so here I go," Patrick said, relieved to discover that Ani was safe even if she was astride a deer. The buck folded onto his knees, allowing Patrick to extend his leg over his back.

"Grab onto the fur at the nape of his neck," Ani said.

"If you say so," said Patrick, and soon buck and doe, old man and young girl were all hurrying to the top of Cadillac Mountain. The animals were swift and light-hooved, leaping with ease, weaving on and off the various trails, knowing instinctively the best and most direct route possible to take their guests. Much like the seals, the bunnies, the squirrels, the chipmunks, the skunks, the dogs Beauregard and Tiny, the birds, and even the bear, the deer had been charged with aiding Kanake-kee.

The jostling was hard on Ani's head, but she ignored the throbbing and concentrated on the path in front of her. Her thoughts raced; we need a plan for when we reach the top since we won't have much time. Oh, I wonder if we will have any time? I can't be too late, not after being so near. She stared down at the cracked face of her watch. Why did my watch have to break now? Why didn't I ask Patrick for the time? What good would his answer have done? For a second time she heard Moon Violet's reassuring instructions: Trust in yourself.

The path was now mostly rocky with a few low-lying shrubs. Ani spied the occasional cairn, or pile of rocks, maintained by the park rangers to keep visitors on the trails and away from fragile plant life. Oftentimes a fake cairn is created or one is destroyed, resulting in hikers losing their way. But these animals followed their own course, and Ani was filled with gratitude.

"Ani," Patrick said, "we're almost there."

The doe crested the hill and Ani was faced with the most

unbelievable sight. The stars and the moon twinkled brightly above the summit, casting a warm glow on the pink granite, while the ocean shimmered underneath the bright night sky. She had seen the view during the day and at sunset, but never in the middle of the night, especially with a full moon. There was not even a wisp of a cloud in the air, which was remarkable given that most days the fog rolled in heavy when the sun went down.

Ani's deer, panting and sweaty, approached a flat boulder and rolled her head, allowing Ani to slide off her and stand safely on the rock. The buck gently bent his tall legs and lowered his body to the ground. Patrick dismounted and fondly patted the buck on his side. "Thanks, it's been a real pleasure." The animals scampered off into the night, beautifully blending into their surroundings.

"Ani," said Patrick, "did we just ride up Cadillac on a doe and a buck?"

"Yes, we did, and that's not the weirdest animal experience that I've had since arriving on the island."

"It isn't?"

"I'll explain later, but now we need to get your book and see if we can find out where to offer the amulets."

Patrick removed his backpack and opened the zipper. He took out his book, still wrapped safely in plastic, and opened it up. He handed Ani his flashlight and together they scanned the pages, hoping to find any clue as to where they should go.

"I'm afraid to ask, but how much time do we have left?"

Patrick viewed his watch and said, "You don't really want to know. Suffice it to say, we need to hustle."

"From what I can recall from my translations from Professor Sol's book, I think we are looking for the exact center of Cadillac Mountain." Ani tapped the open pages and shone the light on the drawings. Patrick leaned in to inspect. "See how these drawings on the edges represent all the amulets that we found as dictated to me from Amelia's book?" Ani pulled the flashlight back to illuminate the outer drawings that formed a circle using both of the pages. She named each one for Patrick, starting with the first amulet that she and Eliza found by accident. "First is the silver sand dollar, then the blue sapphire. Next is the green tourmaline we found at Thunder Hole. Then we have the bald eagle feather, and last the bear tooth we found when you rescued us from Porcupine Island."

"Yes, I see them all."

"Now look here," she said, "this drawing here represents Cadillac, the big upside down *V*, but in the middle of this," she pointed, "is a small circle with a solid *X*. And I think that the Abenakis must mean the exact center of the top of Cadillac. Somehow we need to find the *X*. I'm guessing that it must be some kind of a rock formation that resembles an *X*. Does this make sense to you?"

"I'm not sure, but I have a hunch. Tourists naturally come to the summit, which is about twenty feet in that direction." He pointed to the left from where they were standing. "Everyone assumes that this is the true summit, but actually this is where it was easiest to put the parking spaces and a trail that loops the top where several trails come together."

"Really?"

"I think the actual center and highest point is located behind the park store and rest area, which is directly in front of us on the other side." He took the flashlight from Ani and directed its beam toward the store.

"You lead the way with the light, and I will follow behind with the book," said Ani.

"Are you okay to walk without your sneaker?"

"Yes, I'm fine, thanks."

The two set off to find the true summit of Cadillac, and Ani allowed herself to feel a glimmer of hope. Please, please, please, let Patrick be right, let us find the exact spot and be able to leave the amulets in time, Ani thought. Her shoeless foot caused her stride to be slightly off, and she had to skip-hop to keep up with Patrick, but she ignored her physical complaints and focused on finding where *X* marked the spot.

"Here," shouted Patrick, "It should be around here."

Ani joined him and they scoured the area for anything

that resembled an *X*. After each turned around completely and Ani's hopes for an easy discovery diminished, Patrick said, "You take the light and cover the ground closely in this immediate area clockwise. I can see fine with the moon and the stars, so I'll start on the other side of the store and loop around counter clockwise. Yell out if you see anything, and I'll do the same. If not, we can meet back right here, okay?"

"Yes, good idea."

Patrick handed her the flashlight and disappeared from sight.

Ani pointed the light and walked a short distance from the store before she started searching. She swept the flashlight up and back, making sure to cover the area as carefully as possible, following the light with her eyes scrutinizing every inch of the ground. In her mind she started at twelve o'clock and next moved to one, then two, three, four, five, and six. At six she waited and listened but heard nothing but the wind, which had picked up during the few minutes they had been looking for the *X*. At seven o'clock she saw a shape off to the left. It has to be Patrick, she thought. Maybe he found something.

"Patrick, is that you?" she yelled out. "Did you find the *X*?" The person moved closer but when he did, she knew instantly that it wasn't Patrick. This person's movements were sudden and jerky, and she recognized the gait immediately. The hairs on the back of her neck and arms stood at attention. Why would he be here?

"Well, if it isn't little Ani, Ani Banke girl," a tinny voice called to her.

"Professor Sol, is that you?" Ani said tentatively, trying hard to project confidence.

"Yes, yes, yes, it is, my little friend. And what, pray tell, are you doing here here here, on the tippy top top of Cadillac Mountain at night and tonight of all nights?" He was repeating his speech as he had done earlier when they had met at Maine Oceanic College. He moved near and then inched back before finally stepping even closer to Ani.

"I, I, I," Ani said, "I'm surprised to see you," she managed to say.

"Doing some late night reading?" he said, and with cat-quick reflexes, he snatched Patrick's Abenaki book from her hands and rested it against his chest. He used his chin to flip through the pages. "Oh, my, my, my, methinks someone has been reading ancient Abenaki lore."

Ani shone the light directly into Professor Sol's face, casting an eerie and unnatural glow, highlighting his completely pink and shiny skin, the screaming red hair now standing straight up, and his bloodshot eyes. She gasped and said, "No, I, er, ah, found this book while I was out hiking and night bird watching. I mean, while I was with Patrick O'Leary, and we got separated, but I'm sure he'll be here any minute."

Seemingly oblivious to what she was saying, Professor Sol shouted, "Oh you lucky, lucky one, you special Kanake-kee!" And at the mention of her Abenaki title, Ani's mouth opened in horror.

How did he know this? she wondered.

"Yes, tis true, tis true, I can see by the look on your face. You are Kanake-kee. I didn't believe that it was possible, but I should know better myself as now the impossible is most cer, cer, certainly possible."

"I don't know what you're talking about, Professor Sol," Ani said, her voice quivering. She backed up a few steps as he moved even closer. "Why don't I come see you tomorrow at your office and we can talk more about—what did you say—that I'm Kayak-kee?" Ani hoped using Eliza's word would fool Professor Sol.

"Now, now, now, that sounds lovely, doesn't it?" he said as his voice grew higher and louder. "But tomorrow will become a day for the record books, a real his-story event or should I say lob-story." He cackled maniacally at his own play on words.

His laugh sent shivers up and down Ani. Where is Patrick? I need to keep Professor Sol talking, just enough until I find what I'm looking for, and then we can get him to a psychiatric hospital because clearly he is having some kind of a mental health breakdown.

"Lob-story," said Ani. "That's really very clever, Professor Sol, ha, ha."

"Clever, is that what you think this all is, something clever? A practical joke for you and your sister and your little Spidey-boy friend?" he yelled, getting nearer to her face. Ani took several steps backward, and reaching eight o'clock, she scanned the ground with her flashlight. Oh, how she wished she would find an *X*, but she saw only flat rock without any marks.

"No, I …"

"As Kanake-kee, you must know the legend behind the Abenaki Lobster Tale, and yes, yes, yes, it's all very clever indeed. How sweet, and agreeable, and fabulous it was as the lobsters willingly agreed to go back to the sea since the poor Abenakis—oh boo hoo, I'm crying a bucket full of tears—couldn't live in the ocean. The lobster tribe decided to go back to whence they came as long as the Abenakis took care of the land and blah, blah, blah." He crept closer to Ani, who stepped back to nine o'clock and secretly glanced at the ground. "And they all got together and created a beautiful and powerful orb, made from the rose quartz found right here at the top of Cadillac, to solidify the arrangement and cleverly, oh so cleverly, cleverly, cleverly they buried it deep within the base of the mountain." He took a few more steps in Ani's direction.

Now ten o'clock, she thought as she slid backwards and swept the light over the ground, but found nothing.

"And, and, and, and …" Sol's speech became even louder and more animated. "But it wasn't all hearts and flowers as some members of the lobster tribe didn't want to leave the land and wanted to battle it out, lobster against man, man against lobster, and let the victor stay on the island. But the dissenting tribe was outnumbered, and we all had to go back to the sea!" He waved dramatically at the ocean.

Odd that he said "we," thought Ani. Who is we?

"The tribe of dissenters was a strong and loyal tribe and one that everyone should have listened to because now, now, now, look at the mess that has been created. The covenant has been stolen and lo the problems: the town is crying, people are missing, and tourists are not spending their American dollars! Oh my." He placed his hand exaggeratedly over his mouth. "The scientists don't know what to do, and then the silly mil, mil, military are coming and are going to drop NC 241 and destroy the lobster population."

He smiled and smacked his thin tight lips together making a tsk, tsk sound. He sidled even closer to Ani, who again walked backward, reaching eleven o'clock. Ani watched until he turned his head, and then she secretly shone the flashlight across the area, expecting to find nothing. She was stunned to spy a pencil-sized crack running directly underneath her feet. Stealthily, she looked up at Professor Sol, who was working himself into a frenzy, ranting and raving and swinging his arm around wildly. Ani nodded to let him know that she was listening and waited for her chance to glance back at the crack, tracing it with the flashlight, and bingo, the crack intersected with another larger crack to form a perfect *X* about three feet to her right.

That's it, the *X*. It has to be! I just need to distract Professor Sol so I can explore the spot. Where is Patrick? What is Professor Sol going on about?

"And they think, think, think that a little poisonous gas will hurt us." He chuckled in a menacing manner. "How wrong they will be. It might slow us down, but it can never kill us. What is put in mo, mo, mo, motion, once started can never be stopped." He paused, aware that Ani was not paying attention to him. "Hey! I'm talking to you, you, you great Kanake-kee!"

Ani tilted her head sideways and said, "I'm listening to you, Professor Sol, and I hear that you have much to say this evening, but I'm afraid I'm going to have to end our conversation and get going now to search for, for, other nighttime creatures." She sauntered nonchalantly to the right, or as nonchalantly as she could with one sneaker missing.

"Not so fast, my young Abenaki meddler, busy, busy, busy bee." He grabbed Ani by the shoulder, stopping her in her tracks. "Come into my parlor, said the spider to the fly, or the lobsterman to the lobster. Ridiculous name for part of the lobster trap. Abby, abby, absurd!"

"Ouch! Hey," Ani cried as he pulled on her injured shoulder. "Let go of me!" She attempted to pry his fingers loose, but his grip was impressively powerful. As she wriggled her body sideways, the neck of her T-shirt slipped down, revealing the leather strap.

"What's this?" Professor Sol screeched and hastily released Ani's shoulder. She stumbled backward, losing her footing before righting herself. Professor Sol swung his right leg behind her, preventing her from moving in any direction.

"What are you doing?" she screamed.

"I'm taking what is rightfully mine," he said and then lifted the strap over her head, revealing the suede pouch filled with the precious amulets.

"Give those back," Ani demanded, grabbing at the pouch.

Professor Sol held the bag high over his head. "Finders keepers losers weepers," he sang and slipped the pouch around his own neck, tucking the bag beneath his sweater-vest. "And there is nothing you can do about it."

"Patrick!" Ani yelled, but Professor Sol clapped his hand over her mouth. He smelled horrible: a cross between rotting fish and seaweed. Ani gagged and he clamped down even harder on her mouth. His skin felt cool and hard to her lips.

"Oh, you won't be needing to cry out little, little one. No, no, no need for histrionics. We all know, know, know that you know, know, know more than you say you know so no, you won't be calling for anyone."

With her sneaker-shod foot, Ani kicked Professor Sol hard in his left shin, and he loosened his grip. She immediately kicked his other shin, and the professor doubled over in pain. Then Ani pulled the leather string with all the strength she could gather against his neck and broke it and pulled free the amulet pouch from underneath his shirt. She pivoted and tried to get away, but Professor Sol was fast, lightning fast, and reached her within seconds, tearing the pouch out of her hand. Ani screamed.

"You can run, but you can't get away," he said.

Ani was paralyzed with fear. Her instinct told her to run, but she knew he would catch her. She also knew she couldn't leave the amulet pouch.

"Ani?" Patrick called. "What's going on?"

Professor Sol whipped around toward Patrick's voice and listened. "What's this?" he hissed at Ani. "A gardener friend to help the little sapling in her time, time, time of woe?"

"Patrick, over here!" Ani cried.

"Leave her alone if you know what's good for you!" Patrick said. He sounded stern and serious, much like he did when he had discovered Ani in his shed. "I said," he repeated louder, "leave her alone!"

"Bossy, bossy, bossy pants. Why is everyone telling me what to do?" Professor Sol roared.

"Ani, are you okay?" asked Patrick, "Did he hurt you?"

"I'm all ..." Ani spoke, but Professor Sol cut her off.

"She's fine, fine, fine. We're just catching up, see. Ms. Banke has been busy, busy, busy these last few days, and she's filling me in on all the things she's done."

"Ani, come here," Patrick said. She moved toward him, but Professor Sol seized her arm and pulled her back behind him.

"Now wait a gosh darn min ..."

"Thwack!" Professor Sol clocked him on the forehead, and Patrick dropped to the ground like a stone.

"Patrick!" screamed Ani, rushing to his side, but Patrick didn't respond. He was out cold. A dark liquid emerged from his forehead. "What have you done?" she cried, "He's bleeding."

"Tsk, tsk, a small price to pay for a huge pay, pay, pay off in the end." Ani began to weep, but Professor Sol continued his tirade. "For years we have waited for the right time, and that time is now. We did not want to leave the land. We wanted to stay and fight, fight, fight. But the ruling tribe, Retsbol, which is *lobster* backwards for those keeping score at home, had the final say. My father and my father's father and his father's father and so on and so on have all promised to fight to get back to the land and take back the island, which is rightfully ours. And soon I will be rejoined by my fellow lobstermen. Alone no more! I am ready for you!" he yelled out to the harbor.

Afraid he would hurt Patrick again, Ani retreated from her injured friend's side. "What do you mean, Professor Sol? Who is Retsbol and who is we?" Ani needed to keep him talking and have him follow her back to the *X*. She thought if she could get him to stand near the *X*, even if he had the amulets, she could still offer them to the gods. She remembered Amelia had said something about Retsbol when Ani first met her in the orb. *Beware of Retsbol,* she had warned.

"We? We? You are not part of we!" he shouted, spittle spraying from his mouth.

Ani took three more large steps away from Patrick and Professor Sol followed her. Excellent, she thought, guessing that they were now on the circle somewhere in the area of four o'clock. If I cross over and up, I can get back to eleven and the mark. She decided to ask another question.

"I don't understand what you're talking about. Can you please explain to me what you mean?"

Infuriated, he roared like a wild animal. "Have you not heard a word that I've said? Not so clever after all, huh? My name is Bert Sol, that's B-E-R-T-S-O-L. Anagram for *LOBSTER*!"

Ani's eyes widened in astonishment. "No."

"I'm part of the lobster tribe that didn't want to retreat to the ocean, and I have been waiting, waiting, waiting until the time came—and come it has—to reveal my true, true, true self!" he bellowed. He tore off his ugly sweater-vest and button-down shirt. He then flung out his missing arm, which wasn't missing at all, and Ani watched in abject horror as his arm unfolded slowly and transformed into a giant-sized lobster claw, clicking and clacking open and shut.

Ani shrieked.

"Victory is ours!" he screamed, his voice shrill and threatening. "Go ahead, drop your canisters and watch and see what happens! We're immune to anything you can throw at us. NC

241 will only increase our reproductive ability and our growth!" Professor Sol closed his pincher claw dramatically and poked at Ani with his left hand.

"Now all I need to do is dispose of these amulets." He shook the bag vigorously. "Dropping them over the side of the mountain should do nice, nice, nicely." His body awkwardly twitched. "Ah, good, the antennae are coming." He stretched out his neck and his jaw shut tight. He then emitted a low squeaking noise from the back of his throat, and two pointy antennae pushed their way out from the top of his head and spun wildly, brushing Ani's face, hair, and shoulders. Exhilarated, he screamed.

She swatted at the annoying appendages and stepped back, but Professor Sol pursued her. Soon they were both going around in a circle, just as Ani did before when looking for the X, only this time she was terrified, terrified he might dispose of the amulets, and terrified he might really harm her as he had harmed Patrick. Oh Patrick, she said silently, please be all right.

"Why don't you let me take the amulets, and I will see that they are destroyed. I can throw them into Thunder Hole. That will make it impossible for someone to find them," Ani said, trying anything to keep him talking and moving toward the X.

"Why don't you let me take the amulets," he mimicked her in a childish high-pitched voice. "That's a swell, swell, swell idea, Kanake-kee, but not gonna happen." He snapped his pincher close to her face. His body shuddered violently again. "Here comes the tail." He grinned and bared his teeth, grunting like a wild boar as out popped a colossal lobster tail, which curled up behind his legs. "It feels fab, fab, fabulous to be back to my original self. He scratched his body with his remaining fingers and pop, pop, pop, pop, four lobster legs protruded from his chest.

"Oh, no!" Ani yelled, and shone her light away from the horror show exploding before her very eyes. She moved a few more steps sideways, and scanned the lit area, expecting to see Patrick sprawled out on the ground, but he wasn't there. She spotted the trail of blood from his injury, but he definitely was not where she left him. Her heart skipped a beat. She had hope.

Distracted by his lobster transformation, Professor Sol didn't notice that his victim no longer lay on the ground. "Oh, yes," he said, responding to Ani's "oh no." "Yes, yes, yes!" And three more legs popped out of his chest—seven in all wriggling and wiggling and writhing at Ani.

"Well, looks like I'm almost done, and as much fun, fun, fun as it has been catching up, up, up, up," he paused and leg number eight burst out of his chest, "your time is finished. And if you would be so kind as to keep walking backwards, I will just shove, shove, shove you off the side of the mountain." He clacked his pincher claw demonically in front of her nose. Ani squealed as Professor Sol, or what used to be Professor Sol, pressed forward, legs and antennae whipping around, prodding and jabbing at her. "I promise, you won't feel a thing. That is, until you hit the ground." He laughed uproariously.

Suddenly, Ani saw a form appear behind Professor Sol. It was Patrick! He's alive, she rejoiced in her mind. Patrick put a finger to his lips to signal Ani to be quiet.

"On second thought, I want to be at the shore when the gas is released, so I think I'll just use this," Professor Sol said, waving his deadly pincher claw. "And snap, snap, snap."

Patrick, with hedge clippers in hand, snipped off the threatening claw right at the shoulder, severing it from Professor Sol's torso. Sol screamed as his blood spurted wildly from his body and the severed claw, now lying on the ground.

"A gardener is only as good as his clippers," Patrick said, and Ani grimaced.

"No, no, no!" Professor Sol screeched and collapsed as blood spattered all three of them.

"Ani, hold the tail steady while I tie his legs." Patrick pulled off his own shirt and wrapped it tightly around the wound. "Ani, give me the flannel shirt. We need to stop the bleeding." She handed his shirt to him and watched as Patrick ripped it into several strips and wound it around the other makeshift bandages. "That's the best we can do for now." Professor Sol moaned, his red eyes shut, and all movement stopped.

"Patrick, he's part lobster!"

"Yes, Ani, I see that, but we can't worry about this now. You have only ten minutes left to offer up the amulets."

"He took them from me with his normal hand."

Patrick reached around Professor Sol's body and was relieved to discover that his clenched fist held the leather string attached to the amulet pouch. Patrick handed it to Ani.

Ani took it and stuffed it into her pocket.

"I found an *X*, at least I hope I did."

"Well, go to it," Patrick said.

Ani frowned, worried about Patrick and his head injury, which was still bleeding.

"I'm fine, Ani, just a bad bump. I'll stay with Professor Sol. Go. Hurry. And good luck!"

Ani whirled around. Where's eleven o'clock? I need to find eleven, she thought and flashed the light toward where she sensed the *X* was located. Up and down, back and forth, she swung the light, but couldn't find the *X*. "Where are you?" she said and looked up to the beautiful night sky. "I need to see the *X*." A breeze danced across the mountain's summit, followed by a low rolling mist. Ani could feel the moisture envelop her and watched her light dim in the haze.

"No, please, no. I'll never find it in the fog."

She breathed deep, relaxing breaths and closed her eyes. Her racing heart slowed and her mind focused. Help, I really need help, she prayed. Time is running out and the fog is coming in. Show me the way to the *X*.

She waited for something to happen, but soon was disheartened. The fog was increasing, thicker and heavier with each moment. She moved to the left, then switched and headed right. Which way? The fog added to her confusion. Concentrate, she scolded herself and paused. Left, I feel like I need to move left. Ani cautiously followed her gut and took a few steps to the left. The expression "as thick as pea soup" sprang to her mind as she could barely make out her hand in front of her face. She wandered, kicking at the mist with her feet, wondering what to do next. She swung her hand through the fog, attempting to clear a path, and brushed something soft with her fingertips. She pulled back her hand, afraid of the soft something, and then it happened. A burst of electric energy rushed through her body, awakening her senses. She inched nearer to the softness and repeated her action of waving the mist away. The fog parted and revealed a black bird resting patiently on the ground.

Ani recognized the bird as a peregrine falcon, one of Maine's endangered species. The overuse of dangerous pesticides had almost eradicated them. They nested along the cliffs of Cadillac Mountain and they were efficient sharp-eyed hunters. The bird blinked her eyes, almost hidden by her bluish-gray hood. She stared at Ani and thrust her wings up and open, the tips dark and pointed, in a span close to four feet wide. She opened her yellow beak and screeched. She blinked again and then lifted off, swallowed by the mist.

Ani leaped to the spot where the peregrine had been standing and retrieved the amulet pouch from her shorts pocket. She held it up and spoke aloud what came first to her mind: "I am Ani Banke, Kanake-kee, and I am here to graciously bestow these amulets upon you." Her voice echoed and rolled away, carried by the fog. Nothing happened. Then she cleared her throat and added, "the powerful gods of Cadillac!"

The mountain rumbled directly beneath her feet. Ani's legs buckled from the vibration. It feels like an earthquake, she thought, tightening her hold on the pouch. Then the ground cracked and gave way. "Help!" Ani screamed and fell into the mountain, vanishing from sight.

* * * *

"Let's see about this," said Dr. Banke, extending his hand for the jackknife. Roonie handed it to him and Eliza pursed her lips. Her father, never known to be handy with tools unless they were scientific instruments, approached the door. "I'll just stick this in here," he said, jabbing at the side latch and ignoring the keyhole center, "and I'm sure I'll have us out in a jiffy." He jiggled, poked, and prodded, and then proudly proclaimed, "There, that should do the trick." He attempted to slide the door open, but it wouldn't budge. "Strange, I thought I got it in there good," he said, examining the tool.

"Dad," Eliza said kindly, "why don't you let Roonie try? He's had a lot of experience fixing things."

"Right, yes, very good," he said, giving the tool to Roonie. "It's tricky," he warned.

Roonie took the jackknife and slid the screwdriver back into place. Then he popped open the nail file. He placed it directly into the door lock, turned it a bit to the right and a bit to the left and presto, the lock released. Roonie smiled and cautiously slid the door open. "I'm sure you helped, Dr. Banke," Roonie said.

"Yes, glad to help out, son," he said. "Now let's get back to the command center. We need to stop the detonation."

Lobster fact: *If peregrine falcon mating or nesting behavior is observed in Acadia National Park, certain trails are temporarily closed to avoid disturbing the birds. These measures are helping this magnificent creature make a triumphant comeback in the park and contributing to the success story of the Endangered Species Act.*

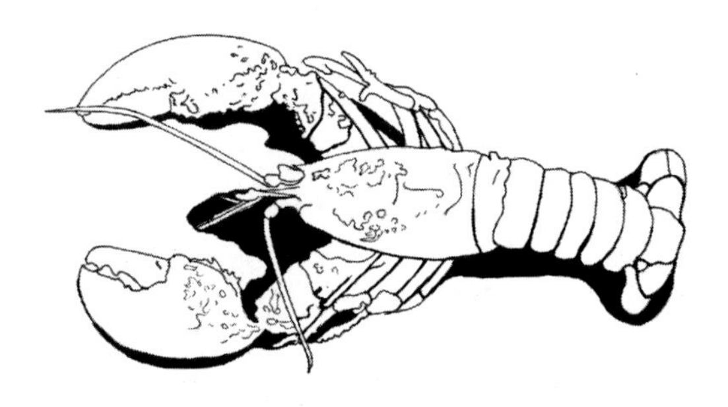

Chapter 49

Barton and the Lobsters

Ani plunged down, arms and legs waving wildly yet not touching anything but air. She felt like Alice falling down the rabbit hole, or like Alice with a concussion and an injured shoulder who had just gone a round with a scary lobster-man falling down a hole inside a mountain. She recognized the sound of her own heartbeat drumming in her ears, her body alert and pulsating with adrenaline and fear. The speed at which she descended pushed her lips back wide into an unnatural grimace while cold moist air whipped by her face and rushed into her nostrils and through her clenched jaw. Her mind tried desperately to adjust to what was happening to her. She guessed she was falling to the base of Cadillac, the place where the sacred orb was buried before Barton stole it and discovered Amelia trapped tight inside. She fell through darkness, even though her hand gripped tightly to a flashlight. Her arms had shot straight up and over her head, the force of falling so fast, she was unable to bring them down to shine Patrick's light ahead of her.

"Ouch!" Ani cried, her voice echoing eerily throughout the cavernous darkness as she landed abruptly on something soft and cushy. Soft and cushy and wet, the "ouch" more a reaction to the shock of landing than to feeling any real pain. She tried to stand, but her feet slid clumsily on what she imagined to be seaweed, the feel and the stench both familiar and strangely welcome. She wobbled as her knees bowed, and then she collapsed in a heap and catapulted awkwardly down again, any attempts to right herself completely unsuccessful. Soon the seaweed vanished, replaced by cold stone, and she now tumbled headfirst, rolling and twisting like she was on the giant slide at the water park not far from her home in Woods Hole. Wincing from her injured shoulder, she flipped over onto her back and turned her body around so that she was going feet first as she spiraled down. She directed the flashlight in front of her, illuminating pale, pink-hued walls covered with primitive drawings. Abenaki, she wondered? Yet she was traveling too fast to be sure.

Just as the summit had unexpectedly opened and started her free fall, the stone surface suddenly leveled out and then curved upward, allowing Ani to decelerate, but her ride ended abruptly as she shot out into midair, breaking free from the slide for a few seconds before dropping several feet onto a hard cave floor. Her landing sent ripples of pain through her shoulder and head and dislodged the amulet pouch from her shorts pocket. The pouch ripped open and the amulets spewed out and scattered on the cavern floor.

"Ouch!" Ani cried again, gripping her shoulder and rolling over before slamming into a wall. Silver stars danced temporarily around her head. Ani blinked hard a few times, and ignoring the stars and the pain, she hurriedly shone the flashlight around to recover the precious amulets. Within a few seconds, she retrieved all five, and after a quick inspection, she returned them to the pouch, cinching the bag tightly shut with her own hair elastic before tucking it back into her shorts' front pocket. That should keep them secure, she thought.

Her surroundings resembled the underground grotto the cormorants had helped them reach when they were looking for the green tourmaline underneath Thunder Hole. But this spot was darker and narrower. Stalactites, in all shapes and sizes, hung precariously from the ceiling and water dribbled sporadically from them, hitting the solid rock floor and loudly emitting a drip-drop echo as waves pounding against rocks roared in the distance. Ani licked her lips and tasted salt. She glanced at her watch, forgetting that it was broken from her earlier fall on the

Gorge Trail. She didn't need to see the time to know she had only a few minutes, if any, left before the NC 241 was detonated in the harbor. From where she stood, Ani saw three tunnels veering off in different directions. Which do I follow? she wondered, frustrated that she had to make yet another choice. She heard a faint click-clacking coming from the left path, or was it just a loud drip-drop from the stalactites? Should I go that way? Or maybe this center tunnel, she thought, and shone the light in that direction, hoping to see anything, a clue, a sign, but just what she wasn't sure.

Think, Ani, think, she chided herself. But she felt nothing, nothing but cold, tired, and sore. She pointed the light down the third tunnel and was discouraged to see that it looked exactly like the other two. Another loud splat of water dripped on the rock in front of her bare foot. Ani automatically looked up to see where the drop originated and noticed faint red markings on the top of the entrance to this third tunnel. She moved closer to angle the light directly on the area and was elated to discover primitive patterns running along the curved top of the wall. She recognized the drawings instantly: Abenaki. Ani didn't stop to try to figure out what they meant. Instead, she took it as an omen that she was headed in the right direction. She raced down the tunnel, forgetting about her fatigue, her injuries, and the time. Along the way she spied more ancient Abenaki drawings and smiled to herself, feeling certain she had selected the correct path to the place where she would offer up the amulets.

After only a short distance, the tunnel led Ani to a small, circular cave, veiled in a white mist. Her body tingled with excitement. "This is it!" she exclaimed and stepped into the center of the room, unable to see anything because of the haze. Without any warning, she slammed her bare toe into a solid mass that she supposed to be stone. "Ouch, ouch, ouch," she cried, grabbing her foot and hopping up and down. Her erratic movement swirled the haze up and away, exposing the object that Ani had stubbed her toe on, a large flat wheel, pink in color with flecks of black, gray, and white, and measuring about three feet in diameter. It was resting on a boulder as wide as the wheel and about two feet tall. Ani ran her hand over the smooth, cool stone. Granite, she thought, it must be granite, found right here on Cadillac. Ani pointed the light at the stone and was astounded to see five shapes carved out of the granite and spaced evenly apart.

"The amulets," she said softly, her breath parting the mist around her. In awe she touched the stone wheel a second time, already knowing deep inside what she would discover. Indented in the wheel were a flat round shape, the silver sand dollar, followed by a much deeper round shape, blue flame, the sapphire from Blueberry Hill. Her hand glided over the next indentation, a cylindrical shape for the green tourmaline prism, and next a thin, long shape with subtle ridges just perfect for the bald eagle feather, and finally, the familiar pointy indent of a tooth, the black bear's tooth. Tears welled in her eyes as the importance of what she was about to accomplish resonated within her.

"This is for you, Eliza and Roonie." Ani thrust her hand into her pocket and grabbed the amulet pouch. "And you too, Patrick and Moon Violet." She slipped her hair elastic off the pouch and spread the top open. She pulled out the first amulet she could get her hands on, not caring which one it was, and placed the eagle feather into the feather outline on the granite slab. It fit perfectly. Next, she took the silver sand dollar, which reminded her of Whiskers and his friends, first when she and Eliza swam with them at Seal Beach and second when they helped rescue them from the lobsters at Bar Island. Again, the amulet matched exactly its allotted place. Then she retrieved the green tourmaline recovered from Thunder Hole, and it too, slid effortlessly into its appropriate space.

Ani once again reached inside the bag, her fingers eagerly searching for either of the remaining two amulets. She touched the sharp points of the tooth, clasped it with her thumb and pointer finger, and placed it in the tooth-shaped cutout on the Abenaki wheel. With only one more to go, Ani rejoiced. Excitedly, she stuck her hand in the bag, anxious to remove the final amulet, but couldn't find it! Her fingers darted in and around the inside of the bag, but still she found nothing. Frantic, Ani turned the bag inside out and felt a lump on the side. "Blue flame," she shouted and held up the amulet. The light from the flashlight, now resting on top of the granite wheel, illuminated the stone.

"What's this?" Ani asked, perplexed that the supposed blue flame was now a muted red color. "I must have picked up the wrong one when I landed."

Ani whipped around and sprinted back through the tunnel to where she was so brusquely dumped moments before. I have to hurry, she thought. I'm most definitely running out of time. Ani reached her destination and waved the light on the floor near where the amulets had spilled out. So intent on finding the blue flame, she did not hear the approaching footsteps. Finding nothing and feeling discouraged, Ani got down on her knees and swept the area with her hand, hoping to feel the amulet before she saw it and then get back promptly to the granite wheel.

"Lost something, my child?" a chilling voice called to her, echoing through the cavernous grotto.

Ani screamed, shot up, and turned toward the intruder. "Who's there?" she shouted and flashed the light in the direction of the ominous voice. She recoiled when she recognized Barton framing the left passageway. He wore a flashlight headband, which made his appearance even more startling, casting overlarge shadows behind Ani on the grotto walls. His hair, normally tidy, was tousled and stood straight up, making him look like a mad scientist from one of the old black and white movies her father sometimes made her and Eliza watch. Upon further inspection, Ani noticed that his white dress shirt was ripped and covered with dark stains. He was holding the orb underneath one arm while in his other hand he held the blue flame.

"Oh, it's you, Mr. Baxter," Ani said, trying desperately to sound calm while inwardly feeling anything but. "Sorry for screaming, but you startled me. How ever did you get here?"

"That's none of your business, but since this is the end of the line for you and your snooping around, I guess I will let you in on a little Baxter family secret. These caves have been connected to my family's estate since it was built in 1870. However, I only recently learned of their existence, and let's just say they have come in quite handy, quite handy indeed."

He gloated as he looked around the cave, and then he looked wistfully at the orb, and finally he turned his attention to the amulet. "Perhaps this is what you are seeking, yes?" he taunted, twirling the precious sapphire in his right hand, the blue color shimmering and dancing around the cave from Ani's flashlight beam. "I might give it to you if you come closer," he teased. Ani lurched forward, but Barton's menacing laugh stymied her. "On second thought, I think I'll keep it," he said, cackling. "I welcome the lobsters back to their rightful home."

Tentatively Ani crept nearer to him and said, "As you know, the lobsters are simply getting too large, and people have been injured, some fatally. My sister, Roonie, and I have been trying to help the Abenakis solve this problem and if I can just have the blue ..."

"Silence, whippersnapper!" he snarled, his voice loud and booming, reverberating in the chamber, almost matching the thunder of the ocean waves crashing against the cave walls. "And that goes for you, too," he shouted at the orb, using his body to shield the orb from Ani's sight.

He must be talking to Amelia, Ani thought, so she is still in the orb. Ani needed to get both the sapphire and the orb to help free Amelia from her captivity. She astutely sensed Barton's instability, but she was also aware of the urgency to act swiftly. What to do, what to do? She pleaded with her mind to come up with something clever, but any scenario she imagined ended in disaster. She could rush him and leap up and grab the blue flame, but that might make him drop the orb or he could throw the amulet away, and she would be unable to locate it. She could plead on behalf of Amelia in the orb. He obviously had feelings for her based upon what Patrick had told her. But given the way he had just shouted at the orb, he might not be in a sentimental frame of mind. Frankly, from his appearance, he looked like he had gone over the edge, much like Professor Sol. She hoped he wasn't going to turn into a lobster, too!

Ani decided to use reason as her safest choice. "Mr. Baxter, sir," she said, "we really are running out of time, and we've all worked incredibly hard to collect the amulets and, and ..." She was distracted by a clicking noise, much like one she had heard earlier, only this time it was louder and nearer than before. "I would like you to give, I mean, please give me the amulet, and then I will be on my way, sir."

"I know all about what you and your sister and your little Spider-Man friend have been doing. All about it." He leaned closer to the orb and addressed Amelia. "I guessed what they were doing and I was right. I'm always right. You see that now?" Then he bragged to Ani. "There isn't much that happens on this island that I don't know about. Despite the fact that I hired the bumbling Thibodeau brothers, Lyle and Daniel, to follow you, idiots the both of them, I was always on to your game."

"The bug guys?" Ani said. "Game, sir?"

"Stop playing coy with me, missy, and besides, it's immaterial now." He shook his head vigorously and the light from his headlamp fell haphazardly on the floor, the ceiling, the walls, and Ani. Ani held up her hand to shield her eyes from the blinding light. When it moved away from her, she edged nearer to both the amulet and the orb, trying to position herself within reaching distance of the blue flame and to see if Amelia was still within the orb. Maybe Amelia could convince Barton to relinquish the sapphire. Ani also hoped she might find a way to free Amelia from her rose quartz prison.

"I know what you're up to, and now, unfortunately, your game is over," Barton said, rolling the blue flame between his fingers.

"But, Mr. Baxter," Ani said, "what about the NC 241? Surely you don't want to ruin the harbor? You have companies, properties, and other businesses that will be destroyed."

"Rubbish, girl! They won't be destroyed. The gas is perfectly fine, well, most likely fine. You see, I own the company that distributes NC 241. How do you think the military decided to use it? I gave them quite a discounted price. I'm known throughout the great state of Maine for my philanthropy. It was so wonderfully easy. Like taking candy from a baby. All that money and all the accolades. And of course, it was the least I could do. My chemical company, NC Industries—*NC* stands for Northeast Chemical—developed this gas and coincidentally needed some method for testing its effectiveness. And regardless of what happens, I am going to be rich. Well, richer than I already am. Lucky for me, I also own a lobster processing plant. It has been working overtime since the lobsters began migrating to MDI. The lobsters have been practically walking right into the plant and into the deep freeze. I have complete dominance over the Maine lobster market and will be crowned Lobster King once the dust settles, or should I say gas settles, and I will raise my price, making my lobster meat the most expensive and most desirable in the world."

Ani gasped at Barton's confession. This was worse than she imagined. He is a monster, just like the growing lobsters he has created, she thought. He's never going to give me the sapphire, never. I have failed. I failed them all. Ani felt miserable, and she sobbed as tears cascaded down her face. She struggled to remain standing and not collapse on the floor and weep.

"I took the covenant. Yes, I did, I took it and I would take it again!" he declared. "And I found my precious Amelia." He held the orb up for Ani to see. Amelia stood defiantly within, her hands on her hips. "I know you found her when you and your foolish father and your dimwitted sister came for dinner. The cabinet door was open, just a tad, but open nonetheless, and I knew then and there that you had to be watched and had to be stopped!"

He continued, "Amelia denied that you had discovered her, but I could tell she was lying. I always could tell. Even when we were kids." His voice got softer. "She didn't approve of lying."

Amelia faced him and clasped her hands together as if

in prayer. "Barton," she cried, her voice so faint that Ani could barely hear her, especially over the waves and that annoying clacking sound. "I beseech you."

"Enough," he hollered at the orb, coming to his senses. "Enough. I can't take your demands anymore." He turned to Ani. "I tried to get her out, but I can't break the spell. No one can. I'm going out of my mind trying," he whined, sounding like a petulant child.

Ani had an idea. "What if we both return the sapphire and the orb together?" she said. "Perhaps that will release Amelia."

"That won't work. Nothing will. And besides, I like keeping her close to me, close to me and away from Patrick." He frowned at the mention of his rival's name. "Patrick will be jealous, just like he always has been, jealous of me because I have Amelia all to myself, forever, for eternity. And I have the lobsters right where I want them, stupid crustaceans, and I have beaten the Abenakis at their own game. They took what I held to be most precious from me, and I have taken their rights to the land from them!" He held both the orb and the blue flame high above his head.

And just as he uttered his last victorious sentence, a dark presence loomed behind him, and Ani knew precisely what had caused the relentless clicking noise. A gargantuan lobster, at least seven feet tall, its hard shell glistening, stood behind Barton, with its enormous right claw click-clacking, opening and closing spasmodically.

Ani dropped to the cave floor in terror. Her flashlight hit the rocks and the bulb smashed, extinguishing her only light source. She scrabbled backward. Barton, recognizing the fear on her face, pivoted to find the mighty crustacean towering over him.

Barton's scream was cut short as the lobster's massive claw clamped down around his exposed and vulnerable neck. "Ah, ah, ah, no!" Barton managed to squeak out, as his headlamp threw bursts of light all over the grotto before slipping off his head. He released his hold on both the blue flame and the orb. They crashed to the floor. The sapphire bounced a few times and rolled within reach of Ani. She dove across the floor and gathered it up. The orb shattered as it hit the hard stone ground, and the substance sustaining Amelia oozed out, soaking the area around it.

Barton, struggling against the lobster, saw the orb smash into pieces. "Amelia!" He screamed her name, "Ameliaaaah," he wailed and then succumbed to his attacker, who ruthlessly dragged him down the tunnel away from Ani and the blue flame and away from Amelia and the broken orb.

"Ani." Ani heard her name, ragged and faint, coming from what remained of the orb. "It's not too late. Go to the wheel. Go."

Ani picked up Barton's headlamp and turned it toward the voice. She discovered Amelia, her small body gasping for air, leaning against a piece of the orb, with fluid spilling from its multiple cracks in all directions.

Ani cried, "I can save you, Amelia. Tell me what to do, oh please tell me what to do." She wept uncontrollably now, giving herself over to her grief completely.

Amelia fought to speak. "You are Kanake-kee. Do not worry about me. My fate has been determined since I went through the door. Please, child, go, go to the wheel. It is your destiny." Amelia took another deep, labored breath. "Go," she demanded, and then her eyes closed and her body went slack and slumped over the side of the broken orb.

"Amelia, no, no," Ani screamed, sobs wracking her body. "No!" she shouted again, slamming her left hand in anger, the hand that held Barton's headlamp. The light went out, thrusting Ani into utter darkness.

Go, it is your destiny. Ani heard Amelia's words in her mind. She stood up, holding the blue flame tight in her hand. I need to finish what I started, what we all started, she thought, remembering the help she received from Eliza and Roonie. She headed toward what she thought was the correct tunnel, but instead walked headfirst into a wall.

Frustrated, she said out loud, "I need light," lamenting that she broke the headlamp in her fury and grief. Instantly she heard buzzing coming from the opening where she first entered the caves of Cadillac. The buzzing got louder and louder with each passing second until a ball of light appeared in the hole.

"Whoosh." The light rapidly filled the area.

"Fireflies!" Ani exclaimed. "They sent me fireflies." Hundreds exploded into the cave and around Ani, buzzing and humming, circling and dancing, until the entire space was brightly lit.

"Come on," she called to them and raced down the tunnel on the right, worried now that she might be too late, that the NC 241 had been detonated, its destruction already on its way to ruining the harbor. The fireflies brightened Ani's every step, surrounding her in brilliant, dazzling light.

Once again Ani found herself at the ancient wheel. The mist was still heavy, but Ani waved it away with her arms, exposing the wheel waiting for the final amulet. Ani kissed the blue flame, which reflected the light emanating from the insects and sent blue rays bouncing around the chamber. Ani dropped the sapphire into its appropriate space, and with the placement of this amulet, the wheel lowered, the mist turned black, and Ani heard a great rumbling.

"Oh, no, I must be too late," she said. "The gods of Cadillac are rejecting the offering." The rumbling increased, and Ani felt the ground shift beneath her feet.

"What is happening?" she cried out, swaying to and fro. Suddenly, a giant stalactite broke free from the ceiling and crashed down, hitting Ani on her head and knocking her unconscious for the second time that night.

* * * *

Dr. Banke, Eliza, and Roonie erupted into the command center and charged toward the abort button. The timer read 00:11—eleven seconds— as Dr. Banke rushed past two midshipmen before being stopped by the commander himself.

"Settle down, settle down," the commander said with his

thick arms wrapped tightly around him.

Dr. Banke struggled. "Unhand me!" The two officers they had encountered when they first came on board the vessel grabbed Eliza and Roonie.

"Let me go," cried Eliza.

"Me too," said Roonie, squirming in the grasp of his captor.

"Sir," the officer monitoring the underwater sonar system said to the commander. He removed his headset and tapped the computer screen in front of him. "The lobsters are receding. They're moving back."

The commander released Dr. Banke and walked to the screen. "Let me see." All eyes focused on the green screen as the sonar signal swept over the image of the ocean floor. The officer was correct; the lobsters were leaving the area.

"Unbelievable, but you're right. They're actually retreating," the commander said.

Dr. Banke, noticing that the timer read 00:02, lunged for the button and pressed it down with all his might. Operation Lobster Annihilation, NC 241 was aborted once and for all.

Eliza shouted, "Hooray for Ani! She did it!"

Roonie cried, "Yay, the harbor is saved!" Both kids jumped with abandon, elated, and ran to Dr. Banke, who gathered them into his arms and twirled them around, laughing and shouting, overcome with sheer joy.

"Ani saved the harbor. Way to go, my girl, way to go," he shouted proudly and gave Eliza a high five. "You all did it. Thank you, and thanks for making me believe."

Eliza grinned. "Let's go find Ani, Dad, the true Kanakekee, our hero!"

Lobster fact: *The biggest recorded lobster was caught off the coast of Nova Scotia and weighed 44 pounds.*

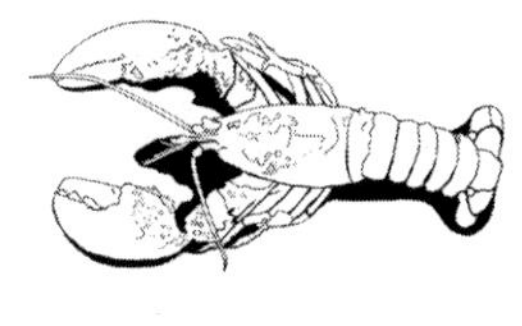

Chapter 50

Always End with a Picnic

Robin Banke pulled her rented car over at Stewman's Lobster Pound just outside of downtown Bar Harbor. She couldn't explain why, but she had been thinking about lobsters since landing at Bangor International Airport early that morning. She felt fatigued from her travels but relieved to be in Maine and closer to the girls and her husband. After the seagull incident at the site, her body had been jostled up and down while traveling the dusty old mining trails in a rickety, open-air jeep back to the lodge in Montezuma. Once there, she had tried unsuccessfully to reach George. This only increased her desire to get to Maine, and she had hurriedly packed her suitcase. As luck would have it, Robin was able to catch a ride from a colleague meeting his wife in Santa Fe for a few days' respite from his dig near the Gallinas River, about fifty miles from Robin's own site. From Santa Fe, she got on a short flight to Albuquerque followed by a two-hour layover before boarding a red-eye for a direct flight to Boston.

Once in Boston, Robin had felt comforted to be home, well, close to home anyway. She had purchased the *Boston Globe* newspaper and a hot coffee from her favorite coffee shop at Logan and boarded a seven o'clock flight to Bangor, Maine. She was remarkably alert, despite sleeping only a few hours on the various plane rides. Even though she was still unable to reach her husband or the girls, she reasoned that George would have tracked her down if something really horrible had happened. Yes, she told herself, he never would keep anything, anything of a serious nature from me. And no matter how hard she had tried to make sense of the flock of seagulls and the feathers, her mind was unable to come up with a valid explanation. And so she had followed her often-bestowed advice to listen to what the heart feels, and knew she had made the right choice by coming to Maine.

The urge to taste some succulent Maine lobster had increased with each minute she drove along scenic Route 3, especially when she entered Ellsworth, a community close to Mount Desert Island, where she had been bombarded with advertisements for lobsters. She hadn't been to Acadia since she was a little girl on vacation with her older sister and her parents. The beauty of a Cadillac Mountain sunset rushed into her thoughts, recalling images from what seemed ages ago to flash before her mind's eye, among them the way the fading sunlight highlighted the pink quartz scattered about the mountaintop before dipping below the horizon while she and her sister skipped along the trails, amazed by how small the boats looked in Frenchman Bay and how much the Porcupine Islands really did look like the prickly backs of porcupines. Funny how she hadn't thought about this time until now, yet the impression still felt so fresh in her memory.

She turned off the ignition and opened her car door, the cool moist air a welcome change from the stifling heat of New Mexico. Robin took a deep breath, filling her lungs, and entered the building. The familiar smell of seaweed and boiling salt water and steamed clams and lobsters washed over her. There's nothing better than to be in Maine in the summertime, she thought.

Earlier, while filling the car up with gas in Ellsworth, Robin had stopped at the famous Helen's Restaurant, a place her parents still talked about, known for its homemade pies. She purchased both a graham cracker and a blueberry pie, a perfect ending to a delicious lobster dinner. If she knew George, they were probably living off take-out pizza and Eliza's boxed macaroni and cheese extravaganza, neither of them very fulfilling, especially after having them over several nights. Robin smiled as she envisioned her reunion with them all.

At Stewman's she ordered five lobsters, one for each of them and an extra one to share. Lost in her own daydream, Robin was oblivious to the fact that the smallest lobster for sale was a whopping four-pounder, when a one-and-a-half to two-pounder was more the norm. She paid the cashier and thanked her. As she turned to leave with her lobsters tucked tightly under her arm in the traditional brown paper bag, she almost crashed into an approaching customer.

"I'm so sorry," Robin said. "I'm hurrying and not paying attention to what I'm doing." She smiled at the woman.

"No need to apologize," replied the patron, a kindly old woman with long white hair tied neatly in a trailing purple scarf. "You always hurry when visiting loved ones, especially when you've been absent for a while."

"Excuse me?" Robin said. "What did you say?"

"I must be the one asking for forgiveness. I'm being presumptuous when I haven't even introduced myself. You must be Robin Banke, Ani and Eliza's mom. You look like both of them actually."

"Yes, yes, I am," a startled Robin said. "And you would be?"

"Again, I feel the need to apologize. I'm just incredibly happy to finally meet you, and I'm forgetting my manners. My name is Violet Cyr. I own the Moon Violet Inn in Bar Harbor, and I am the proud grandmother of Roonie Cyr. He and Ani and Eliza have, have," she hesitated before continuing, "let's just say they have become very good friends while performing some very good deeds, especially Ani."

"Ani? She's all right isn't she? And Eliza and George, too?"

"Nothing that a few days of rest won't cure, but yes, be assured, Mrs. Banke, Ani, Eliza, your husband, and my grandson are wonderful. They will have much to tell you about their recent adventures."

"Adventures?"

But Moon Violet chose to ignore her inquiry and instead said, "Now that I have accidentally, um, run into you, I was wondering if you might give this to Ani?" She held out a white shirt box tied with a wide, deep purple bow.

Robin took the box. "What's it for?"

"Just a little thank you from some friends of mine for a job well done. Ani will explain," she said in response to Robin's clouded expression. "And when she does, listen with your heart, not your head."

"Why, that's what I always say," an amazed Robin said.

Moon Violet beamed knowingly. "Lobsters?" she said, pointing to the paper bag.

"Yes, I thought I might surprise everyone."

"Oh, they will be, ah, certainly surprised," Moon Violet said and raised her eyebrows. "Well, I must be off. Still so much to do," Moon Violet said, holding the door for Robin. "It has been simply delightful to see you again. I mean," Moon Violet caught herself. "I meant to say to meet you, simply delightful."

"Likewise," said Robin, feeling both relieved and perplexed by their conversation. The two exited the lobster pound and Moon Violet followed Robin to her car. "Weren't you going to purchase some lobsters?" Robin said.

Moon Violet looked back toward the pound. "No, I changed my mind. I think I've had my fill of lobsters for the time being."

Robin smiled halfheartedly, unsure of what to make of this strange yet well-meaning woman. She opened the door and placed the gift and the lobsters on the passenger seat, next to her pies. "Well, again, it was a pleasure meeting you, and thank you for letting me know that the girls and George and," she paused here, "what was your grandson's name?"

"Roonie," said Moon Violet.

"Right, Roonie. Thanks for letting me know they are all okay. I've been worried."

"When we are linked to our loved ones, like you clearly are, our hearts and our concerns are always attuned to each other. It's what makes us human."

Robin nodded, unable to think of how to respond to this curious individual. She got into her car and headed directly to the cottage, her heart already lighter from her chance meeting with Violet Cyr.

Moon Violet reached down and picked up a handful of dirt from the side of the Stewman's parking lot. She rubbed her palms together for a few moments, then closed her eyes. "Kinikinik Volcanda Kottliwi, Kwahliwi Tapsiwi, May the Great Creator bless us and smile upon us," she chanted and grinned from ear to ear as she blew the dust from her hands, offering her blessing up to the winds to carry away to the ancestral Abenaki gods. The winds picked up, causing Moon Violet's scarf to swirl around her head. Softer now, with a slight tear in her right eye, she whispered, "God bless you, Kanake-kee. God bless you, Ani Banke."

* * * *

"Let me look at you."

Annoyed, Ani said, "Dad, I told you. I'm fine, totally and completely fine." Disbelieving his daughter, Dr. Banke frowned at Ani. "In fact I've never felt better," she added for good measure.

"Regardless, you and Eliza are not going over to Roonie's grandmother's house. I don't care how fabulous you say you're feeling. The doctor clearly said that you were supposed to rest, relax, and then rest and relax some more. Understood?"

"But Dad," Ani protested.

"Ani, with two concussions, one resulting in stitches, several bruises and cuts, not to mention over a gazillion bug bites, you are staying put."

"Ah, Dad," Ani said. Defeated, she slumped down into the living room chair.

There was a quick knock on the kitchen door. Ani attempted to stand up, but Dr. Banke waved his hand. "Sit."

Ani glared at him, but was actually glad to sit back down. She felt a little woozy when she moved, and as much as she hated to admit it, her head hurt. Not as sharp as last night, but still painful, dull and throbbing. The doctor had told her she would have a powerful headache with occasional bouts of dizziness. Considering all that she went through, Ani knew she was extremely lucky.

As much as she tried to rest, her mind kept replaying all that transpired yesterday and last evening: finding the final amulet and the bear on Porcupine Island, being attacked by the lobsters in the boat, falling down Gorge Trail only to be rescued by a deer. I actually rode a deer, she thought. Experiencing Professor Sol imploding right before her very eyes. Ani shuddered, thinking about how terrified she was when he whipped out his overly large, definitely frightening, right lobster claw and nearly gagged when recalling his absolutely horrid smell.

Her thoughts turned to Patrick. Thank goodness his injuries from being knocked down by Professor Sol were not too severe. She remembered how initially Eliza, and herself, too, if she were being honest, thought the gardener was creepy and mean. How wrong they both had been. Then the peregrine falcon had helped her find the *X* spot, and she had slid down to the Cadillac Mountain Caves. That part was kind of fun, well, until she ran into Barton. At this recollection, Ani's throat constricted and tears sprang to her tired eyes. She was devastated over the orb smashing and Amelia's death and dreaded having to share this news with Patrick.

She sighed and wondered where her dad had wandered off. He hadn't left her since she had been released from the hospital a few hours ago. Her mind traveled back to last night. After Barton had been brutally taken away by the colossal lobster (he still hadn't been found), and the fireflies arrived and lit the path for her to follow back to the wheel, Ani found her memory vague as to what happened next. She remembered setting the blue flame into its allotted spot and then the wheel sinking down as the ground rumbled and shook, the noise deafening, and the stalactite coming loose. She wasn't exactly sure how long she had been unconscious, only that she came to with the help of one very large and excited black dog, who must have made his way through the same tunnels that had led Barton to the caves. Beauregard, who had set her on this amazing journey, had stayed beside her ever since nudging her awake on the cold stone floor. Ani reached down to pet the loyal dog, and he stretched with joy from her soft touch.

Ani wasn't sure why Barton had returned to the caves last night. Perhaps he meant to stop Ani, as her father, Eliza, and Roonie seemed to agree, but maybe, as Ani always liked to find the good in people, maybe he went to the grotto with the goal of rescuing Amelia. Like Ani, he might have hoped that by restoring the orb to where he originally discovered it, in the center of the amulet wheel, he could have righted the wrong he started and Amelia miraculously would have been set free. But maybe, Ani mused, when he found the blue flame stone, Amelia, who knew I had been charged with locating and replacing the amulets, had informed him about my true purpose. Maybe right then and there he feared that somehow the placement of the amulets could foil his grand scheme, and he decided to keep the sapphire from me. Ani would have to resign herself to the fact that she would never know the answers to her many questions.

Beauregard raised his head and emitted a low, protective growl. Ani listened and heard nothing. "It's okay, Beau, it's okay," Ani assured him. Her new friend snorted and lay back down.

Ani continued reflecting on the last thing she recalled before reuniting with Eliza, Roonie, and her father. Her father had been convinced that Beauregard must have sensed that Ani was in distress and had raced to the caves. When Beau found her out cold on the ground, he must have pawed and pushed Ani, willing her to wake up, because when she finally managed to open her eyes, the dog was barking loudly and pulling at her clothing with his sharp teeth. Ani told her father that when she came to, the fireflies had departed and taken their tiny lights with them. Ironically, however, the same stalactite that hit her on her head had left a small crack in the ceiling that allowed for some light from the full moon and stars to shine through and illuminate the cave. Ani had been amazed to discover that the area had completely changed. It now appeared as if nothing had ever been there, no heavy mist, no ancient Abenaki wheel, no center spot for the orb. It had simply vanished, and all that remained was the bare stone floor and a few broken stalactites.

Ani believed then that not only had she missed the prescribed deadline to return the amulets, resulting in the deployment of the deadly NC 241, the likely destroyer of every living thing in its wake, but also that somehow her humble offerings had angered the gods of Cadillac, who retaliated by shaking the mountain with unmistakable rage. This theory, combined with her injuries and the loss of Amelia, had proved too much for Ani to endure, and she had buried her head into Beau's neck and wept. Beauregard had comforted Ani, allowing his young friend to pour out all her sadness and disappointment before eventually backing away, barking excitedly, and repeatedly tugging on Ani to leave and follow him.

Ani sighed deeply in her chair and gazed at her canine hero, feeling an enormous sense of gratitude toward and pride in Beau for his bravery and his perseverance. She remembered how he slowly led her up and out of the grotto, winding and weaving his way through the vast maze of tunnels, until locating the opening that brought them to the surface and refreshing night air.

Along their arduous journey, Beau instinctively recognized when Ani needed to rest. He would stand next to her and wait patiently for a few minutes, and then bark when he felt it was time to move on. Ani would have most definitely fallen asleep had it not been for his encouragement.

As she had staggered sluggishly behind Beauregard, her jumbled thoughts came back to the song Roonie had sung for them after they discovered the green tourmaline. Ani had hummed this faintly to herself, which gave her mild comfort and helped to move her along, despite her body's multiple injuries.

"Tide and time remain still,
When down below, below the hill.
Tunnels carved and caves were formed
For passage to hide from mighty storms
Tide and time will remain still
When down below, below the hill."

Once outside, Ani had absolutely no clue as to where she was or where to go. Her head had pulsated with pain while her vision blurred, and all she had wanted to do was lie down and sleep. She had also desperately wanted to see her mother, whom she missed more than she ever thought possible, and to collapse into her soothing arms. But Beau would not give up and prodded Ani along the path.

When Ani tried to piece together what had happened next, her brain felt cloudy and distant. Her father had filled in the gaps for her while she was still in the hospital. After stopping the NC 241, he, Eliza, Roonie, Ben, and TJ had hurried to the summit of Cadillac. Once on Park Loop Road, they had spied Patrick's truck and had just pulled over to investigate when Beauregard burst out of the trees. His barking and jumping had alerted them all to follow him back into the woods.

TJ had been the first to reach Ani and had collected her in his arms (something Eliza would always be jealous of), and together he and her father had carried her to the car. While Dr. Banke, Eliza, and Roonie had rushed Ani to MDI Hospital, Ben and TJ had driven to the top of Cadillac, breaking through the *Road Closed* barrier, to find Patrick and Professor Sol. Apparently, Ani had been fairly incoherent but kept repeating the words, *Professor Sol, Bert Sol, Lobster, Lobsterman*. Not until Ben and TJ located Patrick cradling Professor Sol in his arms, with a huge lobster claw draped over a patch of shrubbery nearby, did they completely understand what Ani had meant.

On the way to the hospital Ani had drifted in and out of consciousness. Her father had been able to share the wonderful news that the NC 241 had not been released and that this was unquestionably on account of Ani, Kanake-kee, his heroic and courageous daughter. Ani had squeezed his hand before falling into another deep sleep.

After she had been treated for her injuries, including twelve stitches along her hairline for the gash from the stalactite, Dad had informed Ani that Professor Sol had been taken to an undisclosed military hospital for treatment and observation. The military had advised the Bankes, Roonie, Patrick,

Ben, and TJ to keep this information under wraps with promises of receiving a report about the professor's recovery soon. No one had much faith that this would ever happen. Ani, Eliza, and Roonie had briefly discussed this request of keeping Professor Sol's transformation from man to lobster a secret, and all agreed that if they told anyone, no one would ever believe them. Ani was still having a difficult time believing it had happened and she had been there! Beau's ears perked up and he swiveled his head toward the kitchen. Ani listened intently and thought she heard someone whispering and then a giggle, but she couldn't be sure.

"Hey," she called out. "Is anyone there?" She waited, but no one replied. Ani glanced at Beau, who cocked his head and thumped his stub of a tail vigorously against the side of her chair. "You're such a good doggy, good doggy," said Ani, petting Beau's back, which only increased his wagging. She heard the back door slam shut and more giggles from what she guessed to be Roonie and Eliza scurrying away from the kitchen. What was Roonie doing here? Dad was adamant that I not have any visitors.

Ani heard approaching footsteps from the front porch and saw Patrick looking through the side window. He smiled and waved at Ani and then pushed the door open.

"Patrick!" Ani squealed, and Beau barked a few hellos of his own.

"I heard this was the place that heroes hang out." He winked at her and pulled a pretty bouquet of fresh-cut flowers from behind his back. Ani took the flowers and smelled their wonderful fragrance.

"Thank you, Patrick," she said warmly. Ani noticed that in addition to several bruises and scratches, he had some stitches of his own from where Professor Sol had whacked him on the side of his head with his frightening claw. Ani pointed to her wound and nodded.

"Yup, I got some of those myself." Patrick smiled and winced as he sat in the chair opposite Ani.

"Patrick, you're hurt, too. I'm the one that should be bringing flowers to you. Without your help," she paused, her eyes filling with tears until she cleared her throat and continued, "without your help, I never could have done it."

"Rubbish, girl. You and your unshakable determination would have found a way."

The two sat in silence for a few minutes, enjoying the quiet and the satisfaction shared by both for a job well done. Ani knew that in addition to wanting to check on her, he had another reason for his visit. Ani had tried to get up from her hospital bed to see Patrick once Eliza had told her he was there, but her nurse, a strong and persistent woman by the name of Ms. Mary-Lou, would hear none of it and threatened to get restraints if she tried to move again. Eliza had entertained Ani earlier this morning with her imitation of Ms. Mary-Lou, and Ani had gathered that this would go on throughout the remainder of the summer.

"I tried to visit you while you were in the emergency room," Ani said.

"Yes, I heard about that." He scowled at her. "I know your nurse well. She told me about your attempt to get out of bed."

"I just wanted to see if you were okay and to tell you about …," she stared directly at Patrick, tears pooling in her eyes.

Patrick rubbed his head and nodded, his eyes matching Ani's. Hopeful, he said, "You saw Amelia, didn't you?"

Ani nodded, too choked up to speak, her tears glistening down her cheeks. Beauregard placed his head on Ani's lap.

"Barton was there, too?"

"Yes," Ani managed to say. "Yes, he came by the tunnels that run underneath his house. He, he …" She hesitated.

"Go on, Ani," said Patrick. "I need to know what happened."

"He had one of the amulets that I dropped when I fell from the summit. He told me he wasn't going to give it to me and, and, he had the orb."

"Was Amelia still in it?" he asked, bowing his head low.

"Yes."

"And then what happened?" asked Patrick, sounding both serious and apprehensive.

"Mr. Baxter was ranting and raving about the NC 241

and how he owns the chemical company that engineered the dangerous gas, and how he stole the orb and was glad the lobsters came back because he also owned the processing plant, and regardless of what happened after the gas was detonated, he would be the sole supplier of Maine lobster meat and soon be crowned the King of the Lobsters, or something like that. Amelia pleaded with him to give the blue flame to me, but he wouldn't listen to her."

"And?" Patrick asked.

"And," Ani said between sobs, "he said that he wouldn't return Amelia to the place where he first found her because he wanted to keep her for himself and away from you." Patrick said nothing, and Ani continued, "And suddenly a seven-foot lobster appeared from behind and grabbed Mr. Baxter with his claw, throwing him to the ground before dragging him away through a tunnel. He's missing, you know."

Patrick nodded and rubbed his chin. "What happened to the orb?"

"Oh, Patrick," Ani said, her voice almost a whisper, "Mr. Baxter dropped the orb and it shattered. And Amelia," Ani struggled to speak, overcome with sadness. "The fluid was seeping out all over the place and I rushed to her and tried to help her, but she told me this was her destiny. And my destiny was to go put the amulet in the Abenaki granite wheel." Patrick let out a long sigh as if he had been holding his breath. "I wouldn't leave, Patrick, honest, I wouldn't leave her, but she stopped breathing, and I, and I didn't want to let her down so I returned the blue flame to its rightful place. You know the rest from there."

Patrick said nothing.

"Patrick, I'm sorry. I would have done anything to save her." Ani sniffed and wiped her nose with the back of her hand.

Patrick stood and without looking at Ani patted her knee. With great effort he managed to say, "I know, I know, Ani." And he walked toward the front door. "I need to be alone now," he said. Ani watched him open the cottage door, step onto the front porch, and walk slowly down the stairs. She put her head in her hands and sobbed.

Tired from Patrick's visit, Ani closed her eyes and napped. She dreamt about Amelia, lobsters, Patrick, and seals, dreams that were not unpleasant but disjointed, much like her mind felt as she worked to process everything that had occurred. She woke to her father kissing her gently on her cheek,

"Hello, sleeping girl. It's time to have something to eat before you take some more pain medication."

"I'm not hungry, Dad," Ani said, yawned, and closed her eyes again.

"I think you might change your mind when you see the spread we have for you."

"Not Eliza's macaroni and cheese. I would surely have to go to the hospital if I had to eat that again."

"I heard that," cried Eliza from the kitchen.

Ani and her father suppressed a giggle. He lifted Ani, careful of her right shoulder, and called to Eliza. "Come help your sister please."

Eliza entered the living room. "Well, it's about time you got up, lazy bones," she said. "I thought you might just lay around all day. Oh, my." Eliza scrutinized Ani's head. "I'm definitely going to have to fix your hairstyle. You've got kind of a teased, caked-on dirt and dried blood thing going on that simply will not do for our hero."

"The nurse said she could shower later tonight. I think she looks perfect," her father said and kissed her again.

"Please, Dad, not the nurse. I can't take anymore impressions."

"Indeed," Eliza said, breaking into her best Nurse Mary-Lou voice. "A child like you, not following the rules of the hospital, outrageous!"

The girls laughed together, closer from their shared experience and happy to have survived. Eliza took Ani's other side and soon they maneuvered her out the door and onto one of the garden paths. Ani enjoyed the feel of the sunshine on her face and the support of her sister and father with Beau prancing close behind. She guessed they were taking her to the circle of Adirondack chairs where Roonie had initially spied on the girls from above in the tall oak tree, but instead of moving to the right they chose another path, the one that ran along the back edge of the garden, a path she had visited only once before. The hairs on her neck stood up, and she slowed her already slow gait.

"It's okay Ani. Patrick wants us here," Eliza said, sensing her sister's hesitation.

Soon they came around the corner and Ani noticed Roonie and Patrick standing behind a large wrought iron table flanked by chairs with bright colored balloons tied to their backs blowing in the breeze. The well-tended perennial beds were filled with an array of colorful blooms, which added to the festivity of the garden celebration. At the center of the table was an enormous vase filled with flowers much like the bouquet given to her earlier, geraniums, snapdragons, zinnias, and daisies, Ani's favorite, and she knew that Patrick had been responsible for this. The table was covered with a white linen cloth and loaded with all of Ani's favorite brunch foods: blueberry muffins, blueberry pancakes, popovers, French toast, waffles, scrambled eggs, bacon, sausage, blueberries, strawberries, and sliced bananas with pitchers of orange juice and chocolate milk to drink.

"Wow!" Ani said. "This is amazing." Though she tried not to notice the thick interlocking brambles covering the forbidden Abenaki wooden door not fifteen feet away from the feast, she locked eyes with Patrick, and he bowed as if to say, *It's all right*.

Roonie chimed in, too excited and hungry to keep silent. "This is all for you! I spoke to my Aunt Kate, and she together with the cook made this for you. Kate knows the entire story of what happened and wanted to help in your rest and recovery." Looking at the food and licking his lips in anticipation, he said, "I guess they kind of got carried away."

"Ya think?" said Eliza, tousling his hair. "But who cares. Let's eat!"

"Yes," said Patrick, who pulled out a chair close to Ani, "for you."

Ani sat and Patrick pushed her up to the table and whispered into Ani's ear so that only she could hear him. "She would want us to rejoice and enjoy the garden." He glanced at the door. "And that's what we're going to do."

Ani patted his hand. Eliza grabbed Roonie's glass and asked, "Chocolate milk?"

"Eliza!" he shouted. "It was an accident!"

"Just kidding you," she said and winked at him.

They all dug in with gusto. Ani, astonished by how strong her hunger was, tried a bite of almost everything on the table. She looked at everyone seated around her, her father, Eliza, Roonie, and especially Patrick, and was filled with great affection for all of them. Her eyes moved back to Roonie and she cried out, "Roonie?"

He turned to her, his mouth filled with blueberry pancakes. "Yeah?"

"I'm shocked! You're not wearing a Spider-Man T-shirt!"

Roonie grinned and stood up, swallowing hard. He pointed to his chest, which read *RED SOX NATION*. "It's time to root for the home boys. My dad says they need all the help they can get."

"You can say that again," quipped Patrick, and they all laughed.

"But," added Roonie, still standing, "Spider-Man is never far!" He lifted his Red Sox shirt up to reveal a bright red Spider-Man shirt underneath.

After a few moments, Patrick cleared his throat and clinked his glass with his knife, signaling the group that he wanted to make a toast. With all eyes on him, he raised his glass and announced, "As a child, I was afraid of this giant door and rightly so, given the circumstances. As an adult, I no longer feared the Abenakis and their strange ways, but I was angry with them, angry and bitter. But today, thanks to Ani and thanks to all of you, I have finally come to a better place." He choked up, but then continued, "A place of acceptance, respect, peace, and belief in their ancient traditions. So here is to Ani, great Kanake-kee, a champion of all, animals, man, and even lobsters."

"Here, here," the others cheered and Beauregard barked.

The sun moved behind a cloud and darkness passed over the happy setting, casting shadows. Ani heard a rustling, and all heads turned toward the brambles and watched in amazement as the persistent, thorny bush twisted before sliding away completely to reveal the wooden door. Ani read the carved inscription:

Rain, sleet, snow, or hail,
Let no man pass this trail
—ABENAKI

When she finished, the rusty padlock swung back and forth, rubbing the wooden door and screeching as it came apart and dropped to the ground. Patrick stood wide-eyed and speechless. With a creak, the wooden door opened, and yellow mist poured out from the widening gap. Out of the mist about twenty feet behind the open door, a small girl with dark plaited hair, missing a single blue hair ribbon, emerged and moved slowly down the path. Ani recognized Amelia immediately, and her body tingled with awe.

"Amelia!" Patrick whispered. "Amelia!"

Amelia walked closer to them and with each step her appearance changed: she grew taller, her cheekbones became more defined, her body filled out. She was aging right before their very eyes. Amelia as a teenager, a young adult, and so on, until Amelia, now the same age as Patrick, looking both different and the same, stood at the threshold of the infamous wooden door, holding her arms out. And before anyone could react, Patrick rushed to his childhood friend, his one true love, and wrapped his arms around her sobbing. "Amelia, oh, thank you, Abenaki gods, thank you." They embraced, yellow mist surrounding them before dissipating in the warm summer sunshine.

Patrick with wet eyes turned to the group, still clutching Amelia's hand. "I'd like to introduce you to Amelia Legere, my long lost friend."

The table erupted with shouts and cries of joy. Ani was the first to reach them, and Patrick stepped back to allow Amelia to wrap her arms around her friend, the keeper of her book and champion of the Abenakis.

Then, from behind the tall lilies, another voice came.

"Hello? Is anyone there? I was told by one of the gardeners that I would find my family here." Robin Banke appeared, set down some packages, and said, "Well, hello, everyone."

"Mom!" Ani and Eliza both cried and ran toward their mother.

"Robin," exclaimed Dr. Banke. "What are you doing here?"

Robin placed her packages on the ground and hugged both of her girls tightly.

"Mom," said Eliza, "have we got a story for you."

She rose and kissed her husband warmly. "I've heard that you," she turned to Ani, "and specifically *you* have had quite an adventure."

Her eyes narrowed as she noticed Ani's head. "Are those stitches? Can someone tell me what has happened?"

"We will, Robin," said Dr. Banke, "but first tell us why you're here."

She smiled at her family. "Let's just say a little bird, or rather, a flock of seagulls told me I was needed at home."

Ani introduced Patrick, Amelia, and Roonie to her mother.

"Nice to meet all of you," Robin said. "And you too, Roonie. Oh, that reminds me." She reached down to pick up the gift from Moon Violet. "I already met your grandmother," she said to Roonie, "and she wanted me to give this to Ani." She handed the present to her.

Ani took it from her mother. "What is it?"

"Why don't you open it and find out?" said Eliza.

"Open it," said Roonie. "My grandmother always gives unusual presents," he said proudly.

Ani slipped off the purple ribbon and removed the lid from the box. She lifted out a simple wooden box that she placed on the table. She raised the hinged lid and found a note, addressed to her, on purple stationary with tiny violets bordering the envelope. She opened the card. "Smells like lavender," she said, bringing the card to her nose. Ani read the contents to herself.

Dear Ani,

On behalf of the entire Abenaki tribe, I would like to thank you for accepting the challenge dictated to you by the Abenaki ancestors of long ago. Your bravery, dedication, and strength are commendable, and you will always be remembered in Abenaki history for restoring harmony and peace throughout Mount Desert Island, specifically for saving the harbor from a deadly catastrophe. It has been an honor and a privilege for all of us, both man and animal alike, to assist you in your quest.

As much as the amulets that you so courageously offered up to the gods were accepted, resulting in calling the lobsters back from whence they came, the fact remains that the orb was taken. This thievery disrupted the flow of positive energy throughout MDI and the entire earth plane. Thus, there are early indications that several urgent situations are developing that may benefit from your special talents. This parchment holds the secrets of many other tribes across the globe. If you choose to receive this gift by opening the contents within, you will signify your willingness to accept your destiny. Choose wisely, for once opened it may not be closed. Your choice, as with anything, is always your choice.

Please never forget what I told you when I first met you. You are Ani Banke, One Who Walks with Animals, Abenaki Kanake-kee.

Kee Matum, Walk in Peace,

Moon Violet

"Well," said Ani's mother. "What does it say?"

Ani replaced the card in the envelope, grinned and looked at Eliza and Roonie. But before she answered, she noticed the brown paper bag next to her mother's feet.

"Is this something else from Roonie's grandmother?"

"What?" asked Robin, forgetting about her own gift. "Oh, right." She bent and opened the bag, pulling out a lobster, which she proudly held up for everyone to see. "Surprise!" she said. "Who wants lobsters? My treat."

"Oh Mom, no, no more lobsters," Eliza said.

Roonie made a face and said, "Yuck, I'm out."

Patrick and Amelia, sitting next to each other still holding hands, laughed in unison while Ani backed cautiously away from the writhing, wriggling lobster, even though its claws were clamped shut with thick yellow elastic bands.

Dr. Banke sprang toward the table, gently took the lobster from his confused wife's hand and placed it back into the paper bag. He shook his head at his wife, smiled, and said, "It's a long, long story, and I promise to tell you all of it later. Let's just say we've already had our lobster quota for this summer and most likely for several more to come."

Robin shrugged her shoulders and returned her attention to her younger daughter. "So, honey, what did the letter say?"

"Oh," Ani said with a mischievous twinkle in her eye, "just some, ah, some suggestions of where we might like to spend our vacation next summer." And with that statement, Ani confidently opened the first parchment page of her new present.

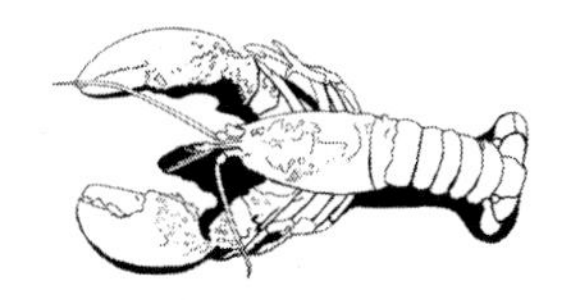

Acknowledgements

Thank you to Jennifer Billings and Robin Gaynor for starting me on the writing journey. A big thank-you goes to Anne Clemens who helped create the three parchments and first told me I should turn my idea into a book. I owe a special thank-you to Robin Perlow, my first editor, who kept me on track, researched the lobster facts, and cheerfully read each chapter. I also want to thank my family, who listened to my chapters over the years, especially Amelia and Julie Nealley and Emmy Jones. Thank you to my nephews, Eli and Jay Legere and Will Nealley for the character of Roonie—you were right! Thank you to Eliza Nealley for the use of her name. Thank you to Mary-Lou Destefano and Nancy Murphy for allowing me to tell the story again and again. Thank you to my mother-in-law, Elaine Jones, for her recipes and to my parents, Del and Bob Rowe, for their continued enthusiasm and support. Thank you to all my early readers; in addition to Bob and Del Rowe, I also want to thank Kate and Jay Legere, Tom and Elaine Jones, Peg Ayotte, Lorraine Fallona, Joanne Fish, Jan and Joy Froding, Rosemary Fugel, Jill and Michael Hallet, Audie Lambert, Valerie McClead, Linda Pomerleau, Melanie Galeaz, Sophie Jones, Beth Sherr, Julie Doonan, Amanda Randall and Kelly Seymour. Thank you to Amanda Jones for her great photography and to Sarah, Dave, and Hannah Belanger for their interest in all things lobster. Thank you to the entire staff at Maine Authors Publishing, including David Allen for his wonderful book jacket design. A particular thank-you goes out to the very talented Thomas Block for his fabulous drawings, which helped bring the characters and story to life. Thank you to Tom, TJ, Emmy, and Baloo, the wonder dog, who always looks good in his lobster costume. An extra special thank you to the splendor of Mount Desert Island, Acadia National Park, and Thuya Garden, whose beauty never ceases to amaze me and continues to inspire me each time I visit.

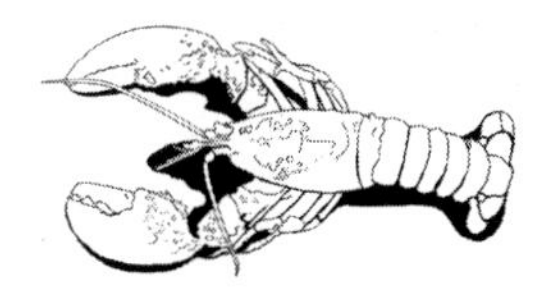

Note from the Author

While many of the places mentioned in this book are real, not all of them are (and none of the people are), and some license has been taken with those places that do exist. Under no circumstances should a reader attempt to venture below Thunder Hole, climb exceedingly tall trees to disturb eagle nests, get trapped on Bar Island, swim with seals, or interact with bears and other wildlife. Caution should be taken too before swimming in the cold Atlantic waters—you might be shocked just like Eliza! But if you are fortunate enough to visit MDI and get to enjoy a delicious lobster dinner, and you happen to spy the distinctive Retsbol marking on the lobster tail, please keep it to yourself. You never know who might be watching.

Abenaki Indians do exist in Maine and also in Vermont, New Hampshire, Massachusetts, and Quebec, Canada. I especially want to thank them for helping to inspire the lobster tale; however, their story in *Retsbol Rises: An Abenaki Lobster Tale* is purely a figment of my imagination. To learn more about the Abenaki Indians and their real history, please follow Ani's lead and visit your local library.